The Deadliest Sin

Also by The Medieval Murderers

The Tainted Relic

Sword of Shame

House of Shadows

The Lost Prophecies

King Arthur's Bones

The Sacred Stone

Hill of Bones

The First Murder

The False Virgin

THE DEADLIEST SIN

A Historical Mystery
By
The Medieval Murderers

Susanna Gregory
Bernard Knight
Karen Maitland
Ian Morson
Philip Gooden
Michael Jecks
Simon Beaufort

Medieval Murderers

SIMON &
SCHUSTER

London · New York · Sydney · Toronto · New Delhi

A CBS COMPANY

First published in Great Britain by Simon & Schuster UK Ltd, 2014
This paperback published 2015
A CBS COMPANY

1 3 5 7 9 10 8 6 4 2

Simon & Schuster UK Ltd
1st Floor
222 Gray's Inn Road
London WC1X 8HB

www.simonandschuster.co.uk

Simon & Schuster Australia, Sydney
Simon & Schuster India, New Delhi

A CIP catalogue record for this book is
available from the British Library

Paperback ISBN: 978-1-47111-438-0
eBook ISBN: 978-1-47111-439-7

Typeset by M Rules
Printed and bound by CPI Group (UK) Ltd, Croydon, CR0 4YY

The Medieval Murderers

A small group of historical mystery writers, all members of the Crime Writers' Association, who promote their work by giving informal talks and discussions at libraries, bookshops and literary festivals.

Bernard Knight is a former Home Office pathologist and professor of forensic medicine who has been publishing novels, non-fiction, radio and television drama and documentaries for more than forty years. He currently writes the highly regarded Crowner John series of historical mysteries, based on the first coroner for Devon in the twelfth century; the fourteenth of which, *A Plague of Heretics*, has recently been published by Simon & Schuster.

Ian Morson is the author of an acclaimed series of historical mysteries featuring the thirteenth-century Oxford-based detective, William Falconer, a series featuring medieval Venetian crime solver, Nick Zuliani, and many short stories set in various historical periods.

Philip Gooden is the author of the Nick Revill series, a sequence of historical mysteries set in London during the time of Shakespeare's Globe Theatre. He also writes nineteenth-century mysteries, as well as non-fiction books on language, most recently *Idiomantics* and *World at War*, a study of the the impact of World War Two on language. Philip was chairman of the Crime Writers' Association in 2007–8.

Susanna Gregory is the author of the Matthew Bartholomew series of mystery novels, set in fourteenth century Cambridge, the most recent of which are *Murder by the Book* and *The Lost Abbot.* In addition, she writes a series set in Restoration London, featuring Thomas Chaloner; the most recent book is *Murder in St James's Park.* She also writes historical mysteries with her husband under the name of **Simon Beaufort**.

Karen Maitland writes stand-alone, dark medieval thrillers. She is the author of *Company of Liars* and *The Owl Killers*. Her most recent medieval thrillers are *The Gallows Curse*, a tale of treachery and sin under the brutal reign of English King John, and *Falcons of Fire and Ice*, set in Portugal and Iceland amid the twin terrors of the Inquisition and Reformation.

Michael Jecks gave up a career in the computer industry to concentrate on writing and the study of medieval history. A regular speaker at library and literary events, he is a past Chairman of the Crime Writers' Association. He lives with his wife, children and dogs in northern Dartmoor.

The Programme

The Prologue, in which the pilgrims arrive at the Angel Inn

The first sin:	Michael Jecks tells a tale of Lust
The second sin:	Ian Morson tells a tale of Greed
The third sin:	Ian Morson tells a tale of Gluttony
The fourth sin:	Susannah Gregory and Simon Beaufort tell a tale of Sloth
The fifth sin:	Philip Gooden tells a tale of Anger
The sixth sin:	Bernard Knight tells a tale of Envy
The seventh sin:	Karen Maitland tells a tale of Pride

The Epilogue, in which the pilgrims depart from the Angel Inn

In fond memory of Dot Lumley (1949–2013),
general agent and first editor for all the
MEDIEVAL MURDERER *books.*
Thanks for keeping us all in line.

PROLOGUE

The English say that April is the best month to make a pilgrimage. Once winter is over, the roads and tracks become passable again. The skies lift and the days draw out. People begin to grow restless.

But this particular spring, in the year of Our Lord 1348, was different from other springs. True, the days were growing lighter and longer as they always do, yet the people of England were not so much restless as terrified.

For a time at the end of the previous year it had been possible to ignore the rumours as mere invention, stories created to frighten children. Extraordinary tales were coming out of the east, tales of poisonous clouds that overwhelmed whole cities and even countries, with scarcely a human being left alive to tell the horrors he had witnessed. But because there were often reports of fantastical things out of the east it was not so hard to dismiss these new alarms.

Then the accounts of mass dying began to arrive from nearer at hand. The cloud of pestilence reached out of the Levant and crept round the shores of the Mediterranean Sea, from Greece to Sicily to Genoa. According to some, it had already taken hold of the port of Marseilles and the city of Aix and even Avignon, the seat of the Pope. His Holiness commanded penitential processions and prayers, to no avail. The citizens of that holy site fell as rapidly as the inhabitants of the most pagan places beyond Christendom.

The pestilence had not yet reached England and many comforted themselves with the notion that the sea would keep them safe. Or they believed that God would not permit them to be afflicted precisely because they were English. (After all, hadn't He provided them with a great victory over the French at the battle of Crécy less than two years before?) But the better informed or the more hard-headed knew it was only a matter of time before the sickness reached their island shores. Indeed, as the spring of 1348 turned to summer there were rumours that the infection had already taken hold at the ports in the far west of the country.

And when it did arrive at the place where you lived ... what then?

Neither prayers nor practical measures had any effect. You might bar the gates of your town and turn visitors away, but the pestilence, in all its cunning, found ways to circumvent every precaution. It was said that people could contract it merely from the glance of an infected victim. Some who had been nowhere near any sufferer fell sick nevertheless and died. And how they died!

Death took two equally dreadful forms. In this it might be likened to a pitchfork, for though you might avoid being impaled on one of its prongs you would most surely find yourself squirming on the other. Many vomited up copious quantities of blood from the lungs and died very soon afterwards. The rest endured fever and delirium before great swellings erupted in their necks or armpits or groins; after several agonising days they too perished.

If death by pestilence was like being impaled on a pitchfork, the question was: who was wielding it? Everyone knew that this familiar implement was one of the tools of the demons in Hell. Now it seemed as though the Devil himself were ranging across the earth, twitching his tail and flailing about with his pitchfork. More thoughtful, religious individuals were aware that such things happened only with God's permission. And since God was permitting His people to be punished with these terrible forms of death, then it could only be because they had committed terrible sins, and then committed them again and again. Deep-dyed in wickedness. they rejected with laughter or contempt every opportunity for repentance provided by a generous, forgiving God.

If some individual had the temerity to ask whether all the citizens of Genoa or Aix or Avignon – down to the last man, woman and child – had committed sins deserving such terrible punishment, the answer given by the thoughtful and religious was that God's purposes were inscrutable.

The only recourse for those English waiting in fear for the pestilence was to pray more earnestly and live yet more devoutly. Of course, not everyone was pious. Some carried on as usual, either because they were resigned to events or because they believed themselves to be God's favourites and immune on that account. A surprisingly large number decided that, if the end was really coming, they might as well enjoy themselves and blotted out their remaining days on earth by drinking and gambling and whoring.

And then there were those who hoped that God's wrath might be averted by going on a pilgrimage. Even had they the leisure and means, there was no question of travelling overseas; for example, to the holy cities of Jerusalem or Rome. So it was fortunate that there were shrines and sacred places closer to hand.

*

Not far from the north coast of Norfolk stood a famous shrine to Our Lady. Inside the priory at Walsingham was a chapel that sheltered an image of the Virgin and the Holy Child. The light of many candles was reflected in the offerings of gold, silver and jewels that bedecked the image. Though made only of wood, she was capable of working miracles. Everyone knew that prayers at Walsingham were especially efficacious, for the shrine possessed relics beyond compare, such as the Virgin's milk preserved in a phial on the high altar of the priory church, or a finger joint belonging to St Peter. The Virgin herself had commanded a healing spring to flow forth near the chapel. It was not only ordinary folk who journeyed to pay their respects there; it was often visited by Edward III and the kings of England before him. If there was any single shrine in England that might be propitious for those hoping to ward off the pestilence, then it was surely Walsingham.

So it was that, in the spring and summer of 1348, streams of people made their way from all over England to this sacred site. Most made careful preparations before embarking on their pilgrimage to ensure their families and homes, their farms and other businesses were in good hands. In return, they promised to pray for those left behind and to bring back some protective token. Routes had to be planned and stopping-places decided in advance; the devotion of the pilgrims would be increased if due reverence was paid at the churches and lesser shrines on the way to Walsingham. There were even a few, particularly among those dwelling not far from the shrine, who declared they would walk the entire distance on bare feet.

If you could view these pilgrim parties from high above, you would see them moving along different tracks with a single-minded discipline and shared sense of purpose, moving like currents of water until they converged in larger streams and then in still larger ones before turning into a river that, flowing in from the south, overwhelmed the little town of Walsingham.

But if you were to come down and observe them at eye-level, if you were actually to walk with them and listen for a time, you would soon realise that not all of these good people were driven by a sense of devotion. Indeed, not every man and woman was going to Walsingham but simply happened to be travelling in the same general direction and was staying with a group of pilgrims for companionship and safety on the road. Among the pilgrims, not every man or woman's purpose was a holy one. Even at this moment of great peril, with the pestilence beginning to stalk across the land, there were those who treated the pilgrimage as a fair-weather jaunt or a chance to escape their domestic obligations, or perhaps an opportunity to keep company with a neighbour's wife under pious cover. And the many groups of pilgrims would, for certain, have included a few individuals hoping to profit by the whole enterprise, since souvenirs brought back from Walsingham – or supposedly brought back – would have an especial value to those who stayed behind at home.

One day in early July, a certain group of pilgrims, made up of several smaller bands and numbering altogether about three dozen people, was still several days' journey away from Walsingham. Some had come from places to the south and west, such as Cambridge and Newmarket and Bury, but others had travelled much further.

Now they were not so far from the town of Thetford, which is just over the southern Norfolk boundary. The pilgrims were at a point in their journeying when many would have welcomed the chance to stop for rest and refreshment, particularly as they were on the outskirts of a town that, though not large, still boasted an inn. This establishment, called the Angel, was known to two or three of the group, who were busy recommending it to their companions. The food and drink were reliable, they said, and the landlord was honest and friendly. Another reason for making a halt was that a storm might be on the way. For some time, the travellers had been aware of whispers of thunder beyond the level horizon.

Yet, because several hours of daylight remained, others in the group wanted to press on to Thetford, which was much larger than this place – called Mundham – and therefore offered more possibilities for overnight lodging. Thetford was also a desirable spot in itself because, like Walsingham, it contained a shrine to the Our Lady at the Cluniac priory.

As they entered Mundham, a bank of dark cloud suddenly welled up above the forest that lay on the far side of the straggling town. Thunder boomed, this time from nearby. The day was warm, and the pilgrims were dusty and sweaty, but within moments their garments and exposed faces were buffeted by gusts of colder air and drops of rain driven sideways. In a few more moments, it was as if a dark blanket had been thrown across the sky and the drops turned into a downpour. The few people loitering in the main street of the township and idly observing the arrival of the pilgrim party had already run for shelter, together with the dogs that had been enjoying the late afternoon sun.

There was no discussion now about whether to stop or continue walking and, as one, the pilgrim group made for the Angel inn whose wooden sign rocked in the wind. The company scrambled beneath the arched gateway and into the courtyard, already turning into a mire, and then inside the shelter of the hall that lay on the far side of the yard. A couple of locals were already sitting drinking at the long trestle table that occupied one side of the high, spacious chamber. They looked up from their mugs with a mixture of smugness and annoyance at these new arrivals.

The landlord, whose name was Laurence, was a cheerful man, not only for professional reasons but by nature. He and his wife made the pilgrims feel welcome straight away, congratulating them on their piety in making the trip to Walsingham and saying that after a long day's journey they must be ready to take the weight off their feet and to sit down and be refreshed. The couple ushered the pilgrims to the long trestle table, indicating to the two local drinkers that they should budge up, and swiftly pressed a second table into service because there were so many guests. The newcomers were served bread and cheese and wine or ale by a boy and girl whose resemblance to the landlord and his wife showed plainly enough whose they were. All the while the rain rattled against the high-beamed roof and draughts of wind penetrated ill-fitting shutters to lift the rushes strewn across the floor. A fire was going and some of the travellers clustered near it to dry off their clothes.

Now Laurence was faced with a problem, even if it was quite a desirable one for an innkeeper. This was not the first party he had hosted on its way to Walsingham and he welcomed this influx of potential overnight guests but could not accommodate them all in the timber-framed wings that flanked the courtyard of the Angel. How to encourage some of the pilgrims to stay, others to go? In this situation, Laurence thought of business and not of the purpose of the pilgrimage. Like everyone else he feared the pestilence and its effect on trade, if it struck, to say nothing of whether it might touch him and his family personally. But so far the plague had worked to his advantage because the general alarm it produced somehow seemed to shake people up and to provoke more coming and going than usual.

As they helped to serve the food and drink, Laurence and his wife swiftly sensed which of the pilgrims were inclined to turn this halt into an overnight stay and which of them wanted to brave the weather and reach Thetford before darkness fell. With hints and nods, the husband and wife – well-practised in this kind of quiet persuasion – agreed with the desires of each group. Yes, madam, it does make good sense to remain here at the Angel in Mundham where your comfort and security are guaranteed. Indeed, there have been recent whispers of thieves and outlaws operating in the woods between here and Thetford. And to others they said they admired their devoutness in wanting to get on with their journey to Walsingham as speedily as possible.

Sometimes it was possible to tell just by looking at people which ones were not likely to stir any further that day. For example, there was a white-bearded man in the company of a younger one and, though the older man seemed very alert, something about the way he turned his head to catch at sounds suggested to Laurence that his eyesight must be very imperfect. He surely would need to stay the night. Then there was that attractive woman – not English, Laurence thought – who definitely wouldn't wish to expose herself or her well-cut clothes to the mercy of a violent summer storm. And there was a hatchet-faced churchman – a prior, no less – who looked unlikely to put up with a moment's more discomfort than he had to.

In a short space of time the band of pilgrims split into two, half waiting only for a pause in the downpour before resuming their journey, and the remainder, complaining of tiredness or sore feet or just wanting the certainty of a bed for the night, deciding to stay. It helped that they seemed already to have sorted themselves instinctively into different groups, one at one table, one at the other, with a group also clustered about the fire, and another two or three who seemed to prefer their own company on the fringe of each party. Laurence rubbed his hands with pleasure, calculating how he would fit those who looked likely to remain into the beds in his two chambers.

So it was that after an hour or so the pilgrim band divided, with the leavers retrieving their bags and staffs and picking their way across the Angel yard, now sticky with mud, and out into the main street of Mundham. The rain had ceased for a moment, though there were still rumbles of thunder in the distance. The rays of the evening sun shot through ragged holes in the cloud.

Those left behind ordered more food and drink and talked a little more loudly or rapidly, perhaps to reassure themselves that they were doing the right thing in staying behind. There were several hours of daylight left, no need to go to bed yet. Besides, it was pleasant to be warm and fed and to talk at leisure while receiving the hospitality of these excellent innkeepers. Whether it was because the remaining pilgrims were generally more cautious and reflective people, or had other reasons for not travelling on, the general conversation soon took a more serious turn. Although you might try to forget the pressing matter of the pestilence, you could not do it for long, and so it was here at the Angel inn at Mundham. Once again the same questions came up, as they surely recurred in thousands of conversations and exchanges taking place across the country every day.

Why was God allowing the pestilence to attack His people?

How might it be evaded?

Or, if it could not be escaped, how might its effects be minimised?

Someone had heard of a most infallible method, involving the gathering up of the contents of piss-pots and privies and the pouring of the mixture into a great brass cooking pot. Drape yourself with a towel, said this individual, and hang your head over the cauldron. Breathe deep and long until your gorge rises. Then, as soon as you have recovered, repeat the treatment. The noxious vapours will not only harden you against the pestilence but the vomiting that will likely result has the benefit of purging your body of any dangerous elements. The more fastidious pilgrims turned up their noses at this treatment but, even so, a number of them made a mental note of it.

From physical remedies the talk turned to spiritual ones: to human sin and divine salvation. There was discussion about which sin, out of the seven deadly sins, was the worst and so the most deserving of God's punishment. Some said it was pride, others wrath or envy. Gluttony was scarcely mentioned – after all, the pilgrims were still eating and drinking. Lust was referred to, but in passing, and with an embarrassed snigger or a wry look. Rather in the way that the original pilgrim party had divided in two by instinct, so now it seemed that there was a natural tendency for this woman to denounce one particular sin, or that man to turn his attention to another, until not a single one of the seven was left unmentioned and commented on. Settling in for a longer session, several of these same pilgrims indicated that they might have stories to tell, each of which would prove the wickedness of the sin that he or she was proclaiming as the very worst, the most damnable.

Seeing an opportunity, their host, Laurence, who had by now made himself one of the party, suggested that the guests should tell their tales. After all, the long summer evening had scarcely begun. (There was plenty of time to purchase more refreshment, he might have added.) 'Why don't we have a proper contest?' he said. 'As they do in universities and such learned places, but not all dry and dusty. A contest of storytelling, told by people with real knowledge and experience of life. As,' he said, looking round with a beaming smile, 'I can see all of you ladies and gentlemen have knowledge and experience.

'Yes, let us tell stories of sins, and then it might emerge which one is the best. That is, the worst . . .'

Though the idea was received with enthusiasm, there seemed to be a reluctance to go first, as if each speaker feared being judged not for his storytelling but for the sin that was its subject. Then from the group clustered around the fire came the sounds of urgent discussion . . .

The First Sin

He had listened to the anecdotes and rumours told by the other travellers with half an ear while they were trudging along the road, but once they reached the inn, Janyn Hussett glanced about him and shook his head as he settled himself near the fire, trying to ignore them.

These folks were all full of piss and wind. They wittered on about their feelings, their lives, as though nothing else mattered, but they were shallow, insubstantial people. If he had any choice, he would leave them. He wasn't one of them. They had no idea what life was like for men like him, for men like Bill and Walt and Barda. For those who had died.

He sat and stared at the fire. Flames were licking up the faggots from the twigs beneath, and he was reminded again of the fires about Caen after the terrible sacking of the city, the wailing and weeping. And those horrors were early in the campaign, long before the astonishing victory at Crécy, and then the capture of Calais itself. His was a life of horrors: war and bloodshed, power and fear.

But now? Now it felt as though his life was ended. He had fought and killed, and when Calais fell, he had enjoyed a brief spell of happiness, but now God was punishing him – punishing everyone. Janyn's wife and little babe were only two among the countless bodies that littered France's villages and towns after the arrival of the Terrible Death, 'atra mors'*, or what the French were calling the* 'morte bleue'*. So many: all tossed into the mass graves in cities like Calais, or left to rot in the fields and lanes uncared for, since all the others had already died. The horror would never leave him, he was sure. God had decided to punish them all. But Janyn knew others who suffered even more than he himself. One man had thought himself responsible, and suffered in his own private hell.*

That was his curse.

When the travellers started this stupid game, asking about the worst sins, Janyn almost shot to his feet and left the room, struck with the urge to vomit. Scenes appeared in his mind, pictures of the corpses at the roadside, women screaming as they were raped, soldiers laughing and queuing for their turn, a nun's corpse decapitated, babies . . . the world was full of sins. The deadliest sins? They were all deadly. Wherever men went, they brought evil with them. For a while he had been happy with his wife. He had been content. Seeing the miracle of pregnancy and birth, feeling the wonder as he held for the first time his little pink, mewling son, he had thought life could not offer anything so marvellous and awe-inspiring. Then the joy in his heart had almost crushed him. He adored his wife and son so much, he would happily have died for them.

But now both were gone. God had taken them.

Janyn Hussett wanted to shout at the other pilgrims: 'You know what I think? I think you have no idea what real life is like! Look at you, all of you! Sitting here in comfort, out of the rain, whining about the weather . . .'

But he held his tongue. He held his hands to the fire and gritted his teeth. It was better not to speak, but to hold himself in resentful silence, ignoring their vapid maunderings.

But they would keep going on about their pointless, stupid, irrelevant lives.

'Friend, you are very quiet,' one of the pilgrims said to him. 'Tell me, where do you hail from?'

Janyn looked up and snapped, 'What is it to you where I come from? Why do you want to know?'

'Please, friend! I was being amiable, that is all,' said the man. He was stocky, serious-looking. His name was Nicholas. 'We are all friends here, aren't we? We are making a long journey. It would be good to know you better. Then, if we meet again, we can exchange stories about our lives.'

'Exchange stories?' Janyn said with contempt. He took a stick of kindling and broke it, hurling the halves into the flames. 'What stories do you want? Tales of death and horror? Shall I tell you how I have seen nuns raped and slaughtered like so many sows? Or children taken from their mothers' breasts to have their heads dashed against a wall? Is that what you would hear? No: you don't want that. You don't want to know my story.'

'I would hear it,' Nicholas pressed him quietly. 'Come, friend, we are all here together. You are a man of much experience, I'd wager. I would value your tale. Which sin do you think is the most terrible?'

'Why do you ask me that?' Janyn demanded. He was wound tight as a cog's rigging as he leaned forward, his hand straying to the knife at his belt.

Laurence saw his hand's movement and the innkeeper shook his head, smiling and holding his hands up pacifically, but stepping forward to prevent a fight. 'Hoy, friend, he means nothing by it: nothing. But we were talking about the deadly sins. From the look of you, you must have a view on such things. Which would you say was the worst?'

'I have seen all the sins imaginable committed while I was in France. There are men there who have sought to offend Christ and His saints every day with their debaucheries,' Janyn said, grimacing. 'Ach, no! Why do you want me to speak of them? I would forget them all.'

'You were a fighter in France?'

This was the prior, the churchman with the sharp face. He sat at the other side of the fire, smugly arrogant as he eyed Janyn – like a judge presented with a felon of notorious fame.

Janyn sneered and turned his attention back to the flames. 'A pox on your cockiness! If you were in France, you wouldn't survive above a day,' he muttered. Then he looked up, his dark brown eyes fixed on the rest of the group as he spoke, glowering with a fixed intensity that spoke of pain and anguish. 'What can you know of the horror, the suffering of the men out there? How many of you have been told to slaughter prisoners? To butcher men and women, aye, and their wains? Not one. You cannot appreciate how war changes a man, how it twists him and torments him, until he is utterly broken.'

He was a grim-faced little man. Like many a peasant, his face was leathery and tanned from exposure, but there was a hard edginess to the lines on his face.

'You want to know what I think, then? I'd say lust is the worst.

Because it's lust that leads to murder and slaughter. Lust for women, lust for gold, lust for power. All come to the same: lust! And one man felt sure that his own lust brought about the plague that hunts all men now.'

'Tell us your story, friend. Show us what you mean.'

He stood, caught between the urge to leave them there in the chamber – and the desire to tell them all. He was almost ready to flee the room but, just then, Laurence passed him a green-glazed drinking horn, and he took it and stared into the pale-coloured ale. There were bubbles and swirls in the drink, and suddenly, as clouds might form the appearance of a cog at sea or a man's face, he saw her again: Pelagia, the Frenchwoman with the neck of a swan, the body of an angel. He saw her face as clearly as he saw the flames in the fire.

It decided him. With a gesture of defiance, he tossed his head back and drained the horn in one. He could tell them a tale to make them sit up and listen! A tale of . . .

Lust

War is evil for many, but most of all for the people who want no part in it – he began – the women and children. They suffer from the unwanted attentions of men; they are raped and slain by invaders, or they're killed by their own because they can't fight, or they starve because food is kept back for the men who will fight. That is what Calais was like. A foul city, full of scared, fretful people. When we got there, the place was already encircled by our King's host, but the fear – you could taste it in the air.

Men react differently to things like that: the smell of fear. Some are like hounds. If a hound senses another is scared, it'll push it around, snarl, growl . . . anything to make it know who is the master, who is the villein. Some men are the same:

if they can tell another is petrified, it gives them a feeling of power. In the army, there were many men like that. Some beat their men, some would brawl and bellow, bragging about their conquests, while others would enjoy a man's terror in silence. They would stand quietly and observe as a man shivered and shook. They are the ones to watch, the ones who will tease and torment, and twist the knife a little deeper, enjoying every squeal of terror, every rictus of agony.

I knew a man like that at Calais, a man called Henry the Tun. The centener.

At Crécy, I was a vintener myself, responsible for twelve men by the end of the campaign. They were all that was left of two vintaines of forty archers under our banneret, Sir John de Sully, but my boys were badly mauled during the flight to the north. We were harried all the way from Paris by the French King's armies, and the people of the towns came out and attacked us as we drew near. There was never a spare yard that wasn't fought for.

After Crécy, things eased a bit. We had destroyed the French on that battlefield, and when we finally left it we were filled with joy. The country was ours, with all the wealth. Even poor archers became rich. And we soon had more men arrive to fill the gaps. My own vintaine needed new blood more than most, and we had seven new fellows join us. But then I was struck down with a fever, and I had to take to a wagon. My men were sent on before me, and I rattled along in their wake like some kind of pathetic infant, with only a pair of brothers to help me: Bill and Walter from Southampton. They were recent recruits, sent to help win Calais after our losses on the long march. I didn't know them, nor the men we travelled with, and, at the first opportunity, I left the wagon and took up a horse. I wanted to rejoin my men. With the brothers, I tagged along behind another vintaine that was passing, and soon I was introduced to their centener: Henry the Tun.

He was a short, thickset man, with a heavy belly that stuck over his belt like a sack of oats bound at the middle. His face was round and ruddy, with cheeks as red as the apples that made his favourite drink, cider. A nose like a plum, and jowls like a mastiff's gave him a pleasing appearance. He looked jolly, a genial, jovial man like a Bacchus come to earth. His eyes were constantly creased as though in great humour – but when a man looked into them, it was clear that there was nothing there. No kindness, no humility, only an overweening greed and desire.

When we were within eyesight of the town, he sat back on his mount and breathed deeply, before pointing to it and grinning at me and his own vinteners. 'There, boys, that's where we'll make our fortunes,' he said.

One of his sergeants, a man called Weaver, looked over at the town. Most of us in that army were good at grumbling. We'd fought all the way from the coast down to Paris and, like I say, been chased away from there all the way to Crécy. There we won our famous victory, it is true, but the cost was high. We lost many friends, good friends, on that march homewards, so we felt entitled to grumble.

Anyway, Weaver was there at the front with Henry, and as he looked out over the town and the army, he drew his face into a sneer. 'The King wants that? I wouldn't pay a clipped penny for the whole place.'

'Shows how much you know of things like that,' Henry said. He sat back in his saddle, gazing ahead of him, that smile on his thick lips, like a glutton presented with a whole roasted suckling pig. 'It's the King's delight, is Calais, and should be yours, too, Weaver. It'll be an easy sail home from here. You can almost see England over there.'

Weaver, he just grunted. All we could see was a greyish mess. Could have been clouds, but more likely it was the thick smoke rising from all about the town. When you have a few thousand Englishmen in an army, you have a mess. Weaver wasn't stupid enough to argue. We'd all seen others who'd argued with Henry. They hadn't done so well.

Anyway, Weaver, he said nothing. I thought it was because he didn't want to be beaten, but when I looked at him, I saw why. He was staring down at a figure by the side of the road. A young woman.

Like I said, war is a horrible thing for the poor souls who work the land it smothers. That's what war does, it engulfs whole lands; and the poor people who live there, they're like cattle. Captured, milked dry, and killed. Of course, for women and children, it's worse. They are little better than slaves to an invading army, and any can be taken or slain on a whim. I saw enough of that kind of casual brutality on the way to Calais. Even English boys who were there to help support the fighters were often beaten for no reason, just because the soldiers knew they could.

This girl had been brought up well. She had soft skin on her hands, and her knees were unmarked. She wasn't a peasant's child, I could see that from the first. But her clothing was rough, tattered stuff that would have suited a maid from a plague vill. You know what I mean. We've all heard of folk who've lost their families since the plague. In France, I've seen worse: girls and boys without their fathers, who've had to fend for themselves for months until they starved. All with swollen bellies, their faces pinched and grey. Well, this girl had the same ragged clothing, but her belly was flat, her face still haughty. It was a wonder she had not learned humility yet, I thought. After all, a girl with that kind of manner appeals to many men.

You can imagine how a girl like her would have found life under the English boot. She had been brought up to enjoy all the finer things: good food, wine, servants. Suddenly she was homeless, wandering with the refugees trying to escape the English. Us.

Who was she? No one. She had been raised in some town or other – mayhap it was Caen – and was daughter to a fuller. He was a good, kind man, apparently, but, as our army approached, he insisted that she should leave with her mother and two brothers. He was to remain to look after the town with the rest of the militia, so she said when I got to speak with her later. She and her mother and brothers took a heavy purse of coin, and set off on their way.

But God had set His face against her.

'Friend, you are feeling out of sorts,' said Nicholas. 'Wait, let another tell his story, and take some ale and a rest.'

'I am fine,' Janyn snapped. He wiped a hand over his face, remembering, and his voice grew softer as he looked about him at the expectant faces. 'It is a hard story, though.'

'We have heard such tales before. The men lusted after her, and—'

'You think to tell my story for me?' Janyn snarled.

'No, I—'

'Listen and you may learn something new about men,' Janyn stated.

He could see her again in his mind's eye as he spoke. A lovely girl, she was. Slim and perfect as a birch. In her life, he knew, she was raised to wealth. There was nothing unwholesome about her. Nothing spoiled, unlike the devastated country they had marched through. Janyn had seen war in all its forms, but to walk about a country in which every farm had been burned, all the stored crops stolen or ravaged, all the cattle driven off or slain – to walk about that ravaged landscape hurt his soul. He felt as though he was taking part in the systematic rape of the country.

She was just one of the countless thousands who had lost all. Both brothers and her mother had been killed by marauding bands of English, and it was a miracle she wasn't found and raped and killed in her turn, but by keeping to the night hours and hiding during the day, by degrees she made it to Calais. Not that she was any safer when she reached it.

The girl was found by King Edward's men just outside the city. Like so many, she had been cast out of Calais when the English appeared. Many had been thrown from the gates as soon as it was realised that the English were coming to lay siege. No spare mouths would be allowed to remain inside the walls. Those who were refugees from the surrounding countryside were evicted, sometimes forcibly, so that the stores would last longer for the garrison and people of the town. This was no time for the kind-hearted support of those less fortunate; rather, it was a time to callously guard one's own security. And food must be kept for those who came from the city or those who could guard it. She was neither; she was a foreigner.

She had been flung from the gates, her money and little pack of meagre belongings stolen from her. She would soon be dead, so why leave her with goods to enrich the English? Better to keep them in the town. Too scared and tired even to weep, she took to whatever cover she could find out beside the road. But there was no protection out there, between the lines of English invaders and the city walls. Not a tree, not a bush. The weather was dreadful, and soon she was shivering with the cold and damp, petrified of what would happen when the English caught her. She had heard much of their brutality.

As the first English hobilars appeared, she was found and taken away, out of bowshot of the town's walls, to be held with other prisoners. She expected there would be little sympathy for her and her companions. The English could not afford to waste good food on her and her like. She would be fortunate if she was only raped and killed quickly. Others endured days or weeks of torture.

But Janyn saw her, and he felt a little flare of compassion. He had been marching for miles, and the last thing on his mind as he approached the town was a woman. All he wanted was a chance to sit down under canvas and pull off his sodden boots – but the sight of her touched something in his heart, a sense of tenderness. It was the same, he saw, when he looked into the faces of Bill and Walter. They all felt the same attraction to her. For his part, Janyn reckoned he wouldn't get any rest unless he saw that she was safe. The thought of her being raped was intolerable, somehow.

Henry and Weaver were riding on with the rest of the centaine as Janyn dropped from his saddle. Bill and Walter waited on their mounts.

'What is your name?' he asked as he approached her.

She looked at him with the fear naked in her eyes. Men here were only interested in what they could take.

'Come, maid, what is your name?' he said.

Her gaze dropped. 'Pelagia.'

'It is a pretty name.'

She looked up at that, anger searing her face. 'How would a man who burns and murders recognise prettiness?' she spat.

Janyn's days were full enough after that. He was glad to see that the girl and the other prisoners were not slain immediately, but instead were released. The girl Pelagia was set free on the second day, and Janyn saw her again that morning.

There was a gaggle of men who organised provisions in this section of the army, and Janyn was at the wagons collecting food when he noticed the slim figure staring desperately at the wagons with their precious cargoes. Her face was tragic. She had no money, and no means of earning it – bar one.

Janyn walked to her and smiled, but she looked straight through him as though he wasn't there. Only when he hefted the wrapped bundle in his hands did she show interest. It was a fresh loaf, and he held it out, nodding to her as he pulled the linen from it. The aroma of warm bread seemed to fill the space between them, and he held it out again. 'Eat – please.'

She struggled with her feelings. How could she not? These were the men who had destroyed her city, who had probably caused the death of all her family, and now this man offered food in exchange for . . . she knew what he would want.

'Leave me!' she spat, and turned.

'Girl, just take it and go,' he snapped. He broke the loaf in two and threw one piece to her. She caught it quickly, and would have said more to him, but Janyn had already stalked off angrily. He only wanted to help her. To have his offer of aid thrown back in his face was demeaning as well as insulting.

Why? Why would anyone want to help a young woman in her predicament? She was young, fresh, beautiful, a reminder to him of when he was younger and in love, perhaps. Or maybe it was because he thought he saw in her a dim reflection of his own mother. Whatever the reason, he only wanted to aid her. She had a need of food, and would find it hard to come by here, with the English taking everything for miles around. It was foolishness to refuse his offer, no matter what she thought he was like.

He set her from his thoughts. She didn't deserve his efforts, he thought. The ungrateful wretch could go hang.

If there was any justice, that is what would have happened. Janyn would have gone through the siege and never seen her again. She would have been found stealing from a baker's or from a butcher's, and would have been hanged on the spot. Janyn would never have been tormented by the sight of her again.

But life was never so straightforward.

He came to see her every so often. She had become a familiar face about the camp after a few days, and while men occasionally leered at her and tried to get close, they always found themselves reluctant to get *too* close. There was something about her that made a man keep away. Not exactly fear – the men of King Edward's army were not scared of any woman – but a sort of grating on the nerves. When they spoke to her, or made lecherous comments in the hope she would respond, she said nothing, but she had a look that spoke to many of them; it was the kind of stare a witch might give. It was as if there was no soul within her breast, no heart, no compassion or feeling. She felt neither terror nor hatred; she was filled with a numbing emptiness that was so cold it would freeze a man who touched her.

Once, Janyn saw three men attempting to persuade her to lie with them. They circled about her, one trying to engage her in conversation, another playing with the binding of his cods and holding out a penny, while the third laughed inanely, waving his arms like a cockerel warning off an interloper in his ring. It was plain enough that if she refused their money they would take her for free.

It was a sight to spark his rage, and Janyn had his hand on his sword as he opened his mouth to bellow at them, but he need not have worried. Even as he prepared to defend her, and while she stared at the men, one at a time, without moving, he saw two others running to her aid: Bill and Walter. They shoved the men away, and her attackers left her like melting snow sloughing from a roof, to go and find easier prey.

It came back to him now, that scene. The ringleader of the men spitting at the ground, another biting his thumb at Bill and Walter, but all three moving off, unwilling to test the anger in the faces of the two men who stood at her side to protect her.

Bill and Walter glanced at each other, then at Pelagia. She stood looking at them, utterly still, and the two men looked confused, pinned under her scrutiny like a man stabbed to an oaken door by an arrow.

'Are you well, maid?' Bill asked at last.

She gazed at him from those fathomless eyes of hers, but said nothing.

'I wanted to help,' he said.

Janyn watched the woman turn and walk away from them. Neither brother made a move to follow her. They watched her as she made her way between the little shacks and carts of the camp. But in their faces, Janyn saw the dawn of adoration.

They looked like men who would cast aside their own lives to protect her.

Janyn knew that there was something between the brothers and the girl from the first moment. Bill and Walter would stare at her, and he wondered at first whether they were planning on making use of her for their own enjoyment. He kept a close eye on them, but soon he realised that these two were not seeking to rape, they were both attempting to win her over in their own ways.

The older of the two, Walter, was a heavy-set man. If he had been a tree, he would have been an oak. Brown-faced and with a thick, black beard and slanted blue eyes that gleamed under his brimmed felt cap, he had heavily muscled arms and short, stubby fingers. Although he was a massively strong fellow, he had already gained a reputation for kindness – he was the first to share any food or drink, and when he did capture the enemy, he always brought them in alive.

His brother was not the same. Bill was a harder man, with the slim, wiry strength of a birch tree. He had lean, narrow features, and while he was as dark of hair, there was a tinge of brown in his beard and moustache that wasn't in Walter's. Unlike his brother, Bill had long, slender fingers, and his arms and thighs looked as strong as reeds compared to Walter's powerful build, but Bill was a ferocious fighter. Janyn saw that himself often enough in the little fights about Calais. Still, while both were very different men, neither gave him any cause for concern.

Not for their fighting prowess, anyway. It was different when it came to love.

Janyn was wary with all his men when it came to Pelagia. She was aloof, holding all the men in contempt, but for some, especially Walter, this served as a spur to his desire for her. It was not a rough, demanding lust, but a deep infatuation that tore at him whenever he saw her. Janyn could see it, and just as clearly so could the other men. However, Bill adored her too, in his own quiet manner. When she walked about the camp, Janyn could often see the two brothers, their eyes following her slim figure.

Seeing their competitive desire for her, Janyn had thought they might come to blows, yet their fights were not with each other, but with any other man in the vintaine who threatened Pelagia or who tried to force himself into her company. The two brothers were protecting her, and she seemed to appreciate their help as much as she did Janyn's own calm defence.

Perhaps all would have been well, were it not for Henry the Tun.

Henry was not a man to hold a secret. He was content to tell his tale to any who would listen, and he had spoken of it to Janyn on many occasions. His life had been full of incident, but he was a senior commander in the King's army now, and safe. Besides, along with his age and experience, he had confidence in his prowess and authority. His tale was known to many. It was a source of pride to him, a proof of his strength and valour, he thought.

Henry had been born the son of a cooper in a village called Cleopham, some few miles from London. When he was old enough, he had travelled up to the city, and there he was apprenticed to a barrel-maker, but the work didn't satisfy him. He was a bold, roistering fellow who loved ale and women, rather than being tied to a master who ordered him about and made him work at tasks in which he had no interest. Henry was not remotely interested in sweeping and cleaning, or learning how to split and shape barrel staves, nor in binding barrels with willow. He wanted money to enjoy himself with friends in alehouses lining the Southwark streets. And there he got to know the women.

There were so many of them, and they were enthusiastic companions to a man with money. The Bishop of Winchester's lands south of the river were full of brothels and individual women making their own way, usually supporting their pimps with their income.

It was one of these who got Henry into trouble.

He had been with the boys in London during the excitement of a riot. King Edward II, the King's father, was realising that his reign was coming to an end, and when Walter Stapeldon, Bishop of Exeter, was slain in the street like a common felon by the London mob, Henry and the other apprentices went on the rampage. They swept down Ludgate Hill to the Fleet River, and broke the shutters of all the shops on the way, beating up anyone they met. Any men who wore the insignia of the hated Despenser family were grabbed and tormented, or battered with canes and clubs on the way.

Henry saw one man dart into an alleyway. Catching a glimpse of Despenser's arms on his tunic, and full of ale and cockiness, he chased the fellow until he managed to crack him over the head with his club. The man fell, tumbling to the ground, and Henry kicked him a couple of times for good measure before cutting his purse free. It had a pleasant heft to it, and he opened it to find plenty of coins.

Later, he went with his new-found wealth to the stews of Southwark, and there he met the woman.

God alone knew what her name was. She must have told him, but he couldn't remember the morning after. He was brutally drunk: as fighting, swearing, rotten drunk as any man had ever been. And while he was stumbling into walls, shouting and laughing, he yet wanted a woman, this woman.

She was a saucy-looking little slut, with a head of thick straw-coloured hair and eyes the colour of the cornflowers he used to see in the fields about his home when he was young. He used to pick them for his mother. She liked to receive little gifts like that and, seeing the whore, he was reminded of those little acts. He wanted to find her something pleasant. There were no flowers here in the muddy, noisome streets. Little could survive amongst the cart tracks and faeces. Human, cattle, swine, dog and cat excrement lined the ways. Any plants would be trampled underfoot in no time. But he wanted to get her something.

He had plenty of money in his purse, he remembered blearily.

'Maid, come with me. I'll buy you a drink. I'll buy you a new coif or something . . .' he blurted.

'You're too drunk,' she said.

'I am. You come with me, and you can be too. I've money, look!'

He held up his purse and jingled it so she could hear the coins inside.

Her eyes widened. 'I'll come with you.'

'Which is the best tavern in the street?'

She indicated a building with a large bush tied over the door, and he walked with her to it, stumbling only a little as he went, but as they drew nearer, he was shoved, hard, and a man pulled the woman away.

'You bitch! You don't leave your place over there. You know my rules!' the man shouted.

He was a big man, heavy in the belly, but with the thin, wiry frame of a smith.

Henry pushed himself to his feet. When he felt his head, there was blood running in a thin trickle where he had struck a stone as he fell. He stared at the blood.

'Get back, bitch!' the man said again, and shoved her.

Henry was too full of ale to take care of the likely outcome. He drew his knife and struck the cock-bawd. Later, he heard that he slammed the blade into the man more than twenty times, but for all he knew it could have been once or a hundred times. He didn't know what he was doing. The ale was driving him.

That was the end of his apprenticeship. He realised, as he stood looking at the crumpled body before him, that he must flee, that this was the end of all he knew. The whore, after giving a muffled squeak of alarm, began to shriek like a banshee, claiming that someone had murdered her husband, and men began to appear in the street. A horn was blown, and men began to gather.

Henry had to run faster than ever before in his life. He didn't take the risk of returning home to collect his meagre belongings, he just ran and ran, up to the river, over along the shoreline, until he found a wherry and begged the oarsman to take him to the other side. A handful of coins persuaded the man. Within a few hours, Henry was safely on board a cog, feeling the waters roll her side to side, bound for Gascony.

He had never looked back.

There were many men in the army with irregular marriages. These women who joined the men in the camps were known as 'marching wives'. Some of them were keen to stay with just one man; some were enthusiastically promiscuous, perhaps because they felt safer knowing that several men would look after them. There was less risk that their investment in time and effort would prove to be pointless. After all, it took only one arrow to remove their asset.

Janyn had never taken a woman. He had seen them, the sad, grey-faced widows and children, tagging along after the fighting men. Some put on a show of courage and enthusiasm, but for the most part they were weary, shocked, terrified women, many of whom had seen their menfolk hacked to death in front of them. Janyn had early on sworn that he would never force women like them to share his blanket with him. Yet there were times, as he listened in the darkness to other men grunting and rutting, when he envied them.

For certain, some of the women did enjoy their status. Sometimes the younger ones could be prickly and acerbic, but when they chose their mate, they were enthusiastic. So long as they hadn't witnessed the slaughter of brothers and parents. That did tend to change them.

Many of these marching wives were happy to join the army. They came not from villages that had been pillaged, but from towns further away. Their lives were already mapped out for them: marriage with a local boy, life under a despotic mother-in-law, a patriarchal father-in-law, who would often hold incestuous desires, all of them ready and waiting to force the young wives into prolonged servitude. And for what? So that they could become brood-mares for the village. Nothing more. They were valued as highly as a bitch in whelp – not even as highly as a cow in calf, for a cow brought milk, meat and money. A bitch would only bark and snap. Little surprise, then, that the more enterprising young women would slip their leashes and run to join the army. There, they were valued as companions and lovers.

But Janyn would not take them. He was content with a simple financial relationship with one of the many whores, but he would not become emotionally entangled. It would take only a moment's reflection on a husband's, brother's or child's death for a woman to turn into a knife-wielding avenger, and he had no wish to share his bed with a vengeful harpy. Sex with a woman who might bear a grudge for her man's death – that was a risk he could happily live without.

For that reason, when Pelagia joined him in the camp the day after the three had been scared away by Bill and Walter, the men of his vintaine were surprised. They knew their vintener's opinions about the marching wives. But none dared say anything. The grim expression on Janyn's face was enough to dispel any potential humour.

He had come across her lying huddled beside a tree that evening, already cold, shivery, suspicious and wary. She had no cloak to cover herself, nor yet a thick tunic. Instead, she huddled for warmth closer to the tree. It was like clutching ice in the hope of heat.

'If you don't find a man to protect you soon, you'll be taken by someone less understanding. If you're not careful, I'll wake up one morning and find your body. I don't want that,' he said, and shuddered at the thought as though it were a premonition.

She gave him a long, slow stare. 'What do you want from me?'

'I would have you live. That is all,' he said. 'There has been enough death about these fields. Just live, woman, and I will be content.'

She rose stiffly, and shivered again. He led the way without turning to see if she was behind him. She could have slid away into the welcome concealment of the surrounding trees, for all he knew, but he continued traipsing on until he reached the circle of his men. There, he turned, and found that she was a mere four paces behind him.

'Lie down there,' he said to her, indicating his own blankets. The thick fustian was scratchy and rough, and he saw her eye it doubtfully. 'It's all there is,' he said. 'If you want to keep warm, you must roll yourself up in it.'

He said nothing more that evening. As she settled herself, wrapped in the coarse cloth, he sat nearby, his back to a tree, his steady gaze fixed on a point in the distance. Walter brought him a little pottage, but for the most part the men left him to his bleak meditations. Only one person didn't seem to hold him in awe. When he glanced down, he saw that her eyes were still fixed on him. Feline, she seemed, and he could not tell whether, like a cat, she appreciated his protection or doubted his intentions.

Henry the Tun had not thought of the woman in the days since his arrival at Calais. He had been too busy with his men. He had never been an ardent womaniser as such. There were too many other distractions for a man like him. As he strode about the encampment and as he sat in the hastily erected tavern drinking sack, he had no time to think about women, and Pelagia had been little more than a bundle of rags in the ditch when he first caught sight of her, but then, one day, he saw her again, and this time he wanted her.

Henry the Tun took women when the urge washed over him, but he was no cruel ravisher of innocents. Those taken prisoner as the army marched tended to be safe from him.

He had little use for them, in truth. Women were necessary on occasion when he was free to indulge his natural desires, and that was all. He preferred the whores who were more likely to be compliant than determined to avenge a dead lover or relative.

With men he was a natural bully. Janyn knew him of old, and knew that Henry was a bold and fierce fighter. He liked to brawl and wrestle, and even when sober, he would join in a gladiatorial battle. He was no coward: that was not one of his faults.

His boldness, his conviction of his own strength and authority, led to his intimidating and bullying others. If there was a ready target for his bile, that fellow would suffer. If a stable-boy mishandled his pony, that boy would receive a clout over the ear that would send him flying, but when he was drunk, Henry would use any as the target of his vicious cruelty.

He was a keen drinker and, when deep in his cups, he was vicious. He would pick on any man, even one of his own company. No matter that the fellow was stronger than most, Henry would willingly take him on. And often, when he had taken more wine than he should, his thoughts turned to other pleasures.

That night he was feeling comfortably amorous after a few pints of wine, and walking back from the tavern, he was feeling a warm glow. His men were content, his purse was full, and all was well with his world. Perhaps he should go to the stews and find himself a woman. There were wenches down there who would be willing enough when they saw the weight of his purse, but it was growing harder to find one to slake his desires. As his reputation was passed from one slut to another, it grew ever more difficult to persuade one to let him lie with her. No woman willingly slept with him above once or twice when he was deep in his cups, because for him the height of ecstasy was to inflict pain while he rutted.

The roads from one place to another were well marked out by then. All about the town of Calais, where the English were camped, a makeshift town had been thrust up. Now there was a regular market, with peasants from about the countryside bringing in some goods, and more appearing from English ships. Wine, ale, clothing, and – blessed Mary! – even new boots materialised. At the same time, ale-houses and taverns appeared, their barrels set up on wagons or simple trestles, and the men tramped along paths that were soon solid-packed earth roads. Gutters ran alongside the older, long-established roads, and it was into one of these that Henry stumbled drunkenly.

Cursing, he stood and staggered from the filth back to the road itself, and began to make his way back to his men, but now he found his path was blocked by a slowly trundling wagon, and he must stand aside.

At the side of the road here, he saw a group of huddled figures, and in their midst, he saw her: the girl.

He didn't recognise her immediately. At that first glimpse all he saw was a woman with a long, willowy throat, her hair indecorously loose over her shoulders, without wimple or coif. She must have appeared a very lewd woman, sitting there amongst a company of men. Who knows? Perhaps he thought her a common marching wife, or even a whore.

Janyn saw Henry at the side of the roadway, and immediately felt the prickling in his belly that warned of danger.

Henry was a strong man, the commander of a centaine, responsible for the wellbeing of his men, but he had no actual friends, only men to be commanded. Janyn's was a lonely enough position, answering to the commands of his banneret, but trying always to keep the men beneath him happy and keen. It wasn't always easy, and for a man more senior, like Henry, it was still more difficult. There was no camaraderie for the leader of a hundred. Above him was his lord, Sir John de Sully, who was himself a stern commander, but a knight had his own circle of companions. Henry had none, only the loneliness of authority.

Seeing him there, Janyn thought Henry had a wistful look about him. Perhaps that was it: sometimes a man just wants to stop, rest, take some comfort. That evening, as drunk as a churl at the harvest festival, Henry perhaps sought only that at first: companionship. Perhaps that was all he ever wanted from a woman. A moment's freedom from responsibility, a spurious friendship. And only later did he come to want to inflict pain to increase his own delight.

When his eyes lit on her, he saw not a prisoner, not a piece of meat, but a young woman of delicacy and beauty. Perhaps, like Janyn, he remembered a vision: a summer's day, a river bank, the scent of meadowsweet heavy on the air making him drowsy as he sat with his head resting in the lap of a woman such as this. It was the kind of memory to take a man's breath away. A lovely, enticing memory of a time long gone, when a boy could meet a girl and they could enjoy the natural pleasures without shame.

It is often the way that a man will form a picture in his mind, when he is all but befuddled with drink, and he won't realise that the object of his affections doesn't share his dream. So it was this time.

He made his way to them.

'Maid, I have a mind to take ye,' he said, belching and dragging at his belt. He was far gone in his cups that night, and once he had the idea of a bout with the maid, nothing would dissuade him from his determination.

'She's not for sale,' Janyn said. 'She's not a slut from a tavern.'

'Shut your mouth, unless you want to feel the King's justice for answering a King's officer,' Henry said. 'By Christ's balls, she is lovely. Maid, I want you. Won't you come with me? I'll look after you better than these churls!'

'Centener, go!' Janyn said.

'Go swive a donkey,' Henry said.

Henry had lumbered forward like a man almost in a trance. His lips were moving, but Janyn couldn't hear a word, only a roaring in his ears that muffled all sound. There was a moment when he felt suffocated with rage, and thought he was going to fall down, but then an intoxication of fury propelled him forwards, and he found himself face to face with Henry.

The centener didn't look at him. His attention was focused entirely on the girl, and as Janyn thrust himself before him, Henry stopped and blinked as though confused to find that another man was in his way.

'She is not for sale,' Janyn grated. 'Leave us alone.'

'You are trying my patience,' Henry said, his face reddening. His jaw jutted as he leaned towards Janyn. 'Get out of my way, you cat's turd.'

'You try this, and I'll have you broken,' Janyn said. 'All my vintaine here will stop you.'

'You would stop a King's officer? You think so? I'll come back with three vintaines, man, and I'll take her over your dead bodies!'

'Try it. You'll be the first to die,' Janyn hissed.

There was a moment's shocked pause. Janyn could feel

the tension like a taut bowstring as he stared at Henry. There was a creak and a slight click, the familiar sound of a bow being drawn taut. Janyn knew that behind him at least one man had nocked an arrow.

'Hear that, Centener? You try to strike me down, or try to steal her from us, and you'll be dead before you've taken two paces. Now go!'

Henry the Tun's face went utterly blank. The colour left his features like water running from a leaking bucket, and Janyn could almost imagine he was facing a ghost. The thought made him shiver.

'You'll regret this,' Henry said quietly. He stood, studying Janyn for a long moment, his eyes empty of all emotion. For a while, Janyn held his breath, convinced that his centener would draw steel and try to stab him, but at last, Henry retreated. After some paces, he turned and walked away, but before he had taken more than a few paces, he stopped again.

His eyes took in all the men there: Janyn, the bowman behind him, and the woman, and he nodded as though reminding himself of all their faces, before chuckling to himself and striding off.

Was he evil? Janyn considered that again now, sitting before the fire. He always wanted to see the good side of any man, where possible. In the past he had taken raw, savage men, and from them honed sharp, competent warriors, and he would like to think that there was more to Henry than he met at first sight, but he knew, even as he considered the man, that there was no point.

Some men may be overtaken with rage in an instant and forgive in the next. Henry was not of that mould. He took his hatred and viciousness and nursed it to his breast until it became a focus and concentration of his anger.

Henry was filled with bile and spite at that moment, that was certain. To be forced away from his chosen prize by a few meagre churls from another vintaine, and by one of Sir John's own vinteners, was demeaning, and that alone incurred his wrath. But to leap from that to declaring him evil was a long jump. Janyn knew that many men, thwarted of their desires, could be vicious. Some would lie in wait for a victim and take revenge for a slight. Many would punish a man by any means. Henry did none of these. He was fixed upon a different revenge. If he could not take her, he would have those who protected her destroyed; he would have her destroyed in time. But he would take her. He had no doubts of his abilities there. He would recognise no bounds to his rage at his humiliation. No, he would see how to get his revenge, and when he did, he would see them all utterly ruined, and they would see his hand in their destruction. He would gain satisfaction in their horror. And he would ensure that they knew he would have her regardless.

That was the mark of his cruelty. Not that he would stab or punch in a moment's rage, but that he would nurse his hatred and black bile to himself and nurture them, and let them grow and fester, until they took him over entirely.

Henry did not think himself evil. His life had been one of fighting and struggling, but he was only a man, making his way as best he could.

Arriving in Guyenne after he fled London, he had been happy. He had enjoyed his time there. The warmth, the wine, the women, all were to his taste. But a man needed a career as well. He had no trade, but he was good, he learned, at fighting, and he began to take part in the little tournaments for money. He would take on all comers, and his speed and lack of fear usually gave him the victory. Whether he fought with swords, daggers or fists, Henry soon learned that he had an edge over most men.

It was that which led to his joining the King's men. He fought for many of the noblemen of his day, spending much of his time with Sir John of Norwich, but then he met Sir Walter Manny, and joined his forces. Ten years after the murder of the man in Southwark, Henry was on a ship once more, and fighting with Sir Walter against French ships near Sluys. They won a victory at Cadsand and, from that moment, Henry knew his vocation. He was a fighter for the King.

As the war continued and conflicts spread, he found himself advancing ever further. He joined as an infantry fighter, but then gained a pony and a bow. From there he became vintener, and gradually built a reputation for steadiness in battle, for a cool head, and a ferocity unequalled in Edward's host. Henry was as fierce as a tiger when he was placed with an enemy before him, but that enemy could be a Frenchman or a recalcitrant fighter from his own vintaine. A man who did not fight for him would often be forced to fight against him. He held an iron discipline in his unit, and all who disliked it were forced to respect it.

When he rose to his current post, it was because the old centener was too incompetent for his own good, let alone the men he was supposed to lead. He couldn't lead the men into a tavern on a good day. On a bad day, he was too swine drunk to bother. More and more often it was Henry who took the men and led them himself, while his own men rallied them when a sudden reverse struck. And one day, the old man was in the line, fighting, when a sword caught his belly and opened him like a paunched rabbit.

That day, Henry took the top job. It was his right. It was his reward, he felt, for having endured the laziness and cowardice of his predecessor. He had to kill the man for the good of his unit and that whole arm of the King's host.

In all these last years, no one had dared gainsay him. No one had thought to refuse him anything he demanded. And this miserable cur, this mewling kitten, this streak of piss, this Janyn Hussett, dared to stand before him and deny him the woman he should have as a right!

He would have her. He wanted her, and no one would stand in his way.

No, he did not think himself evil. He merely did not consider how any action of his own would affect other people. He didn't care.

Janyn and his men could guess that no good could come of this.

'Well, Janyn, by my faith, you've dropped us right into the shite this time,' Barda muttered, taking the arrow from the string and putting it back with its sheave before reaching up to unstring his bow. 'Ballocks to that! I didn't come over the water to fight my own folk. I thought I was going to fight and kill the King of France's men.'

Barda atte Mill was a short man, with a fuzz of grizzled hair circling his bald pate. About his cheeks and chin was a thick growth of beard as if to compensate for his hairless skull. His eyes were shrewd and kindly, with enough laughter creases to make him look like a modern Bacchus.

'What would you have had me do? Let him take her?' Janyn demanded, glancing round at Pelagia.

She was still staring after Henry and, when she felt his eyes on her, she threw him a cursory look before bending and continuing with her work preparing vegetables for the pot.

'Aye. If it makes our life easier,' Barda said. His eyes were narrowed as he peered after Henry, but there was no humour in them. 'It's a mistake to go upsetting the man who commands you in battle, Jan.'

'Don't talk of her like that,' Bill said. His face blackened with his mood. 'Would you see the poor maid raped by that son of a dog?'

'I'd prefer to see her open her legs wide for him rather than see us suffer his anger.'

'Perhaps. But I wouldn't let him take her,' Janyn said.

'Is she your wife?'

Janyn didn't answer that.

'Well, I hope she's worth it in the end, Vintener,' Barda said, and walked off.

Bill and Walter stood together, muttering in low voices, their eyes drifting off to where Henry had gone, but Janyn squatted with his back against a tree and closed his eyes. After the rush of excitement, he felt light-headed and slightly sick. He had been so close to drawing a knife that he could feel how it would have been, to have stabbed and slain the centener. There was a metallic taste in his mouth at the thought, just like he had after a battle.

Pelagia was over at the fireside, and Janyn opened his eyes to watch her. She was entirely unaffected by the presence of the men about her, as if she knew that she was safe with them. Sitting amongst them, she pulled her hair up, away from her neck. She had a fine neck, Janyn thought, like a swan's. Pale, long, slender, it looked vulnerable. He wanted to kiss it. It was rare for him to be attracted to women, but this one had something, an inner strength like a cord of hemp that kept her together. Even when threatened by Henry, she had shown no fear. Perhaps it had been throttled from her. The tribulations of her last weeks, losing her family, seeing her countrymen slaughtered all about her, maybe that had had the effect of squeezing all her feelings from her, so that now there was nothing left at her core but a savage determination to survive.

There was something in her eyes that he saw occasionally. A gleam, as if she entertained a thought that gave her solace. Perhaps it was a dream of quiet and rest, a view of an all-but-unattainable peace. For he was sure that there was little peace in her soul usually. Not during her waking hours. While she slept, she looked as though she was calm enough. Sometimes he had seen her lips curl into a gentle smile . . . but other times she gave muffled screams and moans as she thrashed from side to side. And always, as soon as she woke and took in her surroundings, any happiness faded until her eyes took on that distant harshness once more. Hers was not a soul at rest.

Janyn desired her, yes, but he would not go near her. She was a focus and target of danger. He could feel it about her. She could bring only disaster. Barda was right: they should throw her from the vintaine, send her away to fend for herself.

Except if Janyn were to do that, he would lose the support of newer recruits like Bill and Walter.

Barda had walked to her. As Janyn watched, he hunkered down beside her. 'Maid, do you want food?'

She said nothing, but Janyn saw her give him a slanted smile and a flash of her eyes. She knew she had him already. Like a spider watching a fly willingly land on her web.

It was a thought that made Janyn shiver with sudden trepidation.

It was in April that things grew more troubling for the English. Janyn could remember it with such clarity: the mud, the constant dampness, the grey faces of the troops forced to endure.

All that winter the weather had been foul and, in March, when their spirits were at their lowest, came the news that they had all feared: the French King had taken up the great crimson banner of France, the Oriflamme of St Denis. With this flag in the hands of the French, they could not be defeated, some said in hushed whispers – but they had borne it with them at Crécy, and there it had served them no useful purpose, as others said. These loud denials, however, could not change the increased tension that affected the English with the news of the gathering French host.

But after March, there was nothing for weeks. Snippets of information came to say that Flemings and French were fighting on their borders, and occasionally there were tales of sea battles, of English convoys being savaged by the damned Genoese, but more often the news was of victories by the English. Even when French fleets tried to force the blockade and bring food to the starving population of Calais, they failed. At last, in late April, the English captured the last piece of land encircling the town: the Rysbank. With this narrow spit of sand taken, the English could control the whole harbour with cannon and other artillery. It was the beginning of the end for Calais. The English had their mailed fist on the throat of the town, and they were slowly strangling it.

A few weeks later, the French made a last attempt to rescue

their town. A fleet of fifty or more ships set sail – cogs and barges laden with provisions – all guarded by galleys full of fighting men, but before they could approach the stricken town they were met with a larger English force that sank or put to flight the whole convoy. Not a single ship reached the garrison of Calais.

For the people of the town it was dismal news. The commander, Jean de Vienne, wrote to his king to say that there was no more food left in the town, and that they must resort to the horrible expedience of human flesh or die. A terrible, grim letter, it was, as the English soon learned.

It was entrusted to a Genoese, who tried to slip from the town at night in a small boat to make his way to Paris, but before he could pass by the English lines, he was seen. English ships were launched in pursuit, and he was captured, although not before he had bound the letter to a hatchet and hurled it into the sea. But at low tide the message was discovered, still tied to its weight, protected by its oilcloth wrapping, and the letter was read by King Edward. He resealed the letter, placing the mark of his own seal on it, and had the letter dispatched to King Philippe. It was a flagrant challenge, and the King of France took it up.

He mustered an army, at least five-and-twenty thousand strong, and marched to meet the English.

It was a few days later that the call came for the English in Janyn's vintaine to gather their weapons. There were rumours of an army marching to meet them, and while it was scarcely to be thought that it could equal the size of the army they had destroyed at Crécy, still, a host of French knights was a force to be reckoned with.

'They're coming up the road there,' Janyn was told.

He and the other vinteners and centeners from the force with Sir John de Sully were gathered together in a wide space behind a wagon-park. Men were standing on wagons and carts to listen as Sir John, tall, hawkish and lean, told them of the danger approaching.

'They are coming slowly, we believe. I doubt me not that after Crécy they will be keen to show us that our success there was a mere chance. They will have as many knights and men-at-arms as they can gather together in so short a space. It will not be easy for them, for we slaughtered their army. There can be few fighting men in the whole of the French King's northern lands.'

Next to Janyn, Barda grimaced, then muttered, 'The French King's son had an army. He was bringing that up here in a hurry. What if this is his army? Battle-hardened and powerful.'

Janyn said nothing. Barda was his most trusted companion from the vintaine, but there were times when his grumbling and complaining were annoying.

Sir John was continuing: 'So we have to hurry and meet them. We have to assess their speed of march, gauge their size and abilities. If need be, we shall have to make them pause on their march. The siege is essential, and nothing can be allowed to prevent us from taking Calais. No matter what this army may be. But we do need to know all we can about it so we can find the best way to deter it. Are there any questions?'

The usual few hands rose, with queries about the food and provisions for the march, but all issues were soon resolved and a basic plan agreed.

'So, off we go again.' Barda grunted. 'Always us at the foreground. The army likes us to be the bleeding spearpoint, doesn't it? And when we're blunted, other bastards can claim the sodding glory.'

'We'll be fine,' Janyn said as they made their way back to their men.

'You know what I think? I reckon the King knows he can replace any number of men over here. So many English would be glad to come and join in the sack of Calais that he will never lack for men. And after Calais, well, it'll be easier to launch an attack with a town already colonised, won't it? He doesn't care about you and me, Jan. He thinks he's got the country by the short hairs as it is.'

'Perhaps.'

'No "perhaps" about it, old son. Take my oath on it. We are the dispensable vanguard. He can lose any or all of us. Right now, we're the most experienced of his soldiers, but he'll throw us at the enemy, like a lure to the French hawk. We can be discarded – just so long as we hold them back for a little while, until the King's host is ready to receive them.'

'You're too cynical,' Janyn said.

'You think so? You're too trusting, man. You're gambling, but you're gambling with your life,' Barda said harshly. 'And ours, too.'

It was a thought that would return to haunt Janyn later.

The vintaine was packed and ready in short order. Janyn looked about him and assessed their strength, studying each man and his weapons.

Although they had marched hundreds of miles to get here, and then endured the winter over the long months, they did not have the appearance of men worn out by their journeys and privations. Still, there was the usual grumbling and complaining. Will of Whitchurch, a scrawny, ill-favoured malcontent with the look and sound of a whining cur, muttered loudly as he packed about: 'These gits. Why don't they send in the Welshies, eh? Just about done, me. Nay, but they'll send us all in until we're all jiggered. They can't risk the Prince's little darlings, can they, oh, no. But us, they can throw us into every battle.'

'You should be honoured, Will,' Janyn said.

'Honoured, Jan? Just why should I be that?'

'You've done so much, they think you can win the battle all on your own, man. We're only here to guard you so you can fight and hold them all back.'

'Oh, ah. Ycs, I can see that. I'll bloody have to, because we're all going to dic, but I'll tell you this: you'll go before me, man! I'm not getting my throat cut by a Genoese quarrel-chucker! Not me!'

'I doubt you will,' Janyn said, and meant it. There was something about the wiry little fellow that inspired confidence in his ability to survive any number of disasters. They had already come through a series of battles on the way here, and not many of the original team were still alive.

It was only when the men were mostly packed and had already begun to wander off to the muster that Janyn realised Pelagia was standing silent. She looked like a statue. Her hands were balled at her side, and she held her body tense, unbending. Her face was stiff, and Janyn thought her jaw looked like a clenched fist, the muscles were so taut. He was about to go to her when he saw Bill and Walter. Bill wandered to her, his head low, glaring at the world from surly eyes.

'Maid, what will you do?' he asked.

She looked at him, then gave a long, slow stare about the

rest of the English camp. 'If I stay here, how long can I survive?'

Janyn made a quick decision and crossed to them.

'We can introduce you to some of the other men,' he said. He could take her to some of the other marching wives, let them help her. It would take no time for her to find a new 'husband'. But the brothers stared at him. They both knew what would happen to her there. They didn't – she didn't – want that, and neither did he. He remembered the day he had given her half his loaf. He had admired her even then. With Janyn's vintaine she had not been forced to pay the marriage debt. She had made no vows to bind her to any of them, and her time with the men had been one of armed neutrality. She held no feelings for Janyn or the others, and while he had no need to protect her, yet he felt some affection for her. To discard her would be like throwing a chicken in the midst of a pack of dogs. They would squabble and bicker over her until the strongest consumed her.

Bill's head dropped, and Janyn could see the man's despair. They all knew what would happen if they left her. But marching to a battle was a matter of hard effort. They had no time to concern themselves over the woman. And in a fight, Janyn didn't want his men worrying about the woman left behind with the camp. He had seen that all too often before: men fighting while half their minds were fixed on a woman. All too often it led to the man being killed.

'Vintener, we can't leave her,' Walter said firmly.

Horns were blowing to signal the march. Janyn made a quick decision. 'If you bring her, she's your responsibility,' he said.

'Aye,' Bill said quickly.

Janyn could see how Bill's mind was working. The thought

of leaving her here filled him with horror. If she was left to the mercies of the English army, she would be ravished and probably dead inside a day. It had taken Bill and his brother to rescue her from three drunken men before now. She could do nothing to protect herself if she were left alone.

Janyn could almost see these thoughts chase themselves across his face.

'Will you come with us, then?' Bill demanded gruffly.

'What else can I do?' she said.

They did not journey far. They marched on horseback with full packs and the spare arrows and bowstaves packed carefully on their carts, one to each vintaine, and the few women and children trudged along behind.

Looking back along the lines of troops and women, Janyn was hit by a feeling of happiness.

'Glad to be rid of the place for a while?' Barda asked, riding at his side.

'It's the stench of the latrines – I never could abide that,' Janyn said, but it wasn't only that. It was the feeling of grim, relentless misery that encompassed the area about the town, and more than anything else, the unremitting boredom of daily duty in the army.

'Aye,' Barda said, breathing deeply. 'It's good to be on a horse again, and to be riding, even if we will be riding into danger.'

Behind them, kneeling on the bed of the cart, he could see her: Pelagia. Beside her, as though guarding her on the way to her wedding, were Bill and Walter, flanking her on their ponies. Janyn was quite tempted to bellow at them to leave her and join the main column that straggled its way along the road, but there was no point.

He could see why they kept near her. She looked lovely.

'What?' Barda asked, seeing the direction of his gaze.

'Should I do something about them? Look at them: drooling over her like a pair of dogs after a bitch,' Janyn said.

'What, are you jealous? Jan, get a grip!' Barda chuckled to himself. 'You met her, you allowed her into our vintaine, and you stopped the arsehole Henry from raping her – what more do you want? Are you jealous of the lads?'

'Of course I'm not.'

'But she does look beautiful, doesn't she?' Barda said. 'She gives the brothers something to fight for. No Frenchman will get to her without knocking them down first.'

'I'm worried about Bill. She never gives him a look, but I'll bet he's never stopped thinking about her.'

'I think Walter is smitten as badly, and yet she gives them no affection, no sign of any desire to be with them, only a cold, distant demeanour.'

'I don't think Walter hoped for anything from her. When she first came to the camp, he just sought to protect her from the other men.'

'Is this all about them – or is it you, Jan?' Barda asked.

'Me?'

'When Henry came to us, it wasn't Bill or Walter who stood before him, it was you. Is that the problem?'

'No!'

It wasn't because he wanted her. If he'd wanted a woman, he could have found himself one. Any of the Winchester Geese who followed the army would be good for a quick release. They were able, willing, and quick, generally, just like the whores of the Bishop of Winchester's stews from whom they took their name.

Pelagia was not like them. She was a mystery. Other women demanded attention and craved companionship, but

Pelagia just seemed to exist. She desired nothing from any of the men in the vintaine, and only showed a calculated disdain when any tried to get too close to her. The rest of the time, she remained with their group as though she was sister to their whole unit. There was no offer of sex or even friendship, only a firm independence.

She was not like other women. He didn't get the sense that there would be any pleasure in pursuing her like a sensualist determined to gain another notch on his bedpost. Other men talked of the thrill of the chase of a fresh woman, but Janyn had never been interested in that kind of exercise. He was content to concentrate on his work. One day, perhaps, he would go to England and seek a wife, but not here, not in this godforsaken land of burned crops and slaughtered animals. This was no place to think of settling, it was only a country to be tamed, and that profitably.

Sometimes he thought he saw something in her face. Perhaps a flash of sadness, or a look of quick despair, but it was so fleeting, he could not swear to it. Perhaps it was just his mind trying to make sense of her, of her feelings and of what drove her on.

He didn't care, anyway. Whatever it was that she wanted, he wanted none of it.

'How was the battle?' Laurence asked. The other pilgrims were hushed by the tale as Janyn paused and topped up his drink from a jug.

'The French did not have enough men. Nothing like enough. By that time, I suppose our King had some thirty thousand men under arms. It certainly looked it, with men all about the town itself, and more arriving every day. But the French had gathered together a scant twenty thousand.'

He nodded to himself pensively. 'Even if they could synchronise their attack with a sortie from the men in the town, they wouldn't have had enough. Their army was demoralised before they saw the English. Who wouldn't have been, after the shattering defeat of Crécy? And while they may have hoped for a diversion from Calais itself, the people in the town were already enfeebled by the siege. Hunger and despair tore at them, and those who still had strength enough to wield a sword would still never have reached the lines of archers ringing the town.

'So I say it again, they didn't have enough. But from where we were, it looked like they had enough to trample us into the mud.'

The French King had to make a display, if only for his honour's sake. So he marched his men up the road to the town. And the only thing stopping him at that moment was Sir John de Sully's little force.

The old warrior was then in his sixties or so. His scarred and worn face displayed no fear that Janyn could see, only a boyish excitement. 'We'll stop them there,' he said, pointing to a narrowing in the roadway.

The road leading to the higher ground outside the town had to pass through a wood before passing a small quarry. Beyond the quarry a hamlet had stood, but now the single stone building, the church, was the only one remaining. All the others had been burned, and even the church itself stood blackened and ravaged, like a sole surviving tree after a forest fire. The tower remained, but the building itself was a husk.

'An ambush?' Janyn asked.

'Yes, Hussett. We'll have our archers here at the front, and as they enter the quarry, we'll loose the arrows. It'll blunt their ardour, eh? The front ranks will run to cover in the quarry, and we can keep aiming arrows at the men coming. They will be pushed on by the press of men behind them, and we can kill many of them as they keep coming.'

Janyn nodded. It was the way the English fought. The archers stood their ground while their enemies ebbed under their withering assault. He moved off to prepare his men.

The two brothers were still there, and now he saw that when Pelagia went to speak with either, it was to Bill that she naturally turned. Walter was left sullenly glowering nearby while she spoke with his brother, her hand resting naturally on his forearm.

Janyn turned away. It was none of his business, but he disliked the idea that she might be breaking the close bond between the two lads.

The first that Janyn knew of the attack was a shrill scream in the night that jerked him from his slumbers.

They were all settled by early evening, his vintaine taking a patch of turf close to the wall of the old quarry. Their cart was nearby, and their weapons all laid close to hand. Bow-staves lay on the ground beside many of the archers, the strings held about their throats or kept in their purses, against the threat of the dew dampening them. As Janyn lay back, his head on his pack, he could see the men. Wisp and Barda stared into the flames from their campfires as they lay wrapped in blankets, and Bill and Walter were a little further off, their faces lost in the glare of the nearer fire. Janyn had dozed off staring at the coals and glittering sparks.

It was foolish to be so arrogant. A few successes against the French and all believed that they were secure, even here, lying out in the open. They should have known that even a cowed enemy would not hesitate to attack a force much smaller, and yet no one had thought to post a guard. All were asleep as the first cry came.

As soon as he heard the first high, piercing shriek, Janyn was up, flinging aside his blanket and bellowing at the other men to gather their weapons and follow him as he sprang forward.

The roadway was already a scene of confusion. Half-asleep archers were milling in the near darkness, while some few blundered around gripping blazing torches in their fists, rubbing the sleep from their eyes.

Janyn hurried to the line nearer the French army, but there was no sign of fighting there. All was peaceful, so far as he could see. A small group of French peasants lay hacked and bloody in a heap near the front line of the English, and two sentries were dead.

'What happened here?' he asked a man-at-arms.

'We all heard a cry, and when we came here, we found this little force. They were probably just here to cut a couple of throats, steal a purse and make their escape. We were lucky: someone behind us heard them and gave the alarm.'

'Hardly behind you,' Janyn said. It was a stupid comment to make. Unless the French had infiltrated the English camps and killed someone in their midst. And yet that first cry, he could have sworn it had not come from this direction. 'Must be the way the hill curls around us. The quarry. Rock can make noises seem to come from an odd direction.'

'If you think so, Vintener,' the man said without conviction.

'Right,' Janyn said, watching as the men pulled the bodies about, one with a war-hammer giving each skull a good blow for good measure. There was no time to take prisoners up here.

Looking at the dead, he felt sad. It was such a pathetic little group: farmers and peasants who were determined to strike their blow for the defence of their realm. When they were confronted and joined battle, they were soon forced to flee, leaving many of their companions dead or squirming in their own blood, their hatchets, bills and sickles left on the ground. If the French Army of the King was no match for the English force of arms, how could these fools have thought that they were capable of doing them damage?

When it was clear that all was safe and not further attacks could be expected that night, Janyn returned to the camp with his men, but when he looked around, he realised that the woman was not where she had hidden.

Pelagia was gone, and so was Bill.

Even now he shuddered at the memory of the shock that coursed through his body at the sight. Bill's bed roll was left open just as so many others were all about; each man, hurrying to his feet, had thrown aside his blankets and grabbed his weapons in a hurry to get to the fight. But Janyn could not remember seeing Bill at the road or up at the front line. 'Walter, where is your brother?' he demanded.

'I don't know, Vintener,' he said, but in his eyes there was a terrible anguish as he looked to where Pelagia had been lying.

'Your brother took her, didn't he? Christ's bones, the shriek that woke us, that wasn't the French, that was Bill. He's killed her, hasn't he?'

Walter hesitated. It was enough for Janyn. He had seen the look in Bill's eyes over the last few days. The longing and desperation that had gradually turned to greedy hunger. He wanted the woman, Janyn was sure. And now he felt sure Bill had taken her.

'Walter, if you find your brother first, you'd better make sure she's all right, because if I learn Bill's hurt her, I'll see him hang!' he said.

'What do you mean? Bill wouldn't hurt her any more than I would,' Walter said haltingly. He was almost pleading.

'You'd better hope that's true if you don't want to watch Bill hanged from a tree.'

'What do you want to do, Jan?' Barda asked. All banter had ceased at Janyn's tone of voice. Now the men stood watchfully.

Where they were, the quarry wall encircled their little camp, but there was no way to tell where the two could have gone. Had they fled together, he would have left things as they were. The loss of one lovesick man was one thing, but if he had snatched Pelagia to rape her, Janyn would see to it that Bill paid.

'Jan?' Barda said again. 'Do you want us to find them?'

'How'll we do that at this time of night?' Janyn said. It was the middle watch of the night, when the darkness was at its blackest, and even the best hunter and tracker would find it difficult to follow a trail. Janyn knew he was no master huntsman. Besides, he and his men had been installed here to help protect the road, and that they must do.

'You want to leave it till morning?'

'Yes. For now we all need to rest,' Janyn said, striding to his blankets. He wrapped himself in them, spreading a heavy cloak over the top, and closed his eyes, seeking sleep.

But he sought it in vain.

Janyn took himself back to the next miserable morning, and as he did so, he felt his face hardening.

He had been furious when he learned what had happened. The shock to discover he had been fooled all that time. And then the slow realisation that he had been wrong again. Even now, the worm of disgust squirmed in his belly at the memory, and his voice grew colder.

'I had trusted those brothers as much as any other men in my vintaine for months. I had done all I could to help them, and then I took Pelagia under my protection too.'

The attractive, well-dressed woman in the pilgrim party – her name was Katie Valier – nodded encouragingly, absorbed in his tale. 'You approach the end of your tale, friend? Round it off.'

'Very well,' Janyn said shortly.

It was still dark when the screams and shouts started afresh. All the vintaine was roused at once, and they collected their weapons and moved to the front in support of a small company of men who were beset by the vanguard of the French army.

Janyn recalled that battle as a series of disjointed little fights. There were never more than a couple of hundred men from either side. It was mostly a matter of brutal hand-to-hand combat with small groups of Frenchmen. Janyn fought with his teeth gritted, his belly clenched, stamping down on feet, stabbing, butting his shield into a man's face, then hacking at a man fallen at his feet. As day broke, he and the vintaine was thrust backwards, and Janyn saw Henry over to the further side of the vintaine as the fighting began to wane and the French who were still capable began to drift away, fighting as they went.

The men gathered about Janyn, faces pale from exhaustion, weary from too little sleep and too much fighting. For some time none of them could speak, but all stood panting, their fingers still gripping their weapons with the death-grasp of men who knew they could be under attack again at any moment. They all had a need for rest after their exertions, but even as the reinforcements arrived and the first of Janyn's vintaine began to drop to the ground, a series of fresh calls came from further up the line, and they hurriedly clambered to their feet again and ran to the alarms.

It was after the last of these small frays that Janyn was called to a small pavilion some yards from the road. 'Hussett? I have need of your men,' Janyn was told. It was his master, Sir John de Sully.

'Sir?'

'Take your archers to the right of our front. There seems to be a small party of French archers over there, near the edge of your quarry. They're loosing bolts into our flank. I want you to go with your men and remove them.'

'Yes, sir.'

'But be careful.'

'Yes.'

He saw at the pavilion's door a quick movement, and caught a fleeting glimpse, no more, of a figure that stalked away. It was impossible to be certain, but it looked like Henry.

The men were soon arrayed with bows at the ready, quivers full, and they made their way slowly about the edge of the quarry, climbing the steep hillside through mixed brambles, thorns and thick undergrowth between the slender boughs of young saplings. Overhead great branches rustled in the soft, soughing breeze. All that Janyn could hear was the noise of men breathing heavily, cursing, slipping and cracking twigs.

Their way was not easy. Loose stones and soil moved underfoot, sending more than one man sprawling on his face. They were trying to approach the French from the north, looping around in a great circle so that they could attack from the rear of their enemy, but even as they reached the top of the hill, they realised their mistake.

Before them and to their side was a large company of Genoese crossbowmen lying in wait. Loosing their quarrels from safety behind trees, they unleashed a sudden attack that knocked six of Janyn's men down in the first instant.

It was a hellish place to try to fight. The trees shielded the men from the sun, and the thick vegetation meant none of Janyn's men could see a target. But every instant a solid thud told of another bolt slamming into a tree trunk, or a damp sound like a wet cloth thrown against a stone heralded a fresh scream of pain as a bolt struck a man.

Janyn tried to rally the men and charge, but it was impossible. On the ground before him, he saw other men. Another vintaine had been here to storm the Genoese, and they too had been killed. In only moments Janyn had lost half his own men, and now the Genoese were picking off the remainder. With too few men to assail the crossbowmen, and with the English handicapped by their great long bows here in among the trees, Janyn had little choice other than to call the remnants of his men to him. He was himself struck in the calf, and began to hobble away, helped by Barda, who stopped and turned to loose an arrow at every other step, taking one Genoese in the throat, whose slow, agonised death persuaded the rest of the pursuit to take more care.

As they made their way through the trees, sliding on the scree and tripping over roots and branches, Janyn's mind was empty of suspicion. But then, as they came closer to the quarry, he slipped on something soft and fell to his hands and knees, winded. It was some little while before he could turn and take in the sight.

In a deep hole formed where a tree's roots had once clung

to the soil, he had stumbled over an accumulation of loose branches. Leaves dangled from them, still full and fleshy. They had been cut recently. A bolt hurtled overhead as Janyn leaned down, a leaden sensation in his belly.

'What are you doing, Jan?' Barda demanded.

'Shut up. Just keep them back,' he said, pulling branches and twigs away. 'Christ!'

'What?'

Janyn didn't answer, but squatted back on his haunches, staring down at the pale features of Pelagia. 'At least now she is at peace,' he mumbled to himself.

She had the look of a woman deep in sleep. If it weren't for the nakedness of her lower body, the blood on her thighs and belly where her murderer had slashed and stabbed at her, Janyn might have thought she was only resting.

'Who did this?' Barda demanded. He was staring down at the body with horror in his eyes. 'Shit! Was this Bill?'

'Who else could it have been?' Janyn asked. He heard the whistle, thump, as another bolt slammed into a tree. 'The two of them disappeared in the night. I suppose Bill got away after this. He took her, raped her, and fled before we could catch him.'

There was a sudden cry from over on their left. They crouched, and then began to crawl through the thick bushes towards the source of the sound. There they saw a pair of Genoese holding an English archer, while a third calmly spanned his bow and set a bolt ready.

Before he could lift it to aim, Barda's arrow passed through his head. The man was hurled to the ground by the impact, and then Janyn was hobbling forward, pulling his knife from its sheath, while a second arrow flew and took one Genoese in the cheek, spinning him about and making him fall.

Janyn's knife was up and he grabbed the last man's arm, pulling the man off-balance and slamming his knife into the man's liver and kidneys, stabbing again and again until the fellow stopped moving.

Standing, panting, he looked about him to see that the other man was dead. Two more arrows had hit him in the back of the neck and spine and, although his body twitched sporadically, there was clearly no life in him.

'Come, quickly!' Janyn hissed, and grabbed the man from the ground.

It was not until that moment that Janyn paused to glance at the man he and Barda had rescued. For an instant, he gaped, and then he leaped forward and rammed his fist into the boy's belly. 'That's for her, you son of a whore!'

Barda had to pull him away and hold him back. 'Let's get away from here, Jan. Come on, this isn't the time or the place.'

Janyn stood with his jaw clenched so tightly he thought a tooth was loosened. Then he turned on his heel and set off down to the camp, leaving Barda to help the boy.

The rage bubbled and fizzed in his blood. There was a hollowness in his belly, and his heart was thundering like a galloping horse in his breast as he strode on, all thought of the Genoese put from his mind. It was only as he reached the English lines and saw a column of men marching forward towards him that he remembered the trap in the trees, and paused to warn the commander of the men.

Back at the camp, already the main assault had been turned away, and now the only sign that there had been a battle was the mound of corpses, as Englishmen picked up the French slain and piled them one upon another. Janyn marched to his banneret's pavilion and stood outside while

Sir John finished buckling greaves and pulling on his gauntlets.

'You removed them?' Sir John asked.

'No, sir. They were too numerous, and in the trees there, there was little we could do to protect ourselves. They were well positioned.'

'Never mind. The main assault has failed, anyway. I'm surprised, though. Your centener thought you would easily win through.'

His words took a moment to register, and then Janyn thought again about the figure hurrying from the pavilion earlier, before he and the men went to outflank the Genoese. 'Henry? He suggested us?'

'Yes. He said your men were best placed. He said you were freshest and ready for a little excursion up into the woods. Why? Is there a problem?'

'No, sir,' Janyn said. 'Did you know someone else had tried that route before? There were many dead on the ground already.'

'I had not heard, no. That is annoying – we could have saved you and your men, if we had been told.'

'Yes, sir.'

Over at the carts, he saw Bill lean up against a wheel, his arms draped over the wheel. Janyn thought to himself how he would see him whipped later, until the skin was flayed from his back. It was clear enough what had happened. The boy had taken Pelagia, hoping perhaps to run away with her, and then raped and killed her when she refused. The murderous scum had hidden her body to hide his guilt. In his mind's eye, Janyn saw the scene: Bill half-dragging the woman up the slope after him, all for lust. All for desire for a woman who didn't want him.

But as he'd noticed, she did seem to want him. Janyn could only assume she wanted to imitate a nun, and when Bill got her up on the hillside, she didn't want to open her legs to him. Perhaps she was scared of the idea of the army approaching, or maybe Bill's lust was alarming to her. Whatever the reason was, she refused him. And he, craven cur that he was, forced her.

Although that too seemed unlike him. Janyn stood, staring over at the cart. Bill had a gash on one cheek, and even as Janyn watched, the lad turned, draping his hands over the top of the wheel as though crucified.

He had never shown violence towards her. He had never even displayed much lust. Rather, he held a simmering bitterness towards anyone else who looked at her. The only man of whom he appeared to hold no jealousy was his brother. That was natural, after all. Brothers could maintain their friendship even in the face of rivalry.

But there was another man who had shown his lust. Henry had been violently angry when the vintener refused to allow him to take Pelagia. He expected to be able to rape her, and had even made threats when he was thwarted. And today, for some reason, he had recommended Janyn and the others to go into that terrible wood.

It was coincidence, Janyn told himself. Why would Henry want to kill off the vintaine, especially Janyn? It made no sense, except he knew Henry. They all did. If he felt snubbed or insulted, his brutality in revenge could be boundless.

Janyn was suddenly assailed by a sense of revulsion so intense, he had to grasp a nearby tree and cling to it, waves of nausea running through his entire body.

'It was him,' he said. 'Damn his eyes, Henry tried to get us all killed!'

Barda saw his sudden lurch, and hurried to his side. 'Jan? Are you all right?'

'By God's cods, Barda, I think little is well,' Janyn said.

Henry was with his commanders when Janyn approached him. The other vinteners were about him, and Henry looked at Janyn sidelong.

'Thank you, centener,' he said. 'My men appreciate being sent up to the ridge.'

'What are you talking about, Jan?'

'You'd had your own men, or another man's vintaine up there already. Their bodies are all over the hill. We'd already fought all morning before light, but that didn't worry you, did it? You were happy enough to be rid of us, I suppose.'

'You always were an insubordinate bastard, Hussett. Your father was a trader in second-hand clothes, and I suppose you're little better. Well, if you don't like the army, you shouldn't have joined the King's forces.'

'I joined my master, Sir John, to come here,' Hussett said. He looked about the other men with casual deliberation. 'But he wouldn't have sent me to have me killed with the callous disregard that you did.'

'Me? What are you saying?'

'That you wanted your vengeance because you wanted the woman Pelagia. You were prepared to kill us all to have her, weren't you?'

'You've been drinking too much cheap wine!'

'She's dead. But perhaps you know that already. She was killed and set down in a hollow last night. Where were you? Did you go up there to kill her, and then tried to have me and all my vintaine wiped out so you could hide your murder?'

'Now you're talking hog's turds!' Henry said, and set his

arms akimbo. 'You say I killed the maid? And what of it if I had? How many other men and women have we all killed? You think I'd have run with my thumb up my arse in case a peasant's mongrel like you learned of it? Get your brain to work, man! You think I'm scared what you or anyone else thinks? Go swive a goat!'

Janyn was about to launch himself at the man, but Barda put a restraining hand on his breast. Then Janyn paused and considered.

There was merit in Henry's words. Why would he worry about killing the woman?

'You tried to have all my vintaine wiped out just so you could have her to yourself, didn't you?' he said wonderingly. 'It wasn't just to hide her murder – it was simple lust. You wanted her, and you were prepared to kill me and all my men just so you could take her.'

'You have no way of knowing what I would or woudn't do,' Henry said, but now his voice was colder.

'You were prepared to have Sir John's force depleted just so you could rape the woman.'

'She would have been willing enough,' Henry said with a smirk. 'The women always are.'

Janyn nodded. He set his jaw and gazed at all the other vinteners standing with Henry. 'You all heard that. He wanted to sacrifice us, his own men, so that he could grab the woman. Like David and Bathsheba. A corrupt leader prepared to see his own men slain just so he can steal their women. We all know where we stand with him.'

'Get your arse out of my sight!' Henry spat. 'That is villeiny-saying of the worst sort, you—'

'You accuse me of villeiny-saying?' Janyn said mildly, but then he launched himself forward. Barda grabbed his arm as he flew past, and another vintener caught him by the shoulder and neck, keeping him back. 'Get off me! Leave me alone! He's safe enough from me – for now!'

'You're finished!' Henry said. 'I'll see that you're ruined, Hussett! You won't fight here with the men ever again, you little shite!'

Janyn nodded. As he was released, he tugged his jack and hosen back where they had been jerked tight. 'I will never fight for you again, Henry. I don't mind a Frenchman killing me, but I won't die from your bile.'

He stalked away, and Barda had to trot to keep up.

'Do you really think he did that?' he asked.

'Who doubts me? Sir John told me as much. He wanted to see all of us die in a trap up there, Barda.'

'He won't do that again.'

'No,' Janyn said. The two glanced back over their shoulder to where the centener was expostulating with his other commanders. 'No, he will not last long in the next fight.'

Janyn and Barda found Walter not far from the front line with the rest of the vintaine.

'Have you heard about your brother?'

'What, have you found him?' Walter said.

'Yes. He wasn't far from her body.'

Walter nodded, his face empty, and then, very slowly, a tear formed. 'I couldn't let him. I'm sorry, but I couldn't . . .'

'She was going to marry him?'

'I think she enjoyed the attention we both gave her. It gave her satisfaction to see men bickering over her, and when it was me and Bill, she was pleased to see how she could make us both suffer for love of her.'

'It wasn't love. Love doesn't mean raping a woman and then killing her.'

'I didn't want to kill her! I didn't mean to! I only wanted to keep her for my own! I thought if I took her, and showed her how much she meant to me, that maybe she'd marry me. I made her take me, but then, when I was spent, she looked at me like I was a turd, and told me she would enjoy telling Bill what I'd done. I saw her then for what she really was. It was your fault, Jan! You brought her with us – you should have let us leave her behind! Why did you bring her with us? It's ruined us all!'

'What will you do?'

'I don't know.'

'Your brother knows?'

'When I took her, he saw us leave, and followed us. I had to strike him down before he could find her. I knocked him down, and covered her over. I hoped he wouldn't realise it was me!' He was sniffling now, snot gathering at the tip of his nose. He wiped it away angrily. 'I didn't want to hurt him. I was just desperate. And lonely.'

'You did better than hurting him,' Barda said. 'You nearly had him killed. The Genoese found him up there and would have killed him. And when we found him, Jan nearly killed him, too.'

Janyn stopped. His eyes were fixed on the flames as though he could see the faces from long ago deep in the flickering light.

'Well?' Laurence asked quietly. 'What happened? Did the two brothers forgive each other?'

'Only one need forgive,' the Austin canon said. 'That was the point. His lust drew the man Walter into dishonour and deceit, and made him knock down his own flesh and blood.'

Janyn shut his eyes in disgust, then stared up at the friar. 'Did you understand nothing of my story?' he said harshly. 'You think it was all that cut and dried? It was lust moved them all: simple, animal lust. Henry wanted the woman, and he was prepared to kill anyone to slake his desire. Bill wanted her too, and he would have killed anyone who threatened her. He would have taken her if he had the courage, but instead his brother decided to take her for himself. Not because he was worse than the others, but because his lust overwhelmed him sooner. And what else? Why were we all there in France? Because of the lust of two kings for the same city. We are all consumed by lust. Even Pelagia, who wanted revenge like Henry wanted her body! We were all consumed by lust. And then the plague came, and Calais was consumed. This plague, it is a proof of God's displeasure with us. All of us!'

'What happened to Henry?' the landlord enquired after a moment's thought.

'He died a short time later. His centaine was in the thick of a battle, and he fell.'

'From a blow before him or behind?'

Janyn curled his lip without humour. 'If you were a man in his hundred, and you heard about him sending an entire vintaine to its doom just because he wanted a woman, would you want to fight with him?'

'What happened to the brothers?'

'What would you have done? Was there any purpose to be served in punishing one? I didn't have to, in any case. Bill refused to speak to Walter, and a week or so later, Walter was found hanged in a barn near Calais. He couldn't bear the guilt over what he had done. And then, he couldn't bear his brother's contempt either.'

'Did his brother survive?'

'Bill took his money when Calais fell, but when the peace was agreed, he went away. I heard he joined a fraternity of mercenaries. He didn't feel there was a life for him back here.'

'What happened to you?'

'Me?' Janyn stared into the flames. 'I swore I wouldn't fight any more after Calais. I took up a little alehouse in the town and built good

custom with the English garrison. I promised myself I'd forget war, and for a year I was happy. I married Alice, my lovely Alice, and she bore me a son.'

'Are they in Calais still?'

'Oh, yes. They will always be there. Both perished when the plague came. So I came here on pilgrimage. To find peace.'

Aye, he said to himself: peace – calm after the fighting. A pilgrimage to beg forgiveness.

Forgiveness for slaying his own centener in the midst of a battle; forgiveness for all the Frenchmen he had killed, some in anger, some in cold blood; forgiveness for the rapes and tortures, for the abbeys and churches laid waste, for the nuns left raped and slain in the burning embers of their convents.

And for failing the young French woman who had sought his protection.

The Second Sin

Every man in the party had at some point surreptitiously ogled the woman who now moved forward to offer her story. Her clothes were of the finest cloth, and their cut betrayed an origin in the Mediterranean. The south of France, perhaps or one of the northern Italian city-states. She was a mature woman without being matronly, for her waist had not grown thick, as did that of others of her age. Perhaps she had never had children. She was attended by a younger woman, but no one could say whether she was a servant or a daughter. The more discerning males amongst the gathering might have come to a consensus about her age, and supposed she was past her fortieth year, but only just. All would have been surprised to learn she was actually in the middle of her fifties.

Her hair was blond with a hint of gold to it, but no white, and her face was healthily rosy and unlined. When she spoke, her voice rang like a small silver bell, and her Italian accent was obvious.

'I want to tell you about the corrosive effects of that most deadly of the seven deadly sins – greed.'

Here she paused for effect, and cast her pale blue eyes around the gathering. No one challenged her contention that this particular sin was the most deadly. Not yet, anyway. They would reserve judgement until her story was told. Satisfied that she had their full attention, she went on.

'This is a story often told by my grandfather about a time when I was a young woman living in Venice. Niccolo Zuliani had travelled to the ends of the earth, and seen many wonders. Great palaces where a thousand men may banquet at a time, a robe made of salamander that can resist fire, and a black stone that burns better than logs. Some said he told lies, or at the very least embroidered so heavily on the truth that it would have hardly known itself if it looked in a mirror. I like to think that everything he spoke of was the literal truth. Whatever people may have thought, this story is certainly one I can verify the truth of myself, as I was involved in its unfolding, as you will eventually see.'

The small group of travellers leaned closer to her to hear the tale of . . .

Greed

Nick Zuliani was bored. Though he was more than seventy years of age, his mind was as sharp as it had ever been. He had recently returned from a small Greek island owned by the Soranzo family, where he had performed a service for Giovanni Soranzo, who was now the Doge of Venice. Since his return, his days had been full of idleness, and he yearned for something to occupy his mind. Even his dearest love, Cat Dolfin, was tired of his sighs and his constant wandering through the rooms of her home, Ca' Dolfin.

'You're like some tiresome ghost, always interrupting my peace, Niccolo. Do stop it.'

Zuliani sighed some more at the rebuke, knowing that if she addressed him by his full name and not as Nick, she was seriously annoyed. Then, seeing Cat's reaction to his further sigh, he satisfied himself with a silent grimace.

'Perhaps you are tired of having me around. You should throw me out on the street like some homeless beggar.'

He was indeed homeless, and had been for some time. Since, that is, his own house had been burned down in a fire set by a man seeking to mask his deliberate disappearance. In that conflagration, Zuliani had lost almost everything he possessed, including most of the wonders he had brought from Cathay. Still, at the time it had been a boon, in that it had resulted in him finding and moving in with his long-lost love, the aristocratic Caterina Dolfin. At the same time, he had also discovered the existence of his granddaughter, Katie.

He cast his mournful gaze on the still slim and attractive woman, who as a young lady he had left pregnant when he had skipped Venice over some misdeed or other. His only excuse at the time was that he had not known of Cat's delicate state when he had fled. Cat returned his soulful look with a steely one of her own. She pursed her lovely red lips.

'Don't push your luck, Niccolo.'

Then she sighed, knowing what was behind his irritating behaviour. He needed to be busy, and the only thing that truly excited him was the pursuit of trade and the growth of money.

'Oh, very well. I will loan you some money, just so that you can lose it on some hare-brained scheme, like you have with your own money.'

Zuliani flashed her a smile.

'A promissory note will be enough, and I shall be out from under your feet and on my way to the Rialto in an instant.'

She quickly picked up a quill before he could change his mind.

'So this is about a Venetian's greed for money,' said one of the pilgrims gathered in the Angel tavern in Norfolk. Katie frowned, annoyed that the thread of her story, so soon started, had been broken already.

'Not at all. There is no sin in honest trade, as any Venetian will tell you. Listen, and you will soon learn what sort of greed I am telling you about.'

It was not long before Nick Zuliani found his way to the Rialto. The great wooden bridge was at the centre of the early settlement, and was now the commercial heart of La Serenissima. On its sturdy planks strode impecunious merchants seeking the funds for trading ventures that they could not afford on their own. Any Venetian with a little money to invest could have a share in such trade. Artisans and widows, even the aged and the sick, could enter into what was called a *colleganza*. This might take the form of a simple partnership between two merchants, or that of a large corporation of the kind needed to finance a trans-Asiatic caravan. It might run for a short, agreed period or might be an *ad hoc*, ongoing arrangement that would be dissolved automatically when the venture was complete. Whatever the constituent parts of the partnership, it was founded on trust and was inviolable. Even one involving an immense initial outlay, or several years' duration and considerable risk, could be arranged on the Rialto in a matter of hours.

Zuliani walked up and down for a while assessing the merchants who were on the bridge. They were mostly young men such as he had once been. He too had stood here, eager-faced and keen to find someone past their prime who could afford the money but not the time or effort to travel to the corners of the globe for profit. Now he was on the other side of the fence – one of those aged men too weary for long journeys in pirate-infested waters. He listened in on a couple of merchants who were already trying to persuade the people around them to take a chance on making their fortune.

One, a raw-boned man with a face that looked as though it had been chiselled out of rock and been around the world, was expounding the virtues of trading salted North Sea cod, Rhenish and Bordelais wines, and Breton salt with oil and rice from ports in the Mediterranean. Zuliani knew such a *colleganza* would provide steady profits, but what he sought was excitement, even if it was of the vicarious sort. The other merchant he turned to was a fresh-faced youth with long, black hair that kept blowing across his eyes in the wind that swept up the Grand Canal. He spoke of cotton from Syria and North Africa, and silks from the East. Zuliani's heart began to beat a little faster. He moved closer, the eager eyes of the young trader spotted him and his spiel grew more expansive.

'Remember that at sea there are no toll duties as there are on routes overland. A sea route costs a twentieth of an overland route, and all we have to fund is the basic cost of fitting out a ship, freight charges, and sailors' wages – which are precious little.'

As he said this, he nudged the well-dressed man standing next to him and laughed. The man did not respond, his face keeping its solemn cast as he twisted the ring on his thumb, so the trader swallowed his joke and pressed on.

'The more valuable the cargo, the greater the profit. I am proposing a *colleganza* that will sail as far as Antioch and Tyre in order to benefit from the silks that come from Cathay.'

At the mention of that far distant empire, Zuliani was won over to this young man's proposition. Memories of his own travels around Cathay at the instigation of the Great Khan, Kubilai, flooded his mind. He elbowed his way to the front of the crowd that had gathered around the young merchant.

'I will have some of that trade, young man.'

The trader eagerly grasped his hand.

'You are a wise man, sir, and I shall not let you down. My name is Bernardo Baglioni, and yours is . . .?'

Zuliani hesitated, fearful that his name and reputation would draw too many into the venture and dissipate the profits. He produced the note signed by Cat.

'Let's merely say I am acting on behalf of the Dolfin family.'

Baglioni's smile broadened. It was not often that someone from the *case vecchie* – the old aristocracy of Venice – got involved in trade.

'Then I am honoured at such an association. Come, let us adjourn to a taverna and seal the deal.'

The well-heeled and solemn man with the thumb-ring also stepped forward. In an accent that suggested he was not Venetian, he also proposed part-funding the deal.

'My name is Agnolo Rosso.'

Zuliani was surprised that someone so formal and reserved

should wish to participate in the sort of risk suggested by Baglioni, but he wasn't worried. There was enough profit in it for at least two big partners. Besides, the trader no doubt already had a few small investors in his pocket too. He nodded at the other man, and all three strode off the bridge and towards the nearest hostelry.

A week later, over a meal prepared by Cat's cook, and in the presence of both Cat and his granddaughter, Katie, Zuliani expanded upon the brief report he had given on his drunken return to Ca' Dolfin the day of the business deal.

'Baglioni now has a large galley commissioned with a capacity of over a hundred and fifty tons and more than a hundred oarsmen to speed it on its way. He will be loading soon with goods for the outbound trip. Now that he has my money . . .'

Cat gave him a sharp look, and he corrected himself.

'Now he has your money and Rosso's, he can fund the whole trip all the way to Antioch. Though when I saw him yesterday in the evening, he seemed a little nervous. It was as if he didn't want to speak with me.'

Katie thought that must be normal for a young man on his first big *colleganza*, and told Nick so.

He shrugged. 'Maybe so. But his captain, Saluzzo by name, behaved in the same way, avoiding me like they both had something to hide.'

Cat ignored his caution. She was more interested in the other big investor.

'This Agnolo Rosso, he is a Florentine, did you say?'

Zuliani nodded. 'With a name like that he has to be. And he certainly doesn't speak Venetian.'

'And he put up a matching sum to mine?'

Again, she got a nod of agreement from Zuliani. Katie put down a sweetly honeyed chicken leg, sucked her fingers, and asked Cat what she was puzzled about.

'Oh, nothing, Katie. It's just unusual for a Florentine to get involved in a *colleganza*. Though I suppose that, where there's money and a profit, they are not far behind us Venetians.'

She plucked a grape from the large bunch on the table and popped it in her red-lipped mouth. Zuliani gulped down the last of his wine and yawned in an ostentatious way.

'Time for bed for an old man like me.'

He cast a meaningful glance at Cat, which Katie saw too. It made her laugh.

'I'm not too young to know what you adults get up to when you retire early. Just don't keep me awake by making too much noise.'

Cat pretended to be scandalised, and chided Katie for her coarseness. But she still gave her a wink as she and Nick left the room arm in arm.

Zuliani looked dishevelled the next morning, and his eyes were red-rimmed. It must have been a good night, but he was determined to be up early. Baglioni's galley sailed that very morning, and he wanted to be on the quay to see it off. He explained his superstition to Cat.

'See it off, and you will see it back safely. That's what I say.'

He grabbed a hunk of fresh bread, and hurried out, his fur-trimmed robe flapping round his legs. Katie secretly followed him at a more demure pace. The sun was just coming up over the sea where the galley was soon to go, and the morning mist turned it a rosy red. A few people stood on the quay to watch the oars dipping and swinging in rhythm as Bernardo Baglioni's galley set off into the lagoon. Zuliani shaded his eyes against the sun, and nodded with satisfaction. An old man stood leaning on a stick only a few yards away. He commented on the trim nature of the vessel.

'A good ship with a fine crew, though she looks heavy in the water.'

Zuliani cast him a sharp glance. 'Laden with goods to make my fortune, I hope.'

The old man grinned, the lines on his face creasing up like crushed paper.

'Mine, too. Though I dare say, looking at that fine robe of yours, you will have more at stake than I do.'

He stuck out a hand made rough and knotted with manual labour.

'Marco Baseggio, retired shipwright.'

Zuliani took the offered hand and, squeezing it firmly, felt the calluses that years of carving wood had worked on to its surface.

'No matter how much, or how little, you have invested, if it's all you've got, it's an awful lot. Here's wishing us both good luck.'

The old man nodded, and made off down the quay, relying on his stick to steady him on the cobbles.

The months of waiting for the merchant galley to return would have been anxious ones for Zuliani, if it hadn't been for a curious event that took place some weeks after the galley set off. Katie was seated in her room reading a work by a new Florentine poet called Dante Alighieri. Some might have thought she was reading his love poems, being a girl of no more than seventeen. But *Convivio – The Banquet* – was about the love of knowledge, and what is more it was written not in stuffy Latin but a local dialect of Italian. The language of the people. It is difficult to imagine how that excited Katie's young soul. She was so engrossed in the book that she didn't hear the visitor to Ca' Dolfin arrive, and closet himself with Zuliani. It was only when her grandfather was leading him back out that she heard their voices echoed in the reception hall. There was an entreaty from the visitor that what he had spoken about should be kept secret. This aroused her curiosity immediately. She put her precious copy of Dante upside down on the table to preserve her place, and moved to the door of her room, which gave out on to the reception hall and the doors to the water gate. But by the time she looked, the visitor was out of the gate and in his boat. She waited until the sound of an oar slapping through the water of the Grand Canal told her that he had gone, and then dashed out to speak with Nick.

'A secret. Do tell.'

Zuliani took her arm, and they strolled back towards her room.

'The trouble with telling a secret is that it's then no longer a secret. So you end up destroying the very thing you are charged with keeping.'

Katie tugged on his beard, which was more grey than red by this time.

'But I know you can't keep a secret long, Grandpa. So you might as well tell it to me now.'

He laughed that deep, throaty laugh of his. They were now in Katie's room, and he saw the book carelessly laid with its pages open facing downwards. That was bad for its spine and he picked it up. He read out a few lines from the place she had been reading, chortling as he did so.

'"Since knowledge is the highest perfection of our soul, in which our supreme happiness is found, we are all by our very nature driven by the desire to attain this." Dante Alighieri shouldn't be the one to lecture on perfection of the soul. He was at the head of the White Guelph faction after they defeated the Ghibbelines in battle, you know, and was as greedy for power and influence as any Florentine.'

Katie knew Nick was talking about the struggles between those who supported the Pope and those on the side of the Holy Roman Emperor. But she didn't want to know about Dante's allegiances. Only what the mysterious visitor had told her grandfather in secret, and she wasn't going to be diverted by a discussion about the greed of a poet. He could see the determination in her eyes, and knew she was as stubborn as he was. He sighed heavily, knowing he would have to tell her eventually.

'Very well, it will be our secret. They want me to be on the Council of Ten.'

Katie couldn't believe her ears. The Council of Ten had been set up after the failed coup of a couple of years back purely as a temporary measure to ensure public safety. There had been a fear that in its anxiety to avoid a concentration of power in one man, the republic had ended up with an unwieldy bureaucracy. Almost all the Doge's decisions had to be ratified by the Great Council, which numbered around a thousand people. It was so cumbersome a process that it could not make decisions quickly, and the coup had almost succeeded because of this. That it had failed was mainly due to its own incompetence, and some underhand work by her grandfather. The Ten was then set up so that urgent matters could be resolved more swiftly and decisively. But the Council was still an elected body.

'Won't you have to stand for election?'

Nick smiled enigmatically. 'Of course, but when I was a youth I worked out a way to circumvent the convoluted system to elect the Doge. I almost made it work, too. So getting on to the Ten will be simple in comparison.' He pulled a face. 'Though I'm not sure I want to do it.'

'Why not? You've always complained that the *case vecchie* run everything. That the old order keeps the common citizens out of the positions of power. Now you can change all that.'

'I know. And that's why I was wondering why they asked me to stand for the Council. Maybe I will just be a token commoner. And it's only for a year, anyway.'

'But you would have a turn at being the head of the Council in that year.'

He burst out laughing. 'It's only for a month, and I would be one of three equal leaders. And the leaders have to stay out of society for the whole month to avoid the risk of being exposed to bribery.'

Katie grinned. 'Oh dear, a month in Granny Cat's company. What a burden.'

He punched her arm playfully. 'You always win the argument with your impeccable logic. You're right – I should do it. But I hope Baglioni's ship returns before I'm the co-leader. I would hate to be in purdah and miss our triumph.'

As it turned out, the ship came back much sooner than Zuliani had expected, even before the election. News of its arrival brought members of the *colleganza* down to the quay, along with the idle onlookers who liked to see what wonders a trading vessel had brought with it. Everyone peered anxiously at the galley until the sly smile on the face of the captain, who stood at the stern, told the story. The trip had been a success, and had been made in record time, too.

Zuliani missed the galley's unexpected arrival because he was busy pressing palms at a gathering at the palace of the grandiose Tron family.

Unused to such exalted company, Zuliani had recruited Cat Dolfin into accompanying him. She was a member of that social élite formed by the *case vecchie*, and so was at ease with the Trons. And all the others who attended the gathering – the Tiepolos, the Dandolos and the Gradenigos. In the presence of such silken opulence, and expensively clad men and women, Zuliani nervously tweaked the collar of his stiff new *jaqueta*. Cat smiled at him indulgently at first, but slapped his hand away when he began to pull at the arse of his new hose.

'Don't go behaving like some common labourer just to prove a point,' she warned him through her gritted teeth, 'or you'll never be elected.'

'If I have to wear this gear all the time, I don't think I want to be on the council,' Zuliani growled. 'Who's that over there?'

Cat looked over to where Zuliani was pointing. A small group of young men, fashionably attired in silk brocade, were bunched around a much older man. The object of their admiration, not to say sycophancy, had a lined, long face and an imperious Roman nose. Cat thought he was probably over sixty, and his expensive clothes spoke of wealth and power.

'I don't know, but that's Domenico Valier standing next to him. He's my nephew, and as weak as his uncle – my husband – was. I can soon get out of him who the old man is.'

Zuliani almost restrained her, but she was across the room, smiling and touching sleeves courteously and at the same time intimately in a way he was incapable of. He didn't like her talking to the Valiers. It reminded him of his failure to capture Cat for himself. They had been lovers forty years ago, but then Zuliani had fled Venice under a cloud, leaving Cat pregnant. She had been forced to marry Pasquale Valier, who had brought up Zuliani's child – a son – as his own. Though it had all been his fault, Zuliani still resented Valier having taken his place, even though the man was now long dead. He deliberately turned away from Cat as she moved closer to her nephew, and began to press palms with others in the grand chamber. He decided that, if he pretended he was a trader selling a *colleganza* to gullible men with money, he could win the inbred *case vecchie* members over to his side. After rubbing shoulders with Kubilai Khan, getting on to the Council of Ten shouldn't be all that hard. Just as he was tiring of his task, Cat Dolfin returned to his side. She bussed his cheek.

'You have been doing well without me, I see.'

He shrugged his weary shoulders, but still grinned wolfishly.

'It would seem I have what it takes to be a politician, after all.' He paused. 'So who was he?'

She looked at him archly. 'Who?'

'You know who. The old man with the big nose.'

She ran a finger down the front of his new silk doublet. 'Are you jealous? You know what they say about the size of a man's nose reflecting the dimensions of his other organ.'

Zuliani quickly looked around, hoping no one had heard Cat. He wondered if this was what the conversation was like all the time amongst the old aristocracy. Cat laughed at his discomfiture.

'Never mind. Your ... nose ... is quite big enough for me.'

'Caterina!'

She cast her eyes up to the ceiling high above their heads to signify her delight at his impatience.

'Very well. To business, if you insist. The old man is Antonio Perruzzi himself.'

Zuliani's eyes widened. 'Of . . .?'

'Of Perruzzi's bank. In fact, you could say he *is* the bank, to which, they say, the English king is so indebted that if he paid off what he owes it would bankrupt his whole kingdom.'

Zuliani frowned.

'What's he doing in Venice?'

Cat took his arm and led him out of the chamber.

'Doing what he always does, no doubt. Making more money.'

'There's nothing wrong with that. It's what we Venetians do best. What do you think we expected of the money invested in Bagnioli's *colleganza*?'

Cat waved a deprecatory hand, as if the money she had loaned Zuliani was of no consequence. But despite her gesture, he knew the loan was important. The Dolfin family, of which Caterina was the last living representative bearing that name, was no longer wealthy. Of course she should have been a Valier after her marriage – and had been for a number of years – but on Pasquale's death, she had returned to her own illustrious name. Zuliani had pondered asking her to marry him and take his name for herself and their granddaughter, but so far had been afraid to broach the subject. A Dolfin was always a Dolfin, even if this one was his lover too.

As the day was still warm and the sun bright, they began to walk along the quay from Ca' Tron towards the Arsenale.

It was then that Zuliani spotted the galley, which was unloading on the quayside.

'It's Baglioni's vessel, and it looks as though he has returned with a hold full of goods.'

He rubbed his hands briskly, and gave Cat a pleading look. She sighed at being abandoned, but was resigned to Zuliani's natural instincts.

'Go on. Go and find out how much Baglioni has earned for us.'

Zuliani grinned his thanks and, leaving Cat stranded on the quay, he pushed through the crowd, which had gathered to gawp. He was soon at the gangplank of the galley, carefully noting the bundles of silk that were being offloaded. Making a mental calculation as to the return on his – on Cat's – investment, he cast around for Baglioni. There was no sign of him, but he spotted Saluzzo, the ship's captain, hanging from the rigging. Zuliani called out to him, and the man looked round. His face clouded over a little when he saw Zuliani on the dock. But then Saluzzo soon put a cheerful grin back on his face, and nimbly dropped on to the deck of the galley. He strode over to the gangplank, meeting Zuliani on the quay before he could set foot on the ship. He shook his hand vigorously.

'A good trip, master, with a well-bought stock of silks and cotton to sell on to the German traders. You will profit well by it.'

'I am glad to hear it, Saluzzo.' He looked around the quay. 'Where is Baglioni?'

Saluzzo looked around too, as if he expected to see the trader on the dock, though his eyes said otherwise. He shrugged.

'He was here a moment ago.'

Zuliani wondered if Baglioni's absence was a sign the trader planned to short-change him over his deal. It certainly looked as if the man was avoiding him, and perhaps in the process of falsifying his records. But then, just as his suspicions were mounting, he heard Baglioni's voice behind him.

'Messer . . . Zuliani?'

He turned to be met by the beaming face of a successful trader, who was eager to share his good fortune. And it seemed he had divined Zuliani's real name.

'It is Niccolo Zuliani, is it not? You should have told me who you were when we made the contract instead of hiding behind Dolfin money. I would have been proud to havc Messer Zuliani as my partner.'

Despite wishing to keep his identity a secret, Zuliani was flattered by Baglioni's effusiveness. He didn't think at the time to wonder who had revealed his identity.

'Please. I am an old man, whose glory days are in his past.'

'Never! You have shown you can still spot a good business proposition when you see one, if I may say so. I will prepare the accounts in a few days when the silks and other cloths are sold on the German market. But now, I am afraid you must excuse me.'

Zuliani could tell that, though Baglioni was engaging him in conversation, his eyes were elsewhere. He watched as the young man strode across the quay, his posture betraying his nervousness. Then he saw why. The solid figure of Marco Tron stood in the shadows of the buildings that bordered the quay. Baglioni hurried over to him, shook his hand, and they both disappeared inside the building behind them. His actions left Zuliani wondering if the Tron family had invested secretly in the *colleganza*, too.

'Big money demands full attention.'

Zuliani turned, and saw that the owner of the voice was the old man who had put his life-savings into the *colleganza*. He struggled for a moment to remember the man's name, but then it came.

'You are right, Baseggio. But who cares? We will both reap a tidy harvest from this business too.'

The old man shrugged. 'But the big man . . .' He stuck out a finger to point at where Tron had gone. '. . . will get a whole lot more.'

He passed a professional eye over the galley, which bobbed sluggishly on the lapping waves of the lagoon.

'There's more than meets the eye on that vessel.'

Zuliani wasn't sure what he meant, but assumed the old man was just jealous of the bigger slices he, Tron and Rosso were taking. As for himself, he could calculate what he stood to make, and was entirely content with the deal. He passed a few more words with the old man, and wandered back to Ca' Dolfin and Cat's company. The rest of his day was passed agreeably in drinking to his good luck, and the pleasures of the flesh.

The election to the Council of Ten was only a few days away, so, the next morning, Zuliani was distracted from the more lucrative business of calculating his profits with considerations about whose palm he should grease. But before he could be on his way, there was a loud knocking at the Dolfin street door. Cat's elderly steward, Donato, eventually answered the persistent hammering, and Zuliani heard loud voices in the hallway, as Donato tried his best to keep whoever it was from entering. Unsure why the old steward was being so obstructive, he poked his head out of the room.

'What is the matter, Donato? Show our visitor in.'

The steward appeared at the end of the passage, his face red and his arms waving.

'It's a mad woman, master. She wants to see you, but I don't think you should.'

'Why ever not?'

Before the old man could reply, a matronly woman came up behind him and pushed him peremptorily aside. She spoke up with a strident voice, edged with hysteria.

'Because he thinks I am too common to see the inside of the Ca' Dolfin, that's why.'

Indeed, the woman was shabbily dressed in a brown woollen dress that was tattered at the hem, and her headgear was worn and in holes in places. But she was more care-worn than careless of her appearance. She was poor but not ashamed of her status in life. Zuliani could see recent grief in her face, and was intrigued what had brought her to him.

'It's fine, Donato, I will see the lady.' He took in her strained look. 'And I think she would benefit from a little of the good Rhenish I know you still have stored away in the cellar.'

The old steward looked scandalised that Zuliani should be offering his mistress's best wine to the woman. But his sense of duty took over, and he bowed his head graciously and went about his task. Zuliani took the woman's arm, feeling it trembling with shock now her anger had subsided, and guided her into the main room of Cat's palatial residence. When she had sat down, and Donato had brought the two goblets of wine, he set about finding out what this incident was all about.

'Now, tell me why you came to see me. I guess it is me you want, not anyone else, mistress . . .' He paused. 'I don't even know your name.'

The woman took a deep gulp of the wine, and sighed as it slipped down her throat. She wiped her mouth on her sleeve.

'I am Francesca Este, Messer Zuliani, and, yes, it is you I want to see. It's about my father.'

Zuliani frowned, not recalling an Este as someone he knew, and guessing he would have nothing to do with the elections. The woman saw his puzzlement, and explained.

'Este is my married name. Before that I was a Baseggio.'

Zuliani knew that name. So, the old shipwright with the stick was her father.

'Ahhh. How is old Baseggio?'

The woman's face crumpled, and a tear ran down her cheek.

'He is . . . dead.'

'Dead? Good Lord, I'm sorry. When? Tell me what happened.'

After gulping back a few sobs, Francesca Este told her story. It turned out that the old man had been found that very morning floating face down in the Rio della Celestia close to the Arsenale. When his body had been fished out, there was not a mark on him to suggest foul play. So the authorities assumed he had fallen in accidentally, and informed his daughter accordingly.

Zuliani frowned, and asked the obvious question. 'So, why are you here, Domina Este? I am sorry for your father's death, naturally, especially after the success of the *colleganza* we both invested in. It's a pity he could not reap the rewards of his good judgement, but I will ensure you receive what was due to him.' It was the least he could do. 'Sometimes these things happen to old men, especially if they have been . . .'

'Drinking?'

Zuliani shrugged. 'I was going to say celebrating his good fortune. I, too, had a drink or three last night. Now, if you will excuse me . . .'

The woman grabbed his arm with a surprisingly firm hand.

'I came to you because my father said you could be trusted, even though we have heard you are standing for the Council of Ten. He said to me that it didn't matter what it looked like, that you would never switch sides.'

'Switch sides?'

Zuliani asked the question, already knowing what was coming. But he still needed to hear it for himself. Francesca Este explained in no uncertain terms.

'He said, as a Zuliani, you would never kowtow to the old hierarchy. That you would stand up for the common people of Venice. Don't let him down now.'

Zuliani was embarrassed, and felt his face going red. Was this what everyone outside the charmed circle of the *case vecchie* thought of his standing for the Council? That he was betraying his origins? If so, he would have to reconsider. He grimaced, and looked the woman squarely in the eyes.

'What makes you think it was more than an accident? I take it that that is what you want to tell me. That Baseggio didn't die by accident.'

She nodded her head, and sure of having gained his full attention, let go of his arm. He rubbed the spot where her grip had dug into his arm ruefully as she told him what she thought had happened.

'We live off the Campo San Biagio, right by the entrance to the Arsenale.'

She was describing the area round the great state-owned

basin that formed the shipyards and armoury of Venice. Its naval power emanated from this dockyard, and Marco Baseggio had given his working life over to building ships in the great basin.

'He had retired on a small pension,' explained his daughter. 'But he still went there every day, and checked on what was being built. Some of the younger men got annoyed at his interference, but the older ones – the ones who had known him at work – respected his opinions. They would drink with him, and swap stories of the old times. He could always make his way home afterwards, even though he had to use his stick. He never fell in any canal.'

'So what made yesterday different?'

'Because yesterday he saw Baglioni's galley in the Arsenale, and he told me it was still riding low in the water. Even after all the silk and cotton bales had been removed.'

Zuliani recalled that Baseggio had intimated something similar to him.

'So it was in the Arsenale to be checked over, in case it had a leak. What is so unusual about that?'

The woman prodded a stubby finger at Zuliani. 'Because it was the early afternoon when he saw the galley low in the water. When my father came away from his usual drinking session with his old cronies some time later, he saw the ship again. He told me the ship was now as high in the water as it should have been in the first place.'

Zuliani frowned, still not quite seeing where this was taking him. He could not fathom the meaning of this change that had meant so much to the old shipwright.

'Could they have merely removed the ballast from the scuppers in order to check the boat out? That would explain its different position in the water.'

'That's what I said to my father, too. He didn't think much of my suggestion, and told me so. He was always irritating people over what he saw as their lack of knowledge about ships. So it was then that I gave up trying to get him to tell me what was bothering him, and ignored him. He came over all sulky, and despite my asking him later what the problem was, he clammed up. All he would say was, if it was just ordinary ballast, why didn't they offload it on the public quay?'

Zuliani began to have an inkling about what had piqued the old man's interest. It was starting to do the same for him.

'He had a point there. But you say he said this to you after he had been to the Arsenale? After he had drunk with his fellow ship-builders and seen the changes in the ship?'

'Yes. As he does . . . did every day.'

'So how did he end up in the Rio della Celestia later that same night?'

The woman smiled grimly, seeing that Zuliani was catching up with her.

'He went out again. After dark. I wish I had known he was going, and that I had taken his worries seriously earlier. He might still be alive now.'

'You think he saw something on his return to the Arsenale, and was murdered because of it?'

She nodded.

'But he still could have fallen into the canal accidentally. Especially as it was dark.'

As soon as Zuliani had said those words, he knew how foolish they were. Not only did every Venetian know very single *calle* and *corte* in La Serenissima, and could find his way around blindfold, Baseggio's home was in the opposite direction from the Arsenale to the *rio* where his body had been found. Francesca Este looked on as the truth dawned on Zuliani. He put into words what she had guessed already.

'He was murdered and his body thrown in the canal to make it look like an accident. But they made the mistake of dumping his body in a canal that was not on his route home.'

'Yes.'

The woman said the simple word with a great sigh of relief. She had finally convinced someone else of the truth of her father's death. Now something could be done about the injustice. Zuliani's mind was racing, and a plan began to form.

'I need to check for myself what they were taking off the galley that required such secrecy. Tell me, did you ever learn from your father if there were any private entrances and exits to the Arsenale? I cannot simply turn up at the gate and demand entry.'

She smiled broadly. 'Oh, yes. Father took me to the shipyards often when I was a child. I played there a lot.'

The woman paused in her story, and noted with satisfaction that the pilgrims and travellers who made up her audience were entirely engrossed in her tale. The fire was burning low, but no one moved in order to feed it. If anything, they were greedy for more of her story. She smiled quietly and went on.

'Nick appeared not to know that his conversation with Francesca Este had been overheard.'

As it was still daylight, and he couldn't sneak into the Arsenale undetected until after dark, Zuliani decided to reconnoitre the area around the great basin immediately. He would need to be sure of his access and escape routes in case of trouble. He strolled down from Ca' Dolfin to the great square facing the Basilica San Marco and the fortified castle that was the Doge's Palace. The four gilded horses, stolen from Byzantium over a century earlier, glinted in the watery sun. They were a powerful symbol of Venice's long reach and history, but Zuliani hardly noticed them. He made his way along the quayside where Baglioni's ship had originally docked, and towards the Campo San Biagio. Poor dead Baseggio had lived his entire life there and inside the walls of the Arsenale, his days measured by the tread of his feet between the two. Zuliani followed the old man's daily journey towards the massive gates of the Arsenale, crossing the rickety wooden bridge that spanned the *rio* that led to the basin.

He stopped on the bridge and peered through the gateway like an old man with nothing else to do in his life but gawp at the business of others. He could see Baglioni's ship, still docked to the left of the basin. It was true that it now rode high and proud in the water, but Zuliani noticed something else. There was an unusual amount of activity both on the deck of the ship and on the quayside adjoining it and it was not the normal bustle of loading or unloading. Zuliani could hear sharp cries carrying over the still water of the basin, alarm sounding in their tones. The men running backwards and forwards across the gangplank between ship and quay were empty-handed, not like dock workers. Until, that is, a limp and heavy shape draped between two men came across the gangplank. A burden that looked suspiciously like a body was being transferred from ship to shore, but Zuliani was too far away to tell who it was. Or even if it really was a body. The two men carrying the burden shuffled into the building on the edge of the quay, and the door was swiftly closed behind them.

Zuliani hung around on the bridge for a while longer, listening to the soft thud of adze on wood as workers across the other side of the basin shaped planks for a new hull. But no one emerged from the Arsenale and he was unable to ask about what had happened on Baglioni's galley. Instead, he gave up his surveillance, and followed the alleys around the outside of the great basin, checking on the ways to get in and out of the Arsenale that Baseggio's daughter had told him about. The best option seemed to be to the north where an old water gate, half hanging off its hinges, would allow an agile person to swing round the gatepost out over the water and on to a narrow ledge inside the great basin. Zuliani wondered if his seventy-year-old body would be up to it. Maybe he couldn't do it by himself, but someone younger could do it with ease and, once inside, help him perform the acrobatic feat without falling in. He knew who he could ask – it was just a matter of making sure Cat Dolfin didn't find out.

Later that afternoon, Zuliani found Katie in her room still reading Dante Alighieri's book. He asked her if she was busy that evening. Of course she didn't tell him she had overheard his whole conversation with Francesca Este, and already knew it was a case of murder he was investigating. So she was surprised when he seemed to hesitate over asking her assistance.

'It is nothing very much, and you may be unwilling to give up your nice warm bed.'

'Oh, Grandpa, now you are intriguing me. Is it something really . . . exciting?'

'Noooo. I just need your help with a small matter that needs more than one pair of hands. But maybe I should not bother you with such a trifle.'

By now, Katie was getting nervous about him withdrawing his request for assistance. Perhaps he was afraid to put her in danger. But then, hadn't he already involved her in more than one murder investigation? And hadn't she seen some gruesome bodies already? She insisted she would not be inconvenienced even if it was a very minor business. Whatever his thinking was over being so uncertain, he began to tell her his plan.

'We will wait until it is dark, and make our entry when the sentries are at their lowest ebb physically and mentally. Some time between matins and lauds will be best.'

Katie laughed. 'What do you know of those monkish hours? You're usually snoring then after a late night of drinking.'

'I'll have you know I am well acquainted with those night offices. The damned chanting in the Church of San Zulian used to wake me up often enough when I was a child. So, if we are to get up then, we should emulate our religious brethren and retire at compline.'

Katie pulled a face at going to bed at such an early hour, but Zuliani insisted. He got up to leave, but had one more word of advice.

'It would be well done if we were to dress in dark clothes, and in your case in the apparel of a boy, like you so much seem to enjoy doing.'

He was making reference to the fact that before they had actually got to know each other, Katie had stalked him dressed as a youth in order to be inconspicuous. And on another occasion, she had done the same thing when called upon to pretend to be his page. But it was true – she did like the freedom of wearing leggings, and not having her limbs encumbered by a heavy dress, and she took every opportunity to do so. She grinned broadly, for she had already thought to dig her boy's clothes out of the chest at the foot of her bed. Zuliani grunted and left her to her change of wardrobe.

After a few hours, when neither of them slept well, they were both sneaking through the dark towards the Arsenale. Katie was in the top and leggings of a boy, and Zuliani in his best black *jaqueta*, which Cat had had made for him. It had been intended to make him a sober-looking individual for the Council of Ten campaign, and Katie was astonished he was intending to wear it for the secret assault on the walls of the Arsenale. So she told him so, but he waved away her objections with a disdainful hand.

'It is the only garment I possess that is black, and besides, it will come to no harm.'

But then, standing as he was at the rusty, half-open gate round the back of the great basin, he began to doubt his certainty. To gain access to the gate, they had first to edge along a narrow stone ledge set above the dank, smelly canal. The waterway ran from the basin, and was in every sense – including that of smell – a back passage out of the Arsenale. While Zuliani paused, Katie skipped nimbly on to the ledge.

'Here, let me go first.'

He didn't make a move to stop her, and watched as she inched along and came up the old, iron gate that hung half off its hinge. Grasping one of the round eyelets that formed the top part of the hinge set into the wall, she swung easily round the obstruction and got her feet on the continuation of the ledge on the other side of the gate. She settled her feet in place, and beckoned Zuliani.

'Come on. It's easy.'

Zuliani expressed a lack of belief in her encouragement

with a groan. Katie held out her hand, and waved him on. He stepped on to the ledge and began to inch closer to her. Grasping the same rusty eyelet, he paused and then swung round as Katie had done. Unfortunately, Zuliani's weight was greater than that of a seventeen-year-old girl and the fixture began to pull out. He groaned, and scrabbled for the ledge with his leading foot. Placing it on the stonework, he grabbed his granddaughter's offered hand and, as the eyelet wrenched free, concentrated on transferring his weight from the unreliable metal peg to her. For a long moment, they both almost overbalanced into the murky waters, then with a lurch they were safe on the ledge. The rusty gate, freed from its moorings, fell into the water with a splash. They tried to still their fast and heavy breathing, and stared into each other's eyes. But no cries of alarm came from deeper inside the Arsenale, where the guards were located, and they breathed more easily. The clumsy break-in had so far gone undetected. They finished their traverse along the ledge to gain the easier ground of the quayside proper where Baglioni's ship still rode proudly at its moorings. Zuliani brushed the rust off his hands, and indicated silently that they should proceed to the tall building next to where it was moored.

Using the shadows, they gained the large archway that formed the entrance to the storage sheds. The heavy oaken double doors looked intimidating, but Zuliani tried the small wicket gate set in the right-hand one and found it opened easily. It seemed no one was expecting intruders in the basin. They were inside in a moment, and closed the door behind themselves. The storehouse was almost pitch-dark, with only the weak light of the moon shining through a barred window set high on the rear wall. Zuliani cast round for a lantern, but there wasn't one.

'We shall have to take a risk and leave the door open or we won't see what we are looking for.'

He turned back to the wicket gate and opened it again. It cast a little more light into the interior, and Katie peered around.

'What *are* we looking for?'

'Whatever it was that held the ship low in the water before it was removed.'

'What if it was just stones?'

Zuliani sighed. 'Then we shall find a pile of stones and be none the wiser for our adventure. But I don't think it will be stones, or why did they bring the ship into the Arsenale before emptying it?'

They began to shuffle around in the darkness, reaching out in front of themselves to avoid bumping into anything. It was Zuliani who made the first discovery – with his shins. He cried out sharply as the corner of something substantial cracked his old bones, but then quickly changed his mood.

'Look at this.'

Katie moved over to his side, and felt out for what had barked his shin. As their eyes adjusted to the gloom, they saw what it was. He had bumped into the first of a long stack of wooden boxes, all of the same size. He looked around, and in the light from the door saw what he was seeking. A long metal bar with a flattened end that the dock workers used to prise open crates. He grabbed it, and jammed it under the lid of the nearest box. Prising the wooden slats upwards, he eased out the nails with a frightening screech. The furtive pair waited with bated breath, but could still not hear any sound other than the soft lapping of the waters against the quay. Further effort pulled the nails free, and the lid came away easily. Zuliani looked inside and gasped. Katie peered over his stooped shoulder.

'It's a king's ransom.'

Inside the crate was a heap of gold coins, gold ornaments and gold bars. Even in the soft moonlight they glowed seductively. Zuliani eyed the contents of the crate, and then looked at the stack. Katie could tell his brain was calculating the accumulated worth of the pile of crates, if every one was as full of gold as the one he had opened. He gave out a low whistle.

'This is more than a king's ransom. It's enough to buy his whole kingdom. We . . .'

He stopped and held a finger to his lips. Listening hard, Katie heard what he had. The sound of men calling to each other out on the quay. Their voices carried easily over the waters of the great basin, so they were probably some way away. But it was obvious they were coming their way. Katie was beginning to get nervous.

'We should go, Grandpa.'

'Just what I was about to say.' But he still hesitated.

'What is it?'

He was looking around again.

'There just one more thing. This morning I saw what I thought looked like a body being brought in here.'

The voices were getting closer, and she clutched at his sleeve.

'A body! It's too late for that. Let's go.'

But Zuliani wasn't deterred, and began to look around the darker corners of the storehouse. With a sigh, Katie set about helping him. With two pairs of eyes, the job would be done quicker, and she reckoned they would be on their way sooner. And it was Katie who found it. Behind the crates she saw a blackened sailcloth with a suspicious hump underneath it. She lifted one corner, and revealed a calloused hand, its fingers curled upwards like a dead spider. On the end of the hand was a tattooed forearm. She pulled the sailcloth further back. The man's sightless eyes gazed up into the moonlight. Not daring to shout, she hissed out for Grandpa. But he was already at her shoulder.

'Saluzzo. The ship's captain.'

He bent to look closer, and then suddenly heard a cry from outside. The men were much nearer than before. And it was obvious they had seen the open door to the storehouse. They were coming their way, and would be on to Zuliani and Katie very soon. Zuliani was still examining the body, and seemed oblivious to the danger. She grabbed his arm and pulled him away.

'We have to go. But how are we going to get out of here? They are at the door and will see us if we go that way.'

Zuliani seemed unconcerned, and with one look back at the body, beckoned his granddaughter towards the rear of the warehouse.

'This way.'

It seemed madness to her to be trying to hide in the furthest reaches of the big, gloomy chamber. With a guard set on the door, it would take the other men no time at all to flush them out. But Zuliani was not going to cower in the dark and await his fate. As he paced around close to the rear wall, the sound of his feet on the ground changed. He stamped to make sure, and was rewarded with a hollow note echoing back to him. He kneeled down and wiped the accumulated straw and rope strands from the stone floor, revealing a ring set in one of the slabs.

'Help me with this. It will be heavy.'

She hurried over to him and helped him heave the slab up by means of the ring.

'How did you know this was here?'

He grinned at Katie. 'Did you miss that when you were eavesdropping on my conversation with Domina Este? She told me all the secret exits from the Arsenale, including those used by the dockers to plunder what treasures were stored in here in the past.'

She had little time to marvel at how he had known she had overheard his conversation with the bereaved woman. He was already ushering her down the open hatchway and into the impenetrable dark below. He followed her down but was unable to get the slab back in place and cursed his luck.

'Damn. We shall just have to hope we have made our escape before they find this hatch. Go that way.'

He pointed to his right where there was a patch of light beckoning. Katie realised they were on a level with the ancient wooden pilings that had been driven ages ago by their thousands into the marshy ground to create a base for building La Serenissima. Sliding over mud and wooden post tops, they slithered towards the beam of moonlight. Finally, they squeezed through some rusty bars and found themselves underneath one of the bridges crossing a canal. She poked my head up, and saw exactly where they were. Close to the rear of the Church of San Martino.

'Damnation. We are in trouble.'

It was Zuliani who uttered the curse, and Katie looked round at him, fearful that they had after all been followed.

'What is it?'

He poked a finger through a gaping hole in his new *jaqueta*. 'I have torn it. Cat will kill me.'

*

With only a day to go to the elections to the Council of Ten, Zuliani had to set aside his discoveries in the Arsenale. He first needed to concentrate on convincing those with a vote that he was a suitable candidate. With his *jaqueta* repaired by Katie's nimble fingers, he started doing the rounds of the good and the worthy, only stopping short of exchanging money in order to court favour. He would have had no qualms about doing this, but Cat convinced him that the old aristocracy would think it too common an approach to the election process. Instead, he should intimate that favours could be carried out for those who voted for him as soon as he was in a position of power.

'Isn't that corruption?'

Cat laughed at such naïvety from her lover. She couldn't believe that Zuliani of all people had said that. The wheeler-dealer *par excellence* was questioning the rightfulness of using – or maybe misusing – a position of authority.

'Merely accepted practice, Nick. You do a favour for them, and when you need one, they will do one for you in return.'

Zuliani's face darkened, and he scrubbed his freshly shaven cheeks.

'All the same, it will be me using my status to gain advantage. I've never been on this side of the fence before.'

Cat patted his arm. 'And you still aren't, yet. So get out there and oil the wheels.'

Still grumbling, he left Ca' Dolfin for his first appointment. Katie looked at her grandma in surprise. She had never heard her grandmother supporting the ways of the *case vecchie* before, even though she was one by birth herself. Cat saw Katie's look, winked and walked off to her room.

The mist was being pushed back out to sea by the sun, revealing La Serenissima in all its beauty. Zuliani poked a finger in the tight collar of his *jaqueta*, and sighed. Being a public figure was harder work than he had imagined. Everyone thought they owned you, and demanded some of your time. He had not been out his door for more than a few moments, and he could already hear the sound of someone hurrying towards him. He turned, a fake smile plastered on his face. When he saw his pursuer was Bernardo Baglioni, he let his mask drop. He could see that the man was terrified.

'What on earth is the matter, Baglioni? You look as though you have seen a ghost.'

The trader's face was indeed pasty-looking, almost green, and his mouth was pulled down in a grimace. His voice came out high-pitched and broken.

'Saluzzo is dead, killed by a fall, they say, from the rigging. But . . .'

His voice finally failed him, and Zuliani finished the sentence for him.

'But Saluzzo was as nimble as a monkey up in the rigging. I myself saw him swinging down from it and landing at my feet with barely an intake of breath. Yes, I know.'

He glanced around, concerned in case someone had been following Baglioni. Though there were several men hurrying about their business, no one seemed to be intent on scrutinising their meeting. Still, it was as well to be circumspect, and Zuliani dragged Baglioni into the dead end of a dark, damp alley that led only to the edge of a canal. In the gloom, Baglioni appeared to regain his composure a little.

'They didn't let me see his body, but insisted that the only marks were those caused by falling from the top of the mast on to the wooden deck. His neck was broken apparently.'

Zuliani tested out the other man's understanding of the situation.

'Then it could have been a tragic accident, after all.'

Baglioni shook his head vigorously, his dark hair flopping over his forehead.

'Never. He was silenced, and I will be next.'

It was obvious to Zuliani that Baglioni didn't know about the old man, Baseggio. And yet he had still come to the same conclusion Zuliani had. He wanted to know more from the trader.

'What reason have you both to be silenced? And who are the "they" that you keep referring to?'

Suddenly, Baglioni glanced nervously back towards the sunlit entrance to the alley where he and Zuliani stood like a pair of thieves. Zuliani could see the indecision on his face. Baglioni was so scared of someone, he was going to back-track. When he spoke, his voice broke like a boy's.

'Maybe I was mistaken and you were right when you said it was a tragic accident. Saluzzo had to miss his footing as some point, being as overconfident as he was.'

All of a sudden, he was suggesting the ship's captain was not as sure-footed as he had first imagined. Baglioni was now anxious to convince Zuliani of this incontrovertible fact.

'Yes, that's it. A simple accident that I have blown up out of all proportion.'

He even puffed out his cheeks and laughed, as though he had convinced himself of his mistake. Not quite making eye contact with Zuliani, he waved his hand in apology and strode back out of the dark alley. However, Zuliani noticed that it was not without looking edgily both ways first that Baglioni walked into the sunlight. Zuliani would have left it there, and planned another strategy to get the truth out of Baglioni, if he had not seen a dark shadow suddenly flit past the end of the alley. His immediate reaction was that someone was walking purposefully after the trader. Someone who had waited for him to come back out of the darkness where Zuliani now stood.

He ran to the end of the alley and looked in the direction Baglioni and his tail had gone. The street twisted to the left only a few yards away, so he didn't see Baglioni. But he did see the end of a dark cloak, flapping in the breeze, before it too was lost round the corner. He hurried in pursuit. The street he was now in ran straight towards the Franciscan friary of Santa Maria Gloriosa dei Frari. Zuliani cursed his old legs as he tried to close the gap between himself and both Baglioni and his dark pursuer. He had a bad feeling about what was happening before his eyes. The man in the cloak was closing rapidly with Baglioni, and there was no one else around to see what might happen.

Zuliani called out a warning to Baglioni, but it only served to aid his attacker. The trader turned round, stopping in his tracks and allowing the man to fall upon him. There was a flash of a blade in the morning sunlight, and Baglioni fell. The attacker ran off diagonally across the small square beside the friary, but Zuliani was close on his heels, cutting him off at the bridge over the canal that ran behind Santa Maria. From under the hood of his cloak, the man snarled, feinting one way, then dodging the other. Zuliani was too slow, and as he twisted round, he felt a sharp pain travelling across his chest. He looked down, and saw that the sober *jaqueta* was slashed from one side to the other. Wondering how he was going to explain the ruined coat to Cat, he fell to his knees and blacked out.

When he came to, he found himself being bathed solicitously by the very person he had last been thinking of. He realised the offending *jaqueta* had been removed, and Cat was washing his bare chest. He smiled and looked up at her, but her face was set in a grim mask.

'Don't think you are going to get away with ruining that coat just because you have been wounded.'

He tried to look down at his chest.

'Wounded? I thought I had died and had gone to Heaven, where beautiful handmaidens were attending to my every need.'

'No, it's just me making sure this cut doesn't turn bad.'

With his chin tucked in, he could now see what Cat was referring to. A red line ran across his chest, bisecting his nipples. She had washed away the blood and little was now oozing out. She proceeded to pour an oily liquid along its length. Zuliani struggled to sit up, howling at the pain. Cat laughed and pushed him back down.

'Don't be such a baby. It's just oil, wine and vinegar, but if it was a good enough remedy for the Greeks, it's good enough for you.'

'I would much rather have taken one of those ingredients internally.'

Cat pulled a face, and proceeded to bind some clean linen around his chest.

'You can do that shortly. When you have spoken to the Signori della Notte. One of them is waiting outside to speak to you.'

Zuliani groaned. The Signori della Notte were a shady bunch who looked into all disorder and crime in Venice. He had fallen foul of them when a youth, being accused of a murder for which he was not responsible. He had been wary of them ever since. It had been only his prolonged absence from Venice, and his subsequent return rich and famous that had resulted in the accusation being shelved. But the Signori had long memories and an even longer reach. They could easily dust down his alleged criminal act. And now he would have to explain to them his presence at the attack on Baglioni. Suddenly recalling what he had seen, he asked Cat to enlighten him.

'Baglioni?'

Cat Dolfin shook her head.

'Dead.'

Zuliani cursed his luck. The trader could have given him a lead on the matter of the mysterious cases of golden ballast, and now he had been killed. Along with Baseggio and Saluzzo. With much more to do, he decided that now was not the time to tangle with the Signori. They could embroil him in a prolonged debate about what he had seen, and who the killer had been. They might even accuse him of making up the presence of another person, and imprison him for the crime. After all, he had been accused once before of murder. It could end up being weeks before he could prove his innocence, and in the meantime, the true killer could disappear, along with the gold. He sat up, feeling the bandages pull tight across his chest.

'Tell whoever is waiting that I am too weak to be interviewed. I am after all over seventy, and this has been a great shock to me.'

'Hmm. I am not sure that will keep them from seeing you. But you do have one other means at your disposal.'

'What's that?'

'I will explain to them that you are shortly to be elected to the Council of Ten, and your friend the Doge would not take very kindly to you being badgered at this crucial time.'

Zuliani was not accustomed to using an elevated position

in society to avoid the Signori. He was more used to ducking and diving like the common man he was. But he liked the idea, and grinned suddenly.

'Excellent. You can put on your most patrician face, and send them on their way.'

Cat laughed at his drawing her into the scheme.

'I am glad you see the sense in my suggestion. At least it beats what you used to suggest I do to protect you.'

'And what was that?'

'That I used my feminine wiles to distract them.'

Zuliani's smile turned wolfish. 'Well, your attributes are manifest in that area.'

She gave him a playful slap in the arm and turned away, giving him a view of a wiggling bottom as she went about her errand.

Ruefully, Zuliani picked up the garment ruined by his attacker, and poked his hand through the long slash. The quilted nature of the elaborate stitching was probably what had saved him from a worse injury, but it meant the *jaqueta* was beyond salvation. He bundled it up, and tossed it aside carelessly. He had never liked it anyway, preferring his old fur-trimmed long gown with its patterned cloth. It had been his favourite garb in distant Cathay, and reminded him of other, more carefree days. Days when he didn't have to kowtow to the wealthy in order to gain their favour. Then, he had been an agent of the Great Khan, with his personal passport and badge of office – the *paizah*. The gold bar, etched with the Khan's command, had been his means of access to officialdom wherever he went in Kubilai's empire. It had been lost in the fire that had engulfed his home recently, along with most of his other treasured possessions from Cathay.

Now, he had to rely again on his wits to achieve his goals. And wits alone would now be needed solve the mystery that had so far caused three deaths. Most recently, Bernardo Bagnioli had been stabbed because he had been deeply involved in whatever plot revolved around the bringing of gold back to Venice. Zuliani had no doubts about that. Baglioni's own fears, expressed so clearly, meant he must have known who he would fall foul of if he spoke up. Unfortunately for the trader, his co-conspirator had decided to stop his mouth anyway. Saluzzo had also been murdered. Zuliani had seen the corpse, and there was no way his death had been an accident. You didn't get three puncture wounds on your chest falling from the rigging, only from a dagger seeking to stop your heart. Saluzzo had met a similar fate to Baglioni, either because he was in the plot as well, or because he had seen too much. Zuliani guessed at the former reason. A ship's captain knew everything that happened on board his ship. He had to, in order to maintain control. Baglioni and whoever the others were would have had to recruit him to the cause too. And ultimately, that had led to his death. That left only Baseggio.

Zuliani believed the old man was innocent of any wrong-doing. The retired shipwright had no reason to be a part of the plot as his only involvement prior to the venture had been to put a small amount of money into it. No, he had been killed merely because he had been too nosy. Just like Zuliani had been. He began to wonder if he too would be silenced. It all depended on whether he had been seen in the storehouse. But even if he had been, he had one consolation after that night's escapade: Kate was safe. No one would have identified her as the youth accompanying him on the break-in.

He sniffed at the three jugs that Cat had used to mix the salve for his wounds, finally identifying the wine. He took a swig, and pulled a face. Though it was not the vinegar in the concoction, it was close to it in the sharpness of its flavour. It must have been the cheapest wine she could find for the preparation.

Cat returned, and saw what he was doing. She took the wine jug from him. 'That was awful wine, and only good to wash wounds with.'

Zuliani wiped his lips with the back of his hand. 'I know that now. Do you have some good wine to take away the taste?'

She gave him a severe look, and told him that the representative of the Signori della Notte had gone. He had reluctantly bowed to the grand lady's wishes.

'But they won't leave it there. You need to find this murderer before you are accused yourself.'

Zuliani shrugged as if he hadn't a care in the world.

'I think I need to do something to cheer myself up. I thought I would attend the Doge's banquet tonight.'

Cat was startled by Zuliani's pronouncement. The banquet was intended to parade the Council of Ten candidates one last time before the great and the good of Venice. Everyone whom Zuliani despised would be there, and she had assumed he would not wish to attend, even if he was still set on getting elected. And she had presumed that recently he had stepped back from the idea. That was why she had been pushing him into the fray at every opportunity. She had hated the idea of Zuliani becoming part of the establishment from the beginning. But she knew the only way to dissuade him was to persist in encouraging his involvement with the corruption that power brought. Now he seemed to want to rub shoulders with those in the highest positions in the republic and their supporters. Had her strategy failed?

'Are you sure you want to?'

Zuliani nodded vigorously. 'Oh, yes. And you will be on my arm, of course. Now go and get dressed in your finest.'

Caterina Dolfin glanced down at the discarded and ruined *jaqueta*.

'Very well. But what will you wear?'

'Something appropriate to my aspirations, I can assure you. Now go!'

Cat was not convinced by Zuliani's choice of clothes. They arrived at the palace's water gate in Rio della Canonica by means of the Dolfin family *barchetta*. In order to get out of the boat, Zuliani had to lift up the long robe he wore. It was a silk gown embroidered with dragons that he had brought back from Cathay. And though he insisted it was proper court dress in the presence of Kubilai Khan, Cat thought it would not impress the *case vecchie*. But as its sumptuous nature outdid her own gown, perhaps she was being overcritical. Having straightened his own gown, Zuliani helped her from the boat, which was swiftly rowed away, allowing more vessels to disgorge other richly caparisoned guests at the Doge's gates. Climbing the grand stone stairs, they made their way towards the hall of the Great Council. The event was already in full swing.

Zuliani cast an enquiring gaze around the hall, and Cat realised that perhaps he wasn't here to impress the old aristocracy after all. He seemed to be looking for someone in particular. She took his arm, and pulled him to one side, allowing others behind them to pass through into the chattering throng. She whispered in his ear, though it was hardly necessary as the sound of a thousand conversations was almost deafening.

'Who are you looking for, Nick?'

'Looking? Why should I be looking for anyone?'

A servant passed by with a tray of wine goblets, and Zuliani grabbed two, splashing some of their contents on the marble floor. He scuffed it with the sole of his boot, and passed one of the goblets to Cat. She pulled a face at his expression of innocence about her question.

'I may have found you again only after many years, but you were always an open book to me in the past and nothing has changed since then. You think the answer to the murders is here in this room, don't you?'

Zuliani smiled, and took a long swig of the wine. When he had finished, he waved the goblet in an arc before him.

'Take a look around this room, and tell me what you see.'

'I already know who I can see, and everyone is in the pages of the *Libro d'Oro*.'

She was referring to the book that listed the aristocracy of Venice, without which entry a person could not serve on the Great Council. Or vote for the Council of Ten. But she didn't need to look around the hall to know that. Zuliani shook his head at her reply.

'You're wrong. There are others here who are not Venetian, but are the support and mainstay of those you identify. There is a cardinal or two here, for example. But that is not what I asked. I asked what you saw, not who you saw.'

Cat frowned, not quite understanding what it was Nick wanted of her. But he didn't keep her in ignorance for long. He waved his goblet again, splashing more wine on the floor, much to the consternation of an elegantly dressed, elderly woman standing close by. She looked his exotic garb up and down with disdain, and moved away. Cat grinned maliciously.

'You just lost the vote of the whole Tron family. That was Sofia, the matriarch of the Trons, and none of her offspring defies her.'

'I care little about the vote, and you know it. You've spent the last few weeks deliberately pushing these people down my throat, in a bid to convince me of their awfulness. And your ploy has been successful. So I know you can see what I see.'

'And what is that?'

'Greed. Not the simple lust for good food and wine. I can understand that sort of greed, and can forgive it. No, they are all greedy for power. And wealth, which brings power with it.'

'I cannot deny that, Nick. God knows, I have lived with it all my life. But if greed is the cause of those murders, and everyone here is driven by greed, how are you going to weed out the killer?'

Zuliani tapped the side of his nose in a conspiratorial gesture.

'By making him reveal himself. Watch this.'

Cat watched as he strode into the crowd of sycophants around the Doge, and began to shake hands like an eager candidate for election. When a hand was not immediately proffered, he grabbed the reluctant man's arm and took his hand anyway. She observed in bewilderment as he worked his way through the inner circle of Soranzo's friends, even grasping the Doge's own hand. Surely he didn't think that the Doge was involved in the murders?

She noted how he held each hand for a long time, always gazing down as he shook it. Soon he had finished with the group around the Doge, and moved swiftly on, shaking hands as he went. She began to wonder if he had gone mad, and was trying to get elected after all, because she had no idea how his actions would help him find the murderer. Unless he was testing for a sweaty palm. All she could do was trail after him as he bore down on Sofia Tron and her family. Once again he was shaking hands, much to the disgust of the elderly matriarch of the family. Now Cat could believe Sofia Tron capable of murder. The look in her eyes suggested she would cheerfully murder Zuliani before the whole *case vecchie*. He did pause for a long time over squeezing Marco Tron's hand, and Cat wondered if Nick had divined something about the man's guilt. But then he moved on.

Soon he had worked his way almost entirely down the hall, until he spotted someone else. It was the banker, Antonio Perruzzi, who had a similar circle around him as had the Doge. They reminded Cat of buzzing flies hovering around a corpse. In fact, it was an apt analogy, because the banker was quite old, and his face resembled nothing more than a skull with parchment-like skin drawn tightly over it. His cheerless smile exposed a set of yellowed teeth, completing the image of a death's head. Of course, none of the sycophants around him would dare to tell him this, and Zuliani for his part seemed delighted to encounter Perruzzi at last. As Cat drew closer in order to listen to Nick, she saw a faint aura of horror creeping over the banker's face as his hand was pressed. He wrestled it away from Zuliani, at the same time responding to his obsequious address.

'I think your entreaties are ill-placed, messer. I have no

influence over the selection of the Council of Ten, being a mere Florentine.'

His voice was grating, and carried a note of disdain. Zuliani responded ingratiatingly.

'I would not say that, Messer Perruzzi. A man of your wealth and influence wields power wherever he desires.'

Perruzzi narrowed his eyes, not sure if what this ridiculous man in his outrageous garb said was meant sincerely, or as a criticism. Cat, who was now at Zuliani's shoulder, smiled at Perruzzi reassuringly. Zuliani meanwhile pressed on.

'You trade in such great amounts of silver coin and gold that we mere mortals can only stand back and admire. They do say that the King of England is so indebted to you that his whole realm could not pay you back what is owed.'

Perruzzi's thin lips tightened so much that they were all but invisible. Even as he replied, he began to cast around for one of his minions to come to his rescue.

'I do not trade, sir, and any debt owed is to the bank, not to myself. Now if you will excuse me . . .'

A hand fell on Zuliani's shoulder, and he looked round to see it was Agnolo Rosso who had come to the banker's aid. He turned, taking the man's hand in his as he did so. He looked down at the heavily ringed fingers, and shook the hand vigorously.

'Rosso, so good to see you again. I hope you got your profits from Baglioni before his unfortunate demise.'

Rosso nodded curtly. 'Yes, as a matter of fact I did. A bad business that. Such blatant street robbery as that would not be allowed in Florence. But I am not in the mood for such depressing matters. How about a drink to celebrate our mutual good fortune?'

A servant with a tray of drinks was close at hand, and

Rosso took two, passing them to Zuliani and Cat, before taking one for himself. Behind him, Perruzzi slipped away into the throng, and Rosso turned his attention to Caterina.

'Tell me, Domina Dolfin, is your granddaughter well?'

'She is very well, Messer Rosso. Thank you for your enquiry. I was not aware you knew I had a granddaughter.'

Rosso's smile was broad, but somehow unreal.

'Ah, well, the Doge mentioned her in conversation. And Domina Tron, also, I believe. There is so much to learn about the grand families of Venice.' He turned his false grin on Zuliani. 'Is she related in any way to you, Zuliani?'

Zuliani's face froze.

'Why would you even ask such a question, Rosso? That would presuppose some family connection with Domina Dolfin, who is, as you rightly observe, a member of one of the grandest families of La Serenissima.' He paused momentarily. 'While I am a mere member of the merchant class.'

Rosso flicked a beringed finger at him.

'And yet you are a candidate for the Council of Ten, and this charming lady is by your side.'

Zuliani shrugged. 'Merely as a sponsor to smooth my path into the top echelons. And you will have to excuse me now. If I am to win this election, I will have to ingratiate myself some more with the great and the good.' He took Cat's arm firmly. 'If you will introduce me to Domina Tron, I should be obliged.'

As he hustled Cat away from the Florentine, she whispered in his ear, 'What was all that about? And if you want to win over Sofia Tron, you are going in the wrong direction. She is over there putting the Doge in his place.'

She indicated off to their left, where the matriarch of the Tron dynasty was bending the ear of a glum-looking

Giovanni Soranzo. The Doge glanced over at Cat Dolfin and Zuliani with a pleading look in his eyes. But Zuliani was in no mood to come to his assistance. He didn't know who to trust any more in this palace of greed. And he was suddenly afraid for his granddaughter, Katie, whose name was apparently on the lips of the Doge and the Trons. Perhaps her presence on his trip to the Arsenale wasn't as secret as he had hoped.

'We are going home, if you want to know. And as swiftly as possible.'

Not wishing to alarm Cat unnecessarily, he came up with an excuse for his sudden change of plans.

'This gang of crooks has depressed me.'

Cat beamed at him. 'I'm glad you said that. I am as tired as you of them all.'

Zuliani did not want to wait for the Dolfins' *barchetta*, so the couple exited the palace by the land gate, and hurried home through the dark streets of Venice. Reaching Ca' Dolfin, Zuliani called out Katie's name, and when there was no response, ran to her room as fast as his ageing legs could carry him. The room was empty, and the only sign she had been there was the book by Dante Alighieri lying open and face down on the floor. It looked to him as if it had been hastily discarded, or dropped in a struggle. He slumped down on the bed beside it.

'What's going on, Nick? Why are you so concerned about Katie?'

Cat stood in the doorway, a dark look on her face. Zuliani hesitated for a moment, not sure whether he wanted to share his fears with her. But then he knew she would never forgive him if he didn't do so and something terrible had happened.

'I know who killed Baglioni, Saluzzo, and the old man. And I think he knows about Katie and me uncovering the secret hoard of gold in the Arsenale. Even if he doesn't, I think he is going to use Katie as a pawn to draw me out, and kill me, too.'

Cat felt the heat of her body falling away, and being replaced by an icy coldness. She leaned on the door frame for support, her legs quivering.

'What is all this about, Nick. Whose gold is it?'

Zuliani took Cat's arm and drew her down on to Katie's bed beside him.

'At first, I thought it was Soranzo, or another member of the *case vecchie* – the Trons maybe – accumulating gold secretly. They are not listed in the *Libro d'Oro* for nothing, after all. But then I began to put Baglioni's trip together with other stories I have heard bandied about for some time now. The big banking houses have been shipping out silver coins by the thousands in order to buy gold at preferential rates in the Middle East and beyond. They seem to care little about the effect on trading here in the West as our coinage disappears abroad. Greed is all that drives them.'

Cat gasped as she realised the truth.

'The Florentines are behind this. That is why Rosso funded Baglioni's *colleganza* – in order to ensure the scheme went ahead.'

'Yes, and behind Rosso stands old man Perruzzi – the greediest of them all.'

Cat clutched Zuliani's arm. 'But then where does this leave Katie?'

Zuliani shrugged. 'My best guess is she is at the Arsenale. They have not had time to move their gold yet. If she had been taken anywhere, it will be there.'

'Then you must find her.'

*

Zuliani didn't have time now to sneak in the way Francesca Este had described to him. Nor was he inclined to be circumspect, not caring this time about being seen. Maybe it would be best if Rosso knew he was coming anyway. So he marched up to the main entrance beside the water gate. Surprisingly, he was unchallenged, and swiftly made his way along the quay to where Baglioni's galley had been moored. It was no longer there, but another vessel was, which was no surprise to him. The galley's purpose had been served, and its secret cargo would now be moved in a different ship to Florence and the coffers of Perruzzi's bank. There had not yet been time to move the chests, and so Zuliani assumed they were still in the storehouse where he had found them.

When he approached the building, he saw that the small wicket gate set in the larger main doors was ajar. It looked so inviting it made him think that he was right concerning the whereabouts of Katie. With such precious cargo inside, the door would not normally have been left unlocked. They wanted him to enter. He edged up to the opening, and peered into the gloom.

At the far end of the storehouse a couple of lanterns lit a shadowy figure moving along the stack of wooden chests that Zuliani had seen on his last visit. It was difficult to see who it was because the lanterns provided only a silhouette. Zuliani inched through the door and tiptoed towards some barrels piled along the left-hand wall, trying to get closer before he revealed himself. As he crouched down behind one of the barrels, he almost cried out as a hand touched his shoulder. Looking up, and thinking he was discovered by one of Perruzzi's henchmen, he was astonished to see a slim, pale face staring at him from under a sugar-loaf hat. The person's hat was pulled well down and the face was in darkness, but a stray blond tress told him all he needed to know. It was Katie in her page-boy garb. He hissed a strangled question at her.

'What are you doing here?'

Katie grinned. 'I might ask you the same question, Grandpa. But seeing as you asked first, I will tell you. I thought you and Granny would be fully occupied for hours at the Doge's party, so I decided it was time to find out if there was gold in all those boxes, and get to the bottom of the matter.'

Zuliani was so relieved to find Katie had not been taken hostage, or worse, he became very angry.

'And you didn't think to speak to me first?'

Katie pouted. 'You would have stopped me coming. And besides, I thought you had given up as you seemed so busy with wheedling votes from everyone.'

'Wheedling?'

Zuliani almost forgot where they were, and had to choke off his annoyed cry.

'Tell me. Have I ever given up on anything as important as three murders?'

Katie thought for a moment, then shook her head.

'No. You are right and I was wrong. But now we are both here, what do we do next?'

'What I do is confront a murderer. What you do is get out of here and go safely back home.'

Katie began to protest, but in so doing managed to knock over an adze that had been left by one of the shipbuilders working in the Arsenale. The loud clunk of the wooden handle echoed down the length of the warehouse, alerting the man they had been spying on.

He grabbed a lantern, and called out. 'Who's there? Show yourself now.'

He began to stride towards where Zuliani and Katie were hiding, his face still hidden by the hood of his cloak. Zuliani pressed the crouching Katie down, indicating she should stay in the shadows, and stood up himself. As he moved away from Katie's hiding-place, he spoke up boldly.

'I'm here, Rosso.' He peered beyond the beam of the upheld lantern. 'It is you, isn't it?'

The man threw his hood back, revealing himself. It was indeed Agnolo Rosso, who was now lit by the lantern he held over his head. He laughed.

'Yes, it's me, Zuliani. Damn you for being such a nuisance. I should have killed you sooner, but I can easily get on with the job now.'

'Just as you did away with Baglioni, Saluzzo and old Baseg gio because they got in your way. Or should I say in the way of Perruzzi, because it is his gold in those chests, is it not?'

Rosso merely smiled enigmatically.

'I would have thought you of all people understood about making profits. You're the legendary Zuliani, who came back from Cathay a rich man.'

Zuliani didn't rise to the bait. It was true he believed in making money from trade, but only in the good old-fashioned way of buying and selling goods. That sort of business always carried with it the thrill of a gamble. Perruzzi and his like did nothing but speculate on money and the fluctuating value of gold and silver. And when the profits were not sufficient, they manipulated the markets. Standard silver coin had been the stable currency of the Holy Roman Empire in Europe since Charlemagne's time. Now it was disappearing into the East at an alarming rate. Zuliani was beginning to see that the massive export of silver coinage from Venice to the East would create severe problems in making payments in trade. But the Florentine bankers were protecting themselves from any difficulties with chests of gold. They were like dangerous sharks swimming in Venice's seas. He answered Rosso's taunt.

'Yes, but I made my money honestly.'

Rosso pulled a face. 'Do you really want me to believe that you never cheated anyone?' He held a finger and thumb a little distance apart. 'Just a little? Besides, what's dishonest about using money to make money?'

Zuliani didn't answer him this time. He prayed that Katie would stay hidden. Rosso took Zuliani's silence as a sign he was winning the argument, and his stance became more relaxed. But then Zuliani saw the man looking not at his face, but over his shoulder. He risked turning his gaze away from Rosso to see where the man was looking, afraid that Katie had been revealed. What he saw was a hessian sack lying by the door to the warehouse, its neck tied up with a heavy rope that was finished in a loop. Zuliani smiled, knowing instantly why Rosso was alone in the building. He had decided that Perruzzi had not rewarded him sufficiently, and was stealing some of the gold for himself. Rosso also guessed what was going through Zuliani's mind. He shrugged, and placed the lantern at his feet.

'Who's going to miss a sackful from such a large consignment? You could help yourself too, and forget you ever saw me here. You could dismiss your suspicions about the deaths of the three men as mere fancy. What do you say?'

Zuliani's instincts told him the man standing before him wasn't going to let him leave the warehouse alive, despite what he was saying. But he decided he would go along with him for the time being, until he could find a moment to get under his guard. And he also had Katie to think of.

'It's very tempting – what you are suggesting, Rosso?'

Rosso's laughter echoed around the warehouse. 'I knew you were a man after my own heart.'

He put his hands on his hips, in a way he hoped would demonstrate his friendliness. But Zuliani could see it put his right hand closer to the dagger in his belt. Zuliani wondered if he could draw his own dagger as swiftly as the younger man. But then Rosso was asking him a question.

'How did you guess it was I who carried out the killings?'

Zuliani pointed at the rings on the hand that was held loosely on Rosso's hip. They sparkled in the light.

'I saw your hand when you tried to stab me, just after you had killed Baglioni. All those rings gave you away. And then there was that ring on your thumb that looks as though it swivels round, leaving the stone on the inside.'

Rosso threw a glance down at his hand, already knowing what Zuliani meant. It was a nuisance, that ring.

'So that's why you were shaking everyone's hand at the Doge's reception earlier. But what of my thumb ring?'

'It matches a bruise I saw on Saluzzo's neck where you held him and choked him as you slid the knife in his heart.'

Rosso looked startled for a moment, then grinned rapaciously.

'So it was you in this place that night. I thought it might have been, but you disappeared without trace before I could get a look at you.'

Zuliani silently thanked God that Rosso and his men hadn't seen him. It meant they were also ignorant of Katie's presence that night. All he had to do now was get out of this alive, and make sure Katie did, too. He saw that Rosso was unconsciously twisting the ring on his right thumb with the fingers of his left hand. It was his moment to strike, while both his opponent's hands were occupied. He slid his dagger out, and lunged at Rosso. But the younger man was quicker, and when Zuliani's stiff right knee gave away slightly, he danced backwards, drew his own dagger and thrust out.

Zuliani grunted in pain as he felt Rosso's dagger skitter across his ribcage and dig into his flesh. His stumble turned into a fall, and he cracked his head hard on the stone floor, dropping his dagger. Rosso smiled coldly as he looked down at Zuliani's prone figure, blood already seeping out from underneath him. He dashed over to the hessian sack he had set by the door, wrapped the loop of rope that tied the neck off around his wrist for safety, and stepped out of the narrow wicket gate into the night.

Katie had been stunned by the swiftness of the attack on her grandfather, but as Agnolo Rosso disappeared, she came to her senses. With a groan of anguish, she ran over to Zuliani's body and grabbed his dagger, which still lay on the ground. She was determined to avenge her grandfather, and the three other men that Rosso had killed. She skipped over the sill of the wicket gate, and saw Rosso walking away along the quay. She ran after him and, just as he turned on hearing her light footsteps, swung a murderous blow with Zuliani's dagger. She missed Rosso's body completely, but as he dodged the blow, he lost his balance and fell backwards off the edge of the quayside. There was a loud splash as he hit the water in the great basin of the Arsenale. Katie looked down into the water, and saw Rosso flailing with one arm, splashing the water around him. She watched in horror as he struggled to disentangle his wrist from the rope binding the sack's neck. Unfortunately, he was unable to get his arm free, and the heavy sack of gold dragged him beneath the waters. A few bubbles broke the surface, and then there was nothing except a ring of ripples growing out from where his body had gone under.

Katie Valier looked round her audience as she concluded her tale of greed.

'You may have guessed that the young girl was me, and I witnessed the price that greed extracts from sinners.'

Every eye was on her, and the fire had been left to turn to a glowing redness. She leaned down and tossed another log on to the glow. It broke the spell, and the old man with the long white beard spoke up.

'I am sorry that your grandfather died, too.'

Katie smiled.

'Oh, Grandpa Nick didn't die. You see, Rosso's knife was diverted by his ribs and left him with just a flesh wound. Hitting his head on the ground knocked him out temporarily, but he was soon by my side to witness Agnolo Rosso's demise.

'"The reward for greed is death," he said to me in a rather satisfied way. "Too much gold is a burden that only served to drag you down."'

'And what of Perruzzi?' asked the old man. 'Did he pay too for his greed?'

Katie had to admit that the banker Perruzzi had escaped any blame for the three murders. Someone on the edge of the group of pilgrims, who was sitting outside the circle of light cast by the fire, made a comment on that.

'Is it not always the way, that the rich escape punishment, while the poor are ground down?'

Katie had an answer to that.

'But then, as you all probably know, justice came to those who were

driven by greed to try to accumulate great wealth at the expense of others. It is only a few years ago that your King Edward reneged on England's debts, and drove the Florentine banks to a collapse. Antonio Perruzzi was a very old man by then, but he lived to see his world fall down around his ears, and died destitute. The sin of greed found him out in the end.'

THE THIRD SIN

It was not long before the old man who had expressed his regret – rather prematurely – about Katie Valier's grandfather, and had asked about Perruzzi's fate, had another question for her. He moved closer to her, and with his eyes strangely not on her but on the glowing fire, spoke quietly so that only she should hear.

'Is it true that your grandfather travelled in the East?'

'Oh, yes. He had many adventures there, and made his fortune. Though that was soon gone when he returned to Venice, for he cared little about keeping it. The fun was in the making of it for him.'

The old man nodded, and stroked his long, white beard.

'I understand that perfectly. But tell me, you said his name was Zuliani?'

'Yes, and he was nothing if not a true Venetian. But he was also proud that his mother was English. And that is why I am in these parts. I am looking for any of his family that might remain in England. They were from Bishop's Lynn, and were called de Foe. The plague has interrupted my journey, but I shall get there eventually.'

'So you are not, like me, on a pilgrimage to Our Lady of Walsingham? Well, I will pray that you are spared this horror. And that the family of your grandfather are, too.'

He reached out his hand as if wishing to reassure her but seemed to grope a little in the air before finding her arm. Before she could say anything, though, he moved on.

'But there is another question I would like to ask. You see, my father and mother travelled in the great empire of Yuan and I was born there.' He laughed and shook his head. 'I don't know if I am English, like my father, Jewish, like my mother, or Chinese by birth.'

Katie Valier was surprised at his confession that his mother had been Jewish. The Church expressly forbade any sort of relations between Christian and Jew on pain of death. She wondered if that was why his parents had travelled far away from England. She was also curious about something this old man had said earlier.

'Tell me. Why did you ask about my grandfather's name?'

'Ah. That is to do with the question I wish to ask. You see, when I was growing up, I was told tales of a Chinese demon called Zhong Kui, who righted wrongs. It was an old tale, but it seemed to have got mixed up with a real-life foreigner whose thirst for justice meant he was called by the demon's name too. His real name – to the Chinese – was Zu Li-ni.'

Katie laughed and clapped her hands like a young girl.

'It must have been Grandpa! He investigated crimes for the Great Khan. He would be so flattered that he was remembered still.'

The old man smiled and nodded his head.

'My father may even have met him. He certainly knew many stories about him. And my father had no small fund of his own tales too. In fact, your story of Zuliani has reminded me of one of them.'

He turned his head to the group of pilgrims, who still sat close to the fire, too bound up in a fear of their possible fate to fall asleep. The old man raised his voice so all might hear him.

'My name is David Falconer, and I have a story to tell which, though it is brief, will get you thinking about another of the Deadly Sins. This one is about . . .

Gluttony

More than thirty years ago, I was travelling through the fabled land of Trebizond. Of course, many tales are told of the place, not least that it was the land where Jason and the Argonauts sought the Golden Fleece. But I have another tale to tell – a tale of a land that was all too real, populated by mortal men with similar failings to our own. It is a tale of murder.

The Empire of Trebizond is a splinter of the Byzantine Empire, which has come to rest on the southern shores of the Black Sea. Barely forty miles deep and two hundred miles long, it is, nevertheless, an opulent and secluded paradise made rich by the trade that flows through it. I came to it from the east by following the Silk Road to Erzerum, where several camel trains came together, bringing dyes and spices from Baghdad, Arabia and India, together with raw silk via the Caspian. This single great caravan of a thousand camels, each bearing three hundred pounds of merchandise, then wound its way over the Pontic Mountains, which protect the back of Trebizond, and down into the city that gazes out over the sea that is its lifeblood. Traders from the west venture there by water on a four-month journey that culminates in the protective, curved arm of the harbour wall. We, as I say, had come overland from the east.

Descending on the swaying back of a mule, I felt almost as though I had arrived by sea, with a lurching feeling of sickness in my stomach. My travelling companion and secretary, the monkish Brother Philip, chattered eagerly as we passed along the edge of the western ravine that protects one side of the city with its tumbling waters. I learned later that the eastern side of the city is similarly protected by another natural moat.

'Master, you cannot imagine the view from here. The city falls away at our feet, and sweeps down to the waters of a great sea. And it is so lush. The trees grow steeply on either side and the colour of the flowers is overpowering.'

Being sightless, I drank in his description. And I shared his excitement, for I could smell the heady scent of pines that grew along the path. That, and the scent of the camel train's contents – pepper, cinnamon, myrrh and spikenard – mingled with the local scent of fruits and musk and incense. It was the very essence of the city I was going to get to know well. We descended the Zagnos valley, skirting the upper town and the Citadel, and broke off from the caravan train to enter the lower town through a grand gateway. Philip led the way and my mount followed obediently. The monk's voice piped up with excitement, describing all he saw. He was barely twenty, and his beard was a mere wisp of soft down on his cheeks. Everything he saw was a marvel to him, but I valued his description of the lower part of Trebizond as we rode through its narrow streets. It seemed the arrival of the caravan was an occasion for celebration. The main road that led back up to the Imperial Citadel was hung with patterned carpets and lined with men in glittering livery. Many walls were covered in holy paintings in ochre and red and dark blue. The inhabitants of this lower town, where the foreign merchants dwelled, were gaily dressed in tight robes quite unlike the loose garments of the West. Their chatter, and the noise of playful children, made it difficult for me to hear what Brother Philip was saying. I asked him to speak up.

'I was saying that we shall have to dismount soon or we shall trample some child underfoot. It is like swimming against the tide. Everyone is making for the gate we have just entered.'

I called out to someone in the throng, 'Where is everyone going, pray?'

A woman answered with a voice that had laughter in it. 'Why, to the Meidan, where there will be games and food stalls to celebrate the arrival of the caravan from the East.'

'Yes, we came with it part of the way ourselves. But I am seeking an official of the Emperor's court. He is the keeper of the Emperor's library, and goes by the name Theokrastos. Do you know where I might find him?'

I had an introduction to this scholar, given me by a Nestorian monk in the Yuan Empire. In truth it was a tenuous connection, for the grimy monk in furthest Tatu had only heard of Theokrastos second-hand through travellers on the Silk Road. But I had heard many stories of the library of Alexios II, Emperor of Trebizond and Autocrat of the Romans, and would use any influence I could exert to get to see it. The woman I spoke to doubted I would see the scholar today, however.

'Everyone in the court will be on the Meidan, sir, and I must go or I will be at the back of the crowd and see nothing of the acrobats.'

I let her go, and dismounted from my tired horse. Philip did the same, and took my reins from me.

'If we look for the sign of the Lion of St Mark, master, we will be sure to find accommodation. The Venetians are acquisitive but generous with their hospitality.'

I agreed and followed wearily beside the horses, as Philip led them down towards the harbour.

It took longer than I had expected to meet George Theokrastos. The Emperor's court was a strange mixture of strict formality and indolence. And its officials were hidden behind a screen of bureaucracy. Written requests had to be made for any meeting, and these documents languished in stacks of similar entreaties, only to be dealt with in the mornings. Afternoons were a time of torpor. I made use of my frequent spare time by walking around the city in the company of Brother Philip. We were fortunate to witness a procession one day as the court made its way from the Citadel to the monastery of St Sophia beyond the western ravine. Philip called out excitedly as servants with golden axes, eunuchs in white robes, and Imperial Guards in shiny breastplates passed before us. We were forced back against the walls of the houses as princes in cloth of gold and black-clad Orthodox priests swinging gilded censers moved slowly by. The air was heavy with incense and excitement.

'Look,' cried out Philip over the buzz of the crowd. 'There's the Emperor carrying a crozier, and wearing a dalmatic with a design of eagles woven in purple and gold thread.'

It was the first time we had come across the Emperor, and I drank in the atmosphere.

The following day, I finally had my audience with George Theokrastos, the keeper of the Emperor's books. I submitted my letter of introduction from Sauma, the Nestorian Christian in the East, and was pleasantly surprised that Theokrastos had heard of him. The letter oiled the ponderous wheels of the Trapezuntine bureaucracy, and Philip and I were soon immersed in Greek and Roman texts that had been rescued from the sack of Constantinople by Flemish soldiers of the Fourth Crusade. We had been allowed into the inner city, the second tier of Trebizond as it were, with only the impregnable Citadel still towering over our heads. But even the library was a palace, with white marble, ivory and gold everywhere. We soon settled into a routine, with Theokrastos bringing us examples from the Emperor's collection like titbits for a valued guest. Philip took each tome in his hand and read while I listened and absorbed the text.

He began with the *Ecclesiastical History* of Salamanes Hermeias Sozomen, which was dedicated to the emperor Theodosius the Younger. It began with the consulship of Crispus and his father, Constantine, and went down to the reign of Theodosius. Sozomen was at one time an advocate in Constantinople, and I thought his style better than that of Socrates. The work was nine books long, and took as many days to read. Philip was coming to the end of the final book, when I heard a commotion in the antechamber to the library. Someone was complaining loudly to George Theokrastos about the foreign merchants in Trebizond. I asked Philip to venture closer to the doorway, and see who was causing the disturbance. After a short while, when the raised voices had quietened down, he came back and told me what he had observed.

'It is a portly gentleman dressed in the finest of robes, all encrusted with jewels, who looks as if he is a person of great importance at the Emperor's court. His face is quite red, and he is practically foaming at the mouth. He was showing the librarian some parchment he had in his hand, and complaining bitterly about its contents.'

My curiosity was piqued.

'Could you make out what it said?'

'No,' Philip replied. 'But the fat man thought it outrageous, whatever it said. He said something had to be done about it, and stormed off.'

I smiled at the idea of investigating the matter. Reading books was getting boring, and I always did like a mystery. I resembled my father in that, for he had solved many seemingly impossible murders in his time. Of course this was not a murder, but I thought I could use it to ingratiate myself into the court. Just as I was wondering how to begin, Theokrastos came scurrying into the reading room. His leather-clad feet made a distinctive sound on the marble floor – small steps heralding his fussy efforts at interesting me in another tome. This time they were swifter than ever, and made me think he was agitated by the recent intruder. He did still come bearing a book, however. His tone of voice was tense, even as he attempted to sound unaffected.

'This may afford you some light relief after Sozomen, Master Falconer. It is called the *Adventures of Clitophon and Leucippe*, written by a Greek named Achilles Tatius.'

In any other circumstances, I would have thought Theokrastos was seeking to make fun of young Philip's monkish temperament. I knew of this work, and heard it described as a dramatic work with unseemly love episodes, the impurity of sentiment of which are prejudicial to seriousness. I would have liked to hear it, but I didn't think Philip could bear to read it without his ears going red. I was just about to suggest that Theokrastos read it to me himself, when I heard him clicking his tongue.

'Forgive me, sir. I am not thinking clearly. Such a work will not be appropriate for young ears to hear.' He sighed deeply. 'I have been distracted, and my judgement has been impaired.'

I took the opportunity afforded by the librarian's admission.

'I heard the commotion outside. Tell me, is there anything I can do?'

During our short acquaintance, I had told Theokrastos of

my interest in recondite matters, so I did not have to convince him I was responding merely out of politeness. His reply was hesitant, as though he was reluctant to reveal a matter that might reflect badly on the Emperor and his retinue.

'Perhaps it is only a trifling affair that would be beneath your consideration.'

I pressed the matter with him. 'I would still like to help, if I can.'

He paused only momentarily, then began to explain. 'The man you heard shouting is Johannes Panaretos. He is responsible for allocating trading licences to foreign merchants, and so holds a very important position in the Emperor's court. Just recently, he has been pressed by the Genoans for greater concessions, and the Emperor has refused. Before you arrived here, Lord Alexios wished them to pay dues on goods they threatened to take away, if they pulled out of dealing with us entirely. The Genoans naturally refused and there was a small skirmish, with the Emperor calling on Georgian mercenaries to attack the Genoan warehouses. The Genoans retaliated and some house down by the harbour were set on fire. Now, Panaretos has received a threat.'

Theokrastos paused in his narrative, and I could tell he was unsure if he was saying too much. I nudged his natural loquaciousness.

'A threat?'

Theokrastos licked his lips.

'Yes. He has just showed me a scrap of parchment on which was written the words – "Death awaits he who hesitates."'

I felt a *frisson* of excitement run up the back of my neck. Perhaps murder was lurking on the sidelines after all.

*

It took a day or two for Theokrastos to arrange a meeting for me with the recipient of the death threat. Apparently, Panaretos had laughed crudely at the thought of a blind man resolving the issue of the author of the note. But the librarian had convinced him to at least speak with me. When I did so, I believe that I convinced him that, being blind from birth, I had tuned my other senses to such a degree that they more than compensated for the lack of sight.

'In fact,' I said to him, 'I believe the Chinese surgeon who plucked me from my mother's womb in terrible circumstances, not only saved my life, but gave me a unique opportunity to do good in the world.'

I don't think it was such platitudes that swayed his decision, but the fact that I could track him enough to appear to be always looking at him. I have been told my pale, blue-green eyes are quite riveting, and nothing can be more disconcerting than a blind man 'looking' at one. In truth, he was easy to follow using just my ears, for he was a fat man whose every movement was accompanied by wheezes and grunts. Even when he thought he was testing me by remaining silent, the whisper of his slippers on the marble floors of his abode was enough for me to locate him.

In the end, Philip and I were invited to a lavish dinner, where there would be present representatives of the major trading partners of the Empire of Trebizond. I was to share the meal with a Florentine, a Genoan, and a Venetian. It would be an interesting evening, especially as Panaretos suspected one of the men to be the author of the message. Which one it would turn out to be was why I was there. But first, I asked to be sent the offending message, so that I could examine it. It arrived on the morning of the fateful meal.

I took it in my hands and felt the quality and nature of

the parchment. I immediately realised it was a piece of a bigger sheet, as one edge was crudely cut. It was also of medium quality, and not of the finest vellum. Probably of goatskin as that was the most easily available local material. The roughness of its surface felt to me as if it was a palimpsest – that is, a parchment sheet that had been used before and scoured of its original writing. If so, it might therefore be possible to discern the writing that has been obscured, and discover something from that. That would be a task for Philip, and I passed the parchment on to him.

'Please read what you can see, Philip.'

'Yes, sir. It says, "Death is waiting for him who hesitates." Just as the librarian said.'

I waited, expecting more from him, but nothing came. I had hoped I had trained him better than that, so I had to prompt him.

'And in what language is it written?'

Philip mumbled an anxious apology, and I could almost imagine his ears turning red as I had been told they did when he was embarrassed.

'I am sorry, sir. It is written in Greek.'

'And in what style of Greek, if you please?'

He paused, and I heard him puff out his cheeks.

'Grammatically, it is correct, but I would say by the hand that it was written by someone whose natural language it wasn't.'

So, it could have been scribed by someone from an Italian city-state – either Florence, Genoa, or Venice. I smiled.

'I was once told of a Florentine, a Genoan and a Venetian who were each left five hundred ducats by a rich man on condition that after his death they would each put twenty ducats into his coffin in case he needed it in the afterlife.

The Florentine and the Venetian duly put in their twenty ducats, and quietly left the room. The Genoan walked over to the coffin, reached in and took out the forty ducats and put in a promissory note for sixty ducats.'

I heard Philip gasp.

'How appalling. I hope he did not get away with such a sacrilegious act.'

I sighed, but refrained from telling the young monk it had been a joke. Though there was a serious intent to my jest. Genoans were renowned for their double-dealing and meanness. Perhaps the one I was to meet had been crass enough to engender fear in Panaretos, when subtlety was a better course. Neither the Venetian nor the Florentine would have surely tried such tactics. But I was keeping an open mind as Philip guided me up the slope that led from the lower city through the gate into the upper city, and past the Panagia Khrysokephalos Church. Panaretos lived as close to the Emperor's citadel as a member not of the royal family may without actually being inside the royal walls. Even so, the end of the street afforded a glimpse of the palace. Philip described what he saw for me with awe in his voice.

'I can see white marble pillars, and a courtyard set with orange and lemon trees, and oleander. There is a fountain in the centre of the courtyard and big, bronze double doors beyond.'

I could sense him turning to face me.

'If it is so grand just on the approach to the palace, how grand must it be beyond the doors?'

I, who had experienced the fabled luxury of the Great Mongol Khan's summer residence called Xanadu, could imagine how ornate it might be through those doors. But it was impossible to describe to an austere fellow like Philip, a monk from northern Greece, who had literally sat on a pinnacle of rock in the Meteora region before travelling east on a mission to convert idolaters, and then becoming my companion. Now, I nudged his arm and reminded him of our goal.

'The delights of Johannes Panaretos' residence will be enough grandeur for your eyes this evening. And you need to keep them wide open for me.'

I knew he lacked the subtleness I needed to interpret every sign that may come our way today, but what he lacked in perceptiveness he made up for with a remarkably retentive mind. What he couldn't whisper in my ear during the evening, I could worm out of him later in the seclusion of our lodgings. It was then he would tell me what the three traders looked like. Apparently, the Florentine, whose name was Giacomo Belzoni, was small, dark-complexioned and compact, with neat and fastidious manners. The Venetian, by contrast, was a tall bear of a man with fair hair, given to sprawling in his chair. His name was Alessandro Ricci. Finally, there was the Genoan, who I suspected the most of the three. Giovanni Finati was stockily built, and probably at home in a ship with his bandy legs and rolling gait. I was to identify them to myself during the evening by their speech, which did seem to fit the word pictures Philip drew of them for me later.

All three were already in Panaretos' house when I arrived, and the wily Trapezuntine forbore from mentioning my blindness. I think he thought it a jest to see which of the Italians would guess it first, and which would be so discourteous as to mention it. No one did. But then I was adept at disguising my deficiency, which I hardly saw as one after so much time. I probably seemed to them just a sybaritic

Englishman relying on his servant to cut up his food and present it to him.

The food, by the way, was excellent. The first course was a compote of hare, stuffed chicken and a loin of veal, all covered in a sauce with pomegranate seeds. This was followed with various pies stuffed full of goslings, capons and pigeons. The pastry case was not as the English served – quite hard and inedible, they are called 'coffins' – but soft and crumbly. It was a delight, therefore, to eat the case as well as the contents. The third course was a sturgeon cooked in parsley and vinegar, which was a joy after such a preponderance of meat. Though I and his other guests were flagging, Panaretos showed no signs of slowing down, and continued to stuff his fat face with all the food that was presented at the table. I could hear his jaws chomping on the delicacies. But, besides the conversation that accompanied the banquet, I was intrigued by the presence of another person flitting in and out of the room as the courses progressed.

Each time a new course arrived, the undoubtedly tempting aromas were accompanied by something more subtle and human. A scent of patchouli oil wafted into the room at the same time that I could hear the slippered feet of someone much lighter than our host drifting round the room. At the arrival of the sturgeon, this person, who had to be a woman – unless it was a young eunuch or made-up boy – passed quite close to me and I heard the rustle of silk. I could bear it no longer, knowing that I could not see what the others did naturally. I interrupted the Venetian, who was talking about the alum mines at Kerasous, and invited Panaretos to introduce the mysterious beauty. It was a calculated risk on my part, for it could have been a catamite, but I didn't think so.

'Are you not going to introduce us to your wife, Panaretos? She looks so beautiful and modest, serving us in silence.'

The fat Trapezuntine grunted in surprise, knowing as he did my affliction, but did as I requested.

'This is Baia Bzhedug, and she is my Circassian beauty.'

The tone of his voice suggested to me that his wife was more a piece of property than a companion. I sensed that Baia was bowing to me as I heard the rustle of her silk robe, but I held my hand out anyway. After a moment's hesitation, I felt the warmth of her delicate and slender hand in mine. I raised it to my lips. The Genoan, Finati, called out his approval of my gesture.

'Bravo, Englishman. You are not such a cold fish as some of your compatriots. During all our trade negotiations, Panaretos never once gave away the fact he had a beauty for a wife.'

I felt the woman's hand tense in mine, and allowed it to slip free. The scent of patchouli oil drifted from the room. Meanwhile, puffed up with pride, Panaretos began to expand on his wife's family history. I could hear his fat lips drooling as he munched on the sturgeon and spoke at the same time. I could almost feel the spit spraying from his gluttonous mouth.

'She is from Sochi, and claims to be a princess. Though in this house, she is my cook and housemaid. Many of the Circassians are no better than idolaters, and have no standing in Trebizond. Still, she is passing pretty, as you say.'

As if to emphasise his point, he chose to call out at that moment, 'Wife, where are the subtleties, the jellies?'

In response, Baia announced her return with the slapping of her delicate, slippered feet on the marble floor, and her aroma of patchouli. With her, she brought jellies, and cream covered in fennel seeds and sugar. I could smell the overwhelming sweetness of the dishes, but refrained from sampling them as I was already full to bursting. Panaretos and the others – including Philip – had no such restraint, and Baia's reward for all her efforts was the sound of the slurping lips of her husband and his other guests.

'Which one do you favour for the death threat, Philip?'

My young companion coughed nervously, and hesitated. It was the day after the banquet, and I wanted to review my impressions of the three traders. I didn't really expect much from Philip, but it was useful for my own thoughts to talk them over with him. If I got bored, I could always ask him to read the opening of the *Adventures of Clitophon and Leucippe*. I would enjoy his embarrassment at least. I was therefore pleasantly surprised when he began an accurate analysis of each man's motives.

'I have heard it said that the Genoan's masters are worried about the lack of progress on negotiating a new set of concessions with Trebizond. Messer Finati is no doubt under pressure to conclude an agreement before the Venetians or the Florentines step in. He could very well be so worried that he resorted to such wild tactics as the letter suggests.'

'Hmm.'

What Philip said could well be the truth. Finati could have gone too far in his anxiety.

'But what of Ricci, the Venetian, then? Is he too under orders to come to a quick resolution?'

'I haven't heard anything about that, sir. But I do know the Florentine trader is ready to pick up the pieces if it comes to a fight between the other two.'

Where was my young monk getting all this information

from? When I enquired, it turned out that he simply listened to the gossip when he was shopping for food. We kept a simple house in the lower part of Trebizond, and Philip both shopped and cooked for both of us. We did not indulge in feasts such as Panaretos did, and therefore had less flesh on our bones than he. The young monk elucidated further.

'There is a square to the east of the town walls where many old men gather, and they speculate on what is happening at the Emperor's court, and with the rival traders. I can take you there, if you wish.'

'Why, do you think me already an old man, who will fit in well with the others?'

I could almost hear the blush creeping over Philip's face.

'I didn't mean that exactly, master. I just thought . . .'

I laughed at his embarrassment, while thinking it was so easy to tease him that it was hardly any fun.

'It's a good idea, Philip. We can go there today, and you can leave me with my fellow old fogies, whilst you go shopping.'

So it was that I found myself in the shade of an oleander in the Meidan, a flat area outside the walls, where at special times festivals were held. But it was also useful for markets, and was laid out with storehouses and stalls providing all sorts of fresh produce. I could smell the mingled aromas of herbs, spices, and cooking meats. In the distance, I could hear a curious set of sounds that mingled horses' hooves with men's cries and the cracking of hammers on something wooden. I leaned across to a man who sat to my left, proffering my best guess at what was going on.

'Tell me, what is that game being played?'

The voice that replied was cracked and old, but still retained much of the man's vigour from another time.

'It is called *tzykanion*, and originates in Persia, they say.

Some call it *pulu.* The players on horseback have to drive the ball with those long mallets from one end of the pitch to the other.' He snorted. 'Like all games, it is pointless.'

I nodded my head in agreement, though I could hazard a guess that cavalry warriors would find it useful training for real battles. I didn't say so, though, for I wanted my companion to respond to my next question.

'Games for boys, played by men who should be more concerned with making money.'

I could tell the old man was nodding his head. So I had got him right, and he was a former local trader with opinions to air. I stared in his direction in a way that suggested I was deeply impressed by him and his opinions. He was not to know I could not see a thing.

'And who is making the most money in Trebizond now? Apart from the Emperor, of course.'

A dry rattle emanated from his throat, which I took for a laugh.

'Well, the Genoans are always the most avaricious, but the Emperor is trying to rein them in. Recently, I think the favoured ones have become the Venetians. Though there is not much to choose between any of them. They do say there are four kinds of people in the west. First, there are the Genoans, who keep the Sabbath . . .' He paused for effect. 'And everything else they can lay their hands on. Then, there are the Venetians, who pray on their knees . . . and on their neighbours. Thirdly, there are the Florentines who never know what they want, but are willing to fight for it anyway.'

Another death rattle suggested he liked his own joke. And knowing he had not finished, I gave him the lead-in to the punch line.

'You said there were four kinds of traders.'

'Ah, yes. Lastly, there are the English, who consider themselves self-made men, thus relieving the Almighty of a terrible responsibility.'

I laughed politely, and refrained from telling him I was, at least in part, English. I continued to draw him out about the trade delegations in Trebizond.

'So tell me . . . Who do you think has most to lose, if the Emperor changes his mind about allocating trade concessions?'

Another voice broke into our conversation. It was another old man, who must have been sitting at the further side of my joke teller. His was a fruitier voice with a more solemn tone than the first man's.

'It's no good asking him that, friend. George has lost his marbles, and couldn't tell a Genoan from an Englishman, if they were pissing on him.'

I heard George mumbling a protest, and spitting on the ground. At least, I assumed it was on the packed earth of the square and not in the face of his detractor. I moved my unseeing gaze to the new man.

'And how would you know the difference, sir?'

The man laughed. 'I know it well enough to make you out for an Englishman. Though your clothes suggest a more exotic origin. The other end of the Silk Road, perhaps?'

He was obviously a very observant person, and his identifying me as an Englishman brought a fit of coughing from my first conversationalist, whose joke had been at the expense of my fellow men.

'Damn it, you might have warned me, Theodore.'

So, my new acquaintance had a name as splendid as his cultured tones. I acknowledged his observations.

'I have recently come from that part of the world, it is

true. But you are only partly right about my Englishness. My grandmother was Welsh.'

This splitting of hairs, important only to the inhabitants of Britain, silenced both old men for a while. Then Theodore answered my original question for me.

'As for who will suffer most from a reversal of trading rights, then it has to be said it would be the Genoans. But it is not the Emperor who will bother himself with such tedious business, but his courtiers and advisors.'

'Men such as Johannes Panaretos?'

I threw the name into the conversation, hoping to see what it would bring out. And I was not disappointed. The harsh laughter of the first man broke in.

'Panaretos will advise the Emperor to do whatever he has been bribed to say. And he will choose to do it in the afternoon, when the court is in a state of torpor brought on by slave girls, hashish and opium. If he has time, that is, from stuffing his mouth with the richest food that Circassian beauty of his can provide.'

A sound of admonition came from Theodore, advising his friend to keep his voice down. I guessed it was not wise to jest out loud concerning the behaviour of the Emperor and Autocrat of the Entire East. There could be spies everywhere. I did have another question for my new-found friends, though.

'Is bribery the only way of bringing court officials to a particular point of view?'

Theodore grunted, and seemed reluctant to reply. But his friend George had no such inhibitions.

'You mean would a Genoan trader threaten Panaretos with violence to keep the concessions?'

I nodded. 'That is indeed what I am asking.'

Before George could reply, Theodore broke in on our conversation. From the rustling of cloth, I guessed he had put a cautionary hand on his friend's arm. His question to me came in a strained tone of voice.

'Do you know something we don't, sir? For if you do, and it affects a servant of the Emperor, I suggest you raise it with the authorities.'

The moment for confidences had passed, and I imagined I was not going to get much more gossip in the circumstances. A strained silence hung in the air, and I stretched the stiffness out of my legs. I was glad that it was not long before Philip returned, and I rose, thanking my interlocutors for their time. Their mumbled replies were in stark contrast to their former pleasure in meeting me. As I walked away with my hand on Philip's arm – I was not certain of the path in this new part of Trebizond – I reminded him of his task concerning the palimpsest.

'Have you examined the parchment with the threat on it more closely yet?'

'Oh, yes, I did, master. I took the opportunity of the bright sunlight this morning to hold it up against the sun.'

'And what did you see?'

'There was some writing underneath the words of the threat that were impossible to make out. But as the message was quite short, there was enough blank space to decipher what had been scraped away.'

Either Philip was drawing out the conclusion in sheer delight at his cleverness, or was too stupid to know when he was annoying me. I stopped him, and turned my most fierce gaze on him. I know that it perturbed him, as he was never sure if I was truly blind or not.

'Come to the point, Philip.'

He stumbled to correct his error.

'Sorry, Master Falconer. The original parchment was a letter from someone whose name I could not make out, but the recipient's name was clear. It was definitely addressed to Messer Finati, the Genoan trade delegate.'

I smiled at having cornered the sender of the threat so easily. In fact, it had been so easy that I was a little suspicious. What if one of the other delegates had laid their hands on a perfectly innocent message addressed to Finati, and concocted the anonymous message in order to cast opprobrium on the Genoan? Philip's thinking was not so convoluted, and he was eager to act on his discovery.

'Shall we tell Master Panaretos?'

I wasn't in such a hurry, and recommended caution.

'No. Let us observe all three for a while longer. It is not as if Panaretos' life is really under threat.'

How wrong my casual statement proved to be.

In another few days, spring eased into summer and the blossom drifted off the cherry and pear trees, scattering on the ground. The Imperial court made its annual pilgrimage from the citadel to the monastery of Panagia Khrysokephalos and thence to the St Sofia monastery beyond the western ravine. We witnessed the passage of the Emperor, and Philip described his appearance in detail to me, right down to the strings of pearls that depended from his golden crown.

On taking another trip to the Meidan, my young companion encountered Panaretos' Circassian wife, who was also out shopping for tempting foodstuffs.

'Look who I have found, master.'

His speech took no account of my infirmity, but on this occasion I needed no eyes to tell to whom he was referring.

The scent of patchouli oil was enough. I rose from the bench on which I was sitting, and bowed low.

'Mistress Baia, I am honoured by your presence.'

I heard the swish of her silken robe, which I knew she wore in the Trapezuntine style – narrow and close-fitting. The slight hesitation in her speech suggested that she was a little embarrassed at Philip's apparent insistence that she speak to me. Therefore I filled the gap with mindless chatter for a while.

'Tell me what you are preparing for your husband today. What delicacies have you purchased at the market?'

I heard the rustling of produce in her basket, which must have been held by a female servant, for I could detect another scent in the air. But this one was a sort of scrubbed, plain aroma proper to a slave. Besides, I knew that a lady of Baia's status would not venture out alone. When she spoke, her voice was low and sonorous.

'I have dates and figs and raisins. And the makings of jellies, for my husband has a sweet tooth and likes red and yellow ones. So I have sandalwood for the first, and saffron for the second sort. Of course, I start every meal with subtleties made of sugar. Johannes would be angry if I didn't.'

She hesitated again, knowing she had said something about their relationship that should not have been revealed.

'But tell me, sir, have you discovered who sent the message that so troubled him?'

Wishing, I think, to impress the Circassian beauty, Philip started to blurt out the truth of the matter, but I interrupted quickly.

'We have made some progress, but there is a long way to go yet. Perhaps we could call in on Panaretos and discuss the matter further with him.'

'Oh, indeed, sir. You are welcome at any time.' I sensed a little smile in her voice. 'And I can always accommodate your appetite, for my husband is fond of his food and always has a plentiful supply. In fact, when he is anxious – as he is now – he is inclined to eat even more than usual. It is my pleasure to see that he is not displeased in such circumstances.'

'Good. Then, if we may, we will come this evening and inform Panaretos what we have discovered so far.'

Baia mumbled her shy acquiescence, and the scent of patchouli oil drifted away from me across the square.

The meal that evening was a simpler affair than the banquet we had been provided with the last time we were in Panaretos' house. But it was delicious nevertheless. It was clear that his wife had made a great effort to present us with Circassian delicacies, beginning with a delicious round of Circassian cheese, which was moist and tasty. I complimented Baia on her selection, but Panaretos merely grunted and demanded something more substantial. Philip spoke little, and I wondered if he was tongue-tied in the presence of Baia's obvious beauty. The next course was made up of two stews of chicken and turkey in a mouth-watering sauce made of garlic and red peppers. With the appearance of meats, Panaretos was mollified, if not silenced, for the sound of his slurping became quite disconcerting. Though both I and Philip demurred at the next dish – apparently some sort of Italian pasta parcels filled with beef – Panaretos continued his gourmandising. Inevitably, the jellies that Baia had planned followed before we retired to Panaretos' private domain. Through a barrage of not-so-discreet burps, he enquired finally if we had found out who had threatened him.

'There is no simple answer to that, I am afraid to say. I could tell you through whose hands the parchment has passed, but that is no guarantee that it was written by those same hands.'

Panaretos was not satisfied by my response, and insisted I name the source of the parchment.

'The original document must have passed through the warehouse of the Genoans, though I still have my suspicions that either Belzoni or Ricci may have made use of the palimpsest to cause Finati trouble. More investigation is required. Tell me, have you had any more death threats?'

Panaretos ignored my last enquiry, brushing it aside with a desultory wave of his hand. Instead, he chose to pick on the name of the man he had suspected all along.

'Finati! I knew it. The Genoans think they can gain further concessions at the click of their fingers. They think me a dog who will sit up and beg if I am beaten hard enough. Well, they have a lesson to learn, and I will teach it them. They have already refused the Emperor's customs officials the right to inspect their stocks, and keep their warehouse locked and barred against us. Now they threaten a high official of the Emperor with death. I must report this to—'

His angry diatribe was suddenly cut short by an alarming gurgling sound from his gut, and deep groan that turned into a belch on his lips. He shifted in his seat, and called out for Baia.

'Wife. For God's sake, bring me the rhubarb powder at once.'

He winced as he turned in his seat towards me. I knew this, for his foetid breath was suddenly in my ear, and he spoke in low tones. I could hear that his voice was strained.

'You must not say anything of this to anyone, especially not to that old gossip Theokrastos, Falconer. And now I must ask you to leave, as I am unwell.'

'Yes, of course. But you should not act until I have checked on the activities of the Florentines and Venetians first.'

Panaretos was in no mood to argue.

'Yes, yes, yes. Do as you see fit.'

He turned away, and I was no longer drowning in his bad breath. He called out for Baia again.

'Woman, where are you?'

Baia hurried into the room in a cloud of scent. She clearly had the medicinal preparation with her, for she explained why she was delayed.

'I have mixed the rhubarb root with some dried figs in order to make it more palatable. Here, let me help you.'

Panaretos was obviously by now in agony, but was not prepared to accept the embarrassment of being ill in the presence of guests, and of having to be assisted to eat.

'Damn you, woman. Just give the bowl here.'

Philip and I hurried discreetly from Panaretos' inner sanctum, leaving Baia with her thankless task. As we walked home, arm in arm, I spoke to Philip.

'It is a shame we did not get a chance to talk to Mistress Panaretos.'

'Why is that, master?' Philip sounded puzzled.

'I should like to have known if there had been any other threats against her husband's life, or unusual occurrences in the last few weeks. I think Panaretos is reticent about telling me anything more, and even regrets recruiting me to find out about the written threat.'

'But why should he do so?'

'Because he is becoming sensitive about his position in

Trebizond, and how he appears to foreigners. Perhaps if he appears weak to the Emperor, his position will be in jeopardy. His present malady was also an embarrassment to him.'

Philip's next comment was censorious in the extreme, coming no doubt from his austere upbringing as a monk.

'Then he should pay more attention to how much he eats. Even in the few months we have known him, I can assure you he has got fatter and fatter. Now he reaps the reward of his gluttony.'

Thinking of the mistress of the house, and her desire to please her glutton of a husband, I had an idea about how I might gather information about any possible further threats on Panaretos' life.

'Philip.'

'Yes, master.'

'Do you think that, when you shop tomorrow, that Mistress Baia might be shopping, too?'

Philip's response was all too quick, and betrayed something of his feelings for Panaretos' wife.

'Oh, yes, sir. She is always in the square. I often . . .'

The young monk paused, realising what he was admitting to. And I was certain that he was beginning to blush to the tips of his ears. He was cautious in his next enquiry.

'Why do you ask?'

'Because I want you to ask her if there have been any other threats since the parchment was sent.'

The relief in his voice was evident, and he must have been glad that his revelation had not resulted in my censuring him.

'Ah, yes, master. I am sure I can do that.'

I bet you can, I thought, imagining it was a perfect opportunity for the love-struck young monk to engage the

Circassian beauty in conversation with good purpose. But that was for tomorrow. For now, I was glad of a brisk walk to work off the excessive amount of good food that I had consumed.

The next morning, Philip was eager to carry out his task, and rushed me off to the Emperor's library as soon as we had broken our fast. Once seated in the marble hall, I could tell he was champing at the bit. So I arranged for Theokrastos to read to me instead of Philip.

'Go, Philip, and use your wiles on the lady.'

He coughed nervously at my words, and hurried out, his sandalled feet slapping on the floor. Theokrastos laughed quietly.

'Did you know that his ears get quite red when he is embarrassed?'

'Indeed I do. It has been observed by others. Now, what do you have for me?'

The librarian settled in his seat, and I heard him opening a heavy tome. I could even smell the dust of lack of use rising from it. I sneezed.

'This is the treatise of Cyril, Bishop of Alexandria, entitled *Against the Blasphemies of Nestorius*. It is in five books.'

I sighed, thinking of Sauma, the Nestorian monk in far-off Cathay, who had given me an introduction to Theokrastos. His heretical form of Christianity was about to be ripped apart, and I was about to be bored stiff. I leaned back, and closed my sightless eyes.

Philip took an inordinate amount of time shopping, and I became a little annoyed that he left me so long with the monotonous voice of Theokrastos. In the end, I suggested that the librarian might like to wet his throat after such exertions. He took the hint, and brought us both some very nice sweet wine from the island of Kition, sometimes known as Alashiya or Cyprus. The wine must have loosened his tongue somewhat for I learned a few things about Trebizond that I didn't know before. And some interesting news about the matter I was investigating.

Eventually, Philip did return full of apologies. As he spluttered his tale of woe, Theokrastos whispered in my ear, 'His ears are bright red. In fact, they are as red as the wine we have been drinking.'

I brushed aside the young monk's apologies, and thanked Theokrastos for his hospitality.

'Come, Philip, we must leave George to his duties, and return home.'

As we left the library, Philip began to tell me what he had learned. As he guided me through the crowds that thronged the narrow streets of the lower town, he explained.

'Mistress Baia was most co-operative, master, and even invited us to eat with Panaretos tonight. But I fear she did not have much to tell concerning the campaign of intimidation against her husband. She said that the letter we have already seen was the only threat that her husband had received.'

I frowned, and wondered what this meant in the light of what Theokrastos had told me. Philip's news, from the lips of Lady Baia, needed some consideration. In the meantime, I needed him to accompany me to the warehouses of our various suspects to enquire more closely into the pressures they were being put under by their employers. Even with hundreds of miles separating Belzoni, Ricci and Finati from their home cities, and letters taking months to travel between them, they must still have felt the heavy breath of their employers on their neck. Each trader would have been sent on the long journey to Trebizond with orders to achieve certain goals, and to return without reaching them could prove disastrous. A good reason to employ threats as well as cajolements.

I didn't want to play my hand with the Genoan, Finati, too soon, so I decided to drop in unannounced on Alessandro Ricci first. With Philip leading me along the unfamiliar streets that dropped down from the top of the lower town to the harbour, I began to smell the odour of fish. It got stronger and stronger, until we must have been close to the quayside. I told Philip what to look out for.

'The Venetians' warehouse will be painted with the sign of the Lion of St Mark. You will not be able to miss it – it rather fancifully has wings.'

'I know it, sir. It was a familiar sight in Byzantium. If you recall, it was I suggested we seek it out when we arrived in Trebizond.'

'Yes, indeed, of course you did.'

I recalled that Venice had once been the master of Byzantium, but that it had not been so for long. However, it was no doubt long enough to have made its mark on the city and its people.

'Here it is, sir.'

We stood at the doors of the Venetians' warehouse.

'Tell me what you see, Philip.'

There was a momentary pause while he looked round, then he described what he saw.

'The store is large, and there are plenty of goods in it, but there is room for much more.'

I could smell spices – cinnamon and pepper, chiefly – and

the slightly different aroma that I identified as the bark and dried insects used for dyes. I had become used to the smells of such products on my long journey along the Silk Road.

'And silk? Does Ricci have raw silk here?'

I had walked into the warehouse on my own to take in the aromas, and Philip was soon at my heels.

'Yes. I can see some bolts of silk over to our right.'

'Then these are just the purchases made from the same caravan we travelled here on. Not the result of any major negotiation with Panaretos.'

'No indeed, Master Falconer. But I can tell you what I do expect to get, if you wish.'

It was the voice of Ricci himself, who had come in behind us. I turned round to face him, aware of his position in the doorway by the change in light his tall body created. It was my only visual sense, and necessitated bright sunlight to provide it to me.

'Messer Ricci, you have caught me out being nosy. Alas, my studying of the books in the Emperor's library sometimes becomes boring, and I can't resist poking around the lower town to see what I can find.'

Ricci moved away from the doorway, and I followed his steps on the flagstone floor with my unseeing eyes.

'I hardly think there is anything here to assuage the thirst of a scholarly mind.'

'Oh, but trade is such a fascinating subject.'

He came out with a sort of belly laugh that suggested he was a man who liked a drink, and a good story.

'Forgive me, Falconer, but trade is hard work. Frustrating and rewarding in equal degrees, it is true. But I would hardly say it is fascinating.'

I heard the clink of glass on glass, and guessed from the

aroma that he was pouring a good Rhenish into some goblets. Philip slipped between myself and Ricci, artfully taking my glass and pressing it into my hand without allowing the Venetian to sense my disability. Then the young monk declined his own proffered glass. Ricci grunted, and clinked my glass with his. I drank a draught, and reckoned it a good red wine. With this and the Commandaria I had drunk with Theokrastos, I was beginning to feel quite drowsy. Ricci explained that the wine was a consignment he had brought to Trebizond, being all part of his reciprocal trade with the Emperor. I nodded my head in understanding.

'And how is the trade – between you and Trebizond, I mean?'

Ricci moved close to me, and all but whispered in my ear, 'Moving swiftly to a conclusion actually, but don't tell Finati. I am mostly interested in the alum trade out of Kerasous. The weavers of Bruges will pay well for it as a mordant for their dyes. After the Emperor's little spat with Genoa that resulted in some fisticuffs, Panaretos is under instructions to offer Genoa's concessions to Venice, as long as we pay the proper dues.'

'Which you will?'

Ricci laughed, and audibly downed a great glug of wine.

'Of course, we will. Anything to get one over Genoa. Finati will be going home empty-handed.'

A final draught of wine went down his throat, and I thought I had all I wanted to know. Though there was one other matter that perhaps Ricci could enlighten me about.

'What of the Florentines? Is Belzoni going to get what he

wants, or could he be as frustrated as Finati, and capable of similar extreme measures to get his way?'

I almost heard the frown creasing Ricci's face.

'Extreme measures? I don't know what you mean. For all of us trade is trade – we are not warriors. No, Belzoni will be glad with what sweepings-up he can get after my deal is concluded. After all, he will be more than satisfied that the Genoans – who are in league with the French here and in Italy – will go home with nothing.'

I downed the rest of my Rhenish wine, and thanked Ricci for his hospitality. I left, thinking he had been wrong – trading was indeed a fascinating subject. Our conversation had told me a great deal. Enough to set Panaretos' mind at rest. It only remained for me to confront Finati with the facts, and then I would be finished. But that was for tomorrow. Tonight, Philip and I had an invitation to a banquet.

The meal turned out to be a special occasion, for Lady Baia was present from the beginning at the table. She had not been relegated to the kitchen, nor was she being used as a serving maid. I detected her patchouli-scented presence from the very start, but as if I needed any confirmation, Philip spoke up eagerly as he guided me into the room.

'My lady, we are delighted by your presence.'

I could detect the catch in his voice, and wondered if his ears were already glowing. I added my own thanks at her invitation, and bowed in the general direction of her and the stronger scent that hardly hid the odour of the sweating Panaretos. His voice wheezed breathily as he spoke to me.

'I am told, Master Falconer, that you have been questioning the Venetians about the constant threats on my life. Did you draw any conclusions, or are you still reluctant to come to a decision on who it is wishes me dead?'

I heard a faint rustle of alarm from the lips of Baia, and a quiet remonstration at her husband's boorishness. But Panaretos clearly waved her concerns aside.

'This . . . man was presented to me as some expert on deductive logic. So let him expound his theories.'

I knew the slight hesitation between his first and second words hinted at his desire to say another word. His inclination had been to pour scorn on my sightless state, and wonder how he could have let a blind man even begin to investigate the perpetrator of the threats. For multiple threats there had been – Theokratos had just told me so. Baia had deliberately misled Philip, but before I could ask her why, she broke the awkward silence that hung over us.

'Look, the warners are being served. We should sit.'

Philip subtly guided me to my place and sat at my elbow. He expressed delight at the sugary subtleties that had been brought to the table as a warning the meal was under way. I had no sweet tooth and declined the carved delicacy, but I could tell that Panaretos had no such reticence, and was cracking the sugary sculpture in his no doubt ravaged teeth. I could smell his bad breath from where I sat. I told him of my discoveries as we awaited the first course.

'I have no doubt that the document you showed me at the beginning of this enquiry was made to look as if it was written by, or at least on behalf of Messer Finati. He will be much vilified when he returns to Genoa without a renewal of the trade contracts that formerly applied.'

Panaretos laughed harshly, and smacked his lips. The broth was being served, and he was already spooning it into his maw, along with lumps of bread torn from his trencher.

I revelled in the aroma of mace and cinnamon that drifted from the bowl placed before me. I tasted the soup appreciatively, noting the flavour of chicken, and the thickness of it that had been achieved with mixing in bread crumbs and then sieving most carefully.

Philip whispered in my ear, 'He is surely twice as fat as when we first saw him. His chins have multiplied till they rest upon his breast, which is itself of a womanish roundness.'

I was sure the young monk was extra critical of our host due to his enchantment by the man's wife, but I am sure his assessment of Panaretos was essentially truthful. The man's gluttony was causing him to expand like some blown up bladder. Apart from expressing his delight at my findings – which I was not sure he understood – he spoke little, addressing more the plates that came forth inexorably from the kitchen.

The next delicacy was crustardes of herbs and fish. A pastry case enclosed pieces of fish stewed in lemon water to which were added walnuts, parsley, thyme and lemon balm. I don't suppose that Panaretos had time to taste any of the subtle flavours in his pursuit of excessive consumption, but I complimented Baia on the concoction.

'I am pleased you like it so, Master Falconer.'

I could get little else out of her, though, and was unable to question her about the more veiled threats that had dogged her husband from the time of the first clear warning contained on the parchment. Theokratos had told me that Panaretos had complained about one particular incident that his wife had reported to him. She had been with her maid in the fish market down by the harbour, and a hooded figure, dressed like a foreigner, had said that she should tell her husband to hurry up and sign the trade deal or he wouldn't have a pretty wife any more. Perhaps she had refrained from telling Philip this because she was afraid the threat might be carried out if she spoke of it to anyone but her husband. Whatever the reason, Panaretos was not going to give me the chance to ask her.

The next course was a heavy stew called monchelet. Neck of lamb pieces had been stewed in a large pan in a wine and herb stock, along with chopped onions, then the sauce had been thickened with egg yolks. The meat was tender and glossy, and once again Panaretos soon began to demolish his portion. I could hear his breathing, stertorous and heavy, and then he belched. I wondered if he had reached the limit of even his gargantuan appetite. Baia's announcement of the final course told me.

'We have a blanc manger next, darling, made from pounded chicken breast flavoured with sugar and almonds.'

'Good. I am still hungry.'

I silently marvelled at Panaretos' capacity for ever more servings of rich food, and was ready to decline anything more than a spoonful of the sweet, tempting dish that crusaders had first encountered in Outremer years ago. I was not, however, faced with such a dilemma. Before the blanc manger could be brought, we heard a disturbance in the kitchens, and the sound of running feet. One of Panaretos' servants came into the room where we sat, and called out a warning.

'Master, we have been warned that pirates from Sinope – the Emir's men – have attacked the harbour. They are woring their way up the hill towards us. What shall we do?'

Panaretos lurched to his feet; I could hear his breath

quicken in alarm. But before he could give any instructions, his voice became nothing more than a strangled gurgle. I heard his chair crash over, and the cry of alarm from the servant. Then I heard the soft thud of a considerable body landing on the marble floor. I called out to Philip, groping for his arm.

'What has happened? Philip, tell me.'

It seemed my companion was completely unable to respond, other than to stutter a few meaningless words. It was a female voice that cut calmly through the panic.

'It looks as though my husband has had an apoplexy. When he rose from his chair, his face turned bright red, his eyes bulged out of his head, and he collapsed. I am afraid he also vomited all down his robe.'

Her tone was unusually calm in the circumstances, and she seemed to be observing a scene in which she took no part, nor had any interest in. Perhaps the shock of such a sudden series of events had overwhelmed her, and she would break down and weep as soon as the consequences struck her. But I was not so sure.

'What of the Emir of Sinope's pirate band? Should we not flee for safety?'

The scent of patchouli came closer, and I felt a feminine hand on my arm.

'Oh, I don't think there is truly any danger. The gates to the lower town will have been closed already. The Emperor must be protected at all costs, and we shall be safe enough here. The servants are such ninnies, and run around in fright at the slightest danger.'

I heard her sit back at the table.

'Would you like some blanc manger?'

*

The old man sensed all the eyes of the assembled pilgrims were on him, boring into him. He hoped he had told his story well, and that the correct conclusion had been reached. It was the woman, Katie Valier, who spoke first. He had known before she even uttered her opening words that it would be she who would guess the truth.

'Panaretos ate himself to death, and that was the reward for his gluttony.'

Falconer smiled.

'Oh, it was more than merely his gluttony that killed him. You see, I travelled to Genoa on Finati's ship, and he swore to me that he never wrote the threatening letter, nor acted in any other way to coerce Panaretos into accepting a trade deal. It only confirmed my own conclusions, which Panaretos did not give me time to expound upon. I could have told him who was threatening his life, but he died before I could.'

Katie was quick to see his point.

'Then it was Baia who wrote the letter, and she also made up the other threats in order to scare her husband.'

One of the other pilgrims piped up, not fully comprehending the enor mity of Katie's suggestion.

'But why would she do that? I know that from what you tell us, Master Falconer, that he mistreated her. But what would she gain by making him even more fearful and angry?'

The old man could tell Katie was looking at him in an understanding way, so he completed the story.

'Because when Panaretos was agitated he turned to his main comfort, which was not his wife, but food. And she gladly complied with his wishes. Over several months, she fed him rich food in ever increasing portions that made him fatter and fatter until the merest exertion brought on an apoplexy. She murdered him just as effectively as if she had used poison or a knife, but it was a much more subtle way to do it that meant she was not even suspected. Except by me, and I saw no reason to tell anyone my suspicions. You see, it was the slowest and the kindest murder I have ever witnessed.'

The Fourth Sin

'Lust, greed and avarice are grave sins indeed,' said John Wynter, prior of the Austin canons in Carmarthen, a tall, hatchet-faced man who had nodded approvingly at the punishments meted out to the wrongdoers in the previous tales. 'But there is one graver yet.'

Wynter had strong opinions about sin, which was why he had been prepared to leave his comfortable monastery when all sensible folk were closing their doors and huddling together in the hope that the deadly pestilence would pass them by. It had not been his own lapses that had driven him east, of course: he had been appointed by his Prior General to sit in judgement over others – at their sister house in Walsingham.

'A sin worse than greed?' asked Katie Valier sceptically. Outside, an owl hooted in the night, as if agreeing with her. 'Or lust and avarice?'

'Sloth,' hissed Wynter, 'is the deadliest sin.'

'I hardly think so!' declared Katie. 'You are wrong, Father Prior.'

'It is the most deadly transgression because of its insidious effects on the soul,' boomed Wynter in the deep, sepulchral voice that had made many a Carmarthen novice quail in his boots. 'And I do not refer to simple laziness, but to an emptiness of the soul.'

'I do not understand,' said Katie, shaking her pretty head. 'Why should—'

'It is a spiritual apathy that will lead even good men to Hell,' interrupted Wynter. 'And I shall prove it. Here is a tale I was told many years ago. It describes what happens to those who allow sloth to rule them, and will be a warning to you all.'

He glanced around, saw he had his companions' complete attention, and began with his tale of . . .

Sloth

Autumn 1205, the Austin Priory of Llanthony, Monmouthshire

Prior Martin had many vices, but the one that disturbed his monks the most was his determination to enjoy an easy life. He disliked making decisions, and had a nasty habit of postponing them until they no longer mattered, while any problems brought to him were dismissed with an airy wave and the injunction to ask God for a solution instead.

Unfortunately, that would not do for the matter that currently troubled the monastery – one that his canons felt would not have arisen if Martin had not been so lazy. Their daughter house in Gloucestershire had grown rich and fat under its powerful patrons and energetic leaders, and was clamouring for independence. It could not be given. The 'cell' at Hempsted was an important source of revenue, one Llanthony could not afford to lose.

The canons stood in the refectory, hands folded demurely inside their sleeves and their heads bowed, although all were in a state of high agitation, because a deputation from Hempsted had just arrived – a dozen sleekly arrogant monks who looked around disdainfully, comparing Llanthony's cracked plaster and leaking roofs to their own palatial dwellings. They were led by Canon Walter, a ruthlessly determined man who would do anything to be Hempsted's first prior. He was unwell, as attested by his pallor and damp forehead, but that did not make his ambition burn any less fiercely. He was aided and abetted by Gilbert, his monkey-faced sacrist, who intended eventually to step into Walter's shoes – and better a prior's shoes than those of a mere deputy under the thumb of Llanthony.

Also among Walter's entourage were two royal clerks, sly, slippery individuals there to ensure the King did not lose out on any deals that were made between the two foundations. The royal treasury was always empty, and King John's officials were assiduous in sniffing out sources of free money on their monarch's behalf. The Llanthony men only hoped that Martin would not accede to unreasonable demands just because he could not be bothered to do battle.

Walter and his companions were not the only ones who had braved the wild Monmouthshire hills to visit Llanthony. Bishop Geoffrey had also arrived. He had been prior of Llanthony himself before being elevated to the See of St David's, and although he was a likeable, friendly man, it was expensive to keep a prelate in the style to which he was accustomed, and his company was an expense Llanthony could have done without.

Then there were three knights who had requested a few nights' respite as they travelled west to join the military garrison at Carmarthen. They were battle-honed Norman warriors who had reacted indignantly when Prior Martin had evicted them from the guesthouse to make room for the bishop. Their surcoats showed them to be crusaders, and such men were known to be dangerous and unpredictable. The monks did not like them, and wished they would go.

'You must make sure Martin stands firm,' whispered Almoner Cadifor to Sub-Prior Roger, although he suspected he was wasting his breath. Roger had followed Martin's example, and was shockingly indolent. 'We may not survive if we lose Hempsted.'

'Not even the King will dare strip us of our most valuable asset,' said Roger with a complacent smile. 'If he tries, we shall appeal to the Pope.'

'Of course!' Cadifor sagged in relief. 'Martin has already contacted Rome to outline our position, so His Holiness will certainly find in our favour.'

Roger's expression was sheepish. 'Martin has not written yet, but I shall suggest he does it tonight. Or tomorrow, perhaps.'

Cadifor's jaw fell. 'But he promised to do it months ago, and you pledged to ensure it was done! We discussed it at length in chapter meetings, and you—'

'Do not rail at me,' snapped Roger. 'You, who cannot possibly understand the trials and tribulations that running a large foundation like ours requires.'

Cadifor was so astounded by the statement – it was common knowledge that he did far more to ensure the monastery's survival than anyone else – that he could do nothing but gape as Roger waddled away.

'I recommend we retire to the chapel, to pray for our future,' he said stiffly to his brethren, once he had found his tongue again. 'I think our home is sorely in need of petitions.'

They did as he suggested, but it was not long before whispered conversations broke out. Why had Walter brought so many monks with him, and why were royal clerks in his retinue? The King had always preferred Hempsted's manicured splendour to the bleak beauty of Llanthony, so had he decided to back Walter's bid for freedom? The muttering stopped at the sound of clattering footsteps. It was Oswin, their youngest novice, racing up the nave.

'I eavesdropped on Martin's meeting with the Hempsted

monks,' he blurted. 'I know it was wrong, but I wanted to find out what was in store for us.'

'What did you hear?' demanded Cadifor, overlooking the fact that he should not encourage such unseemly conduct by asking questions.

'They came to present a writ from the Pope, giving Hempsted its independence. We have lost! Walter has become *Prior* Walter, and he is here to lay claim to numerous farms and manors that he says now belong to him.'

There was an immediate clamour of consternation, but Cadifor silenced it with an irritable gesture. Oswin had more to report.

'Prior Martin told Walter that he should have warned us of his plan to petition His Holiness,' Oswin went on. 'Walter replied that he had, but that Martin had ignored the letter.'

'There *was* a letter from Hempsted,' recalled the cellarer. 'Back in March. I saw Martin reading it, but when I asked what it was about, he told me it was nothing.'

'Martin knew we would be furious,' Oswin continued. 'He called Walter a greedy pig, so Walter slapped him. Martin slapped Walter back, but much harder, and threats were made by everyone before things calmed down.'

'Oh, Martin is indignant now,' said Cadifor bitterly. 'But we would not be in this position if he had written to Rome as he promised. He was too lazy – and so was Roger for failing to ensure that he did his duty. Damn them both!'

'What will become of us?' asked Oswin tearfully. 'Will we starve?'

'Hopefully not,' replied Cadifor. 'We shall have to tighten our belts, of course, but we did not take the tonsure to live in luxury.'

No one seemed particularly comforted by this, but the bell rang for vespers, so they took their places in the chancel. Before they settled down to their devotions, there were many angry whispers regarding what would be said to Martin at the next chapter.

But Martin did not live to hear them. He was found dead the following morning, just before the meeting at which the formal separation was to be discussed. There were no signs of foul play, but few thought his death was natural. The visitors claimed he had been killed by his own canons. His canons accused the visitors, citing the unseemly fracas in the solar. The knights did not escape censure either: they had been offended that Martin had evicted them from the guest-house, and such men were sensitive about slights to their dignity.

Martin was carried to the church and laid in a coffin, but prayers were perfunctory, as everyone's thoughts were on the upcoming meeting. This took place in the chapter house, and was a lengthy, acrimonious event. There was not a man among them who did not storm out at one point or another, so when it was over, no one could claim to have sat through the whole thing. Even Bishop Geoffrey, who had offered to mediate, had thrown up his hands in despair after several hours of continuous bickering, and gone to lie down until he had his exasperation under control.

Eventually, it was over, and the Hempsted men were preparing to leave when there was a yell from the church, and Oswin hurtled out, gibbering about desecration. Everyone hurried inside to see that someone had scratched a message on Martin's casket: 'Sloth is the deadliest of sins.'

'It certainly was for him,' muttered Cadifor. 'It saw him murdered.'

Winter 1208, Carmarthen

The weather was glorious – cold, crisp and clear. A pale sun shone in a cloudless sky, and the winter-bare trees were coated in rime. The carpet of dead leaves on the forest floor crunched underfoot, and the air smelled clean and fresh.

'It will snow soon,' said Sir Philipp Stacpol, whose crusader's surcoat was spotlessly clean and whose armour gleamed, even after two nights of sleeping under the stars.

Sir Symon Cole, constable of Carmarthen Castle, cared nothing for such gloomy predictions. A guilelessly optimistic man, he lived for the present, and could not recall a time when he had been happier. His wife and children were a constant source of delight, there was peace in the region he governed, and he was riding his favourite horse. His naturally ebullient spirit soared, and he began to sing.

'You tempt fate with your unseemly cheeriness,' warned Stacpol waspishly. 'It is never wise to be too joyful. Bad luck will certainly follow.'

Cole laughed. 'It already has, Stacpol. Your horse is lame, and our hunt has ended early.'

'I meant real bad luck,' said Stacpol darkly. 'Like a visit from the King or a rebellion. Or worse yet, an intricate political problem.'

Cole winced. He had scant talent for diplomacy, but fortunately he had married Gwenllian, who was the cleverest person he knew, and she excelled at dealing with such matters. He smiled fondly when he thought of her. It had been an arranged marriage that neither had wanted, but they had grown to love each other, and now he felt blessed to have such an intelligent, insightful wife. He had been

Carmarthen's constable for two decades, and knew he would not have kept the post for so long without her.

When they reached the top of the hill, he dismounted to gaze at his town, which stood a mile or so distant. Over the years, he had replaced the castle's wooden palisade with stone curtain walls, and would raise a new gatehouse in the spring. He had already built handsome living quarters for his household, and clean, airy barracks for his men. It was a fortress to be proud of, and he was glad that old King Henry had made him constable – and glad that Henry's successors, Richard and John, had renewed his appointment.

Of course, he had had his differences with John, whom he considered weak, treacherous and fickle, but that had been years ago, and their quarrels had long been forgotten – by Cole, at least. And John? As far as Cole could see, His Majesty had his hands too full with rebellious barons to worry about a distant Welsh outpost. As long as Carmarthen's taxes were paid on time, the region was left to its own devices.

He tore his eyes away from the castle to look at the rest of the town. It was a sizeable settlement, with a busy market, a good bridge across the River Tywi, and a thriving quayside that could accommodate sea-going vessels.

A short distance north-east was the Austin priory. Recently, the canons had rebuilt their perimeter walls and purchased a new set of gates. Cole kept good order in the area, and his marriage to a native princess meant relations were better between the Norman invaders and the resident Welsh than in many places, but trouble was not unknown, even so. The priory, with its pretty chapel and handsome cluster of buildings, would be an obvious target for marauders, and Cole thought the Austins wise to strengthen their defences.

His companions came to stand next to him: Stacpol, breathing hard because he had been obliged to lead his lame horse while the others had ridden; Sergeant Iefan, who had fought at Cole's side for so many years that he was more friend than subordinate; and Elidor and Asser, solid, reliable men from Normandy. Cole was about to mount up again when he saw a dark smudge above the priory. He narrowed his eyes against the glare of the sun.

'Is that smoke?'

'The monks must be burning rubbish,' said Stacpol.

'That is too big a fire for rubbish.' Cole reached for his reins and vaulted into the saddle. 'The priory is under attack!'

He jabbed his spurs into the horse's flanks and was away, ignoring the others' yells for him to wait. He dismounted when he neared the monastery, and crept forward on foot, too experienced a warrior to rush headlong into a situation without first taking stock. He reached a good vantage point, and began to assess what was happening.

The priory gates had been set alight, which accounted for the smoke. Then the remnants had been kicked aside and invaders had surged in. So much for the new defences! Peering through the gap, Cole saw a tall but stooped Austin barking orders, while Carmarthen's prior, shorter by a head and not nearly as imposing, harangued him furiously. The rest of Carmarthen's monks – fifteen of them, with roughly the same number of lay brethren – had been ordered to stand outside the chapter house, where they were being guarded by soldiers.

Cole turned at a sound behind him. It was his knights and Iefan. All four were tightening the buckles on their armour and checking that their swords were loose in their scabbards, ready for battle. He briefed them quickly.

'There are about twenty soldiers – mercenaries, by the

look of them – and a dozen Austin canons. I have never seen any of the monks before, but that thin, lanky fellow is obviously in charge. And for some reason, Londres, our bailiff, is with them.'

'Londres!' spat Iefan. 'Trust him to be involved where trouble strikes.'

Londres had arrived in Carmarthen five years before, officially appointed by the King to collect fees and fines. It had been obvious from the start that his real remit had been to spy on Cole and itemise any failings, but Gwenllian was efficient, and Londres had found nothing untoward to report. He had grown increasingly frustrated as time passed, desperate to find something, anything, which could be used as an excuse to return to Westminster.

Unfortunately, the King had long since forgotten about the bailiff and his mission, and Londres had been left to fester. He was deeply unpopular in the town, because he was dishonest, selfish and sly. The inexorable passing of time had made him more bitter and angry than ever, and recent weeks had seen him brazenly demanding unlawful levies, and flouting the constable's authority at every turn.

'I recognise the tall monk – he is Prior Walter from Hempsted,' said Asser. He turned to Stacpol and Elidor. 'Do you remember him from our journey here three years ago? We had stopped to rest at Llanthony, and he arrived to declare Hempsted's independence.'

Elidor nodded. 'The Llanthony canons told me later that he had *purchased* the necessary documents from the Pope – Hempsted's freedom was won by deceit, not merit. Since then, he has been expanding his empire, riding all over the country to inform churches, villages and manors that they are now under his control.'

'For the tithes,' explained Asser, seeing Cole frown in puzzlement. 'His monastery is twice as rich as it was when he took over, thanks to his diligence.'

'And it seems that Carmarthen Priory has just become his latest conquest,' finished Elidor.

'On what grounds?' demanded Cole, full of indignation.

Elidor shrugged. 'He will have a document to prove his case. He always does.'

Cole's first instinct was to storm the place and oust the invaders. Four knights and Iefan would be more than a match for mere foot soldiers. But the mention of documents stayed his hand. Clearly, this was a matter that required diplomacy, not brute force. He turned to Iefan.

'Fetch Gwenllian. She will know what to do.'

Gwenllian was relieved when Iefan appeared. She was perfectly able to manage the castle in peacetime, but she had received reports that a contingent of soldiers was moving in Carmarthen's direction. Then she had seen the plume of smoke. She had ordered the castle secured, the armoury opened, and the townsfolk had been invited to take refuge in the bailey, but Cole was the one who did the fighting, and she did not know what to do next.

She heard Iefan's report in the solar, where she had gone to be with her children – three boisterous sons and a daughter who was the apple of Cole's eye. They were not alone. Bishop Geoffrey had turned up the previous day on an official visitation. Gwenllian had not known that the prelate was coming – he tended to travel after Easter, when the roads were better – but it had not taken her long to discover that Cole had, and that the hunting trip had been timed to coincide with the prelate's arrival. Cole had nothing against Geoffrey in particular, but he found clerics dull company in general, with little to say about important matters like horses, dogs and warfare.

The bishop had been entertaining the children, to take their minds off the trouble outside, and they had been enjoying themselves. The younger ones sat in his lap, while the older pair hung on his every word. There was a chorus of dismay when he announced his intention of accompanying their mother to the monastery.

'Stay here, Your Grace,' Gwenllian advised. Geoffrey was no longer young, and she was not sure what to expect from the situation. Moreover, Cole would not thank her for lumbering him with an elderly churchman if he was obliged to do battle.

'I am not afraid,' Geoffrey declared, although his unsteady voice suggested otherwise. 'And the priory is in my See. Of course I must be there to defend it.'

'But my husband wants to assess the situation before taking action. Look after my children until we discover what is happening. Then we will send for you.'

Geoffrey was reluctant, but Gwenllian convinced him eventually. He gave a wan smile when the children whooped their delight at the prospect of keeping him a little longer.

'I have heard rumours that Prior Walter was spreading his wings,' he said soberly. 'But I did not know that he aimed to spread them in my diocese.'

'Will his claim on our priory be legal?' she asked.

'I hope not! Cadifor is a very good prior, and I should not like him replaced by a less competent man. Or a less likeable one.'

'Nor would I. Did you know that Cadifor was a monk at Llanthony before he came here?'

'Of course – I was once a monk at Llanthony, too. We were there together.'

Gwenllian had forgotten that. 'Yes – you were prior before Martin, the man whose legendary laziness lost Llanthony her wealthy daughter house.'

Geoffrey nodded. 'I repelled Walter's bids for independence when I was in charge, and now I see what power has done to him, I realise that I was right to resist his demands. Such lust for expansion makes me very uneasy. But go now, and send me word as soon as you can.'

The streets were deserted as Gwenllian and Iefan hurried through them, although a few merchants had declined to leave their properties unguarded, risking death to prevent the loss of their riches. They called out to Gwenllian for news as she sped past, but there was no time to answer them.

'If Walter wants our priory for himself, why did he set it alight?' she asked the sergeant. 'It will be no use to him if it is irreparably damaged. Moreover, its residents are monks from his own Order.'

'He only incinerated the gates,' explained Iefan. 'Prior Cadifor refused to let him in, so he ordered them to be burned down. Stacpol, Elidor and Asser, who have met him before, say he is greedy and ruthless.'

'It sounds to me as though this is a matter for the Austins to sort out between themselves,' said Gwenllian uneasily. 'They will not thank us for meddling.'

'Cadifor will – Walter has enforced his claim by flooding the monastery with soldiers. He will certainly want our help.'

Iefan indicated she should remain silent as they stepped off the road, taking a narrow path that led to where Cole and his knights were waiting impatiently for her.

'Walter claims that Carmarthen Priory was founded by a monk from Hempsted in the distant past,' Cole whispered indignantly, 'which means it should be Hempsted's now. He has documents to prove it, one of which bears the King's seal. I just heard him brag about it.'

'Then we must distance ourselves from the affair,' said Gwenllian in alarm. 'The King will accuse you of treason if we challenge his decisions. Let Bishop Geoffrey mediate – he is an Austin, as well as Prelate of St David's. He arrived here the day after you went hunting.'

'Oh, yes.' Cole had the grace to look sheepish. 'I forgot to mention his letter . . .'

'I am sure you did,' said Gwenllian coolly. 'Just as I am sure it was pure happenstance that led you to suggest a hunting expedition the day before he was due to appear.'

Cole started to make excuses, but stopped abruptly and lunged towards the bushes. He shrugged when he returned and saw her questioning frown. 'I thought someone was in there.'

Gwenllian supposed it was a townsman, spying so he would have a tale to tell in the taverns that night. 'Come home, and let the bishop take over.'

'I cannot, Gwen. This priory is under my protection, and it would be a dereliction of duty to ignore armed invaders. Besides, you need to look at Walter's document and tell me if it truly does come from the King. Walter might be lying – Cadifor certainly thinks there are grounds for debate, as he has been yelling about it ever since Walter shoved the tiny thing under his nose.'

'It has been difficult to stand here and do nothing while Walter struts about like a peacock,' said Elidor sourly. 'I should love to storm the place and throw him out.'

'So would I,' agreed Asser. 'Yet I suspect the writ will be genuine. The two men standing by the dormitory are royal clerks. Their names are Belat and Henry.'

He pointed. Belat had long dark hair and was dressed entirely in black; Henry was fair and might have been handsome were it not for the selfish pout of his lips.

'I know them well,' said Stacpol grimly. 'They will turn the King against Carmarthen if they survive our assault, so I suggest we make sure they don't. When we attack, I will kill them before they can slither away. They are . . .'

He trailed off, and Gwenllian could tell that he wished he had held his tongue. Her interest was piqued. She had never liked these particular knights, considering them vicious and stupid, and Stacpol had always seemed the worst. She wondered what business such a mindless brute could have had with John's officials that resulted in him 'knowing them well.' She asked.

'I cannot discuss it,' Stacpol replied stiffly. 'It was a private matter.'

Asser laughed. 'Do not think you will keep secrets from Lady Gwenllian! She will have them from you in no time at all. And if not from you, then from me.'

'No – you will not speak out of turn,' said Stacpol, so coldly that the merry twinkle in Asser's eyes was immediately extinguished.

Elidor looked from one to the other in bemusement. 'Did something happen when we met Belat and Henry at Llanthony then? I remember Walter arriving to declare Hempsted's independence, and those two clerks were there to oversee the matter . . .'

'It was before that,' replied Stacpol shortly. 'Please do not question me further, because I am not at liberty to discuss it.'

Gwenllian's curiosity intensified, and she determined that Asser would be proven right: she *would* have the tale from him or Stacpol.

'Londres knew this was going to happen,' Cole was saying bitterly. 'I can tell by the way that he and Prior Walter huddle together that they have had dealings before. They are in league, and it was doubtless he who suggested that they stage their assault today.'

Stacpol frowned. 'Why today?'

'Because we would have been away hunting if your horse had not gone lame and brought us home early. Perhaps you were right to warn me about bad luck. I should not have started singing.'

Cole insisted on riding into the priory on his best warhorse, determined to make Walter see that he was dealing with professional warriors, not country bumpkins who rarely saw military action. He, his knights and Iefan were an impressive sight in their armour and crusaders' surcoats, and Prior Walter's soldiers blanched – he had been right to predict that they would pose no problem in the event of a skirmish. Gwenllian followed them inside on foot.

There were six men among the invaders who looked important. Gwenllian instinctively distrusted Belat and Henry, thinking they were exactly the type of men the King would hire – sly and deceitful. Bailiff Londres was cast in the same mould.

Walter was lean and cadaverous, with the look of death about him. She wondered if he would live long enough to enjoy the empire he had built, although his burning eyes suggested he would not let ill health interfere with his plans. His sacrist, Gilbert, hovered at his shoulder, reminding her of a monkey with his heavy eyebrows, beadlike eyes and dark complexion.

And finally, there was Roger, appointed prior of Llanthony

after Martin's death, although Gwenllian was not sure why he was present. He was a plump, flabby man with soft white hands. There was something disagreeably lethargic about him, and he regarded Cole and his companions with disinterested eyes, as if he could not be bothered to ask who they were.

Cadifor broke away from his captors and stumbled towards Cole in relief, while his canons cheered, clearly believing all would be well now that the constable was there. Gwenllian was sorry they were going to be disappointed.

'They have no right!' Cadifor was tearful with anger, and as he was usually calm and measured, it was unsettling to see him so distraught. Since taking up his appointment in Carmarthen, he had worked hard to enhance the priory's reputation for scholarship and generosity, and he was greatly admired in the town. 'Walter will not wrest a second foundation from under my nose. Order him gone, Sir Symon. With your sword, if necessary.'

'The only people who can resolve this dispute are the King and your Prior General,' said Gwenllian quickly, lest Symon should think to oblige. 'All we can do is prepare a document outlining each side's case, to help them make their decision. I recommend a formal hearing in the chapel, with Bishop Geoffrey presiding.'

'It is none of Bishop Geoffrey's business,' declared Londres arrogantly. 'Let him stay in the castle, away from matters that do not concern him.'

'You think the fate of a priory in his See does not concern him?' asked Gwenllian icily. 'Especially one belonging to his own Order?'

'Bailiff Londres is right, madam,' said Walter curtly. 'This is a matter for the very *highest* authorities. Mere prelates and constables will meddle at their peril.'

'I am sure you *would* like us to leave,' said Gwenllian, beginning to understand why Symon had wanted to settle the matter by force. 'But we have a responsibility to assess the situation, so we can provide His Majesty with an accurate report.'

'That will not be necessary,' said Belat haughtily. 'My colleague, Henry, will document any proceedings, and his is the account that the King will trust.'

Gwenllian smiled sweetly at him. 'Perhaps so, sir. However, we are nothing if not thorough here at Carmarthen. We shall make our own record, and the bishop will be a witness.'

'I want him here,' added Cadifor. 'He used to be Prior of Llanthony, while Carmarthen is in his See. Thus, he has associations with both foundations, and will be impartial.'

'Unlike those two royal clerks,' murmured Stacpol to Gwenllian. 'You should not trust them as far as you can spit.'

Iefan went to fetch Geoffrey, but Gwenllian knew it would be some time before the elderly churchman arrived – the bishop would want to don suitable vestments for the occasion, and there would be horses to saddle and secretaries to brief. But that was no bad thing, as it would allow time for tempers to cool. All she had to do in the interim was keep the two factions apart.

She said as much to Cole, who immediately ordered Carmarthen's canons to the kitchen to prepare food, while the Hempsted monks were 'invited' to wait in the guesthouse. She expected them to argue, but no one did. The soldiers took the opportunity to slink to the stables, patently relieved not to be doing battle with Norman knights.

'You cannot order Henry and me around,' declared Belat, declining to move. 'We do what we like, because we have the authority of the King.'

'So do I,' stated Londres. He edged behind the two clerks when Cole glared at him, daring the constable to push past them to grab him. Cole might have obliged had Gwenllian not laid a cautionary hand on his arm – Londres was not worth the trouble that would follow. Prior Cadifor also lingered, reluctant to go anywhere while his monastery was under threat.

'I cannot imagine why Walter wants this place,' said Belat, looking around in disdain. 'It is mean and shabby compared to Hempsted.'

'We earn a respectable income from the sale of our wool,' snapped Cadifor, nettled, but his face fell when Belat's expression turned triumphant: the clerk had tricked him into revealing something that he should have kept quiet.

'The King will be delighted to hear it,' said Henry smoothly, 'and will raise your taxes accordingly. Or rather, raise Walter's taxes, as it is now his responsibility to pay them.'

'I will not yield my priory's independence without a fight,' snapped Cadifor, 'no matter what fictitious document you produce.'

'It is not fictitious,' averred Belat. 'As you will discover if you challenge it. Of course, there may be a way round the problem, although such solutions are very expensive . . .'

Cadifor blanched. The kind of 'solution' sold by corrupt clerks tended to impoverish their recipients for years. Gwenllian regarded the pair in distaste. She had met their type before – ruthless, grasping individuals who used the authority vested in them to line their own pockets. She glanced at Londres, not surprised that the dishonest bailiff had elected to play a role in the unfolding drama.

'Of course, it will have to be settled before Bishop Geoffrey arrives and starts to poke his nose into our affairs,' said Henry. 'So make up your mind now. Do you want us to persuade His Majesty to revoke the deed?'

Cadifor stood straight and there was a defiant jut to his chin. 'There will be no need for underhand practices, thank you. We are in the right, and Bishop Geoffrey will not support the King in a matter that is blatantly illegal.'

'He will not,' agreed Gwenllian. Having met the unpleasant Walter, she was now firmly on Cadifor's side. 'And his opinion will be recorded in the transcripts of today's proceedings, which may help to convince His Majesty of the unfairness of the situation.'

Belat and Henry exchanged angry glances, and she saw they had not reckoned on having the views of a powerful churchman included in the account that would be presented at Court. Good, she thought. Perhaps justice would prevail after all.

Belat and Henry grabbed Londres' arms and hauled him away, no doubt to remonstrate with him for not warning them that this might happen. Gwenllian stared absently towards the kitchen, wondering what more she could do to further Cadifor's cause. Cole was standing with Elidor, leaning against the wall with his arms folded, while the other two knights had gone inside to beg for food. Suddenly, Stacpol dashed out.

'Lady Gwenllian, come quick!' he shouted urgently. 'Asser has been taken ill.'

The kitchen was a massive room with two large fireplaces

and lines of scrubbed tables. Pots and pans hung on the walls, and there was a pleasantly sweet smell of simmering fruit. Asser lay on the floor with his eyes closed. Gwenllian knelt next to him, but it took no more than a glance to see that he was well beyond her meagre medical skills – his face was white, his life-beat feeble, and his breathing unnaturally shallow.

'What is wrong with him?' demanded Cole. 'He was perfectly well a few moments ago.'

He grabbed the stricken man's shoulder and shook it. Asser opened his eyes, but they were glazed, and Gwenllian doubted that whatever he whispered in Cole's ear would make sense. Then he went limp. She glanced up and saw Stacpol in the doorway, his expression closed and distant.

'It must have been an apoplexy,' said Prior Cadifor, when Gwenllian had pronounced Asser dead and his monks had intoned the necessary prayers. 'He was a large man who ate too much, and he was excitable. Such men are prone to these sorts of attacks.'

'But he has never had one before,' objected Cole.

'Yes, he has,' countered Stacpol. 'About a month ago. He told me not to mention it, lest you sent him back to Normandy and recruited a fitter man to take his place.'

Cole would have done. He had licence to keep six knights, and could not afford to house one who was unable to fulfil his duties. Gwenllian glanced at Stacpol again, and was surprised by his lack of emotion – he and Asser had been friends. Was he manfully concealing his grief, or was he actually relieved? Asser had, after all, witnessed Stacpol's previous encounter with the royal clerks and had threatened to reveal whatever had transpired.

'How curious that he should die now,' she said, looking

hard at him. Stacpol only stared back, his expression impossible to read.

'Not really,' said Prior Cadifor. 'As I said, such men are prone to this kind of ailment.'

'Especially when they are under strain,' agreed Stacpol, a little too quickly for Gwenllian's liking. 'And today has been full of vexation.'

'Not for him,' countered Cole. 'It was not his horse that went lame, forcing its owner to run about in full armour. Nor was he obliged to solve this business with Walter. All he had to do was sit on his stallion and look menacing, which should not have been too difficult.'

'I refer to the quarrel he had with the cook,' said Stacpol. 'That was vexing.'

All eyes turned to the monk in question, a plump, volatile man named Dafydd.

'Of course I gave him a piece of my mind,' Dafydd snapped, although his eyes were uneasy. 'He ate some of the marchpanes I made for the bishop. Geoffrey loves them, and I always prepare a batch when he visits. But Asser came along and stole a handful before I could stop him. And I cannot make more, because we are out of almonds.'

'He took only four,' said Stacpol reproachfully. 'I am sure they will not be missed.'

'Yes, they will,' argued Dafydd bitterly. 'The bishop ate a lot when he called in to see us last night, so there were only a few left.' He smiled fondly. 'I like to spoil Bishop Geoffrey. He has always been good to us. He will prove a friend over these current troubles, too.'

'I sincerely hope so,' said Cadifor fervently.

Cole wrapped Asser in his cloak, ready to be taken back to the castle, while Cadifor began to pray again for the dead man's soul. The commotion had prompted two of the visitors to emerge from the guesthouse: Sacrist Gilbert from Hempsted and Llanthony's fat Prior Roger.

'Gluttony,' declared Gilbert sanctimoniously, when he heard about the marchpanes. 'Asser should have restrained himself.'

'I love marchpanes,' said Roger wistfully, while Gwenllian gripped Cole's hand to prevent him from making a tart rejoinder. 'They are my favourite of all things. Did this knight eat them all, or are there any left?'

'Yes, but they are for the bishop,' said Dafydd curtly. 'And no one else.'

'I am Prior of Llanthony,' declared Roger angrily. 'It is not for a mere cook to forbid sweetmeats to me. Now fetch them at once.'

'You always were a greedy fellow, Roger,' said Cadifor in distaste, while Dafydd glowered at the prior and refused to move. 'You should beware. Greed is almost as deadly a sin as sloth – the vice that ended up killing your predecessor.'

Fortunately, a clatter of hoofs heralded the arrival of Geoffrey, so a quarrel was averted. Keen to assert his ecclesiastical authority with a show of pomp, the bishop had brought not only his secretarius and the castle scribe, as he had been asked, but a large number of richly clad attendants. They formed an impressive procession, and Gwenllian saw Cadifor's monks take courage from the spectacle.

Walter emerged from the guesthouse, and hurried towards the prelate, ready to begin whispering in his ear. Bishop Geoffrey, however, was more concerned with Asser. He eyed Walter coldly until the prior fell silent, then walked to the dead knight's body.

'Pity,' he said softly. 'Asser was a good man. A crusader, no less.'

Gwenllian did not think the two were necessarily linked, and was of the opinion that most crusaders were violent brutes who should not have been allowed back into the country. Even her beloved Symon had done some terrible things in the name of the so-called holy war.

'He died because he gorged on your marchpanes, Father Bishop,' said Dafydd bluntly, and with a good deal of rancour.

Geoffrey blinked. 'He choked on them?'

'They probably brought about an apoplexy,' explained Cadifor. 'But you have some experience with medicine, Your Grace. Examine him, and give us your opinion.'

The bishop was famous for his skills as a healer, an unusual talent for a prelate, but one for which hundreds had been grateful. He knelt by the body, and Gwenllian was impressed by his calm, competent manner, although he eventually stood and raised his hands in a shrug.

'I see nothing to tell me you are wrong, Prior Cadifor. An apoplexy is the most likely explanation for what happened. Poor, poor man.'

Gwenllian had always liked the Austins' chapel. It was a pretty, silent place with large windows that made it light and airy, even on the darkest of days. It was stone-built, with a grey tiled roof, and boasted some of the finest carvings in the country. Cadifor led the way inside, where he arranged seats for Gwenllian, Cole, the bishop and the scribes. Londres and the Hempsted faction were left to fend for themselves. Walter snapped imperious fingers, and his canons brought him a chair that was far grander than anyone else's. Geoffrey pursed his lips disapprovingly, and Gwenllian saw he was unimpressed with the petty point-scoring.

'Send your scribe home, Cole,' ordered Prior Walter. 'You, too, Bishop. There is not enough room at the table, and there is no need for us all to record what is said. My man, Cadifor's clerk and Henry are more than enough.'

'It would be remiss not to keep our own account,' said Gwenllian, sweetly, aware that Henry and Walter's versions were likely to match, thus casting doubt on Cadifor's. 'Our scribe will stay.'

'So will mine,' added Geoffrey genially. 'He is not doing anything else today.'

'Then it will be the best documented hearing in the history of Carmarthen,' drawled Stacpol, as Londres, Belat and Henry exchanged irritable glances. 'Five separate reports! And I am sure they will all be accurate reflections of what happens here.'

'He has just lost a friend,' whispered Gwenllian to Cole. 'Yet he here he is making snide remarks. Perhaps he is glad Asser is no more, because now no one can tell me what transpired between him and those clerks.'

'You spout nonsense, Gwen,' replied Cole shortly. A facet of her husband's character that annoyed her intensely was an unquestioning allegiance to those he considered to be friends. Few deserved it, and he was invariably surprised to learn that his loyalty was misplaced, or that the 'friends' were nothing of the kind. 'He is grieving deeply, as am I.'

When everyone was settled, Geoffrey asked for God's blessing on the proceedings, then declared them open. Cadifor and Walter drew breath to speak, but Prior Roger was there first.

'It has been a long time since we met, Cadifor,' he said.

'And I know why you came to this desolate backwater – you could not bear to remain at Llanthony when I was in charge.'

'Carmarthen is not a desolate backwater,' objected Cole, offended. He turned to Walter. 'And you must agree, or you would not be here trying to steal it.'

'I steal nothing,' said Walter, tight-lipped. 'I only claim what is lawfully mine.'

'Why did *you* come, Prior Roger?' asked Gwenllian quickly, before Cole could argue. Londres was grinning at her husband's incautious words, and she had no doubt that Henry was gleefully recording them for the King's edification. 'Are Llanthony's affairs still entwined with those of Hempsted?'

'They are,' replied Walter, before Roger could answer for himself. 'Our foundations are very close, and we support each other in all things.'

'If you say so,' muttered Roger. 'Although Llanthony will not benefit from this particular jaunt, and I would rather have stayed home. It may not be very comfortable without the income from Hempsted, but it is better than the open road in January.'

'I imagine he is a hostage,' Gwenllian murmured in Cole's ear. 'Walter brought him to prevent Llanthony from doing anything to harm Hempsted while he is away. Clever Walter! He has left nothing to chance.'

'If I were a canon of Llanthony, I would not be too concerned about putting Roger in danger,' Cole muttered back. 'He is not a very nice man, and I imagine his monks are delighted to be rid of him for a while.'

They stopped whispering when Walter stood, towering over them all. He was a formidable presence, and Gwenllian was not surprised that so many churches and manors had fallen under the force of his personality.

'I, Walter of Hempsted, hereby lay claim to Carmarthen Priory,' he intoned in a powerful voice that rang through the ancient arches. 'My claim is based on history – this place was founded by a Hempsted monk, and was always intended to be a cell. King John agrees, and has furnished us with a writ giving his approval.'

Belat produced a document, a luxurious thing of velum with a large red seal. 'Anyone may look, but no one may touch,' he said. 'We cannot have it "accidentally" torn, and thus rendered null and void.'

Gwenllian immediately suspected that he did not want it examined too closely lest it was revealed as fraudulent, so she went at once to inspect it. Cadifor and Geoffrey did likewise, although Cole did not bother, knowing he could look all he liked, but was unlikely to spot anything amiss – he was a warrior, not a clerk, and was happy to leave such matters to Gwenllian. Unfortunately, she could detect nothing wrong either.

'Perhaps a Hempsted monk did found Carmarthen,' said Cadifor, when everyone was seated again. He made no remark on the document, but his expression was strained: Gwenllian was not the only one who thought it was probably genuine. 'However, I cannot imagine that he intended you to come along a century later and claim it for yourself.'

'Hear, hear,' muttered Roger. Anticipating a lengthy hearing, he had brought some food with him, and the front of his habit was covered in crumbs. 'Now can we go home?'

Gwenllian addressed him. 'Hempsted was still a daughter house of Llanthony when this monk was founding cells. Ergo, it should be Llanthony making this claim, not Hempsted.'

Roger waved a careless hand. 'I suppose so, but that would entail a great deal of work, and such details have never been my forte.'

'No,' said Cadifor acidly. 'Details such as ensuring that Prior Martin wrote to the Pope to contest Hempsted's bid for independence. Carmarthen would not be in this situation now if you had done your duty.'

'It was Martin's responsibility, not mine,' objected Roger. 'And he paid the price for his indolence. He will be in Hell as I speak, in a snake pit, which is the fate for those of a slothful disposition.'

'Are you not concerned that you might join him there?' asked Cadifor archly. 'I know that you have done nothing to improve Llanthony's lot since you were appointed, and its situation has gone from bad to worse.'

'I am not slothful!' declared Roger. 'I just have a pragmatic approach to life, which entails not striving after impossible goals. You should learn from me, Cadifor. The King's writ means you are already defeated.'

'The King can issue writs all he likes,' Cadifor shot back angrily, 'but we are an independent house, and the only man who can decide otherwise is our Prior General. The King's opinion is irrelevant in this matter.'

'Watch your tongue, monk,' hissed Henry menacingly. 'There are many who would consider that remark treason.'

'And there are many more who would consider it the truth,' flashed Cadifor. 'Walter's claim is a contrived nonsense.'

As the argument raged back and forth, Geoffrey appealed for calm. It took him some time to regain control, after which he kept a tighter rein on the proceedings. First, he allowed Walter to state Hempsted's case, and then he indicated that

Cadifor should outline Carmarthen's. When each had finished, Belat was permitted to speak; the clerk embarked on an intricate monologue explaining the King's position. Londres and Henry nodded sagely, even applauding on occasion, although everyone else was bored and Cole did not follow it at all.

Roger was eating again, and Cole nudged Gwenllian when he saw that the portly prior had acquired some of the marchpanes intended for the bishop.

'He has eaten at least ten,' he whispered. 'I doubt there are any left for Geoffrey. Dafydd will be livid.'

Belat droned on, while the scribes' pens scratched steadily, although Gwenllian noted with dismay that the man from the castle wrote far more slowly than the others. Londres smirked when he saw she had noticed, making her wonder whether the fellow had been bribed to be inefficient.

Belat finished eventually, and although Roger continued to slumber, everyone else shuffled and stretched as Geoffrey summarised what had been said. Then the bishop declared the meeting over.

'Reports will now be sent to our Prior General,' he said. 'And the King. Until we receive replies, I recommend that Walter's retinue returns to Hempsted.'

Walter was outraged. 'No! We attended this foolish hearing to be polite, but Belat has made the legal position abundantly clear: the King wants Hempsted to have Carmarthen, so that is the end of the matter.'

'Nothing will be final until our Prior General had passed judgement,' argued Cadifor. 'Until then, you can go home. Sir Symon? See our "guests" off the premises, if you please.'

'I do not envy you, Cole,' whispered Londres gloatingly. 'Your standing orders are to defend the town, but the King's writ demands that you support Walter. His commands are contradictory, and I am glad I do not have to choose between them.'

'I am glad you do not, too,' said Gwenllian coolly. 'You would be incapable of doing so sensibly, and would be an embarrassment to the Crown.'

She turned her back on him, although not before she had seen his cheeks colour with anger.

'Londres is right, Cole,' said Belat smugly. 'You are in a difficult position, and I am sure the King will be interested in how you handle it.'

'It is not the first diplomatic crisis we have managed,' said Gwenllian, nettled by the presumption that Symon would be unequal to the task. 'We have gained considerable experience during the last twenty years.'

'Twenty years,' mused Henry. He was carrying his account of the meeting, and she was amazed by how much he had written. 'Perhaps it is time to retire. A man becomes stale if left in one place for too long.'

'Hear, hear,' said Londres sourly, scowling at Gwenllian. 'And if not, there are many other ways to oust complacent officials.'

'Did they just threaten us?' asked Cole, as the trio walked away together.

'I believe they did,' replied Gwenllian. 'So we must be on our guard.'

Cadifor invited Gwenllian and Cole to eat in the refectory when he emerged from the church, although he scowled irritably when the bishop informed him that good manners dictated that the Hempsted men must be included in the meal, too. His canons served their rivals with ill grace, and

Cole and Gwenllian exchanged a wry glance when they saw one spitting in Prior Walter's ale. She and Cole sat with the Carmarthen men, while the bishop trotted from one side of the room to the other in a determined effort to be impartial.

'I am afraid there are no marchpanes, Your Grace,' said Dafydd, pale with suppressed fury. 'Asser took four, but then someone came along and stole the rest.'

'Roger,' said Cadifor immediately. 'I saw him scoff them all while Belat was pontificating.'

'Where is Roger?' asked Geoffrey, looking around genially. 'It is unlike him to miss a meal. I have never met anyone who enjoys his victuals so.'

'He does not need to eat now,' said Cadifor sourly, 'because he devoured enough for ten men while we were in the chapel. Doubtless he has gone for a postprandial nap. He always was a lazy man. Indeed, Walter's ambitions would have been thwarted years ago if he and Martin had stayed awake more.'

Geoffrey smiled. 'And you would still be Llanthony's almoner – we all know you only accepted a post in Carmarthen because you could not bear to serve under Roger. However, you have performed wonders here, so much good has come from your promotion.'

'But it will all be for nothing if Walter wins,' said Cadifor bitterly. 'Carmarthen will not thrive under him. He will bleed us dry to keep Hempsted in riches, and all I have built will be lost. Damn him! And damn Roger, too!'

The bishop intoned a tactful final grace at that point. Gwenllian and Cole stood, and were about to return to the castle when Walter and Gilbert came to speak to Cadifor. Cole stopped, unwilling to leave if there was about to be another spat.

'An adequate feast, Cadifor,' said Walter coolly. 'But not of a standard that will be tolerated now we are in charge.'

'No,' agreed Gilbert. 'There was sawdust in my bread and a nail in my broth.'

'We are a poor foundation,' said Cadifor innocently. 'Once we have paid our dues to the King and dispensed alms to the poor, there is very little left for luxurious living.'

'Then the poor will have to tighten their belts,' said Walter. He turned to Geoffrey, who was listening with a troubled expression on his kindly features. 'Will you give me medicine to ease the pain in my innards? Your elixirs are far more effective than the ones Gilbert makes me.'

'Your innards would fare better if you did not work so hard,' advised Geoffrey, while Sacrist Gilbert shot his superior a disagreeable glance for his ingratitude. 'Rest and regular meals will cure your affliction, but you refuse to heed my advice.'

'A remedy, please,' said Walter coldly, holding out his hand.

'I do not have one with me,' replied Geoffrey. 'I did not imagine that my medical skills would be needed today, so I left my bag in the castle.'

'I will make you something,' offered Gwenllian, thinking that a tincture of chalk and poppy juice would ease Walter's discomfort. And when he was not in pain, perhaps he would be more willing to listen to reason.

'No, thank you,' said Walter coldly. 'I would rather suffer than accept help from a woman, especially one who hails from this godforsaken hole.'

'As you wish,' said Gwenllian, equally icy. 'Enjoy your night.'

'He is a disagreeable fellow,' said Geoffrey, once Walter and Gilbert had retired to the guesthouse. 'But I did not know you were a healer, Lady Gwenllian. I have always been interested in medicine. Indeed, had my family not given me to the Church, I would have become a physician.'

They exchanged remedies for acid stomachs while Cole arranged for soldiers from the castle to stand guard outside the guesthouse, to prevent anyone from entering or leaving – if the two factions did not meet, then there could be no further trouble that night.

When Cole had finished, he and the bishop went to fetch their horses while Gwenllian waited in the yard. Darkness had fallen, but light spilled from the guesthouse windows, all of which had ill-fitting shutters. She could not help but notice that one was the room allocated to the two clerks. She glanced around quickly, but no one was looking and the shadows were thick. She put her eye to the biggest crack and peered inside. Belat was dictating and Henry writing.

'Slow down,' Henry hissed, stopping to wring his hand. 'My fingers hurt.'

'We cannot,' said Belat urgently. 'The bishop may ask to see our transcript, and we must have it ready.'

'I wrote a perfectly good account the first time,' snapped Henry. 'It exposed Cole as a blundering buffoon, as per our agreement with Londres, and showed Walter to be the rightful ruler of this house. We do not need to copy it out all over again.'

'But I do not want to be part of Londres' plot to topple Cole,' said Belat. 'I think the King has forgotten whatever petty squabble prompted him to send Londres here to spy five years ago, and now His Majesty does not care who rules Carmarthen, as long as its taxes are paid on time. Indeed, ousting an efficient governor may even turn John against us.'

'But we made a financial arrangement with Londres,' argued Henry.

'So?' asked Belat archly. 'What can he do? Complain that we failed to write lies about a royally appointed official? Forget Londres! He can rot here for the rest of his life for all I care. We have bigger fish to fry – namely seeing Walter installed in this priory. The King will not be pleased if his writ is contested.'

'No,' agreed Henry. 'His barons challenge his authority at every turn, and he will not want monasteries doing it, too. But what shall we do about the accounts written by the others? Walter's will match ours, but Cole's, Cadifor's and the bishop's will not.'

'Londres paid the castle scribe to write what we tell him, while the bishop's secretarius is a friend of mine. Four accounts will tally, so Cadifor's will be disregarded. Now write.'

They returned to their work, leaving Gwenllian thoughtful. Then she became aware of a shadow at her side, and was unsettled to see that it was Stacpol, tall and menacing in the gloom.

'They have not changed,' he said softly. 'One day, they will be caught, and then all the lies in the world will not save them.'

He strode away before she could ask about his own dealings with the pair. Then, Cole shouted that he was ready, and led the way through the burned gates with the bishop's retinue following. Stacpol and Elidor brought up the rear with the cart that carried Asser's body.

'Did you see that?' Cole asked suddenly, reining in and staring into the bushes that lined the side of the road. 'That flicker of movement?'

'That is the second time you claim to have seen someone watching us today,' called Stacpol. 'Are you sure you are not imagining it?'

'Yes,' replied Cole shortly. 'Quite sure.'

In the small hours of the morning, Cadifor slipped out of the dormitory and aimed for the gate. The guards Cole had set at the guesthouse pretended not to notice him: they had been told what Walter had come to do, and their sympathies lay firmly with the local monks. Once through the gate, Cadifor hurried to the castle, aiming to put his case to Bishop Geoffrey alone.

He was conducted to the solar. The fire had gone out hours before, so it was cold and dark. It was elegantly decorated, though, and he recognised Gwenllian's hand in the tapestries that hung on the wall and the cushions that were strewn about the benches. It smelled of lavender and sage, and of the fresh rushes that had been scattered on the floor.

The bishop entered rubbing sleep from his eyes, but Cadifor's arrival had also woken others. Cole, Stacpol and Elidor were fully dressed, unwilling to remove their armour while there was trouble in their town; Gwenllian wore a thick woollen cloak over her nightclothes.

'I know this is an odd time for an audience, Your Grace,' Cadifor began apologetically. 'But I could not sleep for worry. I felt I was not sufficiently eloquent earlier – not like Walter.'

'You were eloquent enough for me.' Geoffrey smiled. 'I do not believe Hempsted has a right to Carmarthen. I am on your side, Cadifor.'

Cadifor sighed his relief. 'Thank God! Will you help me to challenge Walter?'

Geoffrey nodded. 'And we shall begin by contesting that deed. I studied it carefully, and I am far from sure that it is genuine.'

'I wish I could agree,' said Cadifor unhappily. 'But it came from the King sure enough. Belat and Henry are disagreeable characters, but they are not fools – it would be reckless to forge that sort of thing when it is likely to be inspected by the head of our Order.'

'Cadifor is right,' said Gwenllian. 'I know the King's seal, and I suspect His Majesty *has* given his support to Walter. Probably for a price.'

'Why is Walter so keen to have Carmarthen?' asked Elidor curiously. 'It is not a wealthy house.'

'Because of our wool,' explained Cadifor. 'Walter's empire has now expanded to include several hundred monks, lay brothers and servants, all of whom need clothes and blankets. *That* is why he set greedy eyes on us.'

'But how did he know about the wool?' asked Cole. 'You only sell it locally.'

'I imagine Londres told him,' surmised Gwenllian. 'He must have heard that Hempsted was expanding, and wrote to inform Walter that Carmarthen is a plum ripe for the picking.'

'Why would he do such a spiteful thing?' asked Cole doubtfully.

'His remit was to catch you doing something wrong, so you could be dismissed,' she reminded him. 'But he has failed. He is angry and resentful, and knows he will only escape from Carmarthen – which he has grown to hate – by discrediting you.'

'Which this will,' said Geoffrey soberly. 'He will either report you for failing to protect the priory from hostile invaders, or for challenging the King's writ. Either will see *you* in trouble, and allow *him* to return to Westminster.'

'Politics,' said Cole in distaste. 'Prior Walter is a fool for letting Londres use him in his machinations. He should have just bought Carmarthen's wool instead.'

'Why, when this writ will let him get it for free?' asked Cadifor bitterly. 'Wool is currently fetching very high prices, so seizing our assets will save him a fortune.'

'It is a pity that John allows his favour to be bought,' sighed Geoffrey. 'He is God's anointed, and should set a better example. No wonder his barons oppose him.'

'The greater pity is that Prior Roger is such a lazy scoundrel,' said Stacpol. 'He should keep his former daughter house in order, but instead, he trails along in Walter's wake, moaning about the misery of winter travel.'

'He is the epitome of sloth,' said Cadifor. 'Like his predecessor, Martin. Did I ever tell you about him? He was murdered on the very day that Walter came to declare Hempsted independent. Later, a message warning against the sin of sloth was etched on his coffin.'

'Murdered by whom?' asked Gwenllian, intrigued.

'The killer was never caught, although I expect the culprit was one of Walter's men, smarting over insults that were issued during a spat in Martin's solar.'

'Walter is slothful, too,' remarked Geoffrey.

Cole blinked. 'No! He is the *opposite* of sloth – willing to do anything to get what he wants.'

'You think sloth means lazy,' lectured Geoffrey. 'But it is more insidious than that. It is a sluggishness of the mind that neglects to do good – an evil that oppresses man's spirit, and draws him away from good deeds.'

'The bishop is right,' agreed Cadifor. 'Walter is bored with himself and his life, and boredom represents an emptiness of the soul and a lack of passion. It—'

'Walter has an abundance of passion,' interrupted Cole, although he should have known better than to tackle two senior clerics about the nature of sin. 'Especially for other people's property. Unlike Roger. *He* is the one who lacks passion.'

'He does,' acknowledged Geoffrey. 'But Walter is so obsessed by enlarging his domain that he fails to appreciate the beauty around him. Overwork is a form of sloth.'

'Quite,' nodded Cadifor. 'It is easier to dedicate one's life to obvious goals, like manipulating monarchs to grant you priories, than to sit back and appreciate God's wondrous gifts. In my opinion, sloth is the deadliest of sins and—'

'We need a plan,' interrupted Gwenllian, suspecting the discussion might last all night if it was allowed to continue. 'One that will see our priory keep its independence without bringing the King down on us in a fury.'

'Oh, I know how to do that,' said Geoffrey. 'We simply find out how much Walter paid His Majesty for the writ, then offer to double it if he agrees to a retraction.'

Cole laughed. 'And this is advice dispensed by a bishop?'

But Cadifor was dismayed. 'Why should we resort to underhand tactics? Walter is in the wrong, and any decent person will see it.'

Geoffrey patted his arm. 'In an ideal world you would be right, but this is one ruled by King John. If you want Carmarthen to remain independent, it will cost you in money.'

Cadifor closed his eyes in despair. 'But we do not have that sort of capital.'

'Then I shall lend you some,' said Geoffrey. 'Not from the

diocesan coffers, as my treasurer will not approve, but from my personal finances. I am not a wealthy man, and the loan will beggar me until you repay it, but it will be worth the inconvenience.'

Cadifor sighed his relief. 'Thank you! Although I fail to see what you will gain.'

'I will gain not having Walter in my See,' explained the bishop. 'Four of my brother prelates have him in theirs, and they say he is nothing but trouble. Moreover, I admire what you have done here, and I should hate it to be undone.'

Cadifor gripped his hand. 'You are a *good* man. I shall pay you back within ten years.'

Geoffrey gulped. 'I hope it will be sooner than that – six months at the most! You will have to drive harder bargains with that fine wool you mentioned.'

'Then all we need do is find out how much Walter paid the King,' said Cole. He frowned. 'I cannot imagine he will be very forthcoming when we ask, though.'

'No,' agreed Gwenllian. 'We shall have to be subtle. Leave it to me.'

Suddenly, there was shouting in the bailey below. Cole opened the window and leaned out, letting in a chill blast of air that had everyone drawing their cloaks more closely around their shoulders. Iefan shouted up.

'You are asked to go to the priory as soon as possible. There has been a death.'

'Who?' asked Cole.

'Prior Roger. Apparently, he fell asleep in the chapel during yesterday's hearing and failed to wake up.'

Cole took Stacpol and Elidor with him to the priory, partly to show the Austins a suitable degree of respect for a deceased member of their Order – three knights made for a better display than one – but mostly because he did not believe that Roger had 'fallen asleep', and he would need help if there were signs of foul play.

'No,' he said, when Gwenllian emerged fully clothed from the bedchamber to accompany him. 'Not this time. You were right to be anxious: Roger's death is unlikely to be natural, given all the antagonism that raged yesterday.'

'Quite,' she said, equally resolute as she pushed past him. 'You will need me if you hope to uncover the truth. You cannot do it alone.'

She was right and he knew it, although he was not happy. 'Very well, but only if you promise not to wander off alone.'

She inclined her head to accept the condition, and they set off. Bishop Geoffrey also insisted on going, to pray over the remains of the colleague he had known for years.

'I neither liked nor respected him as a man,' he said. 'But as a youth, he was a charming, entertaining companion. It is a pity he learned bad habits from Martin. Had he moulded himself on Cadifor, he would have been an asset to Llanthony.'

Cadifor inclined his head at the compliment. 'Yet I do not remember Roger being charming or entertaining, and as far as I am concerned, he had no redeeming qualities at all. But I am sorry he is dead, because now he will never have the chance to mend his slothful ways.'

Cole set a rapid pace through the town. Geoffrey did his best to keep up, but soon fell behind, while Gwenllian and Cadifor panted hard. The knights were not breathless at all, kept fit by their duties. Their vigour made Gwenllian wonder how Asser had managed to deceive them about the precarious state of his health.

They passed the houses by St Peter's church, then the woods that separated the town from the priory, after which Cole stopped, so abruptly that Cadifor cannoned into the back of him.

'Did you see that?' he demanded. 'Someone is moving through the trees.'

'Not this again,' groaned Stacpol. 'There is no one here, Cole. If you saw movement, it was the wind among the leaves.'

'Actually, I thought I saw someone, too,' said Gwenllian, not liking Stacpol's discourteous tone. 'Besides, there is no wind. It is calm and the leaves are still.'

Stacpol regarded her with cold eyes. 'Then you were mistaken as well. It is still not fully light, so it is easy to imagine things.'

She opened her mouth to argue, but Cole was already moving away, so she did no more than favour Stacpol with a glare before following.

They reached the monastery and were admitted by the soldiers on duty. However, they were then made to wait in the yard until Walter and Gilbert deigned to emerge from the guesthouse, an insult that had even the tolerant Geoffrey grumbling. The Llanthony monks were wiping their lips on pieces of linen, suggesting that they had finished their breakfast before attending the officials they themselves had summoned.

Londres, Belat and Henry were with them. The bailiff's face was flushed, and Gwenllian suspected he had spent the night drinking. She regarded him in distaste. He was smug, delighted to be the author of a situation that had seen the King win a handsome bribe from Walter, that had resulted in Hempsted obtaining another foundation, and that had put Cole in a difficult situation. He did not care that it would be the monks of Carmarthen who would suffer for his poisonous schemes.

'Prior Roger is dead,' Walter announced. 'He fell asleep during the hearing yesterday, and Cadifor gave orders that he was not to be disturbed. However, when I went to say matins and saw he had not moved, I poked him. It was then that I discovered that he had passed away.'

'I did suggest we let him be,' said Cadifor, a little defensively as everyone looked at him. 'He seemed tired, and I thought he might need the rest.'

'Liar!' hissed Gilbert. 'You ordered him left because you wanted everyone to see how lazy he was – that he could sleep for hours when he should have been reciting his offices.'

'He did not need me to reveal him as a slothful man,' Cadifor shot back, although the guilty flash in his eyes suggested there was truth in Gilbert's accusation. 'He did that himself, by his own words and actions.'

'Are you sure he was there all night?' asked Cole. 'He did not leave and then go back?'

'How would we know?' asked Gilbert archly. 'We were confined to the guesthouse, allowed out only to pray. However, Roger was in the same position each time we passed him, so he probably died hours ago.'

'So we have a second odd death just as you happen to be visiting a sister house, Walter,' said Cadifor coldly. 'The same thing happened at Llanthony, when Martin died. Do you have an explanation?'

'*I* do not need to provide one,' replied Walter haughtily. 'The incident has nothing to do with me.' He addressed Cole. 'Do you want to see the corpse? We have left it as it was found.'

'Have you?' gulped Geoffrey, crossing himself. 'How very unpleasant! Why did you not move it somewhere more appropriate?'

'Like the refectory or the dormitory,' muttered Cadifor acidly. 'Eating and sleeping were Roger's favourite activities, so where more appropriate than those?'

In the chapel, Roger was on the same bench he had occupied during the meeting. It looked as though he was asleep, but when Cole stepped forward to feel for a life-beat, the skin was cold to the touch. He then examined the body more closely, but found no suspicious lumps or marks, and it appeared as though the Prior of Llanthony had simply passed away peacefully in his sleep.

'He probably ate so much during the hearing that he overloaded himself,' said Walter in distaste. 'Gluttony killed him.'

'And sloth,' whispered Bishop Geoffrey. 'If he had been a more vigorous man, he would not have grown so fat. The great Greek physician Galen warns against the perils of too much food combined with too little exercise.'

He began to recite prayers for the dead, which obliged the other Austins to do the same, although they did so reluctantly. Roger had not been popular, and it was clear that few would mourn his passing. Londres, Belat and Henry stood nearby, muttering together. It looked as though they were arguing, and Gwenllian wondered whether Roger's death aided or hindered their plans. Or perhaps Londres had learned that his accomplices planned to cheat him.

When the monks had finished their devotions, six burly lay brothers carried Roger to a storeroom, where he would be prepared for the journey back to his own foundation.

There was silence after the body had gone, although it did not last long.

'I repeat what I said earlier,' declared Cadifor. 'It is odd that there should be another death at a priory which Walter has wronged.'

Walter sniffed, and did not grace the remark with a reply.

Elidor was thoughtful, though. 'Cadifor makes an interesting point. There were no marks on Prior Martin either, but we all knew *he* was unlawfully slain.' He looked at Cole. 'Do you think it possible that both were poisoned?'

'If so, then it was with a substance that cannot be detected,' replied Cole. 'There are no burns or redness in Roger's mouth or on his hands. However, I can tell you that he was cold and stiff, which means he probably died hours ago – perhaps even during the hearing. We all saw him sitting here with his eyes closed, and he did not move as we walked out past him . . .'

Gwenllian had been making her own assessment of the situation, staring down at the place where the body had been. 'Roger ate stolen marchpanes, but there is no trace of them now.'

'Of course not,' said Cadifor, bemused. 'He scoffed the lot.'

Gwenllian nodded. 'Yes, and I saw crumbs all over his habit. However, there are no crumbs now – his robe is clean. And do not say he shook them off himself, because the floor would be littered with them and it is not. It seems to me that someone has swept them up.'

'Why would anyone do that?' asked Cole, puzzled. Then the answer came. 'You mean that someone has removed the evidence? That the food *was* poisoned, so the killer cleared away any remaining fragments to prevent us from proving it?'

'Specifically, the marchpanes,' said Gwenllian. 'Asser also

ate some, and within moments, he collapsed in a stupor. You woke him, but with difficulty. I suspect Roger also slipped into a stupor, but no one shook him awake, and he passed quietly into death.'

Geoffrey's hand shot to his throat. 'Are you saying that someone put poison in the sweetmeats intended for me?' But then he shook his head. 'No! Asser had an apoplexy. Stacpol mentioned similar attacks in the past.'

'And I stand by my claim,' said Stacpol. 'Asser died of natural causes, and so did Roger. These theories about poisonous marchpanes are ridiculous.'

'I am not so sure,' said Elidor, so that Stacpol's angry glare passed from Gwenllian to him. 'Cole is right: many poisons are undetectable, and I think it strange that Asser and Roger should die so soon after eating marchpanes. Moreover, their deaths remind me of Prior Martin's, and we all knew that he did not perish naturally.'

'Fetch the remaining marchpanes,' ordered Cole, seeing Dafydd the cook among the watching Austins. 'We shall feed one to a rat and have our answer.'

'They have all gone,' said Dafydd, frightened. 'So has the plate. I assumed Roger took them, but now it occurs to me that the killer must have been in my kitchen, removing the evidence of his crimes . . .'

'Clearly,' said Walter, fixing him with an icy stare. 'And if the sweetmeats were poisoned, it stands to reason that the toxin was added where they were made: in *your* domain.'

'No!' cried Dafydd, then relief flooded his chubby face. 'Hah! You cannot accuse me, because I was not in Llanthony when Martin was killed – and if Martin, Roger and Asser died from the same cause, then I can be eliminated as a suspect.'

It was a good point, and Gwenllian watched annoyance flit across Walter's face. Had he wanted a Carmarthen man blamed so that his own party could be exonerated? Or because a killer among Cadifor's flock might convince the Prior General that the present incumbent was unfit to rule, and thus strengthen Walter's justification for seizing the place himself?

'I wonder if messages about sloth will be scratched onto Roger's coffin,' mused Henry. 'Or Asser's. I suppose we shall have to wait and see.'

'My soldiers will be guarding them,' said Cole, although Gwenllian wished he had held his tongue: if the killer was the kind of person to deface caskets, then a trap might have been laid to catch him. He glowered at those who had gathered around. 'But if someone did murder my knight, I will catch him. You can be sure of that.'

'I imagine his death was accidental,' said Walter. 'The intended victim was Bishop Geoffrey, and it is unfortunate that Asser and Roger stole his marchpanes.' He grinned nastily. 'So Carmarthen is home to people who murder prelates! The King will certainly support me now – to oust this evil.'

'Let us not allow our imaginations to run away with us,' cautioned Geoffrey, making an obvious effort to pull himself together. 'No one wanted to kill me.' He addressed Gwenllian. 'And you cannot prove that the marchpanes were poisoned. Not now there are none left.'

'You are right: these theories are nonsense,' said Sacrist Gilbert. 'I admit that it is unusual for two men to die so close together, but it happens. Neither was unlawfully slain.'

'Oh, Roger was murdered sure enough,' said Londres, while the two clerks shot him alarmed glances. 'The killer aims to weaken Walter's case by slaughtering one of his retinue – clearly, he hopes that Roger's replacement will side with Carmarthen.'

'Do not think of accusing Cole,' said Cadifor, when he saw where the bailiff's accusing glare had settled. 'I doubt he cares enough about our priory to kill for it. And do not think of blaming my canons either. None of them was in Llanthony when Martin was killed, which means none of them harmed Roger.'

'No, but you were,' flashed Walter. 'And you could not account for your whereabouts at the time, as I recall.'

'Nor could you,' Cadifor barked back. He turned to the two clerks. 'Nor you.'

A spat followed. Geoffrey stepped amid the furiously wagging fingers, and clapped his hands for silence, but no one took any notice, and his increasingly agitated demands for order only added to the clamour. It was an angry roar from Cole that eventually stilled the racket.

'Enough!' he snapped. 'Such hollering is unseemly in a House of God.'

'So is murder,' said Cadifor sullenly, not appreciating the reprimand. 'My chapel has been defiled.'

'*Your* chapel?' asked Walter. 'The King does not think so.'

'It is mine until the Prior General tells me otherwise,' said Cadifor angrily. 'However, even if he does find against me, it will not be anyone from your entourage who takes my place. It is obvious that one of you killed Roger in the hope of bringing disgrace on me. Well, it will not work – I shall tell the whole world what kind of men you are.'

'Sir Symon is right,' said Bishop Geoffrey, as Walter girded himself up to reply in kind. 'We should take this discussion away from the chapel.'

'Actually, I meant you should stop screeching altogether,'

said Cole shortly. 'I did not mean that you should just go and find somewhere else to quarrel.'

But his words went unheard as everyone aimed for the door. They went quickly, eager to resume their haranguing, and it was not long before he and Gwenllian were alone.

'The more I think about it, the more I suspect the marchpanes *were* poisoned,' she said. Then she recalled the dying knight murmuring in Cole's ear. 'Asser whispered something to you before he stopped breathing. Did you hear what it was?'

'Yes, but it made no sense. First, he said, "Sloth is the most deadly of sins," which are the words that were scratched on Martin's coffin in Llanthony, apparently. Then, he told me that I needed to look for an incongruously sharp knife.'

She regarded him blankly. 'What does that mean?'

Cole shrugged. 'I told you it did not make sense. Perhaps I will ask Stacpol. He is good with riddles.'

Gwenllian did not want to tell him that Stacpol was at the top of her list of suspects – that he might have poisoned the marchpanes so that Asser would be unable to reveal his past dealings with Belat and Henry, and that Roger had merely been unlucky in his choice of filched food. Cole would refuse to listen.

Her thoughts churned. What did Asser's last words mean? Were they the incoherent ramblings of a dying man? Or had he been trying to convey a vital clue? But if Asser knew the identity of the killer, why had he not just told Symon straight out? She sighed. Her husband was right: it made no sense.

The warring clerics took their quarrel to the refectory, where they sat on benches around one of the long tables. They began by interrogating Dafydd.

'You cannot blame my marchpanes,' the cook was declaring, half frightened and half defiant, as Gwenllian and Cole walked in. 'They were made from the finest ingredients, and the bishop ate more than half of them with no ill effects.'

'I did,' agreed Geoffrey. 'They were delicious. You are right, Dafydd: no one poisoned the marchpanes. He smiled his relief. 'Which means that no one wants me dead.'

But Gwenllian shook her head. 'After your first meal, the remainder were left in the kitchen, ready for your next visit. But the kitchen is not secure – anyone could have slipped in and dosed the rest with poison. Is that not true, Dafydd?'

The cook blanched. 'Well, yes, the kitchen is left unattended on occasion, such as when I go to the chapel for my offices, and it is open all night . . .'

'You see, Your Grace?' said Gwenllian. 'It would have been easy for the killer to strike.'

There was a brief silence, then a flurry of accusations. The Carmarthen men blamed the visitors, and vice versa, while Londres took the opportunity to accuse Cole, saying that he had let Prior Roger eat the last of the marchpanes to conceal the fact that the real victim had been Asser. Startled, Cole asserted that Asser had been a good friend. Stacpol agreed, but fell silent when Belat and Henry shot him sly glances. Again, Gwenllian wondered what dealings the two slippery clerks had had with Stacpol in the past.

She ignored the angry voices as she tried to decide who had been the intended victim – Asser, Roger or Geoffrey. She had eight suspects. All but one had been in Llanthony when Martin had died, and all were ruthless, dangerous men who would not hesitate to kill if they thought it would be to their advantage.

Heading the list was Stacpol, because Asser's death meant his dealings with Belat and Henry would remain secret. He was a knight, used to killing, and did not seem particularly distressed by the loss of his friend – and she was not convinced by Cole's explanation that crusaders did not weep. Then, once Asser was dead, Stacpol had neglected to destroy the remaining marchpanes, and Roger had paid the price.

Next were the Hempsted men, Walter and Gilbert, and their intended victim would have been Geoffrey, because they were afraid he would side with Carmarthen – which was exactly what he had done. And Roger? Perhaps they had decided that he had outlived his usefulness, or they had not cared who died, and simply thought that any murder in Carmarthen would discredit Cadifor. Yet Gilbert had been eager for everyone to think that no one had been killed, and that the two deaths were natural. Did he really believe it, or was he just losing his nerve?

Then there were the clerks Belat and Henry, who would be keen to tell the King that all had gone well in Carmarthen, and that the royal writ had been implemented without any problems. They would not want the Bishop of St David's issuing counterclaims. Or had they just tired of Roger's unpleasant character, and decided they could not face the return journey in his company? It was a paltry reason to kill, but Gwenllian had known murder committed for less.

Cadifor was next, although she disliked including him. Yet he had despised Roger, and blamed him for losing Llanthony's daughter house – to the point where he had left rather than live in a foundation where Roger was prior. He had also remarked on Roger's indolence and greed, and would have been in a position to ensure the deadly marchpanes were in a place where Roger would see then. Perhaps the notion that Roger was part of a deputation that aimed to oust him had been too much for Cadifor to bear.

Although Bishop Geoffrey had also been in Llanthony when the first murder had taken place, Gwenllian could see no reason for him wanting Roger dead. Or Asser. Moreover, it had been his marchpanes that had been poisoned, and had Asser and Roger not raided the kitchen, it would be him lying in his coffin. She crossed him off her list.

Her last suspect was Londres. He had lived in Carmarthen long enough to know where to buy toxins, and he had had ample opportunity to sneak into the monastery kitchen. He had thrown in his lot with Hempsted, so he would not want Geoffrey damaging Walter's chances of winning. Or perhaps he did not care whom he killed, and just wanted to create an awkward situation for Cole. He had not been in Llanthony when Martin had died, but he was perfectly capable of mimicking the original crime.

Gwenllian watched her suspects carefully as they argued, but the killer was far too clever to give himself away with a careless word or gesture, and it was not long before she realised she was wasting her time. Afterwards, she and Cole went to the kitchen, and asked Dafydd to show them where the marchpanes had been.

'I did not think it was necessary to hide them,' the cook said. 'Nothing has ever been stolen before. I can forgive Asser, who snagged a few before I told him they were earmarked for the bishop. But not Roger, who knew and took them anyway.'

Gwenllian stared at the table that Dafydd indicated. Like all the others in the room, it had been scrubbed so often that the wood was white. There were scratches on the surface, forming a series of rough triangles. Dafydd grimaced his irritation.

'Those wicked scullions! I have told them hundreds of times to use a board when they slice vegetables, but they are too lazy to fetch one.'

'Are you sure?' asked Gwenllian. 'They look more purposeful than marks made from chopping – there is a distinct pattern here.'

Dafydd peered at them. 'You are right! The rogues did it deliberately, knowing that I shall never prove which of them did it. They are a sore trial to a busy man.'

Cole dropped to his hands and knees and began to peer underneath. It was not long before he released a triumphant exclamation and scrambled to his feet. He held a dead mouse in one hand, while in the other was a slightly gnawed sweetmeat.

'A marchpane must have dropped off the plate and rolled out of sight,' he said. 'However, this poor creature proves for certain that Roger and Asser were poisoned.'

'It does,' agreed Gwenllian. 'Not much of the sweetmeat is missing, which means the mouse was overcome very fast.'

She and Cole remained at the priory for the rest of the day, asking questions of residents and invaders alike, but learned nothing more. They walked home as the daylight began to fade, disheartened because they were no further forward.

'Martin's murder was never solved,' said Cole with uncharacteristic gloom. 'Perhaps Roger and Asser's will not be either.'

'Then those two clerks or Londres will tell the King that you are incompetent,' said Gwenllian. 'And John will dismiss you. I do not intend to give them that satisfaction.'

'Damn it, there is that shadow again!' Cole darted into the undergrowth and was gone so long that Gwenllian began to worry that something had happened to him. She was on the verge of following when he emerged, covered in dead leaves.

'No one was there?' she asked.

'Someone was,' he replied. 'I just could not catch him.'

That night, Gwenllian's mind raced with questions, and she lay staring at the ceiling until the small hours of the morning, when exhaustion finally claimed her. She started awake not long after, when little Alys came to complain about bad dreams. It was a ploy to gain attention, but Cole doted on his only daughter, and obediently went to calm her.

'Eight years old and already your master,' remarked Gwenllian when he returned. 'What will she be like at eighteen?'

'Beautiful,' he murmured drowsily, closing his eyes. 'Just like her mother.'

'I cannot stop thinking about the murders,' said Gwenllian, resenting his intention to go back to sleep while she only tossed and turned. 'I find myself hoping that Londres is responsible, simply because exposing him would see him gone from our town.'

'I suppose it would,' he mumbled. 'But you will solve the case, Gwen. You always do.'

His faith was simultaneously touching and annoying. She liked the fact that he appreciated her intelligence, but there was something lazy about his willingness to abrogate the responsibility to her. He was constable of Carmarthen, and it should be him fretting for solutions, not her. She prodded him awake. Perhaps discussing it would help her see sense in the muddle of facts they had accumulated.

'The poison killed the mouse after a few nibbles,' she began. 'Asser also succumbed quickly, and so probably did Roger. That means the toxin was very strong. How could the killer have laid hold of such a deadly substance?'

'Not from an apothecary.' Cole sat up to prevent himself from nodding off. 'They know better than to sell that sort of thing. However, I can tell you that it was a soporific, because both closed their eyes and drifted gently into death. In the Holy Land, surgeons dispensed soporifics to dying crusaders.'

She blinked. 'What are you saying? That a medicus poisoned the marchpanes?'

'Or someone with access to or knowledge of such potions.'

'Who?' She peered at him in the gloom. 'Not Bishop Geoffrey! I know he said he would have been a physician if he had not entered the Church, but he is more interested in healing than killing. He is no murderer.'

'Then perhaps someone raided his supplies. If he was the intended victim, using his own medicines to dispatch him would have a certain ironic appeal to the culprit.'

'Yes, but he does not have any with him, which is why he was unable to furnish Walter with a remedy for his bad stomach.'

'No, he did not have any at the priory,' Cole corrected, 'because he had left his bag in the castle. So someone could have stolen it from here, although it would have been a daring move.'

She nodded agreement, then began to list her suspects, although she received short shrift when she reached Stacpol. She did not press her case, knowing they would quarrel if she did.

'So of your original eight we can eliminate Stacpol, the

bishop, Cadifor, Walter and Gilbert,' he said when she had finished. 'Stacpol is no poisoner, while the others are monks, and would be too concerned for their immortal souls to kill.'

She gaped at him. 'We have encountered plenty of murderous clerics in the past! Besides, Walter and Gilbert are not very devout men.'

'No, but Walter is clearly unwell, and I doubt he would commit a mortal sin so close to death, while Gilbert will do nothing on his own initiative. We have already discounted Geoffrey, and I like Cadifor. So your list now comprises three: Belat, Henry and Londres.'

She wished it were that simple. 'It is not—'

But her words were lost as he bounded off the bed, suddenly full of energy. 'That was time well spent, Gwen. The murders will be easy to solve now.'

It was another pretty winter day, with a pale sun shining in a light blue sky, and hoarfrost sparkling on the rooftops. Gwenllian spent an hour with the children while Cole dealt with urgent castle business, after which they spoke to the scribe who had taken notes at the hearing. The man began to cry the moment he was summoned, and quickly confessed that Londres had paid him to write an account that would favour Hempsted.

His confession allowed Gwenllian to summon Londres for questioning – it would have been awkward to use the discussion she had overheard between Belat and Henry. The bailiff refused to come, but Iefan was more than happy to use force. The delighted grins of the townsfolk who witnessed him frogmarched to the castle did nothing to soothe his furious indignation, and he was seething by the time he was shoved into Cole's office.

'You have no right,' Londres snarled. 'I am a royally appointed official, and I answer to no one but the King.'

'Symon is also a royally appointed official,' Gwenllian reminded him. 'One with the power to arrest and execute those he considers dangerous to Carmarthen's security.'

Cole chose that moment to draw his sword and inspect the blade. Gwenllian knew there was no deliberate intention to intimidate – he was just tired of being indoors, and itched to be about more manly pursuits – but she said nothing as Londres eyed him uneasily. The bailiff grew more nervous still when Cole took a whetstone and began to hone the edge.

'You cannot execute me,' he declared in an unsteady voice. 'The King will—'

'The King will hear that you conspired to do Carmarthen harm,' snapped Gwenllian. 'And he will be grateful to us for ridding him of a traitor.'

'I am not a traitor!' cried Londres. His face grew hard with spite. 'That honour belongs to Cole, who will either ignore a royal writ or let hostile troops invade his domain. He is the one who will have to answer for his decisions, not me.'

Gwenllian smiled coldly. 'The scribe you corrupted has made a full confession, so do not lie.' She treated him to a dose of his own medicine by adding an untruth of her own. 'He also said that Belat and Henry plan to renege on the sly agreement you made – they will keep what you paid them, but will fail to do what they promised. You are in very deep trouble, Londres.'

The bailiff's defiant resolve began to crumble. 'Everything I did was for the King.' He gulped. 'No one can condemn me for that. If you execute me, you will have to explain yourself to an angry monarch.'

'Perhaps, but it will not matter to you, because you will be dead,' Gwenllian pointed out. 'It is a crime to falsify official documents, and you have been caught red-handed.'

Cole began swishing the sword through the air, to test its balance. Again, it was innocent, but she did not blame the bailiff for thinking that Symon was preparing to hack off his head then and there.

'No,' gulped Londres. 'You cannot—'

'You have chosen the wrong confederates,' she continued relentlessly. 'Belat and Henry will deny all knowledge of this deception, and you will bear the blame alone. You could have carved a nice niche for yourself here, but instead you plotted, connived and bled our people dry with illegal fines.'

'What choice did I have?' bleated Londres. 'The King stopped paying me after a few weeks, so how else was I to live? And as for the Hempsted business – I had to do something to regain John's affection, or he would have left me here for the rest of my life.'

'So you hatched a plot to see Symon discredited, using Walter's greed to facilitate it. You do not care that the priory will suffer as a result.'

'I hate Cadifor,' said Londres sullenly. 'It would not surprise me to learn that *he* killed Roger. After all, Cadifor left Llanthony in protest when Roger became prior. He probably murdered Martin, too, then left that message about sloth. It is a vice he deplores.'

Cadifor had said as much himself, Gwenllian recalled, calling it the 'deadliest of sins', which were the exact words that had been scratched into Martin's coffin. But it was no time to ponder Cadifor, and she turned her attention back to the bailiff.

'You accuse Cadifor, but I think *you* killed Roger. What better way to disgrace Symon than have a high-ranking cleric murdered in his town?'

Londres shook his head vehemently. 'No! I was too busy making sure that my plan was going smoothly. And Roger's death is a nuisance, to be frank. It means that people will look more closely at what happened here.'

It had a nasty ring of truth, and Gwenllian found she believed it, although she was sorry to lose Londres as a suspect. All the fight had drained out of him. His shoulders were slumped, his face was grey, and he looked worn and tired.

'I heard that Walter was looking to expand his domain,' he whispered, 'so I told him about our priory's fine wool. And suddenly, there was a letter demanding to know when Cole might be away.'

Gwenllian recalled how she had been suspicious when she had seen Londres and Walter muttering together after the Hempsted party had arrived. She thought they had been oddly familiar with each other, and she had been right. Moreover, Londres' antics explained why he had been challenging Cole's authority and levying more fines over the last few weeks – he had believed his days in Carmarthen were numbered, and was busily making the most of them.

'So you told him about Symon's hunt?' she asked.

Londres nodded. 'And I wrote to Bishop Geoffrey, so he would be here to witness Cole's disgrace. But that is all I did of my own volition. Everything else has been on the orders of Belat and Henry. I am not a traitor. Ask Stacpol. He knows what that pair are like. They are sly and wicked, and I was powerless against them.'

'You accuse Stacpol?' asked Cole dangerously, gripping

the hilt of his sword so that the blade hovered very near to Londres' neck.

'No! I merely suggest that you ask him about Belat and Henry. He knows all about them, although I have no idea what form their previous encounter took.' A tear ran down his cheek. 'What will happen to me now?'

'You are unscrupulous, corrupt and sly,' said Gwenllian icily. 'And you have admitted that the King no longer cares for you, so he will not object if you hang. However, there is a ship leaving for the Low Countries this morning. We will look the other way if you board it and agree never to show your face here again.'

'I will,' gushed Londres in relief. 'I will leave and never return.'

'But there is a condition. I want to know how much Walter paid for the King's writ.'

'Five marks,' replied Londres promptly. 'Belat and Henry arranged it. May I go now?'

Gwenllian and Cole escorted Londres to the ship. It was ready to cast off, and was soon sailing down the river to the sea. The bailiff did not once look back, giving the impression that he was glad his sojourn in Carmarthen was at an end. Or perhaps it was because a small crowd had gathered on the quay, yelling taunts about his spectacular fall from grace.

'Are you sure you are right to let him go?' asked Cole unhappily. 'He might sail straight to John and tell all manner of lies about us.'

'Unlikely. John is not kind to those who let him down, and Londres has failed in what he was charged to do. He will be far too frightened to show his face at Court.'

*

They returned to the castle to find Elidor waiting. Stacpol had not slept in his bed the previous night, and no one had seen him that morning. Elidor was worried.

'Perhaps he has fled,' suggested Gwenllian. 'He refused to reveal the nature of his past association with Belat and Henry, and he knows we *will* solve Asser's murder . . .'

'Then he would have taken his belongings with him,' said Elidor stiffly, not liking the implications of her remark; Cole simply ignored it. 'He has not gone anywhere willingly, My Lady, and I only hope he is safe.'

'I am sure he can look after himself,' said Gwenllian.

'In an honest fight, yes,' agreed Cole. 'But not against sly knives in the back.'

While Cole went to inspect Stacpol's lair to see if he could ascertain why the knight had disappeared, Gwenllian went to the solar, where she found Bishop Geoffrey with the children. He was playing a word game them, to test their Latin. Alys sat on his lap, while the boys clustered around his feet. Gwenllian watched, amazed that the prelate could entertain such an unruly horde with so little effort. When the game was over, they clamoured for another. Geoffrey obliged, and they were so intent on besting him that they barely noticed Cole arrive.

'Do not worry.' Gwenllian smiled at their father's crestfallen face; Alys in particular always ran to him when he appeared. 'Geoffrey is new and interesting, and has sweetmeats to dispense. They will still be clamouring for a bedtime story from you tonight.'

Cole sniffed. 'I think he should go back on your list of potential killers.'

Gwenllian laughed, and went with him to the priory, to interview the monks and lay brothers again. But it was a fruitless morning. Walter claimed he was too busy to be bothered with such nonsense, but ordered Gilbert to ensure that his people were not browbeaten. Gwenllian disliked the dark presence at her elbow, and tried various ploys to make Gilbert leave. None worked, and the sub-prior stuck with them like a leech. She was relieved when the last Hempsted man had been questioned, and they were able to escape.

They met Cadifor in the yard. He was uncharacteristically subdued, which he confessed was due to concern about how to repay the bishop's loan of ten marks – double the five that Walter had paid the King. His wool fetched good prices, but that year's money had already been earmarked for other things, and it would not be easy to raise such an enormous sum.

'And what if John takes the money, but refuses to honour the arrangement?' he asked worriedly. 'Walter has powerful supporters, and his demands will carry more weight than mine. Moreover, John will not want to annoy a wealthy place like Hempsted, knowing that it is far more likely to make him generous gifts than poor Carmarthen.'

Gwenllian had no answer, because Cadifor was right. She left Cole to interrogate Walter's soldiers, and wandered away, watching Belat and Henry sitting together in the winter sunlight. They returned her gaze with smug arrogance, but declined to be drawn into conversation, even when she informed them that Londres had revealed all before fleeing.

Belat shrugged. 'If he is no longer here, he cannot speak against us. And what value is the word of a corrupt official, anyway? Your bailiff is a scoundrel, and there is not a man, woman or child in Carmarthen who will say otherwise.'

*

Visiting the priory had been a waste of time, and Cole was disheartened as he and Gwenllian began to walk back to the castle. He stopped when he reached the woods that separated the priory from the town.

'I know you are there,' he called. 'And you are eager to talk to me, or you would not be dogging my footsteps. Well, I am ready to listen, so show yourself.'

Nothing happened, and he was about to walk on when the leaves parted and a youth stepped out. He was an Austin, but his robes were torn, his face was smeared with mud and his hair was matted. He was shivering, and looked miserable.

'Come,' said Cole kindly. 'There is hot soup, dry clothes and a fire at the castle.'

'I will be seen,' whispered the boy, glancing both ways along the track with frightened eyes. 'I cannot go with you.'

'Seen by whom?' asked Cole, but the lad only stared at the ground and would not reply. 'Here is my cloak. Wrap it around you, and cover your face with the hood. You will be safe with me, I promise.'

The youth hesitated, but the prospect of warmth and food was too tempting to resist. He drew the cloak around him, then trotted obediently after them to the castle. They took him to the office, where Cole grimaced when he heard Alys and the bishop singing together. It was a song he had taught her, but it sounded better with Geoffrey's tenor than his toneless bass. The Austin ate three bowls of stew, and when he had finished, Gwenllian indicated that he was to start talking.

'I am Oswin,' the lad obliged. 'From Llanthony. I was a novice when Martin was killed, but I have taken my vows since, so I am now a canon. I overheard the argument in

Martin's solar when Walter declared Hempsted's independence. And I know a secret, which I have only ever revealed to one other person . . .'

'Who?' asked Cole suspiciously.

'I would rather not say. But I can tell you that I shared it for the first time last night.'

'Why not before?'

'Because I was frightened. However, when I heard that Walter intended to steal Carmarthen, I tried to arrive first, to warn Cadifor. But Walter had horses while I was obliged to travel on foot, and I arrived to find that Walter had beaten me by an hour. It was all for nothing.'

'Yet you believe that something might still be salvaged, or you would have gone home,' surmised Cole. 'I have seen you several times, lurking in the bushes.'

Oswin smiled wanly. 'My adventures on the way here have taught me how to hide myself, although you almost caught me.'

'You say you came to warn Cadifor.' Gwenllian spoke quickly, lest Cole should distract him by offering practical tips on evading pursuers. 'About what? Walter's plans?'

'No – about the fact that a murderer is at large.'

'You know who killed Asser and Roger?' demanded Cole eagerly. 'Who?'

'The same man who poisoned Martin. And I was right to be concerned, given that Roger and your knight died in suspicious circumstances.'

'How do you know Martin was poisoned?' asked Gwenllian sceptically. 'We have been told that there was no proof.'

'Because I was with him when he died.' Oswin's voice was unsteady. 'It was my turn to act as his servant, you see, and I was in his solar, dousing candles and closing the shutters.

He was sitting at his table, grumbling about Walter's high-handed tactics while he scoffed marchpanes. Then he stopped talking . . .'

'And?' prompted Gwenllian.

'I went to see if he was unwell. His eyes were closed, so I shook his arm. He woke, but it was an effort, and it was then that he told me the marchpanes had been dosed with a powerful soporific. I did not believe him at first, but he was insistent . . . I wanted to fetch help, but he would not let me – he knew he would be dead before I came back.'

'What else did he say?' asked Gwenllian urgently.

'That the sin of sloth had caused Llanthony to lose Hempsted, which was true – if he had written to the Pope, we would still have a daughter house. Then he told me that a visitor had killed him. It was no one from Llanthony, because we had no almonds. The gift of poisoned marchpanes had come from a guest.'

'Then why did you not report all this to your superiors?' asked Cole. 'Straight away?'

'Would *you* accuse high-ranking Austins and two royal clerks?' asked Oswin archly. He looked Cole up and down. 'Well, perhaps you might, but I was little more than a boy.'

'A high-ranking Austin?' pounced Gwenllian. 'Not one of the ordinary canons who accompanied him?'

'Martin specifically said that his killer was high ranking,' replied Oswin firmly. 'Which means Walter, Gilbert, Belat or Henry. All four of them wanted him dead, so that Roger could be appointed instead – Martin could be stubborn, but Roger is weak and malleable.' He looked miserably at his shoes. 'Martin's death has gnawed at my conscience ever since.'

'It has not gnawed too hard, or you would have done something about it sooner,' remarked Cole.

Oswin winced. 'I told you – I was afraid. But I have done something now: I came all the way here on my own, hoping to prevent another death. I failed, but not for want of trying.'

'What made you think someone else would die?' asked Gwenllian.

Oswin shivered, despite the warmth of the fire. 'The fact that those four "high-ranking" men went to Llanthony on their way here, and ordered Roger to accompany them. Why do that? It made no sense. I could tell they were planning something untoward, because they kept talking in low voices, scheming and plotting . . .'

'They brought him as a hostage, to ensure Llanthony did nothing against Hempsted while its two most powerful monks were away,' explained Gwenllian. 'And of course they were scheming and plotting – they aimed to invade a sister house and claim it for themselves.'

'Then why did they not say so?' demanded Oswin.

Gwenllian smiled at his innocence. 'It is hardly something they could announce, and I am sure your older brethren understood exactly what was happening. Did you talk to any of them before you left?'

'No, because they would have stopped me – or asked me what I knew about Martin's death, which I dare not share with them now. They would never trust me again!'

Gwenllian stood. 'I had better rescue the bishop before Alys drives him to distraction. That must be the twentieth time they have sung that song.'

She ushered Oswin out, and told Iefan to find him somewhere to sleep.

'Damn,' muttered Cole when sergeant and Austin had gone. 'I had eliminated Walter and Gilbert from your list, but now they are suspects again.'

'Only if you believe Oswin's tale,' said Gwenllian.

Cole blinked. 'You do not?'

'I am not sure, Symon. He has kept his guilty secret for three years, and it is odd that he should break his silence now – not once, but twice in as many days. And why does he refuse to tell us who else he has confided in?'

'So what shall we do about his confession – such as it is?'

'There is only one thing we can do: speak again to Walter, Gilbert, Belat and Henry, to see if we can catch them out in an inconsistency. But do not be too hopeful. They have sharp minds, and will not be easy to trip up.'

'You are more than their equal,' said Cole confidently.

Gwenllian asked Bishop Geoffrey to accompany them to the priory, feeling his presence would be a calming influence. They arrived to find Walter with his hand to his stomach, but the lines of pain around his mouth lessened once Geoffrey had requisitioned ingredients from the kitchen to make a soothing tincture, and it was not long before the colour returned to his cheeks.

'You should rest more,' said the prelate admonishingly. 'Take some time to appreciate what God has given you, instead of racing around trying to acquire more.'

Walter shot him an unpleasant look, then refused to answer any of the questions Gwenllian or Cole put. Gilbert followed his example, and they sat side by side with their arms folded and their lips sealed shut. Eventually, Cole threw up his hands in exasperation.

'Perhaps I should arrest you both, and keep you incarcerated until your Prior General tells me who is guilty of killing Roger and Asser.'

'And Martin.' Geoffrey regarded the two canons sternly.

'Symon and Gwenllian are trying to help, and if you have nothing to hide, you need not fear their investigation.'

'We do not fear it,' said Walter coldly. 'We just do not accept their authority to interrogate senior members of the Church. And now, if there is nothing else, we have business to attend.'

He stalked out, Gilbert loping at his heels, and their unwillingness to co-operate served to put them firmly at the top of Gwenllian's list of suspects. After all, why would they be obstructive if they had nothing to hide?

'Let us hope we have more success with Belat and Henry,' said Cole.

He asked a passing lay brother to fetch them, but it was not long before the man returned to report that the two clerks were nowhere to be found. A search of the priory revealed that they had gone, taking all their possessions with them.

'First, Stacpol, now, them,' murmured Gwenllian.

'Stacpol did not take his belongings,' Cole pointed out. He turned to address the monks who had gathered to find out what was happening. 'Who saw them last?'

'Probably me,' replied Cadifor. 'They were in the stables at dawn, but it did not occur to me that they planned to disappear. I assumed they were just checking their horses.'

'I overheard them whispering together shortly before that,' added Dafydd, 'when I went to start up the bread ovens. I am fairly sure they had been outside the priory, and had just come back in – which was odd, given the hour. I heard Belat mention "an Austin in the bushes", although I have no idea what he meant.'

'Oswin,' surmised Gwenllian. 'They must have spotted him, and realised that he would not have made such a journey without good reason. Their guilty consciences led them to flee before there was trouble. So there are our killers, Symon. Will you go after them?'

Cole returned to the castle, and quickly organised patrols to hunt along each of the main roads. He thought it most likely that the pair were aiming for Brecon, so decided to search that track himself. He was just taking his leave of Gwenllian when Oswin approached.

'So it was Belat and Henry who killed Prior Martin?' the lad asked softly.

'We believe so,' replied Gwenllian. 'It seems they spotted you hiding in the undergrowth, and knew the game was up. They fled before they were caught.'

Oswin frowned. 'They did see me, but they thought I was one of Cadifor's canons, sent to spy on them. They were furious, and gave chase. They would have trounced me if that knight had not come to my rescue and . . .' Oswin trailed off, his expression one of dismay.

'What knight?' asked Cole. Oswin did not reply, so he stepped forward threateningly.

'Stacpol,' blurted Oswin. He rubbed his eyes miserably. 'He was kind to me, and I promised myself that I would keep his name out of this vile business. I do not know who to trust here, and I did not want to repay his goodness by putting his life in danger.'

'So he was the other person you told about Martin's death?' asked Gwenllian. 'The one whose identity you declined to reveal earlier?'

Tears brimmed in Oswin's eyes. 'I found myself confiding in him after he saved me from Belat and Henry. He told me to tell you – he said that Lady Gwenllian would know what to do. But I was afraid for his safety . . .'

So that was what the lad had been concealing, thought Gwenllian. It was nothing more than a desire to protect a man who had been kind to him.

'So where is he now?' demanded Cole.

'I do not know. He saw me safely hidden, then went about his business. However, I think he may have gone after those two clerks . . .'

Cole's face was anxious as he strode towards the stables, but there was a clatter of hoofs, and a horseman rode through the gate. It was Stacpol, and behind him staggered Belat and Henry, their hands bound and fastened to his saddle with long pieces of rope. They were bedraggled and exhausted, but still able to blare an indignant tirade.

'We cannot be treated this way!' Belat was howling. 'The King will hear of this.'

'Yes,' said Stacpol grimly, dismounting. 'He will. I have stayed silent long enough about you and your vile misdeeds.'

'Be careful what you say, Stacpol,' hissed Henry. 'The King does not deal gently with those who break their oath of allegiance to him.'

Stacpol addressed Cole and Gwenllian. 'This pair have been defrauding religious houses for years. My oath to King John – who ordered me to turn a blind eye to their activities – prevented me from exposing them in Llanthony, but when I saw them here, I appealed to Bishop Geoffrey. He has released me from my vow, so now I am free to speak.'

The blood drained from Belat's face, while Henry glanced at the gate, as if wondering whether he could dart through it and escape.

Cole frowned. 'Are you saying that the King knows what they do and condones it?'

'I doubt he knows the details,' replied Stacpol. 'But coins are deposited in his coffers every so often, and he asks no questions. However, when the antics of this pair are made public, he will hasten to deny all knowledge of them. He is not a fool.'

'What have they done?' asked Cole. 'Exactly?'

Stacpol began to relate a long list of sly, devious crimes that had deprived monasteries and convents of money. The bishop's secretarius wrote everything down, and the two clerks, snivelling and frightened, were taken into Geoffrey's custody, to stand trial in the ecclesiastical courts. Other secular officials might have argued about jurisdiction, but Cole was glad the matter was to be taken out of his hands.

'I wronged you,' said Gwenllian to Stacpol, when everyone else had gone. 'I thought you were working with them.'

'You had good cause,' replied Stacpol sombrely. 'Unfortunately, I pledged myself to do John's bidding before I realised what kind of man he was – which is why I accepted a post in the westernmost reaches of his kingdom. He never comes here, and I am away from his malign demands. But all has been put right now.'

'Not quite. We still do not know who poisoned the marchpanes. Was it them?'

'No,' replied Stacpol. 'They wanted Roger alive, because he represented easy prey. I wish they were the killers – Asser was my friend, and I want vengeance.'

Gwenllian was about to suggest to Cole that they sit quietly and review what they had learned that day, when Dafydd waddled through the gate.

'You must come to the priory, quickly,' he gasped. 'Prior Walter is dying.'

*

Gwenllian did not think Walter was dying, although he lay in a bed in the guesthouse, surrounded by canons and clerks, busily issuing instructions as to what should be done with his worldly goods when he was in his grave. Geoffrey started to step forward with more of his remedy, but Gwenllian rested her hand on his arm to stop him.

'Wait,' she whispered. 'Let us see what he will disclose if he believes his end is near.'

The bishop gazed at her. 'That would be ruthless – and unworthy of a healer.'

'Yes,' she admitted. 'But I believe he is a killer, and I would like a confession for Stacpol's sake. Asser was his friend.'

Geoffrey's amiable face was deeply unhappy, but he stood aside and indicated that she was to approach the bed. Cole went, too.

'Good,' breathed Walter weakly. He snapped his fingers at his retinue. 'Leave us. You, too, Gilbert. What I have to say is for the constable, his wife and Bishop Geoffrey only.'

Gilbert's expression was dangerous, and there was a moment when Gwenllian thought he would refuse to go, but he bowed curtly, and followed the others outside.

'Well?' she asked of Walter. 'What do you want to tell us?'

Walter addressed the bishop. 'I made a mistake by demanding Hempsted's independence. When I am dead, I want you to get the decision repealed. And do not let Gilbert succeed me – he is unfit to rule.'

'I shall do as you request,' promised Geoffrey. 'Is that all?'

'No. I resign as Prior of Hempsted. As of now, I am just a simple canon, which should work in my favour when my soul is weighed. I should not like the saints to consider me vain.'

'Your resignation is accepted,' said Geoffrey gravely. 'I

shall inform the Prior General immediately. Do you renounce your claim on Carmarthen, too?'

'I cannot – not now the King has issued that writ. I am afraid it will have to become a cell of Hempsted. But it should fare well enough if you keep Gilbert away from it.'

'Why did you summon me?' asked Cole. 'What crimes do you want to confess?'

Walter eyed him coolly. 'I may not have lived a blameless life, but I have done nothing to interest a constable. The reason I called you here is to witness a few deeds for me, ones I do not want the other canons to know about. They are private, you see.'

Cole gaped at him. 'You dragged us here to help with your personal affairs? I thought you were going to tell us who killed Martin, Roger and Asser!'

Walter grimaced irritably. 'I will – after you have helped me with these deeds.'

Cole turned sharply on his heel. 'Good day, Prior Walter. You are—'

'Wait!' Walter sighed gustily. 'Very well. We shall discuss murder first, if we must. I am not the culprit – I am dying, and I am not so foolish as to stain my soul now. And despite what I might have said before, Cadifor is innocent, too. I ordered him watched, as I considered him a danger to my plans. He did not poison the marchpanes.'

'So we have eliminated Londres, Belat, Henry, Walter, Cadifor, Stacpol and the bishop,' said Cole, oblivious to Geoffrey's surprise that he should have been on such a list. 'There is only one suspect left: Gilbert. No wonder you do not want him to succeed you!'

'That is not the reason,' said Walter. 'It is because I just caught him tampering with my medicine. I have been ailing for years, and *he* is the reason why. He confessed it all just now – he has been poisoning me, because he likes being my right-hand man. He thinks I would not need him if I was hale and hearty.'

'So Oswin was wrong,' mused Gwenllian. 'He thought you, Gilbert and the clerks were plotting murder when you huddled together. Instead, you were merely planning your assault on Carmarthen.'

'Oswin?' asked Walter. 'Who is he?'

Gwenllian supposed she should be glad that Gilbert was under lock and key, but the whole affair had been distasteful, and she was in a sombre mood as she sat in the solar that night. Gilbert had screeched, fought and spat when he was arrested, and everyone had been relieved when the cell door had been closed on his curses. Walter had been equally abusive when he had learned he was not dying after all, and that he would make a complete recovery once he stopped taking whatever Gilbert had been feeding him – especially now that he no longer needed to bear the strain of running Hempsted.

'He was livid,' mused Cole. 'I thought he was going to explode.'

He spoke absently, because he was watching Geoffrey teach Alys a game that involved a long piece of twine and a knife. Her brothers were in bed, but she had claimed more bad dreams in a brazen attempt to secure extra time with the adults. Her ploy had worked, because first Cole and then Geoffrey had fussed over her.

Gwenllian smiled. 'It serves him right for including Carmarthen on his list of conquests. All I hope is that the King will accept the bribe of ten marks from Cadifor.'

'He will,' predicted Geoffrey wryly. 'But the money must be

presented to him directly. Cadifor will need a lot more if he recruits corrupt clerks to help him – men like Belat and Henry, who will demand a sizeable commission for themselves.'

Alys began to drowse on his knee. The bishop stared at the fire, rubbing the table with the knife, an unconscious gesture akin to the random scribbles Gwenllian made with ink when she was pondering the castle accounts. But Geoffrey's scraping made a faint pattern in the wax coating, and it was one that Gwenllian had seen before. Her stomach lurched in horror.

'Oh, no!' she breathed. 'The killer made marks like that when the marchpanes were poisoned. We saw them etched on the table in the priory kitchen.'

Geoffrey glanced at the scratches as if seeing them for the first time. 'What?'

'It was you,' said Gwenllian, standing slowly, and acutely aware that the prelate was holding her daughter. Cole was frozen in mute horror. 'You poisoned the marchpanes. You know all about soporifics, because you are interested in medicine.'

'I am,' acknowledged Geoffrey. 'But I use my knowledge to heal, not to harm. Besides, I did not reach the priory until after Asser was dead. I had no opportunity to tamper with them.'

'Yes, you did – when Dafydd first gave them to you,' said Gwenllian. 'You ate half and poisoned the rest.'

'But that was before Walter arrived,' objected Geoffrey. 'How could I know that he and his entourage would appear the following day?'

'Because Londres wrote to tell you,' replied Gwenllian. 'He admitted it before he left. I should have guessed that there was a reason for your visit: you never usually travel in

January, when the roads are poor – you come at Easter. But you made an exception this year, because you wanted to be here when Walter arrived.'

'But why would I—'

'You knew no one at the monastery would touch the sweetmeats, as they would not want to incur Dafydd's wrath. But Roger was a greedy man, and you guessed he would visit the kitchen and take what he fancied. Unfortunately, you reckoned without Asser.'

Cole found his voice at last, but it was unsteady. 'Asser knew what you had done. With his dying breath, he whispered the words that you had etched on Martin's coffin, and he told me to look for the "incongruously sharp knife". Alys, come here.'

'Everyone has sharp knives,' said Geoffrey, tightening his grip on the sleeping child. 'Including you.'

'Yes, and that was Asser's point,' said Cole. 'He told us to look for the *incongruously* sharp one – no churchman should need a blade with as keen an edge as the one you are holding now. Please be careful it. My daughter is only—'

'It is for slicing bandages,' explained Geoffrey. 'A blunt one is no good.'

'It does not matter why you have it,' said Gwenllian. 'The point is that you are a monk, and Asser thought it was a peculiar thing for you to have. He must have seen the scratches when he stole the marchpane, and he, unlike us, realised their significance when he fell ill.'

'If Asser thought I was a killer, why did he not just say so?' asked Geoffrey with quiet reason. 'These riddles make no sense.'

Cole's eyes were fixed on Alys and the knife; Gwenllian had never seen him so white. 'He knew you were nearby, and that you would deny it,' Cole said, his voice unsteady. 'He spoke in code, certain that Gwenllian would work it out. Please release my daughter.'

'Stay away!' Geoffrey brought the knife to rest on the pale, soft skin of the girl's neck. Alys shifted in her sleep but did not wake. Cole retreated until his back was against the wall, holding his hands in front of him in a gesture of surrender.

'Asser was an accident, but Roger was not,' said Gwenllian, aiming to distract the bishop for the split second it would take Cole to leap forward. 'When Roger was dead, you removed the plate from the kitchen, and brushed the crumbs from his habit and the floor. You expected his demise to be deemed natural.'

'It might have been,' snapped Geoffrey, breaking at last, 'if your greedy friend had not eaten the damned things, too.'

His angry voice woke Alys, and confusion filled her face as she tried to sit up and found she could not move. She did not struggle, but only looked at Cole in mute appeal.

'And I know why you did it,' said Gwenllian. 'You killed Martin for losing Hempsted, and you dispatched Roger for failing to ensure that Walter did his duty. They were—'

'Sloth,' said Geoffrey bitterly. 'The deadliest of sins. I hoped the words I etched on Martin's coffin would warn others, but Roger ignored them and so did Walter. And as I said last night, sloth is not laziness, but a sluggishness of the mind that neglects to do good, oppressing the soul and drawing it away from noble deeds. Martin and Roger were indolent men, and thus unsuitable for running priories.'

'Martin was right,' said Cole, taking a tiny step forward. 'He confided to Oswin that his killer was a high-ranking Austin or a clerk. Oswin thought he meant Walter or Gilbert, but you are also an Austin.'

Gwenllian began to gabble to distract the bishop when Cole inched forward again. 'You told us that you had no remedies with you, but what healer travels without the tools of his trade? Of course you had them – and you poisoned the marchpanes. Your claim to have no medicines was a ruse, so that you would not be a suspect.'

'Please,' begged Cole, as Geoffrey stood abruptly and began to move towards the door. 'She is a child. If you want a hostage, take me.'

Geoffrey laughed without humour. 'I think Alys will be rather easier to control. Now, I am going to lock you in, collect my people and ride away. Your daughter will come with us, but no harm will come to her as long as you stay here and do not raise the alarm.'

'How do we know?' asked Cole in a strangled voice. 'You are a killer.'

'Because I give you my word,' replied Geoffrey. 'Give me yours that you will not follow, and she will be returned to you unharmed. Refuse, and I will slit her throat.'

Cole and Gwenllian could see he meant it, and there was nothing they could do as Geoffrey walked out, taking their daughter with him.

The uncertainty of the next few days was dreadful, but Geoffrey kept his promise. Alys appeared one morning in the arms of a bemused cleric, who had been instructed to take her to the castle. She was tired, dirty and bewildered, but none the worse for her experiences. Cadifor and Stacpol were there to witness the family reunion.

'He let me ride in front of him,' Alys said, as Cole snatched her up and hugged her so tightly that Gwenllian feared he might hurt her. 'All the way to Llansteffan. It was fun, but I would rather ride with you. You do not bounce around so much.'

Cole called for his horse, aiming to hunt the bishop down, but Gwenllian laid her hand on his arm. 'This is a battle we cannot win, Symon. Leave it to Gilbert. He has offered to take the tale to the King, and the less we are involved, the better.'

'Gilbert!' spat Cole. 'A man who dosed his friend with "remedies" that made him think he was dying – for years. I hardly think he is someone we can trust to tell the truth.'

'But we can trust him to keep our names from this affair,' argued Stacpol. 'Which is ultimately more important. I learned from Belat that Gilbert cheated the King of some of his taxes while he was Sacrist of Hempsted, so he will want us as far away from Westminster as possible, lest the secret slips out.'

'Yes, let the matter go, Symon,' begged Cadifor. 'We do not want to become entangled in these webs of deceit.'

'On one condition,' said Cole. 'That you do not repay the ten marks Geoffrey lent you to bribe the King. It will be retribution of a sort, because he did mention that not having it would be inconvenient.'

Cadifor grinned. 'It will be my pleasure.'

'Even so,' said Cole unhappily, 'it will be difficult to live with the knowledge that Geoffrey wanders around freely and merrily while Asser lies dead.'

'He has bad dreams, just like me,' piped up Alys. 'He wakes up in the night and howls that the Devil is coming for him. And then he cries himself back to sleep.'

'So he might wander freely,' said Stacpol softly. 'But not merrily. His conscience will see to that. Thank you, Alys.'

'Moreover, he is unpopular with the people,' added Gwenllian. 'His inability to speak Welsh has turned many against him, so his pontificate will not be an easy one. And he will always be wondering whether he will be accused of murder. That is punishment enough.'

'If you say so.' Cole watched Alys scamper away to join her brothers. 'Yet he did teach me something – that it is a sin not to appreciate the good things we have been given. Shall we all go riding? It is a glorious day, and I feel like being outside.'

'What, now?' asked Gwenllian, startled. 'What about the castle accounts, and the plans for the new gatehouse?'

'What about them?' Cole laughed suddenly. 'We have a family, good friends and we live in paradise. Let us enjoy it while we can.'

He strode towards the stable to saddle up his horse, and as he went he began to sing.

Historical Note

Symon Cole was constable of Carmarthen in the early 1200s, and Lord Rhys of Deheubarth had several daughters named Gwenllian. Richard Belat and Henry de Rolveston were royal clerks, who went to Carmarthen to conduct John's business in 1203. Other 'locals' mentioned in the Welsh Episcopal Acts in the early 1200s are Elidor, Asser and Philipp de Stacpol.

Llanthony Priory was a dangerous place to be during the Anarchy of the mid-twelfth century, so the Austin canons fled to Hempsted, Gloucestershire, to wait the troubles out. However, when it came time to return, some elected to stay behind to form a cell known as Llanthony Secunda (called Hempsted in the story, for simplicity's sake). By the early

1200s, it was as strong and rich as its parent, so it was decided to separate them.

Geoffrey de Henlaw had been prior of both, and oversaw some of the preliminary arrangements for the partition, before he was elevated to the Bishopric of St David's in 1203. He was noted for his medical skills, but Gerald of Wales wrote that he was greedy, violent and corrupt. Geoffrey's successor was Martin, who was replaced by Roger in 1205. The first independent prior of Llanthony Secunda was Walter, who ruled for two years before Gilbert took over.

In 1208, Hempsted decided to expand by laying claim to Carmarthen Priory. The King's blessing was obtained, after which William de Londres, the town's bailiff, led a takeover bid. Carmarthen was naturally indignant, and Prior Cadifor offered John a bribe of ten marks if he changed his allegiance. John seized the money with alacrity, and wrote to Bishop Geoffrey, ordering him to restore Carmarthen's independence.

Interlude

By the time the fourth story, the tale of Sloth, was over and done with, the last traces of the stormy summer light were long gone from the sky. There was no question of listening to any tales of the three deadly sins that still remained out of the seven. Why, to do so, the band of listeners would have had to stay awake and attentive until the sun was rising once more on the other side of the sky! Laurence promised that there would be plenty of time for them to hear about pride and anger and envy on the next day. No one dissented. None of the travellers expressed the wish to get on with their journey at first light. Providentially, it was a Sunday, so the pilgrims would be able to attend St Mary's, to receive the blessing of the local priest and distract the local people of Mundham with their different clothes and accents. In church, they could meditate on the stories they'd heard so far and contemplate their own sinfulness – or, no doubt in the case of a few of the pilgrims, their own worthiness.

Once the pilgrims, tired but satisfied, were ushered by lantern-light to their bedchambers in the Angel tavern, and once Laurence and his wife had attended to the inevitable little niggles, gripes and requests from such a diverse group, the innkeeper rubbed his hands. Excellent, he thought. He reckoned that this Walsingham band was good for another night at the Angel. The weather promised (and he meant, promised) to be just as bad tomorrow. There were three stories yet to be told. The inn was comfortable. There was every incentive for the travellers to stay one more day and night. And Laurence's reasons weren't entirely commercial. He had a story of his own to tell and he planned to be the first of the speakers in the second half . . .

THE FIFTH SIN

Laurence, the innkeeper of the Angel, gazed around with satisfaction. To a man and woman, the Walsingham pilgrims were wearing the well-fed and contented looks he liked to see on the faces of his guests. They had attended the local church, St Mary's. They had exhausted the (not very many) possibilities provided by the little town of Mundham. They had returned to the Angel to eat and drink, and to enjoy a further session of storytelling. Every single one of them, even the hatchet-faced Prior. They were his for another night, especially while the rain continued to pour down drearily outside and the draughts rattled at the shutters. Again the fire in the main hall of the Angel was lit.

Despite the dark, sometimes violent, nature of the stories that they'd listened to on the previous evening, their expressions suggested they were ready for more. More darkness and more sin. Human beings were strange creatures, he reflected. Even when threatened by a pestilence that might wipe them from the face of the earth, they occupied the little time remaining not in prayer but in listening to tales of evil, sin and death.

And, of course, who had suggested this diversion but Laurence himself?

Now it was his turn. He was conscious of the ring of faces looking expectantly at him. He took a slow, appreciative sip from his bowl of wine and cleared his throat.

'Anger is my theme now,' he said, 'and it is right that anger should follow sloth, for sometimes the only way to get a lazy person, a slothful individual, off his fat arse and going about his duty is to grow angry with him – or her. If I find a stable boy asleep when he should be taking charge of a traveller's horse, or if my wife notices that the girl has not replaced the stale rushes on the floor here with fresh ones, then we may grow angry with the offender, for all our mild tempers. I tell you I'd rather be on the receiving end of my own anger than my wife's. You should see her when she's worked up! Yet who is to say that my wife and I are wrong to feel such anger, and to give voice to it?'

A few of the listeners nodded. Perhaps they were remembering occasions when they had chastised their servants or husbands or wives. The landlord of the Angel pressed on.

'What we feel in such cases is surely a righteous anger. And, if I may say it without impiety, this is the faintest shadow of what God Himself feels as He surveys the bogs and fens of human wickedness. Indeed, we must believe that behind the pestilence itself lies God's justified and righteous wrath.

'But I am going to tell you a story of an anger that is quite different from this. There may have been some justification to it in the beginning, but it was bred in the shadows and fed daily with thoughts of vengeance until it grew to a full-sized monster that devoured all around it before turning on its creator. The story I am about to tell you, ladies and gentlemen, is true and it took place not so very far from this little town and not so very many years ago either. It was during that time of shortages and suffering when the father of our Edward III was on the throne. When it seemed as though Noah's flood had come again, and without a rainbow for deliverance. Looking round I can see that scarcely any of you are old enough to remember those days . . .'

In saying this, the landlord was merely flattering his audience. Several murmured at the unhappy memories. Yes, they did recall those days, thirty years ago and more, when the sun never shone and the rain never stopped. With crops failing, bellies went unfilled, and no dog or cat was safe from the quick hands and hungry teeth of the poor. There had even been tales of parents driven mad by the pangs of hunger who killed and devoured their own children. Such terrible things had never happened in the teller's own village, mind you, but they were reported on good authority by a cousin of a cousin or heard from the mouth of a travelling pedlar.

'We must pray to Almighty God,' said the landlord, 'that he delivers us from our present troubles as he delivered us from our woes these many years past.' He waited for the heartfelt 'Amens' to die down, before resuming his tale of . . .

Anger

Like any storyteller, I have to name names and places, too, and because the people are real and, in some cases, still alive, I must sometimes rein in my tongue. Yet believe what I say. In a village called Wenham a few miles distant from here, there once lived a family called the Carters. The land they held as tenants adjoined fields that were farmed by another family, the Raths. The heads of these families were William Carter and Alfred Rath. These families were the two most important ones in the village, leaving aside the people who lived at the manor. And they were absent most of the time attending to their other properties. The Carters and the Raths had once been friends, not good friends, perhaps, but good enough for the working day. Even if it was only self-interest, they helped each other when times were bad and they were glad together in moments of prosperity. Then something happened that turned all this goodwill into sourness.

No one is quite sure what started it. By the time I was aware of the bad feeling, it had already begun. Perhaps some cows belonging to William blundered across Alfred's cornfield and caused a few pennies' worth of damage, or maybe some of Alfred's sheep trespassed on William's pasture. I've also heard that it began with a dispute over a wagon that Alfred Rath had lent to William Carter when they were on better terms. When the wagon was returned in a damaged state, the borrower refused to admit his responsibility but claimed he'd received it in that dilapidated condition.

These cases went to the manor court where both men were fined. Yet honour was far from satisfied, because one man's fine was larger than the other's, so of course the one who'd got off more lightly went round proclaiming victory while his neighbour complained about unfair treatment.

Now, ladies and gentlemen, in such cases it must go one of two ways. Either the disputation and bad feeling gradually die down until things have returned, perhaps not to the old easy and friendly relations, but at least to mutual tolerance. Or things go from bad to worse, with every word or action seen in the most unfriendly light. A reported remark or a casual gesture causes fists to clench and curses to be uttered. Plain accidents or misfortunes, like the sickness of livestock or a chance fire in a barn, are blamed on the old friends even if the evidence runs right against it. So it was with the Carters and the Raths. They lived and worked alongside each other but one family might as well have been on the moon for all they wanted to have anything to do with the other. Then something happened that forced both families together . . . a crime that couldn't help but drag in the two sides . . .

But first, I'd better say a little about the people in this tale. I can remember them clearly, you see, although I was a boy. William Carter was a lanky fellow, who kept himself to himself. He was a touchy man, a choleric one. Everyone knew him for a miser and hoarder. Nothing unusual in that, maybe, but William was the kind of person who'd keep his nail parings, not to prevent a witch getting hold of them, but in case there was a sudden market in nail parings. William Carter's wife, Alice, was almost as tall as he and she had a beaky nose and close-set eyes, which made her look like a handsome bird. It pains me to say this about her, God rest her soul, but she was something of a snob. Her uncle was a priest, you see, and it was whispered that she was actually his daughter rather than his niece. If her husband was silent and watchful, she was a great talker and a gossip.

As for the Raths . . . they were not aloof and they didn't put on airs like the Carters. On the surface, they seemed friendly enough. Alfred Rath was a small man with a round face and cheery manner, though there was a streak of malice in him and he had a wandering eye. His wife, Joan, was a plain woman and strong in her own fashion. She knew her own mind. While her neighbour Alice Carter gossiped in a way that some might say was mean-spirited, Joan looked out for the goodness in people, even when there was very little goodness to be found. Joan Rath had a cousin who was a doctor of physic, Thomas Flytte, and you could say that he is central to the story, because of what happened.

But before I say anything about Flytte, I need to tell you of the incident that turned the hostility between the Carters and the Raths into hatred. It happened towards the end of a wet, gusty market day in the village. Business had finished early on account of the rain – it was always raining then, remember – and the stall-holders were in the alehouse drinking away their meagre takings. There were quite a few of the villagers there as well, including William Carter and Alfred Rath. They were on opposite sides of the room, of course. Didn't even acknowledge each other's existence.

Suddenly, a woman burst in and announced to the world that she had lost her purse on the outskirts of Wenham. She said it was missing from her belt. Missing, not stolen, because she'd been walking alone and no one had been near her. The spot where it probably happened was at the junction of Nether Way and Church Lane, where she'd had to jump aside to avoid a great pool of water. She'd gone back to look for it but without success. There wasn't much money in the purse, but it had value for her because it had been her mother's. All this news came out in a single gushing flow, like the rainwater pouring off the eaves of the alehouse. She was obviously in distress, but nobody cared much. I don't know whether she expected the alehouse to empty out while its occupants went into the rain to help search the place where the two lanes met but, if so, she was to be disappointed. Nobody moved and there were more shrugged shoulders than expressions of sympathy.

After a moment, Alfred Rath remarked in a casual voice but one still loud enough to be heard by everyone in the room that he was sure he'd seen his neighbour William Carter earlier that morning standing at the corner of Nether Way and Church Lane. Perhaps William could help in this matter? William Carter looked startled but didn't deny he'd been there. As I've said, there was a streak of malice in Alfred Rath and, realising he had the advantage, he started to add colour to his story. Yes, he said, scratching his head as if to aid his memory, he had definitely seen his neighbour stooping and peering as if in search of some item that he'd dropped. Furthermore, he'd witnessed him pick something up and put it in his pocket.

The woman made for Master William, relief on her face. 'Oh, do you have it, sir? I shall be eternally grateful if you do,' she said. 'It was my mother's purse, hinged it is, and made of wool and silk. You can have the coins inside as reward but I would dearly miss that purse.'

William Carter looked uneasy, as though he was indeed guilty of picking up the woman's purse. He hadn't denied any part of Rath's account, not searching the muddy ground nor slipping something into his pocket. Spots of red glowed in his cheeks. He glanced round at the ring of faces, all waiting for an explanation. It was obvious that he had to say something. He cast a glance of pure hatred in the direction of Alfred Rath. Eventually, he fumbled under his cloak and brought out from beneath it . . . a short length of rope.

'Here you are,' he said, and there was a mixture of anger and embarrassment in his tone. 'This is what I picked up at the corner of Nether Way and Church Lane.'

He held up the pitiful fragment of rope so that everyone in the alehouse might see it. There were titters and sly comments. Someone said the rope was too short even for a noose. Indeed, it was too short for any practical purpose. The whole piece would have been used up by the act of tying a knot in it. It must have been cut from a longer length for tying a bale or leading a packhorse, and discarded in the road as worthless. But most people were aware of William Carter's hoarding habits. He couldn't help himself. He'd bent down for the rope and tucked it under his cloak out of instinct. And now that instinct was making him look miserly and petty in the eyes of the villagers. With another furious glance at Alfred Rath, he strode out of the alehouse, flinging the length of rope to the floor as he went.

A few of the more thoughtful customers might have felt a little sorry for Carter. Even I felt sorry for him, a boy, not daring to show my face but tucked away out of sight in a corner of the alehouse. He wasn't a thief – unless picking up a useless bit of rope makes you a thief – but he was something that is almost as bad: a laughing stock. And a proud man like William Carter feels such an insult, feels it strongly, especially when he's brought it on himself. Even Alfred Rath looked less eager now and he did not join in the general amusement that he'd caused. Perhaps he knew he'd gone too far. Too late for that, though.

From that day on, there was bitterness between the Raths and the Carters, and especially between the men of the households. Oh, and what about the woman's purse, you ask, the keepsake from her mother? When she returned home she discovered that she'd never taken it with her in the first place.

Where was I? Yes, the physician. As I said before I started on the story of the rope and the purse, Thomas Flytte was a cousin of Joan Rath's. He came from a village a few miles away, Woolney, but he'd soon shaken the dust of that place off his feet and gone in search of a better, wider life. He was a learned man, Thomas Flytte. He talked about his studies in Oxford and Cambridge and famous cities across the seas. He'd travelled and lived for long periods away from England, even going as far as the East. He said some of the greatest physicians and writers had come from there. He casually referred to the noble men and women who had applied to him for help – never by name but as the prince of this or the duchess of that – and no one would have thought to ask at the time whether he was inventing these people or whether they really existed.

He made a point of mentioning the elaborate preparations he'd concocted for those great men and women who lived in foreign lands. One, I remember, was a medicine made up not only of gold and silver leaf but of tiny fragments of precious gems like sapphire and garnet, all mixed in a honey or syrup. Obviously, you must be very wealthy indeed even to think of having your physician offer such remedies. Master Thomas had all the answers at his fingertips too. If you were to ask him why gold was good for the heart, for instance, he'd say that the heart was under the influence of Leo, which is the House of the Sun, and that gold is the metal of the Sun. His talk often turned to the subject of gold.

So what was he doing back in a straggling village in a corner of England staying in his cousin's house? Something had gone wrong, that was obvious, even if Thomas Flytte never talked about it. Perhaps one of those foreign princes or duchesses had died under his hands, when he'd promised a recovery, or perhaps he had been involved in some dispute with a more powerful physician in a royal court and come off the worse. Or maybe there was not much truth in his tales of travel and noble patrons, and he'd never gone further than Southampton, casting waters for the wives of shipmasters and town burghers.

If Thomas the doctor of physic had had money once, he did not seem so well off now. Looked at close to, his purple surcoat was so threadbare that you would see through the fabric in places, while the ermine trimming his hood was yellow rather than white and bright. Even a child could see this. Especially a child. Joan Rath persuaded her husband to lend him a mantle against the bad weather. She said it was the least he could do after what the physician had done for them . . . Well, I'll come to that in a moment.

Thomas Flytte had a companion with him, a kind of attendant. This wasn't a student learning physic at the feet of the master but someone whose idea of an effective remedy was more likely to be the point of a dagger than a pestle full of simples. He was called Reeve, this companion. I do not know his given name. Thomas Flytte referred to him as Reeve and so everyone called him Reeve, if they wanted to call him anything at at all, which wasn't often.

Whereas his master, Thomas Flytte, was a short man with a bit of plumpness to him, as if he was still living off the fat of the olden days, Reeve looked as though he'd always been as spare as a fence-post. He said very little. When he did speak, it was as if words were coins, he doled them out so grudgingly. He dressed in drab greens and browns, and I think it was so he could pass unnoticed. I saw him once emerging from the edge of a wood, ducking his head beneath the branches as though he was coming out of his house. He was carrying a rabbit, which he'd just caught, unlawfully, no doubt. It hung limp and blooded in his hand. He saw me looking at him and he smiled a little smile, and I turned cold all over. That was Reeve.

The fact that Flytte the Physician was a cousin of Joan Rath wouldn't have been enough by itself for her to give him houseroom. She hadn't seen him for many years, I believe. Besides, he was accompanied by the disagreeable Reeve and that was enough to put anybody off. Something more was needed. And something more was very soon provided. Almost immediately after he'd arrived in town, Flytte showed that he was more than talk. Joan had a daughter of twelve or so called Agnes, who was sick, almost on the point of death, it was feared. The apothecary from the next town had visited and then the cunning-woman, who lived in the woods nearby, and each of them suggested various remedies, to no avail. The family resigned themselves to Agnes's death. No food had passed her lips, nor had any words, no, not for several days.

Then, as if guided by providence, Thomas Flytte turned up and, within a few hours of examining Joan's daughter and drawing up his charts and grinding his herbs and powders and mixing them in solution and easing a little of it down her unwilling throat, the girl began to stir and to talk a little sense for the first time in days. By the next morning, she had risen from her sickbed and by the afternoon she was once more sitting down to eat with her family.

It was a miracle! Thomas Flytte was modest or clever enough to credit it not only to his own skill but also to some particular herbs, which he had brought back from the East, plants that were not known in Europe. Of course, this made his presence in the town even more interesting. If Joan Rath hadn't offered him his own quarters someone else would probably have done. The fact that Reeve was with him was overlooked, since it was evident that if you took one man you had to take the other.

Mistress Rath was able to provide the physician and his man, Reeve, with a dilapidated cottage, which she had patched up at her own expense and furnished, too. All this was in gratitude for Flytte's care of her daughter, even if it was understood that he'd stay in the place only for a while. He must surely be going somewhere more significant than the village of Wenham, an important man like Thomas Flytte who'd treated foreigners and royalty. Wenham was a very ordinary village with only a small handful of well-to-do inhabitants, apart from the folk up at the manor. And, having properties elsewhere, they spent little time in Wenham but left their business in the hands of a steward. Joan's husband, Alfred Rath, didn't seem quite so glad at the physician's stay, though he had to acknowledge that the man had ability. Some of the villagers went to consult him and paid for it and, although he didn't bring anyone back from the brink of death as he had with Agnes, he impressed them with his talk and his expertise.

Not everyone was happy with Flytte's presence. Of course, William Carter and his family made insinuations about him and said he wasn't what he appeared to be. If they'd dared to, they might have accused him of witchcraft. Even so, I saw William and Thomas talking together more than once, and I think that he too consulted the physician. Then there was the local priest, Master John. Maybe he didn't like the fact that a few of the villagers went looking for help to Flytte instead of him, and he certainly didn't like it that money that might have gone to the Church coffers was instead finding its way into a physician's purse. In his sermons, he preached against Thomas Flytte, not directly at first, but with little digs and warnings against men of science. Parsons don't like doctors of physic anyway, they shy away from 'em as if by instinct. I've been told that churchmen are convinced that doctors do not believe in Our Saviour. There's some saying about it on the edge of my mind but I can't quite recall it . . .

Laurence paused and took a sip from his bowl of wine. And from the circle of listeners a learned man threw in: 'The proverb you are looking for, landlord, is, "Ubi tres medici, duo athei," *which means, "Where you get three physicians together, two will be atheists". Because physicians sometimes search out natural causes for unexplained things, they also encourage people to mistrust miracles, you see.'*

'Thank you, sir,' said Laurence. 'What a wealth of learning and wisdom there is to be found among the visitors to a tavern!'

He paused again to allow his audience to reflect on the compliment before continuing with his story. The pause was interrupted by a cough from the landlord's wife, who was sitting near the back of the audience. It was the kind of cough that meant: get on with it.

There were others apart from the priest who were suspicious or resentful of Thomas Flytte. I mentioned the cunning-woman a while ago. She'd been consulted about

Agnes's sickness, without result. While the land to the south of Wenham was mostly clear, the area to the north was wooded. This wood stretched so far and the trees in it were so dense that it was always called the Great Wood. Anyway, the cunning-woman lived in the Great Wood, and like most such women she was feared as much as she was tolerated. The children in the village wouldn't go near her. But some of the farmers and shopkeepers used to visit her rain-sodden hut to get forecasts for the harvest or to find out which of their workers was thieving from them. She was a strange creature with straggling white hair and touches of a beard, and yet with a hint of breasts too. Though she spoke with a singsong voice, some said she was a man or a gelding. Others said she had been a nun and was a woman of learning and refinement. Her name was Mistress Travis.

Thomas Flytte was very dismissive of Mistress Travis and her kind. He said that such women – and the cunning-men who ply the same trade – were like the stale leftovers of more superstitious ages. Word of this certainly got back to her even as the villagers who considered themselves more up-to-date stopped consulting her, and so the little sums of money and offerings of food she received began to dry up. If Thomas Flytte was concerned about this, or afraid of her power to lay a curse on him, he never showed it. Like his cousin Joan Rath, he was someone who knew his own mind. Then there was the apothecary from the nearby town who'd also been called in to treat Agnes. His name was Abel. He might have been expected to be jealous of Flytte but, in truth, he seemed eager to learn from the much-travelled visitor, keen to pick up whatever titbits of knowledge were going spare.

There was one other individual whose path crossed with that of Flytte the Physician before the crime occurred . . . and before a very peculiar situation arose . . . This other person was a pedlar who passed through Wenham two or three times a year. Hugh Tanner sold saints' relics – bits of bone, fragments of cloth – to ensure good health to your cattle and clean water in your well, and all the rest of it. Unlike a pardoner, he carried no papal bulls, he offered no pardon for your sins and he wasn't extortionate in his demands. On the contrary, he sold his wares quite cheaply, without much bargaining, and people bought them for that reason and because they felt sorry for Hugh Tanner. They were probably thinking . . . you might as well buy one of these for you never know what's going to bring you luck or protect you from misfortune in this life, do you?

He was a fellow with hangdog eyes and a skin as leathery as if he'd been tanned himself. His sales patter hardly deserved the name and yet somehow he managed to make a living from travelling through towns and villages like Wenham. He brought news from other places, which was always welcome, and sometimes he even talked of London. Like the cunning-woman, he was supposed to have the gift, to be able to see things that ordinary people couldn't see. But it was a gift he was reluctant to use, as if whatever he saw was nothing good.

I myself was a witness to the first encounter of Hugh Tanner and Thomas Flytte. Except that it wasn't their first encounter. It was market day again but this time on a spring morning, and people's spirits were light. Hugh Tanner couldn't afford a stall but he settled himself down with his scrip on a little mound at the edge of the village because he judged the flow of people would be best there. It was where a couple of paths from other hamlets came together, and so old Hugh was aiming to catch people before they reached the stalls and spent what little they had. He wasn't a complete fool, was Hugh.

I was there at the edge of the village, with Agnes Rath, as it happens. We were friends, and a bit more besides, but we had to be careful, very careful, over our friendship. I'd prayed for her recovery when she was sick, and despaired with everyone else when she looked to be dying, and then rejoiced when the skill of Thomas Flytte saved her. I looked up to the physician for what he'd done and I tried to engage him in conversation. I went up to him in the street, and welcomed him to our village, which was a bit forward of me. He could have cuffed me for speaking out of turn or simply walked by. But he seemed amused. He stopped walking and started talking, not once but on two or three occasions, and that's how I found out why gold is good for the heart and about those remedies that are made up of precious stones. He was patient with answering my questions, which is more than my mother or father were. From them, or at least from my father, I got blows or silence, mostly. It was Thomas Flytte who predicted I'd make a good tavern-host. He said, you've got to like people and to be unafraid of talking to them and curious about their lives, while knowing when it's time to rein in your curiosity. You've also got to have a business head on your shoulders. Of course, all this went over my own head, business or otherwise, when I was twelve, but years later I remembered it and now you see me, and my dear wife, settled here at the Angel.

Agnes and I were by the village wash-house. This was a tank fed by a spring and covered with a pillared roof but otherwise open to the weather. There was a bit of privacy on the far side of it, and we were lying on the grass enjoying the April morning and feeling the season coursing through our veins. For once it wasn't raining. The wash-house was a good spot to be on market day because none of the village women would be doing their laundry, and when the two of us met we had to meet in secret. We were out of sight of Hugh Tanner and the people passing along the road but could see them by peeking over the stone edge of the tank.

Suddenly, we were aware of insistent voices, overlapping with each other. We peered across the tank. The pedlar and Thomas Flytte were in the middle of an argument. They were talking too low for us to catch even the occasional word but I could hear the anger in both men's tones, like water boiling in a pot. This was surprising because the physician was not only a grave and learned man but also a calm one, while Tanner was not one of those pedlars who shout their wares at the top of their voices but just the opposite. Something about the way the two men were standing quite close together on top of the little mound of grass, and the hissing tones of their speech, showed that they'd met before. In fact, they must have done, because Hugh Tanner had come back to the village that very morning, his first visit for several months, while Thomas Flytte had been there only a few weeks.

Within a few moments, Flytte strode away, and Tanner flung some words after him. They might have been 'Fraud yourself!' but I couldn't say for certain. Then out of the woods came Reeve, the physician's companion. He rarely walked beside Thomas Flytte or even close to him, but was usually trailing at a distance, like a dog following his master while being distracted by other, more interesting concerns. Reeve's presence made you feel uneasy but it also cast a shadow of doubt over the physician. You asked yourself what he was doing with a man like that for a servant.

As he passed Hugh Tanner, Reeve gave him a glance, which the pedlar was unable to return. Fortunately, a couple of market-day visitors appeared and Hugh gladly unpacked his scrip and spread out the bits of rag and bone that even he scarcely pretended were the property of the saints. Meanwhile, Agnes and I slunk off from our trysting-place behind the wash-house without being observed and went our separate ways, arranging to meet later. We couldn't afford to be seen together in the village.

What was the reason the two of us couldn't be seen together? Surely, you must have guessed it by now, ladies and gentlemen – such a quick-thinking gathering of guests and pilgrims as this is? As you know, Agnes was from the Rath family, the oldest of several children. And I . . . I was one of the Carters, the eldest son of Alice and a stepson to William. He was my mother's second husband. I cannot remember my own father, though I do know that he was called Todd. It was from Todd that my mother had gained the farm, which she was allowed to keep as a tenant because she worked hard and, better still, she was able to make others work harder. Then she married William Carter, when I was small. From the time I can remember anything at all, it was William who was telling me to sop up the last spot of grease from the soup bowl or sending me out at night in the rain to ensure the barn doors were properly fastened. By the time I found out that my mother's husband wasn't my father, I'd learned to think of him – and fear him – as a father. So that's how he remained to me.

Well, if my father had caught me in company with Agnes, he'd have beaten me within an inch of my life. And Agnes, too, would have suffered at the hands of her parents. The hatred and suspicion between the heads of these two families extended to every person in them, or was supposed to. I had an example of that a few moments after I parted from Agnes. I glimpsed my mother, Alice, talking with Alfred Rath on Church Lane. It seemed as though they were having an argument for her face was growing red as it did when she was angry and she was gesturing with her hands. Alfred was raising his own hands in an appeasing way but it made no difference and she turned on her heel and came striding towards me. I looked round for a way of escape and saw my father William coming in the opposite direction. Luckily, I was by the lich-gate to the churchyard and so I slipped through there and crouched behind the churchyard wall. Neither my mother nor my father was aware of my presence.

'What were you doing with that man?' I heard him say. His voice had gone very quiet, in a way I'd learned to fear.

'The insolence of that Rath,' my mother said. She didn't sound daunted but indignant. 'He says I need to attend to our boundaries. He says the hedges are overgrown and the fences broken. He is demanding I go and inspect them with him this very afternoon.'

'You'll not go, of course.'

'What do you take me for?' said my mother.

My father grunted in reply, and I thought that he didn't like being reminded of the fact that it was my mother who had taken over the farm from her first husband, and the related fact that people usually went to her first with any complaint or request. Probably my father thought he ought to be the one dealing with any question about the boundaries. Except, of course, Alfred Rath wouldn't have approached him any more than William Carter would have approached Alfred Rath.

My mother's words soon passed out of my mind when I thought of my next secret meeting with Agnes Rath. But fear of the consequences didn't put us off. There's a Latin saying for that, too, and I don't need anyone to provide it for me, thank you. *Amor vincit omnia.* Love conquers all. That was our happy state, Agnes and I. And you should have seen Agnes as she was then! Lithe as willow, with hair that tumbled down like a shower of gold when it was loosened.

You may think I have been talking about my father and mother without the reverence that is their due, calling one a gossip or snob, and the other a miser and so on. Perhaps I have spoken of them without due respect. But they are long dead and I can see them clearly now. They had faults, yes, and which of us does not have faults, God have mercy on us? But they had virtues too. I thought my father was an honourable man, who was prepared to be humiliated in the alehouse rather than be considered a thief. Thank God, he was not aware of the presence of his son that day when he was forced to hold up the little length of rope. We could not have looked each other in the eye afterwards if he'd known I was there. And though my mother may have been a snob it meant that she wanted to see her sons rise in the world, and because she had a churchman as an . . . uncle . . . she made sure I gained a little more learning than I might have been entitled to as a tenant farmer's son. My mother's uncle sometimes gave me lessons himself. I even picked up a few Latin sayings from him.

Agnes and I had appointed to meet towards the end of that same spring day, the day of the market. We had a regular place. It was on the boundary of the land that my father held against her father's. Because of all the trouble between the two families, the hedges that marked the boundary were left straggling and unkempt, as if to discourage trespassers, and it was these same hedges that must have been the reason for Alfred Rath's complaint to my mother.

In a remote spot, almost out of sight of any dwelling, there was a stile. This too was overgrown and broken down. Because there was no coming and going between the two families, no one had bothered to maintain or repair the stile. Agnes and I often met there, and one or the other would clamber over to the opposite side so we might spend time together. In the past there had been a path running on both sides of the stile and linking the two properties, but because of the coldness between Carters and Raths, there was no occasion for it to be used. Except by us.

It was early evening, with the wind shaking the blossom in the trees and the sun sending out his long beams from the west. A heavy downpour of rain that afternoon made everything smell damp and fresh. As I was on my way to the meeting-place, I thought I glimpsed Mistress Travis, the cunning-woman, on another path that bordered our land. She was running and her wild hair was streaming out behind her. It was strange to see her away from the Great Wood and the rain-sodden hut. But I thought no more of her and instead of Agnes Rath. As I approached the boundary, I could see my friend approaching from the other side through the gaps in the hedge. Between us was the stile. It wasn't until I drew much closer that I noticed something draped over the dilapidated steps of the stile. I took them for discarded clothes but, nearer too, I saw that underneath the garments was a figure. At first, I thought he was asleep, then

I thought differently. I shouted to Agnes to stay back but she was already as close as me.

If we had any sense we'd have turned tail and left it to someone else to make the discovery. But curiosity nudged us forward. Besides, I felt that this overgrown gap in the hedge belonged to us, and I was almost angry that another person should have been using it. Even if that person was dead. He was draped over the stile as he'd been if struck down in the act of crossing, with his legs on Agnes's side and his top half dangling down on mine. His head was obscured. I crept closer still and got down on my hands and knees in the damp grass and peered up and sideways at the countenance of the dead man. I already suspected that it was Thomas Flytte the physician but I had to make sure.

The side of his face that was visible to me was swollen and mottled with purple like the colour of the threadbare surcoat he used to wear. There appeared to be a cord buried deep in the flesh of his neck. His eyes were bulging and sightless. It was obvious that he had not died a natural death. It was only later that I had time to experience any sorrow. This was the man who'd spoken kindly to me – and told me I might become a tavern-keeper! Here was the physician who had plucked Agnes from the jaws of death! But at that moment all I felt was a tightness round my own neck. When I heard someone speaking from the other side of the hedge, I sprang up and almost ran away. I thought of Reeve, Flytte's companion, and half expected him to come slithering out from under the hedge. But the speaker was Agnes. I couldn't see her. Not clearly, just an outline. She was more composed than me. When she spoke again there was scarcely a tremor in her voice.

'Who is it, Laurence? It is not my father, is it?'

I suppose she thought this because the dead man had obviously been coming from the direction of her family's land and house.

'Not, it is the physician, Thomas Flytte.'

'What are we going to do?'

'We should raise a hue and cry.'

'Yes.'

Even then, some instinct kept us from moving, though every moment we delayed in raising the hue and cry meant that the murderer of Thomas Flytte could be making his escape from the district.

'Wait, Agnes,' I said. 'We cannot report this together. People would ask us what we were doing at this deserted place, and our secret would be out. Go home and say nothing. I'll pretend I was out here by myself, wandering about, looking for birds' eggs. I'll say I found him, found the physician's body. I will keep you out of the story.'

Laurence Carter paused in his present story. He seemed almost overcome by his words, by the memory of the body of Thomas Flytte hanging across the stile. There was a stir from the far side of the group of pilgrims and a woman spoke up. It was the landlord's wife. She'd already made clear her feelings about her husband's storytelling by coughing and then harrumphing loudly when he was making comments about the long-haired beauty of his youthful love, Agnes.

'That's not how I remember it, husband.'

'No, my dear?' said the landlord.

'No. I remember you were too confused by the discovery of the body to think straight or to have any idea what to do. It was I who said that we couldn't do this together and that one of us should go and raise the alarm while the other went quietly home.'

'Well, it may have been so,' said the landlord.

'It was so,' continued the voice from the other side. By now, people were craning round to look at the speaker. 'And there are one or two other details in your account that were not altogether as you describe them.'

'Perhaps you would like to take up the tale then, Agnes. To tell the truth, my throat is getting dry. I'd welcome another voice – and another drink. Come forward, my dear.'

'Thank you, my sweet.'

Laurence Carter stood aside while his wife bustled to the front of the group. There was some amusement among the Walsingham pilgrims, as well as surprise, to see that the girl he'd been referring to all this while – Agnes Rath – had become his wife. And was still his wife. It was as if a character in a story had suddenly come to life. Agnes Carter cut a very different figure from the lithe young girl with flowing hair, as depicted by her equally young lover. She was a substantial woman well into middle age, who looked as though she'd take no nonsense from any of her servants or her guests. Her shape was concealed by a gown of dull red, like a dying fire, while her hair was tucked away beneath a wimple.

'Oh, yes,' she said, eying the room, 'you are looking at me and all the while remembering Laurence's description of me when I was a girl. Well, if I have changed a little, so has he. Thirty years ago, he was a ... oh, well, never mind.'

The landlord of the Angel, now sitting in comfort as one of the audience, shrugged ruefully as faces turned towards him. He raised his bowl of wine in ironic salute. Whatever the small niggles between husband and wife, it was obvious that they understood each other well. Agnes Carter now took up the part of the storyteller.

There's one thing that Laurence has not told you, which he did not know at the time. But I had it from my mother, Joan Rath. Thomas Flytte the physican was Joan's cousin from the village of Woolney, and his companion, Reeve, was actually his son. My mother said this was common knowledge in the family but something never spoken of. If you looked closely you could see a likeness in their faces, around the eyes. Thomas had fathered the child before he left Woolney as a young man. It may have been his reason for leaving the village in a hurry, to avoid some forced betrothal. When he came back all those years later, by instinct he went first to the village to find that only his son was left. The child had grown to a man, but he was a shy and sullen one, who preferred to keep away from company. He was called Reeve because that was the surname of his mother – her father had been reeve of an estate near Woolney. The lad must have had a given name but, if so, his father never used it and simply referred to him as Reeve, as if to say: you don't really belong to me but to that other person with a different name.

The father may not have wanted to acknowledge the son, but Reeve wasn't to be so easily shaken off. He followed Thomas away from his birthplace and came with him to Wenham, where they were housed by my mother. The villagers assumed he was some sort of servant. Laurence says he trailed after the physician like a dog, and that there was something sinister or dangerous about him. I didn't see that. To me, he was a rather pitiful creature. At first, anyway . . .

My mother also had a story about just why Thomas Flytte returned home after all those years of wandering. She believed what he said because she was truly grateful to him on account of his treatment of her daughter. As I am grateful to him, God rest his soul, for without him, I don't believe I would be standing here in front of you. My mother and the physician exchanged confidences. He told his tales of travel and foreign courts. He showed her a brooch of yellow topaz. The image of a falcon was cut into it. He said that this was to attract the favour of kings. It was his most treasured possession.

Thomas told my mother that he had fallen foul of a powerful man in the court of Edward II. This courtier surrounded himself with a rabble of projectors and forecasters, some of them little better than vagabonds. Thomas Flytte was on the verge of a great discovery in the search for the substance that would transform base metal into gold, but before he could achieve this the courtier demanded the return of some money he had invested in the scheme. Thomas promised the man that if he was allowed to continue only a little longer he would be rewarded a hundred times over but the courtier was not to be persuaded. The physician had already spent the money, and his own besides, on the equipment he needed, so when the courtier began to threaten him with dreadful punishments and vengeance, Thomas had no choice but to return here to his birthplace in an obscure corner of the country. He was lying low, licking his wounds, deciding what to do next.

The landlady, Agnes Carter, paused in her narrative. Like her husband, but in a more genteel way, she sipped at a bowl of wine before returning to her story, and the moment when they'd discovered the physician's corpse.

It was a strange talk we had, young Laurence and I. We did not raise our voices but conversed in loud whispers on either side of the crossing. I had a cooler head than he, I think, so I said that he should go back and raise the hue and cry. In fact he'd be punished if he didn't do that since it was his duty and he was of age. Meantime, I'd return home and pretend that nothing had happened, if anyone noticed my absence and asked. Already I was good at adopting a guarded face – and keeping secrets. Despite what men say, women can keep counsel, you know.

Laurence took to his heels across the fields. But I did not return home straight away. I gazed at the body of the physician, or what I was able to see of it bundled across the stile. I did not mind being so close to the corpse. I almost felt that he should not be left alone, even though I knew I could not be discovered here when the people came. Then I started wondering what Thomas Flytte had been doing out here. Obviously, he was on his way somewhere, going from the little house where he lodged with Reeve to . . . where? Or perhaps, he had been coming in the opposite direction, from the Carters' to the Raths', and had met someone as he was crossing the stile. Or perhaps, some person had been lying in wait for him. I looked at the ground at the base of the stile but it was just tussocky grass. It was coming on to rain again. Close by was a clump of trees and I went there for cover, though the branches were still quite bare.

From where I was standing I had a good view of the protruding legs of the dead man. I looked down and saw something glinting on the ground. I picked it up. It was a tiny sheet of gold, or what looked like gold, set in a frame of wood. On the sheet was engraved the image of a lion. I'd never seen this object before but I recognised it all the same. It was one of the talismans that Master Thomas carried with him, and the sort of thing he bestowed on those he treated. I cast around on the ground under the trees but saw no more items. Had he dropped it? Had someone tried to steal it from him? Surely the little lion showed that the physician had been here under the trees. I could have dropped the talisman on the ground again, but instead I took it.

And now I examined the earth more closely, I saw the mark of boots or shoes pressed into the earth in a place where the grass grew more thinly and where the mud was still soft on account of the wet dripping down from the bare branches. The print of the shoes was deep as though the person standing here had continued for a long time without movement. I shivered. I crouched down and measured the length of the imprint against my outstretched hand. It was nearly twice the length of my hand. Then I stole off towards the corpse and the feet that stuck out on this side. Strangely I did not feel frightened or disrespectful but . . . merely curious. I placed my hand against the sole of the dead man's shoe and realised that whoever it was that had left their mark under the trees it was not Thomas Flytte.

Then I thought I had done enough work for one day and I ran home, before Laurence should arrive back and the hue and cry begin. It was too late to do anything that evening and by the time the first villagers came out to examine the body, the light had almost faded from the sky. Anyway, nothing could be done until the coroner arrived. He attended the next morning. He had come from Thetford, as quick as carrion, eager to see what pickings he might get from the corpse in the way of deodands and fines. I remember his horse; it was a dapple grey hackney. He was accompanied by a servant.

In truth, that scene is clearer and sharper in my mind's eye than anything that happened yesterday. Almost everybody in the village of Wenham, from priest to ploughman to hayward stood in the field close to the stile, the babies in their mothers' arms, the children jostling to the front for a better view. It was a chill morning. The crows circled and the clouds pressed low overhead. But however grim the occasion, and however much sadness there was at the death of Thomas Flytte, you could sense excitement, too. Even the Carters and the Raths buried their differences for a time and exchanged a few words, though they did it warily, as if they understood that an unconsidered remark or a thoughtless move might bring trouble down on all their heads.

The coroner's first question was to confirm that the body had not been moved. No, not moved? Good. So, whose land was it on? On a boundary, marked by the stile. On one side were the fields farmed by the Raths, on the other those of the Carter family. Thomas Flytte was discovered exactly between the two. His head and upper part were hanging down on the Carter side, while his lower half, his legs, were dangling over the Rath portion. It took some time for this to be imparted to the coroner, with both William and Alfred eager to explain, and somehow nudge responsibility for the body towards the other's territory.

The coroner rubbed his hands. Perhaps he was cold or perhaps he was thinking that having two families involved increased his chances of making a profit. Then he ordered Thomas Flytte to be lifted down from the stile and laid out on some sacking, which had been placed on the ground. The overnight delay had caused the countenance of the poor physician to grow more mottled and bloated, while the body itself had stiffened, making it awkward to handle. When he was stripped bare of his clothing and his shrunken frame exposed for his injuries to be openly witnessed and assessed, there were expressions of real grief from the crowd. They came strong from my mother, and from me too. I noticed that even the Carters were affected and that stern old William seemed almost moved.

The Thetford coroner asked if anyone present could say

for certain who the corpse was, though everyone knew. My mother identified him as her cousin from Woolney. Her voice was low but steady now. The coroner proceeded to examine the body more closely and determined for himself that the cause of death was indeed the rope wrapped about the man's neck. It had been tugged so tight that it bit deep into the flesh, which had swollen up and made the cord hard to unfasten. The coroner ordered the attendant who'd ridden with him to retrieve the rope, and I remember it came away from the corpse with a tearing sound. Then the coroner held it up as if daring someone to come forward and claim it. No one did, of course. He kept the rope but it was thin pickings. There were no goods he could confiscate here. Nevertheless, the coroner took for himself, no doubt the topaz brooch, which was in a pocket. I hope he managed to attract the King's favour with it.

No one said so at the time but much later, after the coroner had departed, someone remarked that the length of rope looked like the piece that William Carter had displayed in the alehouse to prove that he had not stolen a woman's purse. The length he'd picked up in the street, when he'd been seen by my father. Even though it had happened a year or more earlier, everyone remembered that moment. Even those who hadn't been present had heard of it. What had happened to that bit of rope? William had thrown it to the alehouse floor in anger and disgust before he stalked out. But had someone retrieved that rope and stored it away to use many months later to squeeze the life out of a man? It didn't seem likely, but somehow it linked the murder of Thomas Flytte to the Carter and the Rath families.

The body was removed and the coroner departed with his servant. The physician was buried in the churchyard.

Master John gave no sign of gloating at the death of a rival but took extra care with his funeral devotions, sprinkling holy water on the grave to drive off the devils that might trouble the burial-place of a man who had died so suddenly and without being shriven. Both the Carters and the Raths paid for daily masses to be said for Thomas Flytte. You could see why my family should do this, but the piety of William Carter caused some comment, considering how tight-fisted he was. People thought he was trying to compensate somehow for the body being discovered on his land. All this while there was no sign of Reeve, the attendant and supposed son of Thomas.

If the keeper of the King's peace had been in the area, he would have looked into the death. But he was not, and so the crime went without investigation.

You couldn't stop people talking about it, though.

And the talk in the village was of who might have so hated or feared Thomas Flytte that he had assailed him and left him dead in that remote spot. Some people mentioned Hugh Tanner, the pedlar. We'd seen the argument between him and the physician while we were . . . resting . . . near the wash-house, Laurence and I, and it appeared that Hugh had lost no opportunity of venting his anger at Master Thomas to all those who stopped to examine his wares, calling him a fraud and so on. Was he responsible for the fatal attack on Thomas Flytte?

Then there was Mistress Travis, the cunning-woman. She had lost some of her custom because of the physician's words. Furthermore, she was feared because she was a strange, strong woman – certainly strong enough to attack a man, and with enough power in her upper arms to wrap a cord round his neck. Some favoured the cunning-woman.

Others whispered that the priest had spoken out in his sermons against physicians and men of science – and they knew that Master John was resentful because offerings that should have come the church's way were being diverted to Master Thomas. But then they recalled the priest's care with the funeral and they reproached themselves for speaking ill of a man of God. And then finally there was Reeve. As I said, almost no one knew that he was Thomas's son but the fact that he was nowhere to be found after the murder was enough to cast suspicion on him.

One thing was apparent, though, or it would have been to anyone who thought carefully about the matter. The physician had not been murdered by a thief, for he had been left in possession of the topaz brooch, which the coroner had confiscated. It was possible that the murderer might have been intending to search for something to take but had been disturbed by the arrival of Laurence and me, coming from opposite directions. But if that was so then surely we would have glimpsed him . . . or her? We said nothing of how we'd discovered the body together, and I certainly said nothing of what I had discovered under the stand of trees near to the stile.

Not until later, when I told Laurence, and once I had we couldn't stop talking. We talked about the murder and, after we'd finished, we talked about it again. It was less difficult for us to meet now. Our families were not so watchful and the days were longer, even if the sun rarely shone. Well, the summer wore on and the death of the physician continued to cast a cloud across Wenham, even though at least one other villager died during those months. His name was Robert Short, I remember. But he was an old man and he died naturally, while Thomas Flytte did not.

Still there was no sign of the King's peace and it seemed that justice would never be done. The gossip and speculation about who the murderer might be began to die down. One person who was cleared of the crime was Hugh the pedlar. He returned to Wenham at the beginning of the autumn and reacted with surprise when he heard of the physician's violent death.

It seemed he'd not stayed long in the village that market day but departed southwards. He admitted he'd known Thomas Flytte in another place, as he put it, and that he thought the doctor of physic was – not what he appeared to be. When pressed, he admitted that he'd encountered Thomas Flytte in London. (And I thought of the story I'd heard from my mother, about the physician and the courtier who kept company with projectors and forecasters and vagabonds. Was it possible that Hugh Tanner was one of them?) But Hugh held no grudge against the physician. If he'd called him a fraud it was only because he'd been called one himself in the first place. Let every man thrive as best he can under the eye of God, was his motto. If Flytte was dead, and by violence too, then he was sorry to hear it. There was such meekness about him and his hang-dog air that scarcely anyone believed he could have choked the life out of the doctor.

If there was a shadow over the village there was a darker one over my own house. My mother grew quiet and no longer wanted to speak good of everybody. She seemed to be keeping separate from my father, and I thought she had been wounded by the death of her doctor cousin. She refused to do anything about the little cottage where the physician had lived with his son Reeve, but let it lie empty and my father did not seem inclined to contradict her. Perhaps she thought

Reeve was going to return to Wenham even though he would have been seized by the villagers if he'd done so. But I don't think my mother ever believed Reeve was guilty. Towards the autumn, she fell ill and grew weak. She spent long periods of every day in bed, so I had to take over many of the duties in the house. I am sure she wondered whether, had Thomas Flytte still been alive, he would have found a remedy for her affliction.

Perhaps it was to clear away those shadows that I wanted to find out what had happened. Or perhaps I felt I had an obligation to the physician who had saved me from death.

I had only two things to help me, and one of them was no more than a memory. There was the little talisman I'd picked up from the ground, the golden image of a lion in a wooden frame. And, though it no longer existed, clear in my mind's eye I had the image of the shoe-marks in the wet earth of the spinney. From their size, I knew they were not the print of the physician's shoes but belonged to whoever had been waiting in ambush for him, for surely no one would stand fixed in one spot under the trees unless they had a purpose. I struggled to see the scene through the eyes of that unknown man – for I was sure it was a man, from the size of the shoes and the violence of the attack – but I could see and understand nothing. Then I thought of the cunning-woman who lived in the woods, Mistress Travis. She had the gift, like Hugh Tanner. But, unlike him, she was prepared to use it. Many villagers went to her to find out things that they could not see for themselves, things happening just beyond the corner of their eyes and even things that would happen in the future. They paid these visits in an uneasy way, sometimes, and in defiance of Master John, but they paid them all the same.

At once, I was seized with the desire to go to the cunning-woman and show her the only thing which I had: the talisman. But I did not want to do this by myself. Laurence and I talked about it, of course. I think there were shadows over Laurence's house too during that summer. His father was even more silent than usual while his mother would not stop talking, and they grated on each other like a knife against stone.

In the end, Laurence agreed to go with me. Perhaps he was as I was, half eager, half afraid to discover the truth.

Mistress Travis, the cunning-woman, was not so fearful to me as she was to some others in Wenham. As a child, I once got lost in the Great Wood and I ran into her, in my tears and panic not realising she was there. Though the first sight of her was terrifying, she spoke soothing words and took me by the hand and led me through a maze of overgrown paths until we reached the edge of the trees and when I saw the chimney-smoke from my home in the distance, I slipped out of her grasp and ran towards it without a backward glance. So I had no reason to be daunted by her. Even so, Laurence and I approached the hut in the woods in great trepidation. If we hadn't been driven by our desire to find out the truth we would have turned and run back home.

It was a late afternoon in autumn and the trees were almost bare. The branches creaked. The way to the cunning-woman's was not so hard to find, for other village folk apart from us were accustomed to beating a path to her door. As I walked, I clutched the talisman with the image of the gold lion. The hut was in a clearing where nothing seemed to grow, as though the ground immediately around it was blighted. The door of the hut was open, or perhaps it could never be properly closed since it hung drunkenly on a single hinge of rope. We came to a halt either side of the entrance. Mistress Travis was squatting on a low stool just inside. Her white hair curtained her face and the bedraggled smock she wore concealed the shape beneath like a tent.

'You are too big to be lost in the woods now,' she said in her singsong voice.

This was directed at me. I was surprised she remembered the frightened child.

'I have my friend Laurence for company,' I said.

The cunning-woman ducked her head slightly. She knew Laurence, of course, even if they'd never spoken. She knew everyone in the village and everyone knew her.

I waited for Laurence to say something but he would not even look the cunning-woman in the face, instead keeping his eyes fastened on the earth, so I stretched out my hand instead and said: 'We have brought you something, Mistress Travis, an offering.'

The old woman put out a palm that was oddly smooth and soft. I placed the talisman in it. She tilted it so that it caught the little light remaining in the clearing. Her eyes were pure blue. She raised the talisman to her nose and sniffed at it. Looking at her, I thought that despite the hairs on her face, she must have been handsome many years ago. I remembered one of the stories I'd heard about her: that she'd been in holy orders and was once a woman of learning and refinement. 'This is not yours,' she said.

'I found it.'

'Where?'

'In a copse of trees near a stile.'

'Where the physician was done to death?'

'Yes,' said Laurence, speaking up for the first time. 'You were there that afternoon, Mistress Travis. I saw you.'

The cunning-woman looked at Laurence. I could not tell whether her look was an admission – yes, I was there – or whether she didn't know what he was talking about. I wondered why he'd raised the subject. Why should she remember where she'd been six months ago? Now she bent her white-haired head over the object that nestled in her palm.

'For sure, it is one of the physician's things,' said Mistress Travis, examining the golden image tucked inside the little frame. 'They say the image of the lion is a protection against the stone. It is also for those of a choleric disposition or humour and all other hot conditions.'

'Then the physician must have dropped it,' said Laurence.

'No,' said the crouching woman. She brushed her fingertips several times back and forth across the little image and she cocked her head, as though she was listening to someone we could neither see nor hear. 'Its story is plain enough if you have the ears to hear it. This passed from the physician's hands into another's. There was no loss involved.'

I thought she meant that the talisman must have been sold or given away, not stolen.

'Whose hands?' said Laurence.

I felt my heart beat faster. Mistress Travis did not reply. She clasped the talisman in both her own hands now and rubbed it gently. She raised her hands to her face and then cradled her cheek against them and closed her blue eyes. She looked like a child trying to fall asleep. Laurence and I gazed at each other. It was growing more gloomy in the clearing and the evening breeze rattled above us. We were startled by a sudden moan from Mistress Travis. Then, with her hands still to the side of her face and without changing her crouching posture on the stool, she started to speak.

'The rain is coming down hard. He is walking along the

path across the fields. He is moving fast because he is eager to see her. Anger and hatred boil up within me and cloud my vision. The rain is coming down hard even under the trees where I am standing and I wipe my hands across my eyes to clear them but I still cannot see clearly. And now he is drawing level with me and all I see is his arms swinging and his legs moving like knives. Soon he will be with her in the dry and the warm and his legs will be moving like knives, and hers too moving against his, and the anger and hatred boil over and spill down my sides. Here, at my side, somewhere at my side, I have a piece of rope that I have been keeping for just such an occasion. No, it is for this occasion now, as he walks past me so fast and then stops close to the stile. He is thinking for a moment how best to get over it without marring his clothes, and now is the same moment when I go and—'

The cunning-woman delivered all this in her usual singsong tone. When she stopped it was in mid-flow, as if she had been cut off by some external force. That was odd because neither Laurence nor I had spoken a word or moved an inch. But even odder was the fact that though Mistress Travis talked of anger and hatred her voice had not changed in its up-and-down style. It was as if she were reading words she did not understand out of a book. Gooseflesh rose on my arms and I felt my hair stir. Beside me, I sensed rather than saw that Laurence was just as horrified as I.

We waited, not certain what to do next. The woman lowered her hands to her lap. She unclasped them to reveal the lion-talisman crouching there, unchanged. Her eyes opened and, after a moment in which she gazed blankly at the two of us standing either side of her doorway, she came back to herself.

'It is getting late,' she said. 'Home before dark.'

We were being dismissed like children. The inner chill I'd felt while she was telling the story was starting to fade, to be replaced by the outer cold of the evening. I wanted to thank her, even if I wasn't quite sure of the meaning of what she had told us. I gestured at the talisman in her hand.

'What do I need it for, Agnes?' she said, passing it back to me. 'I do not suffer from the stone and I am not choleric. Take it back and give it someone who has need of it.'

Even so, I was reluctant to take the thing and she sensed it was because I was frightened of the talisman brooch now and considered it unlucky. Mistress Travis said, 'There is nothing to fear here. It was created to ward off harm and some small trace of that remains. The person who lost it under the trees cannot touch you.'

I reflected that I had already kept the talisman secret for the whole summer without coming to grief and so I took it back and thanked her in my stumbling way. Laurence said nothing. We turned away from the hut and threaded a path back through the woods. It was fortunate we were together and that we were not children, despite Mistress Travis's words, for otherwise we might have been fearful of the gathering shadows and the sounds of animals settling down or stirring themselves for the night.

We waited until we'd reached the boundary of the woods before talking about the cunning-woman. Laurence was of the opinion that it was all nonsense. He said that Mistress Travis hadn't denied being near the place where the murder occurred. Either she was making things up or possibly she had glimpsed somebody lurking under the trees by the stile but had no idea who it was. I reminded him that Mistress Travis mentioned the rope. She couldn't have seen that from a distance. The rope wasn't a secret, he said. Everybody knew how Thomas Flytte had died. The coroner had pronounced on it. In truth, the cunning-woman had seen nothing, she knew nothing. All that business with stroking the talisman and pretending to go into a trance was nothing more than foolery, designed to impress us, and all for the sake of – of . . .

'Yes, Laurence,' I said, 'all for the sake of – what? Tell me. Because she didn't want any money or gifts from us. She wouldn't even keep the talisman. She was still speaking to us as children almost, telling us to get off home before dark. We are hardly worth impressing.'

There was a silence and I could tell he wasn't pleased.

'All right,' he said. 'Then, if we do believe her, it must be the cunning-woman herself who was under the trees by the stile. She was the one lying in wait for Thomas Flytte. Everyone knows she had a grudge against the physician. She's strong enough to have overpowered him and pulled a cord round his neck and choked him. You know some people say she's really a man.'

'And others say that she's a nun. But it didn't happen like that at all. She held the talisman in her hands and, because of that, she was able to see through the eyes of . . . the person who possessed it at the time. Through those eyes, she saw Thomas Flytte crossing the field at a run because it was raining, she saw him pass in front of her and then pause in front of the stile. Or rather 'she' didn't see all this but . . .'

'Have you tried to do that thing, Agnes?' said Laurence, ignoring everything I'd been saying. 'Go on, hold the wretched object, rub it tenderly and see if you have any visions.'

'Don't be stupid, Laurence. I haven't got the gift. Even her enemies admit that Mistress Travis has the gift.'

'Answer me this, then. Why did she suddenly stop at the very point in her story where she was about to tell us what happened? According to you, she can see or pretends she can see through the eyes of the person who is spying on the physician while he strides across the field. Thomas Flytte pauses as he gets to the stile, and then this "person" goes and does . . . whatever it is he does. How convenient that she cannot tell us anything that really matters. She does not see the murder, she does not see the murderer.'

'Not convenient, just fortunate,' I said.

'You're talking as much nonsense as the cunning-woman.'

I wasn't talking nonsense and Laurence knew it, I think. It was fortunate that the cunning-woman had not seen everything in her vision. It meant that the truth was still half-hidden, which was more comfortable for both of us.

'I have been thinking about why Mistress Travis couldn't see the murder being done,' I said, 'and it makes sense. I can explain it.'

'Nothing makes sense,' he said. I waited for him to ask for my explanation, which I was rather pleased with, but he said nothing more. So I was forced to speak instead.

'Remember I told you I found the talisman under the trees, not by the stile? It was close to the foot-marks. I measured those against the boots of Thomas Flytte and it was obvious from the length of them that he was not the person waiting in the spinney. He was shorter than that person. Which confirms the cunning-woman's words. She was looking through the eyes of someone watching the physician. Even the words she used weren't her own thoughts and feelings, but his. It was his hatred and anger boiling over. His idea that the physician's legs were going like knives. But she could only do that for as long as the man under the trees was holding the talisman. When he no longer had the talisman with him then she could no longer see with his eyes. The talisman is her link to . . . that person.'

I paused, waiting for him to agree, but also to catch up with my own rushing thoughts. Then a further detail occurred to me. 'Or probably, he wasn't holding the lion-talisman in his hand but he had it somewhere about him, in a pocket or fastened to his belt, and in his hurry and anger as he reached for the piece of rope, which he kept with him – remember Mistress Travis talked of the rope at her side, though it wasn't her side but his – he accidentally dislodged it and it dropped to the ground—'

'Where it was conveniently found by Agnes Rath,' said Laurence, breaking his silence. There was almost a harshness in his tone.

I said, 'Don't you believe me, Laurence? I found the talisman where I said I did, and the foot-marks, too. I have told you no lie but only the precise truth.'

After a few moments, he said, 'I believe you,' and this time there was no harshness in his voice but only regret perhaps. We were out in the open by now and coming to the point where he would have to follow his path back to his house while I went off to mine. It was half dark, and I was glad to be out of the woods.

'It could have been the pedlar Hugh standing in the spinney by the stile, or Reeve,' said Laurence.

'I don't think so,' I said. It didn't seem to me as though the shoe-marks I'd seen could belong to either of those ragged individuals.

'Very well,' he said. 'But whoever it was who was standing there, why did . . . that person attack Thomas Flytte?'

'Do you remember the cunning-woman's words?'

'Oh, are we back to her again?'

'When she described what she saw with the help of the talisman, she didn't talk about anyone by name but simply 'him'. He was moving fast along the path on account of the rain. His legs were going like knives until they stopped for an instant in front of the stile. But the man under the trees couldn't see clearly. The rain was coming down hard. He had to wipe his eyes to clear them and still he couldn't see properly. His anger cast a shadow over his vision.'

'Yes, yes,' said Laurence impatiently. 'What does that mean?'

'It means," I said, 'that whoever was lying in wait in the spinney was not expecting to see Thomas Flytte. They were expecting someone else.'

We'd come to the point where the paths divided and Laurence went his way and I went mine, without exchanging another word. When I got home, my father was by the gate to the garden as if waiting for my return. He drew me to one side by the water butts under the thatch. He wanted a private talk, away from my brothers and sisters. He asked whether I'd been with Laurence. In the old days, I wouldn't have dared tell him but now the hostility between the two families seemed to have . . . not died away, exactly . . . but the heat and anger had been replaced by a sort of cold sadness.

I didn't tell my father we'd been to visit the cunning-woman but I didn't deny I'd spent a couple of hours with Laurence Carter either. In case he thought I was slacking, I said that my duties in the house were done and my mother, from her sickbed, had not told me to do anything else. My father waved his hand as though none of this mattered. He seemed curious rather than angry. He even asked after

Laurence's mother and father. I was not able to tell him anything at all beyond what I'd heard from my friend, that Alice Carter had grown very talkative while William Carter was even more silent than usual. It was almost dark and I sensed rather than saw my father's unease at that point, and I caught some words he muttered under his breath. They sounded like, 'I should not have done it.' He saw me looking at him and quickly said something about the alehouse and the piece of rope, and I realised he was harking back to that morning when the hatred between the Carters and the Raths had taken poisonous root. The moment when he'd exposed William for a miser, and a ridiculous one at that. I had not been present, unlike Laurence, but the story was known throughout the village of Wenham.

Then my father turned aside, as if he was done with questioning me, and went back indoors. Before I followed him in, I went to the privy-hut, not only because I needed to go there but because my hiding-place for the talisman was a small heap of stones behind the hut. I did not dare carry the talisman with me for fear of losing it, as the person standing under the trees had lost it. The pile of stones behind the privy seemed best. After I'd hidden the talisman, I went inside. I ate something. I went to bed.

I could not sleep among my little brothers and sisters but lay awake listening to their gentle breathing and occasional whimpers. The autumn wind banged the shutters. I thought of what we had discovered, Laurence and I, at the cunning-woman's. I thought of my father's words, 'I should not have done it', and his too quick explanation that he was referring to the business in the alehouse and the length of rope that William Carter had plucked from a muddy path. In my mind's eye, I saw the path that ran from the Carters' to the

Raths' and went beneath a stile, and I thought how, though that path was used only by Laurence and me, yet it appeared curiously worn and trodden on. I remembered something Laurence had told me a little time ago about an odd encounter he'd witnessed in Church Lane between my father and Alice Carter. None of these thoughts made it any easier for me to get to sleep, though I must have done for the next I knew a bright morning light was squeezing through the cracks in the shutters, and so began a terrible new day. And the end of the story.

Agnes paused and the Walsingham pilgrims thought she was merely catching her breath. But, no, judging by the way she looked across at her husband, it seemed as though her part was finished and that the landlord was expected to take up the reins of the story again. Laurence Carter ducked his head in acknowledgement and once more stood to address the group while his wife resumed her old place towards the rear of the audience. Not a few of the listeners regarded the landlord of the Angel in a new light. They saw him as young man, the lover of Agnes, slight and eager. And all of them wondered what was going to happen next. His wife's reference to a 'terrible new day' sounded very promising.

'Thank you, my dear,' he said to Agnes. 'It is more or less as she says, our story. Though I do not recall that I was so unwilling to go and see the cunning-woman in the woods. In my memory it was Agnes who had to be encouraged. But never mind that. It was I who witnessed what occurred on the following day, and I will never forget the things I saw.'

Harvest time was over and all was being secured for the winter. I was working in the hayloft of the barn, which was near our house. I was helping a man called Ralf, who my father had instructed to patch up some rotten planking in the wall. He was using the wood and nails from a broken cart of ours, and I was doing the fetching and carrying for him, toting lengths of wood across the yard and into the barn and up the ladder to the loft and then down again for more. In truth, it was not very onerous work and Ralf let me carry it out at my own pace, which is more than my father would have done. It was a fine early morning in autumn, with the sun low and blazing in the sky, and burning off the mist. It was warm too. It felt like a mockery of the whole rain-soaked year.

Ralf had removed the rotten pieces from the external wall and cut the wood back evenly so he'd have a sound frame for his repairs. He was kneeling on the floor by the space he'd created, his tools spread around him. The morning sun streamed through and tempted me to lie down on a pile of sacking in the far corner. Ralf's back was turned and I was about to take a short rest after bringing up the final load of wood when he said: 'Who's that? What's the matter with him?'

There was enough concern in his voice to bring me to his side. I crouched down next to Ralf and looked. The barn was set to one side of the farmhouse and off behind it. In front of us was the little fenced herb garden, which ran alongside the house and which it was my mother's job to tend. My father, William, was standing at the corner of the garden and staring to the east over the fence palings. He was cupping his hands round his eyes so as to see more easily against the glare of the sun. In the hazy distance was the figure of a man. If he was approaching our farm, he was doing so in a strange, looping style, sometimes veering off the path into one of the fields and then coming back again, sometimes running for a few steps before slowing down to a walk. At one point, he stopped altogether and seemed to be dancing a jig to music that only he could hear.

'Jesus, who is it?' said Ralf. He turned his head and looked at me. He had a grooved forehead with heavy brows, as though his own head had been hewn out of wood. I shrugged to show that I didn't know who it was approaching.

Every village has its share of people who behave oddly, which is perhaps only to say that they don't behave like the rest of us. I was familiar with two or three from Wenham like that, and I knew their shapes and their walks, but this figure was not one of them. It must have been a trick of the light, for with the sun behind him the figure seemed to be on fire himself, red flames leaping off his body. I glanced down at my father. He had lowered his hands from his face and he stood stock-still, grasping the fence. I had the odd feeling that he was waiting.

It was only when the figure was very close indeed that I saw with horror that it was Reeve, the servant of Thomas Flytte. Reeve, the bastard son who'd disappeared at around the time of the physician's murder and who was reckoned by quite a few in the village to be responsible for it. I didn't recognise him for several reasons. I never expected to see him again, and certainly not emerging from the mists of a fine autumn morning. And whatever it was he'd been doing in the months since his father's death, wherever he'd been hiding himself away, none of it had been to his benefit. He'd always been as thin as one of the fence palings that my father was grasping with both hands. Now I could see his ribs, the bones in his arms, his head like a ball on a stick. He was wearing almost nothing. Rags around his feet, a cloth knotted about his middle, some leaves woven in his hair. Worst of all though was that his bare, famished body was painted in streaks and tongues of red. It was this and his strange, jumping progress that made me think he was wreathed in flames. I have never seen anything like it except for many years afterwards watching a play in Norwich. One of the devils on the stage had just the look of Reeve and I could not stay in the market square but had to leave off watching.

The red paint on Reeve's tattered body was blood. Beside me I heard Ralf gasp and some sound came from the back of my throat. Still my father did not move or even flinch. He did not run back to the house where my mother, Alice, was with two small children, a brother and sister to me. For all I knew, there were others inside. I would have shouted out a warning but I could not get my tongue to work. Reeve halted a few feet in front of William. He stood there unnaturally still after all his jerky moving and he stared at my father, who said something. I could not pick up the words clearly because his back was to me and he was speaking low, but they sounded like, 'It is come, then' or, 'You are come, then.'

After that, there was a silence that seemed to last for many minutes but must have been only a few seconds. The silence was broken by a scream. It came from somewhere out of sight but I knew it was my mother at the door of the farmhouse, gazing at her husband and the blood-stained man. William glanced sideways in the direction of the scream and after that things happened very quickly.

From under the cloth about his middle, Reeve produced a knife. Its blade flashed in the sun. He stepped forward and, using both hands, raised it high in the air and brought it down in the centre of my father's chest. I heard the thud of the blow and a great gasp from my father as the air was pushed out of him and he staggered backwards. He fell next to a rosemary bush in the herb garden. The dagger stuck out of his chest. His legs and arms were flailing in the dark green of the rosemary. Another scream came from my mother, and that broke the spell that had kept Ralf and me crouching at the hayloft opening. We turned and scrambled down the ladder, through the barn and out into the open air. By now, Reeve had turned and was running away from what he had done. I heard a chink of something striking the ground and saw that Ralf had thrown a chisel but it landed far short of the fleeing man. Reeve ran along the same path as the one he'd come on. He did not shift around or pause for a jig this time but ran for his life until he was lost in the haze of the morning.

Meantime, my mother had reached my father's body and I stood beside her, confused and uncertain what to do. She was wringing her hands and moaning. William was still alive but there was a bubbling sound emerging from his slack mouth and the blood was welling up around the dagger, which had gone in almost to the hilt. It quivered with his dying breaths. His tunic was already soaked. I rushed inside to get something to stanch the flow, telling my little brother and sister that they were on no account to come outside. But by the time I returned to the herb-bed with some rags clutched in my hand, it was all over. My mother was kneeling beside William, one bloody hand spread over his chest and the other stroking his forehead.

Ralf the carpenter had set off in pursuit of Reeve but the mad man was far too quick for him and he gave up within a few minutes and returned to the farmhouse together with a couple of men from the fields. He had retrieved his chisel and now he was wielding it like a dagger.

Very soon others arrived, drawn by my mother's cries or by the sense that something was wrong. In a stumbling way, Ralf and I told them what had happened and told it again and the numbers of men around the palings of the herb garden grew until we had a large enough band to go in pursuit of Reeve. There were women too by now, consoling Alice and tending to the corpse even though it could not be moved until the Thetford coroner arrived. Among us was Alfred Rath, Agnes's father. He talked quietly to my mother, and his words sounded soothing though I'm not sure she was listening. I thought it showed Christian charity in him that he should be here so quickly to help at the house of an old enemy.

Alfred thought more clearly than any of us. He said that from our description of Reeve and his naked state he could not have been living anywhere close to the village, otherwise he would surely have been seen before now. True, he might have been hiding out in one of the tumbledown buildings dotted around Wenham, but most of them were used for storage or plundered for their wood and stone, and so wouldn't have provided a safe lair. The obvious hiding-place – the only place – was the Great Wood. And that was the direction he'd run towards. Alfred took charge and issued commands. He strode across to the barn where Ralf had been doing his repairs and directed us to pick up whatever implements we could for the hue and cry. Ralf was quick to protect his tools in the hayloft but he did present me with his chisel, telling me to keep it safe. He equipped himself with a stave.

By now there were at least three dozen men and boys gathered together, and all of us eager to give chase. I was so distracted by the hurry and excitement that I had almost no time to think of the death of the man who was my step-father. Later, I grieved, though not for long. Now we set off across the fields, half striding, half running. Almost every-body was clutching a weapon of some sort: staves, clubs, pitchforks, knives. From what we'd seen, Ralf and I, it did not seem as though Reeve could still be armed. He'd left his dagger planted in William Carter's chest, and his clothing was so tattered that there was no place for anything else. Yet, even if unarmed, he was still very dangerous: he was an outcast and a murderer, a man almost naked, painted with blood, and possessed by spirits.

The sun had burned off the mist and we were sweating by the time we reached the boundary of the Great Wood, where Agnes and I had visited Mistress Travis the day before. She lived in a different part, opposite to the Raths' farm, where it was less densely wooded and there were more paths. Even so, I worried for her in the woods with Reeve on the loose, and I wondered at this because yesterday I had been afraid of her and her visions. Now, Alfred Rath halted us on the edge of the trees and split us up into four groups, directing one to go left and one to the right and search inside the boundary, while the other two were to penetrate deeper into the trees, one veering to the east, the other west. He told us to stay tight within our own group and to judge our direction as best we could by the glimpses of the sun. Though the trees were bare, they were clustered together in many places, making it hard to see far.

I was with Ralf and, by chance, we were part of the band that was heading north-east, though any idea of direction stopped meaning much when we were crashing through the undergrowth and fanning out to cover as much ground as possible. We whooped and we shouted and some banged their staves against the tree trunks, as if we were trying to flush out the quarry from his hiding-place through the sheer din of the thing. Yet for all the noise and the company, Ralf and I found ourselves somehow separated from the others.

We followed a narrow path that was piled thick and slippery with yellow leaves until we were brought up short by a pool of blackish water. Only when we stopped to look for the best way round it did we realise that we were alone. In the distance we could hear the whoops and cries of the others. Then the noises died away and we heard nothing apart from the creaking branches and some rustling in the undergrowth. It was as if there had never been anyone in the Great Wood but Ralf and me – and Reeve, most likely. I felt my scalp prickling and my hand tightened round the chisel, which I still held. Ralf prodded at the black pool with his stave and it bubbled and gave off a terrible stench. He looked at me from under his heavy brows and I saw that he was as frightened as I was. For all the thickness of the trees there was some light on the floor of the forest on account of the fine morning. Abruptly, it grew dark. It was only the sun going behind a cloud but the sudden gloom added to my fear. I looked up and I must have gasped or cried out for I was conscious of Ralf staring at me in horror before he too turned his head upwards.

Immediately above us dangled an object that I couldn't make out. Then I saw that it was a pair of naked feet, all clenched and curled up in agony like the feet of our saviour on the cross. Ralf and I staggered back and away from the pool of black water. Once the first shock had subsided, we were able to see more clearly. Hanging from a branch far above us was the body of the man called Reeve. He was absolutely naked now, though he was all scrawled over with the streaks of dried blood. I could scarcely see his face, he hung so far above us, but it lolled down as if he was regarding us from his great height and with his tongue stuck out.

We ran a few yards down the path and shouted. I don't know what we said. I was very glad when some of the others came in answer to our cries, and most glad of all to see Alfred Rath. My companion, Ralf, pointed with his arm stiff and outstretched and then it seemed as though every man and boy in Wenham was crowding through the trees and down the path and teetering on the edge of the black pool and shoving each other aside so as to get a better view of the hanged man.

After that there was no real part for me to play. All work in the fields and in the village stopped with the double deaths and the arrival of the Thetford coroner. My father's body was removed from the herb garden and laid out in our house, with Master John in attendance. Some time later during the day Reeve's body was cut down. It was Ralf who offered to climb the tree. I think he felt that as he, with me, had been the first to glimpse the body he should be the one to retrieve it. He used the ladder from our hayloft. I helped him carry it across the fields and into the Great Wood. He climbed up the dead man's tree and crawled along the stout branch, and with a knife cut through the knots holding up the body. Reeve had hanged himself with the lengths of rag he wore about his middle or wrapped around his feet. Once Ralf severed the ragged noose, the body plunged down and landed half in the pool of black water. Several people who'd been standing too close were spattered with the stinking mud, to the amusement of the rest of us.

Although everybody treated that day as a kind of grim holiday, running between houses and standing gossiping on corners, the alehouse did good business. There was more talk about Reeve than about my father. People shuddered and looked over their shoulders and crossed themselves and said the murderer could not be human, but a monster or a devil in human shape. They said he must have been living wild in the Great Wood – which was surely true – catching and killing small animals to eat raw and besmearing himself with their blood and his own, for he had many cuts and wounds across his body. I remembered the time I'd seen him emerging from the shadows, holding a dead rabbit and giving his little smile.

It was Reeve, of course, who had killed Thomas Flytte in the springtime, choking the life out of the physician and leaving his body draped over the stile between the Carters' land and the Raths'. Although almost no one was aware that he was more than a servant or companion to the physician but instead Thomas's bastard son, everyone remembered the way he'd trailed after his master like a sullen dog. Everyone remembered his silent stare. As to why he had stabbed my stepfather, that was no mystery at all. If Reeve was a devil, then this was what devils did. If he was human, which was doubtful, then he must be mad or possessed, and it was well known that such individuals behaved in ways that were completely beyond reason or explanation. It was a mercy that he had hanged himself and saved the gallows an extra burden.

William Carter was buried in proper fashion in the churchyard, with all due ceremony. Master John reminded us that life was short and fragile – as if we needed reminding! My mother paid for Mass to be said daily for my father. I do not know what happened to Reeve's corpse. Somebody suggested it should be left where it had fallen by the black pond, which was dark and stinky enough to be one of the mouths of hell. But this was not enough for those men in the village who wanted to dispose of it so that it could never return to trouble us. They dumped the body in the back of a cart and took it off somewhere distant from Wenham, as if to remove the taint altogether from the village. They were gone for more than a day and when they returned not a one of them would say what they'd done with it. Perhaps they burned the corpse. Perhaps they buried it at a crossroads after driving a stake through the heart.

No one asked Ralf or me what we'd witnessed from the hayloft, beyond requiring the bare details from us, which we repeated again and again. The figure with the sun behind him, the body streaked with blood, the flashing knife. I didn't tell anyone of the words that I thought my father had uttered as he faced Reeve – 'It is come, then' or, 'You are come, then' – for the words made no sense. No more sense than the way my father stood there without moving while Reeve came closer. He didn't try to defend himself, he didn't rush inside and bar the door. Normally, my father was prickly and quick to take offence. He was a choleric man. But on this final occasion he had stayed to be slaughtered like a tethered beast.

My mother's grief at my father's death did not last so long. By the next summer, she had married, for the third time. Her husband was – Alfred Rath. For Joan had died before the Christmas of that year. So the two families that had been at odds for so long were joined together, after a fashion. Agnes and I became like cousins, true cousins, and no one cared now what we did or how much time we spent together.

A lot has happened in the intervening years, other deaths and births as well. All our parents are dead now, and the land that we farmed is held by our brothers, while Agnes and I are settled here at the Angel. We've often thought about what occurred during that summer and together we have pieced together a kind of story.

'The story is like this,' said Agnes, speaking from the back of the room, so the listeners once more had to crane their heads. 'It might even be true. The individual waiting under the spinney by the stile was William Carter, the stepfather to Laurence. William hated Alfred Rath, on account of their long-lasting quarrels and differences, and especially because of the business of the rope in the alehouse. But above all he hated his neighbour because he suspected something was afoot between his wife, Alice, and Alfred. He could not keep watch on her all the time, he had too much to attend to, but his suspicions grew stronger all the time.'

Agnes Carter stopped and now her husband began to speak. From now on each spoke a few sentences as if they were sharing the tale, as if they really had created it together. Sometimes the Walsingham pilgrims weren't even sure which one was speaking, man or wife.

Eventually, William Carter convinces himself that what he fears and suspects is so, and he decides to act. He knows that the most out-of-the-way path between their two properties is across the overgrown stile. After witnessing the couple meeting in Church Lane that morning, he determines to keep watch near the stile. Were they arguing about boundaries – or were they having a lovers' quarrel? He listens to his wife, Alice, talk about inspecting the hedges and fences and the request from Alfred to meet there. She won't go, of course. Or will she?

He walks out in the afternoon and reaches the boundary between his land – his wife's land! – and he slips over the stile because he wants to catch Alfred Rath all unawares. He shelters under the spinney. While he waits, the rain pours down and the anger boils up within him until it can no longer be contained. When he glimpses a figure he thinks it is Alfred Rath, because of the man's size and because of the clothes he is wearing. The man under the trees fumbles for the piece of rope he has carried for just this moment – what better way to dispose of an enemy than with an item like the one he taunted you with? – and as he does this he lets fall the talisman which the physician had given him as a preventative against the stone and choler and other hot conditions. He runs out of his hiding-place and overpowers Alfred as he stands for an instant before the stile. Except that the man is not Alfred Rath but Thomas Flytte, who has been lent a mantle by Alfred. In the madness of his attack, William does not realise this. Perhaps he does not see what he's done until he has choked the doctor and thrown his body head-first across the stile. Perhaps it is not until later that he realises with horror that he has killed the wrong man.

Luckily for him, there are other possible culprits to hand, like the pedlar Hugh Tanner and the servant Reeve. Both are missing and either of them might have murdered Thomas Flytte. Yet William Carter has not got away with it. He suffers in silence, or an even greater silence than usual. His wife is perhaps uneasily aware of her part in all of this, as is Alfred Rath. That is what her father means when he says to Agnes, 'I should not have done it.' He is not talking about the rope and the alehouse but about his . . . link with Alice Carter. Unhappiness has descended on both families. Joan too pays a penalty even though she has done nothing, and it may be the reason she slowly fades from our sight.

So when William sees Reeve emerging out of the sun and mist that morning, it was as if he'd been expecting him.

How else to explain the way he stayed fixed to the spot or to understand those strange words he uttered: 'You are come, then'? He did not try to run away or to avoid the blow. It was the punishment he felt he deserved, even if he might not have known it was coming at the hands of the physician's son. And there we have Reeve's motive, too. He wasn't a demon or a man possessed by one. He must have witnessed his father's murder or appeared in the aftermath of the scene. He alone knew who was responsible, and that it was William Carter. Reeve took refuge in the Great Wood where he went mad in his own fashion until that morning when he appeared clad in rags and armed with a knife to take his vengeance. He was angry. But not as angry as William Carter when he brooded over the wrongs done to him by his neighbour. In the end, his rage blinded him and he killed an innocent man, an act that led to the deaths of others as well as himself.

'So you see, ladies and gentlemen,' concluded the landlord of the Angel, 'why it is that I say anger is the worst of the seven sins. Like the other sins, it blinds us to our faults and even causes us to believe we are acting rightfully. Then it takes us further, urging us to pick up the nearest implement and to turn our rage into deeds. The injury we do ourselves is made many times worse by the injury we do to others.'

'And here,' said the landlady of the Angel, 'is a token of our story.'

From the depths of her dark red gown, Agnes Carter produced a small object. She lifted and turned it so that it glittered gold in the candlelight. She held it out to the nearest pilgrim.

'Go on, please,' she said. 'Touch the talisman and pass it round. Observe the image of the lion. It is good for the stone and for those of a choleric disposition. A cunning-woman held that thing and it told her a story. Perhaps it will tell one of you another story, a different one.'

The Sixth Sin

The storytelling was now taken up by an individual called Nicholas Hangfield. It was he who had attempted to speak to Janyn Hussett, the veteran of Crécy, at the very beginning. He was a quiet, good-natured fellow in his thirties, stocky and with dark hair. He explained that he'd been born in Bristol but that he'd moved to London, where he worked as a shipping clerk. He liked being near the water and he liked the sight of boats, though you'd never have caught him actually boarding one. Bristol was one of the places in the west where the plague was supposed to have struck and people looked expectantly at Nicholas as though he might have news for them, but he said that he had no family living there now and thus was no better informed than any of them.

'My father, William, God rest his soul, told me this tale many times, especially when I was a child – and when he was bed-fast for months, dying of a creeping inflammation of his lungs.

'In his prime, he had been one of the serjeants of the Sheriff of Somerset, living in Bristol where I was born and brought up. Not yet thirty years ago, in the fifteenth year of the reign of the second Edward, he had been assigned by the sheriff to be an officer to the county coroner and he served him for a considerable time. My father came to know about all the violent, unusual and suspicious deaths in the city and regaled me with many remarkable tales. One story in particular intrigued me and every detail has stuck in my memory – so much so that in many idle moments, I contrived my own conception of the affair, seeing the people in my mind's eye and hearing their voices in my imagination, until I built up a kind of play or masque in my head that was as good as reality. My theme is . . .

Envy

One sunny afternoon in late spring, Robert Giffard was lying on a bench in the garden behind his burgage in High Street, listlessly watching his servant place a goblet on a stool alongside him. It contained no fine wine, but a sour concoction that he himself had ordered the man to make up in his dispensary at the front of the house.

'Had we enough mother-wort in stock, Edward? We were running low.' Robert's voice was weak as he reached for the glass, but Edward Stogursey nodded reassuringly.

'Enough for another dozen potions, sir. And plenty of valerian, too.'

He was the physician's house steward and personal servant, but also acted as his lay assistant in the practice. A stocky man with a square face and cropped brown hair, he had an impassive manner that rarely showed any emotion. As far as he knew himself, he was about thirty years old, but as he had been left as a foundling in the porch of Stogursey Priory, he had no knowledge of the date of his birth. A local widow had taken him in and given him the name of their village in the Quantock Hills, adding the royal Edward for good measure.

As he walked back to the house, he stood aside deferentially as his master's wife hurried out of the door and made for where her husband lay in the sunny part of the long, narrow garden.

'Robert, are you sure this is safe to drink?' she asked anxiously, as she picked up the glass and sniffed at it suspiciously. Eleanor Giffard was a tall, slender woman, a decade younger than her husband's forty years. Glossy black hair peeped from beneath a linen coif, framing a smooth, oval face that had a hint of Latin ancestry.

'It was made to my own prescription, dear woman,' he replied slowly, as she took a sip of the brown fluid, then made a grimace of disgust.

'It's horrible! You know how careful you must be. We should get an extra taster, after what happened in February.'

Her husband made limp gesture of dismissal. 'Edward always tries everything first – and so far, he has remained hale and hearty.'

Somewhat reluctantly, she replaced the goblet on the stool and bent down to rearrange the pillow that cushioned Robert's head.

'You claimed then that someone was trying to poison you,' she said accusingly, 'and now you are ill again.'

'This is quite different from that time,' he countered, a hint of irritation strengthening his tone. 'Then I had yellow jaundice from an excess of bile in my liver. This time, I have palpitations, cramps and trembling. If I am being poisoned, then I intend to defeat it by taking nothing but simple food and drink that cannot be adulterated.'

Eleanor delicately lifted her skirts from the ground and sat down at the end of the bench alongside his feet.

'It seems beyond belief that anyone in Bristol would wish you harm, Robert! You do so much good in treating many people.'

'Perhaps too many! That may be the problem,' he murmured obscurely.

His wife's smooth brow creased in perplexity. 'Too many? How can that be?'

'There are those who are jealous of my success, as you well know. They are envious of the number and quality of my patients and would wish to gather some of them for themselves.'

Eleanor shook her head dismissively. 'You have said this before, Robert, but I can't believe that your colleagues would contemplate murder just to further their own ambitions!'

The physician gave a wry smile. 'They are not my colleagues, lady – they are my competitors! Just as a baker or a tanner competes for trade with his fellows, my medical brothers would cut each other's throats to gain a dozen more patients.'

The handsome woman considered this for a moment. 'I admit that I don't like any of them much – though that scrawny William Blundus seems modest enough and popular with the common folk.'

'Then he might have most to gain from having more patients, especially ones who could pay,' said Edward, cynically. 'But I wouldn't trust the other two, either. Humphrey de Cockville is too full of his own importance and would kill to have some of my richer customers.'

'What about Erasmus Crote?' asked Eleanor. 'He's such a whining, miserable fellow that I could easily see him hatching some devious plot.'

Her husband shrugged and winced as his muscles cramped with the movement. 'Of course, it may be someone who has nothing to do with doctoring. Maybe you have a secret lover who lusts after you and wants to get rid of an inconvenient husband!'

Eleanor reddened and stood up. 'Don't jest about it, Edward! I think we should get an experienced physician from outside Bristol to see you. Perhaps you are suffering from some obscure disease, and not being poisoned at all. That was your diagnosis, but even you are not infallible.'

'Thank you for your confidence in my talents, lady,' he replied rather sourly. 'And who do you suggest we could consult?'

'I hear that the new infirmarian at Keynsham Abbey is greatly to be recommended. The mayor's wife told me that he attended the university in Bologna.'

'Certainly one of the most famous schools,' he admitted. 'Even older than Salerno and Montpellier. I'll think about it, before we decide.'

'And I'll watch the kitchen like a hawk,' said his wife resolutely. 'Nothing will go on your plate or in your cup that I have not tasted myself!'

The physician's house on High Street was in the lower part, just above the bridge crossing the River Avon to Redcliffe. At the top of that street was the High Cross, the focal point of the city, from which four main roads radiated out to the gates set in the city wall. On one of them, Corn Street, three men sat in a back room of the Anchor alehouse. On a table before them stood a jug of wine, a fresh loaf and half a small cheese. They were not real friends, merely acquaintances, their only common bond being that they were members of the medical profession.

'He's no better. I saw him yesterday and he looks worse than last week,' said William Blundus, wrapping his fingers around his wine-cup. 'He has strange symptoms; I don't know what's wrong with him.'

Blundus was a thin man, slightly stooped and though hardly forty, had grey hair speckling his mousy thatch. A sad, lugubrious face was creased with worry lines and his down-turned mouth suggested that he was a chronic pessimist.

The man next to him was very different. A rotund fellow of about fifty, he had a puffy face with rolls of fat beneath his chin like a prize porker. Bald but for a rim of ginger hair around the back of his head, he had a pink complexion from which a pair of gimlet-like blue eyes stared aggressively at the world.

'You don't know what's wrong him?' he repeated in a rasping voice. 'Well, diagnosis was never your strong point, William!'

Humphrey de Cockville's sarcasm was ignored by the others, who were used to his waspish tongue.

'I wish the man no harm,' said the third doctor, Erasmus Crote, though the others knew full well that he was lying. 'But it's an ill wind that blows no good, for I've picked up three of his patients since he's been indisposed.'

Humphrey leaned forward to cut a wedge of cheese with a knife he took from the pouch on his belt.

'It's unfair that profitable work for us in Bristol is spread so unevenly,' he complained. 'Robert Giffard must have twice the number of patients that I see – and he attends upon most of the important families in the city and county.'

'And wealthy ones, as well as being important!' Erasmus added enviously. 'Most of the ships moored along The Backs belong to patients of his.'

Blundus nodded his scrawny head in agreement. 'All my flock are as poor as a village priest – the richest man I have is a saddle-maker!'

There was a silence as they poured more wine from the jug and Crote hacked the loaf into three, putting the two ends in front of his companions, keeping the softer middle for himself.

'I think I'll call to see him today,' he said. 'We must all

show a little concern for one of our medical brethren,' he added piously.

Humphrey de Cockville cackled at his colleague's hypocrisy. 'You want to make sure he's dying, eh? Then you can chisel away a few more of his patients before we get them.'

Erasmus scowled, his long face creasing in dislike of the fat physician. Crote was older than the other two, being in his early fifties. A sour, humourless widower, he always felt resentfully inferior to them. Blundus had trained in St Bartholomew's in London and de Cockville in Montpellier, both prestigious medical schools, whilst Crote had been merely an assistant to a physician in his native Dublin. However, he considered himself equally skilful and prided himself on his ability to treat skin diseases better than anyone in the West of England.

'I merely wish to show my concern for him and to offer any help I can,' he growled.

'And to ogle that beautiful wife of his at close quarters, no doubt!' sneered Humphrey. 'Though you're a score of years too old to be thinking of bedding her if he dies.'

Crote's sallow face flushed with annoyance, partly because there was some truth in de Cockville's taunt. Eleanor Giffard was indeed very handsome, but he would have little to offer her if she became a widow, especially with a dozen rich merchants all eager to snap her up if she became available.

'None of us has a chance there,' agreed William Blundus. 'I have heard that Jordan fitz Hamon has been a frequent visitor to the Giffard household and that the fair Eleanor looks upon him with some favour.'

Humphrey Cockville's pale eyebrows rose up his podgy face. 'Your long nose has been more active than usual,

Blundus! The fitz Hamon family owns probably a third of the ships that ply their trade from Bristol.'

The three physicians were well aware that Jordan fitz Hamon was the eldest son of Sir Ranulf fitz Hamon, and would undoubtedly be the heir to his business, making him one of the most eligible widowers in the city, as well as one of the richest.

'And he's barely forty years of age, not like you two middle-aged paupers!' continued Blundus waspishly.

'You are just a younger pauper!' countered de Cockville. 'Being of the same age as Ranulf makes you no less unattractive to a woman like Eleanor Giffard!'

'Stop bickering about fantasies,' snapped Erasmus Crote. 'It's no concern of ours what happens to Giffard's wife if he dies – we are only concerned with its effect upon our practices.'

This cooled the sniping between the other two physicians and they brought their minds back to the main issue.

'At least there are no other doctors in Bristol and none nearer than Bath or Taunton,' said Blundus. 'So we will have no other competition, unless Eleanor marries some fashionable physician from London.'

'We are talking as if the man is dead already!' complained Crote, who, alone amongst the three of them, showed a vestige of decorum. He rose to his feet and placed a few coins on the table to pay for his ale and food. 'As I said, I'm off to pay a call on the Giffards, both to see how the man is faring and to wish him a return to good health.' He marched out of the room, pulling the door closed behind him to cut off the snide remarks that he knew would follow him.

Humprhey de Cockville glared at the closed door. 'Two-faced hypocrite, he's off to discover how to wean a few more patients away from Giffard, if the man can't attend to his business.'

William Blundus looked thoughtful. 'That man Stogursey that Robert Giffard thinks so much of – he's been holding the practice together these past few weeks, even though he's nothing but an amateur apothecary.'

De Cockville gave a rare nod of agreement. 'It's not right that a mere servant should pass himself off as a doctor. If we only had a proper guild for us physicians, we could put a stop to it. The tanners or the silversmiths wouldn't tolerate such improper competition for half a day!'

Blundus sighed as he reached for the dregs in the wine jug. 'Yes, it's bad enough having the religious fraternity taking trade from us. If the common man can get free treatment from the nearest abbey infirmary, why should he pay a doctor'?

'Let's see what Crote discovers over in High Street,' advised Humphrey. 'Then maybe we can see how best to turn this to our own advantage.'

Erasmus Crote gained very little from his visit to the Giffard household. After barely five minutes there, he was back on High Street again and began walking aimlessly along the river bank outside the city wall as he considered the situation. He had not seen Robert Giffard, or even his wife, for he was courteously, but firmly barred at the front door by the Stogursey fellow.

'I fear, sir, that the master has taken a turn for the worse since dinner-time. The mistress had him taken back to bed, after he had a species of fit.'

Erasmus did his best to gain admittance by energetically offering his services as another doctor, eager to provide help and advice, but the servile apothecary's assistant was adamant.

'I regret that Mistress Eleanor gave strict instructions that he was not to be disurbed, sir. She is with him now, though he has drifted into sleep.'

Crote's argument that the sick man needed urgent medical attention fell on deaf ears.

'I am sure that you are right, sir – and that is why we have sent for an eminent physician, who will visit us in the morning.'

Erasmus noted the 'we', which suggested that the servant was now on an equal footing with the lady of the house. He also jumped on the news that another doctor had been called and for a moment wondered if he had missed a summons, which in his absence might now have gone to Humphrey de Cockville or William Blundus. But common sense told him that this was highly unlikely in the mere half-hour since he had left them.

'And who might that be?' he demanded of Stogursey.

The servant, obviously eager to shut the door in Crote's face, informed him that it was Brother Xavier, the new infirmarian at Keynsham Abbey and a man of high repute trained at the University of Bologna.

Before the door was finally closed on him, he managed to order Stogursey to give his felicitations to his mistress, hoping that her husband would rapidly improve and that if there was any possible help that he could give, she was to send a message to him at any time of day or night. The man, with a deadpan expression that conveyed a total lack of interest, said that he would do so, then Erasmus found himself staring at the oaken boards of a firmly closed door.

Now the physician was walking along the waterfront, the

many ships that were tied up along the wharfs reminding him of Jordan fitz Hamon, who would probably benefit the most if Robert Giffard died and left his desirable widow available for remarriage.

As he loped along, he contemplated the city where he lived and earned a meagre living. Bristol was now the third largest city in England after London and York, due to the maritime trade that made it the busiest port after London. Erasmus looked ahead of him along the muddy river to where it curved northwards through a steep gorge before meandering down to the sea, some seven miles away. The banks were lined with ships, now tilted against the quays as they lay on the mud at low tide. Twice a day, they were able to descend to the sea at high water, to make money for the city and especially the fitz Hamons.

Once again, Erasmus felt it so unfair that while he worked so hard to scratch a living amongst the poorer folk of Bristol, the rich merchants lived off the fat of the land, sitting on their treasure chests of gold and silver, merely from having accumulated wealth. Such wealth begat even more, with no further effort than employing clerks to administer a fleet of ships, manned by sailors who risked their lives in order to line their masters' pockets.

Erasmus Crote sighed and began retracing his steps back into the city, his melancholy being increased by the prospect of having to deal with a handful of patients when he got back to his dismal consulting room. No doubt it would be the usual collection of chronic coughs, scabies and suppurating sores that would bring in a few miserable pence. Just half a dozen of Robert Gifford's rich patients would set him on the road to success.

*

Robert Giffard was in a bad way by the time that the infirmarian from Keynsham Abbey arrived next day. Late in the morning, a placid palfrey arrived at the physician's house carrying the monk, a tall cadaverous man, accompanied by a groom on another horse. He was admitted to the house and at once taken by Edward Stogursey to the sickroom, where Eleanor Giffard was sitting alongside the bed.

She rose to greet the figure dressed in the robes of an Augustinian canon, a black cloak over a white habit.

'My husband is sinking fast, sir,' she said in a low voice. 'I fear he will not see out this day.'

Brother Xavier went to the bedside and looked down at the sick doctor, who lay deathly pale as he lay on his pillow. 'Has he spoken to you today?' he asked Eleanor. 'Has he shown any signs of consciousness?'

She shook her head sadly. 'Last evening he was fairly well and fell into what I thought was a normal sleep. But he has not responded to anything I say today.'

The infirmarian began examining his patient, lifting his eyelids and peering at the pupils. He gently felt the sides of the neck and probed the armpits, then pulled aside the bedclothes and placed his ear on the chest. Straightening up, he courteously suggested that Eleanor wait outside the room whilst he examined the more intimate parts of the husband's body. With the aid of Stogursey, who stood patiently on the other side of the bed, they pulled down the blankets and Xavier carefully surveyed and palpated the belly and genitals. Then the servant gently pulled the body of his master towards him so that the monk could study the back, noting some small haemorrhages scattered over the skin.

'Do you have a sample of his urine?' he asked the doctor's

assistant. Stogursey produced a glass bottle from under a cloth and the Augustinian held it up to the light from the window, studying the colour and sniffing the odour. Realising that Stogursey had a considerable knowledge of medicine, he extracted a detailed history of Robert Giffard's illness from the man. Eventually, with a resigned shrug, he left the bedchamber and went into the hall of the house, where Eleanor Giffard had ordered the servants to bring food and wine for the visiting infirmarian.

'I'm afraid I can't be of much assistance, madam,' said Xavier in a grave voice. 'And I fear you are right about your husband's condition; he is unlikely to live much longer.'

'But what is it that is killing him?' she demanded. 'Could it be some miasma that he has caught from one of his patients? Some are shipmasters who have returned from far overseas.'

The monk shook his head. 'I do not believe so, Mistress Giffard. I think he has been poisoned – but by what, I cannot tell. There are scores, if not hundreds of noxious substances, most derived from plants and herbs, which could cause such symptoms.'

'Have you no antagonist to such an evil thing?' she said tearfully.

Xavier sighed heavily. 'Without knowing what manner of poison it is, that is impossible. I am afraid that many people are misled into thinking that every poison has an antidote, but that is not so. Most methods of treatment are purely arbitrary.'

'Then what can be done? Is he to die without any attempt at saving him?'

'The problem is to discover how the poison has been adminstered,' replied the infirmarian. 'You say that all his food and drink has been tasted these past weeks since you suspected some evil doing?'

Eleanor once again assured him that either she or Stogursey had strictly supervised everything made in the kitchen and had both sampled it themselves. Xavier spoke gently to her for some minutes, though he knew that there was little he could do. After prescribing some bland treatment such as trying to get the patient to swallow white of egg and crushed charcoal, he had little else to offer other than his prayers. Eventually, after taking some refreshment, he mounted his horse and began the journey back to Keynsham. He had promised Mistress Giffard that he would return in several days, but as he made his way to the bridge, he knew that Robert Giffard would be dead before then.

Bristol Castle was on the eastern edge of the city – or to be more accurate, the city was continuous with the castle whose wide moat was fed from the small River Frome, which lay to the north. Inside the curtain wall of the castle was a massive keep, but there were numerous other smaller buildings, both in stone and wood. The sheriff, as befitted the King's representative, had his quarters in the keep, together with the numerous officers who administered both the city and the county of Somerset.

One chamber on the ground floor of this forbidding mass of grey stone was provided for the coroner, Ralph fitz Urse. Like the sheriff, a coroner was a royal officer, who had multiple functions, mostly of a legal nature. He was responsible for bringing cases before the Eyre, the perambulating court presided over by the King's judges. As part of his duties, the coroner had to investigate all deaths that were obviously not natural.

Most of his day-to-day work was carried out by his serjeant, William Hangfield, who had his own small office, little more than a cubicle, just inside one of the side entrances to the keep. This was a small arched gate some fifteen feet above the ground, reached by a wooden ramp, which in case of siege could be thrown down to avoid offering a weak point in the defences.

At about the eighth hour of the morning, William Hangfield was enjoying a quart of ale and a hunk of bread and cheese in the Great Hall, which during the day acted as a central meeting place of both the sheriff's staff and many of the citizens who came to transact business with the officials. Benches and trestle tables lined one wall and those with some influence in the kitchens could obtain food and drink to fortify themselves for the working day. William lived with his wife and small son in a small house on Wine Street, but as he had to deal with coroner's cases in all of the eastern part of the county, he was often out of the city. Today, he had no such tasks, and having just delivered some inquest records to the clerks for copying, ready for the next visitation of the judges, he had decided on some refreshment. He sat at a table, gossiping with some of his fellow officers, feeling relaxed, looking forward to an easy day in this hot weather. A rather short and heavily built man, now in his fortieth year, he had a thick neck and a round, rugged face, with black hair cropped to a horizontal line, in the old Norman style, which was long out of fashion.

He was a sociable man, popular with his friends in the castle and able to get along with his superiors, both the coroner and the sheriff himself. Both of these were not known for their patience or good nature, but William Hangfield was able to avoid any serious brushes with their authority, whilst still managing to get much of his own way in the methods that he employed to go about his duties. He sat with his pottery beer mug in a large hand, discussing the latest news about the ongoing antagonism between King Edward and the barons, who were demanding the expulsion of his favourites, the Despensers.

William's political conversation was suddenly interrupted by the arrival at his side of one of the door-wards. These were servants who stood guard at the entrance to the Hall, to prevent any undesirables from entering.

'William, there's a lad at the gate who says he must see you urgently about a death,' he reported. 'Shall I let him in?'

A few moments later, the door-ward brought a nervous youth to the table, a thin boy about nine years old in the plain but decent clothing of a house servant.

'If it please you, sir, I have a message for the coroner from my mistress,' he said quaveringly, awed by his surroundings. He held out a folded piece of parchment, sealed with red wax.

The coroner's officer took it and broke the seal, rapidly scanning the brief contents.

'Good boy, tell your mistress that someone will attend upon her very shortly. Understand?'

The boy nodded and quickly vanished, glad to be out of the castle, which to most of the citizens had an evil reputation for dispensing unwanted justice.

'More trouble?' asked his drinking partner, a senior clerk in the taxation office.

'One of our prominent citizens has gone to meet his Maker,' replied Hangfield. 'I had heard that he was ill, but not that he was in danger of death.'

'And who might that be?' asked the clerk.

'Our best-known doctor, Robert Giffard. He was very well-regarded, especially by the more eminent residents of the city.'

The clerk whistled through his teeth to express concern. 'He was certainly the best physician in Bristol – not that any of them could do much good – and he was certainly the most expensive!'

William Hangfield finished his ale in one swallow and rose from his seat.

'I had better tell the coroner straight away, as even in death people like Robert Giffard command priority.'

He walked across the hall to a doorway on the opposite side, where a man-at-arms stood guard with a pike. Nodding at the man, William opened the door and went along a passage from which opened a number of doors, one of which was the coroner's chamber. Inside the familiar room, he greeted the old clerk sitting at a writing desk with a quill. This was Samuel of Redcliffe, who had been compiling the coroner's records for longer than anyone could remember.

'Is he in yet?' asked Hangfield. 'There was a Mercer's Guild dinner last night, so I thought he might be a bit under the weather this morning.'

Samuel's toothless mouth gaped in a grin. 'He's in, all right, but in a foul temper.'

The coroner's officer walked to an inner door and, after a perfunctory knock, went inside. The coroner, Sir Ralph fitz Urse, was slumped in the leather-backed chair behind his table, on which were scattered various parchments concening current cases. He was a pugnacious man, built like a bull, with a florid face and nose covered in small blue veins, suggesting his fondness for the wine flask. He had thinning ginger hair and bushy eyebrows of the same colour. Beady eyes sat above drooping pouches of skin and his fleshy lips were down-turned in a permanent expression of bad temper.

William Hangfield was well used to fitz Urse's unattractive appearance and repugnant personality, but for some reason the abrasive coroner seemed to tolerate his officer far more than most other people with whom he came into contact.

'What do you want?' he growled, peering suspiciously from his bloodshot eyes.

'I've had a death reported,' replied William blandly. 'One that's a bit out of the ordinary.'

'Let me see,' grunted fitz Urse, holding out an unsteady hand to grab the parchment that his officer held. Having read the brief message, he looked up at William, who stood in front of his desk.

'I didn't know the bloody man was even ill,' he grumbled, getting laboriously to his feet. 'I could have done with a decent doctor myself, the way I feel this morning.'

'What do you want me to do about it?' asked William. 'I presume you'll want me to go down there straight away?'

The coroner rasped his bristly chin. 'With someone this important in the city, I'd better tell the sheriff. And you'd better see the family and find out why they think he's been poisoned.'

He lumbered towards the door, heading for the offices of Sir Nicholas Cheyney, the Sheriff of Somerset, who occupied several chambers on the opposite side of the hall. As he reached it, he turned to give further orders to his officer.

'A lot of important people in the city will be very put out by the loss of their favourite doctor.' he grated. 'So make sure you get this right, or we'll both be in the shite!'

William Hangfield strode out of the castle and across the

bridge over the wide western moat to the gate at the end of Wine Street. It was becoming warm already and he was glad that he had not worn his cote-hardie. He had on a loose brown linen tunic down to his thighs, being sufficient over his leggings. He had found his chaperon, a cloth headpiece with a tail on the side, too warm and had tucked it into his belt alongside his dagger and pouch. Pushing his way through the crowded street, now filled with porters, beggars, street musicians and goodwives doing their daily market, he reached the High Cross, the junction of the four main roads, and turned left down High Street. He knew every inch of the city and most of the county beyond, so he was able to walk unerringly to the Giffard house, a large stone-built burgage, its size and quality indicating the prosperity of the lately deceased owner.

He knocked on the heavy oak door from which Erasmus Crote had been turned away the previous day, but received no reply. As he was about to hammer it again, a small figure appeared around the corner of the house. It was the same lad who had delivered the message to the castle.

'The household is all at sixes and sevens,' the boy announced. 'The mistress is too upset to organise the servants and Edward Stogursey is trying to deal with some of the master's patients who have turned up for treatment.'

William put his hand on the boy's shoulder. 'Never mind, lad, it will all settle down,' he said kindly. 'But I must speak to someone straight away about your master's death. Do you know anything about it?'

The boy shook his head fearfully. 'Nothing at all, sir. I am only a boot-boy here and am below the notice of anyone in the family. I think Edward is the one you should speak to.'

The coroner's officer followed the lad around the corner

of the house, through a gate into the garden. Behind the main house was a smaller building, which was used as the doctor's consulting room. It had a separate entrance onto the street at the side.

'Edward will be in there, dealing with patients,' explained the lad, whose name was Henry. He led William Hangfield into an open lean-to, where three or four well-dressed people, who looked to be of the merchant class, were seated on a bench waiting to be seen.

An inner door opened and a man whom William recognised as the wealthy owner of a tannery came out. They nodded to each other as Henry darted inside and emerged with a short, dark-haired man. The coroner's officer had seen him about the city and rightly assumed that this was Edward Stogursey. It was common knowledge that this household steward also acted as the doctor's dispenser.

'I think it was you who sent a note to the coroner by the hand of this boy?'

Stogursey nodded and invited the official to enter the physician's room. Closing the door, he motioned William to a stool and stood before him in a slightly submissive attitude.

'Things are very difficult, Serjeant,' he began in a low voice. 'My mistress is naturally beside herself with grief at the loss of her husband in suspicious circumstances and there is no one else in the household but me who can hold things together.'

'Are there no relatives that you can call upon?'

'None hereabouts, sir. My master came to Bristol from London a good number of years ago and his wife is, of course, the daughter of the Lord of Berkeley Castle. They have no children, so there is no one to direct what is to be done.'

'You say "suspicious circumstances", but what evidence is there for that?' demanded the officer.

'The mistress called the infirmarian of Keynsham Abbey to see the master yesterday. He said he was sure it was a case of poisoning, but had no idea by what – or how it could be treated.'

This was news to William Hangfield, and changed the whole nature of the case.

'I will have to speak with Mistress Giffard at once,' he declared in a voice that allowed no argument. 'I realise she is distressed at the loss of her husband, but if what you say is true, then this is an allegation of murder.'

Edward Stogursey nodded his understanding. 'Of course, sir. I'll seek out my mistress now and advise her that she should speak to you.'

William wondered whether it was significant that this servant felt he should 'advise' his employer, rather than inform her. Before Edward could leave the room by an internal door, the coroner's officer stopped him.

'Before you go, tell me exactly how many people live in this house. I assume there are servants like yourself, as you say there are no other family members?'

'There is myself, of course, the most senior servant and an assistant to the doctor in his professional duties, since I acquired some knowledge of the apothecary's trade from him.'

William interrupted him with a question. 'You have no medical training apart from that?'

Stogursey shook his head. 'I have never been to any medical school nor have been apprenticed to a physician. All I know I picked up from working for Robert Giffard, God rest his soul.'

'Who are the other servants?' persisted the coroner's officer.

Edward Stogursey held up his hand to count off the fingers. 'There is Hamelin Beauford, the bottler, then John Black the cook, Edith the housekeeper, Betsy the skivvy, my lady's handmaid, Evelyn – and of course, Henry, the messenger. Outside, we also have a groom, Hugh Furlang, and a stableboy.'

'I will need to speak to them all in due course, but I first have to talk to your mistress.'

Edward Stogursey vanished and about five minutes later, returned to ask William Hangfield to accompany him to Eleanor Giffard's parlour. This was an airy room on the first floor, overlooking the garden. She stood by the window to receive him, tall and elegant in a black gown. He knew her by sight from seeing her at various city functions as although Bristol had about fifteen thousand inhabitants, most officials were able to recognise the upper members of society.

'I regret very much having to trouble you at this sad time, lady,' said William after making a small bow. 'But you will appreciate that this is a matter of urgency, if it is true that there are suspicions of foul play.'

Eleanor inclined her head to acknowledge his apology.

'I understand that you are the servant of Ralph fitz Urse. I am slightly acquainted with him; I think he was a patient of my husband's at one time.'

'Probably for a drink problem,' thought William, but held his tongue.

'I am his officer, appointed to help him by the sheriff. It is my duty to collect facts and report them to him.'

Eleanor motioned him to sit on a stool, while she sank

onto a padded chair at the side of the window. Edward Stogursey stood near the door, as if to act as a chaperon or a guard.

'I was told that he had been unwell for some time.' William began. 'When did this begin?'

As he spoke, he assessed the lady's manner, as he often did with people he was questioning. She was poised, elegant and showed no outward signs of grief in the form of reddened eyes from weeping. However, experience had taught him that this was no guide to a person's true feelings. She sat impassively, her hands folded in her lap as she spoke.

'Until recently, Robert has always been in good health. He loved hunting and riding and his appetite for his medical work was unlimited.' She paused and looked over at Stogursey. 'Edward, remind me when it was that your master first appeared to be ill?'

'Late in January, or perhaps early February, my lady. One day I remarked to him that he looked slightly bilious, and during the following week this became obvious. His eyes became yellow and he had pains in his belly.'

'But he recovered?' asked Hangfield.

This time Eleanor Giffard provided the answer. 'He had to go to London for some meeting of physicians at St Bartholomew's Hospital. He was away for almost two weeks and when he returned, he was free from the disturbances of bile and felt quite well. But within two months, other signs began to appear and it was this that made him think he was being poisoned back here in Bristol.'

'Why should anyone wish to poison a well-known doctor, who does nothing but good in the city?' asked William, in genuine puzzlement.

Eleanor turned up her hands in bewilderment. 'My husband claimed that other doctors in the the city were envious of his prime position as the most favoured physician, but I can hardly believe that.'

'Did he have any evidence of that?' asked the coroner's officer.

She shook her head. 'I doubt it, but he seemed wedded to the idea. It would be a most extreme means of disposing of a professional rival.'

William also thought it an outlandish theory, but he had to pursue all avenues, however bizarre.

'When he fell ill, was he treated by one of these doctors?'

Edward Stogursey spoke up here: 'My master said that he knew more medicine himself than the other three physicians combined and would not let them near him.'

This sounded more than a little arrogant to Hangfield, but again he kept his peace.

'So what happened? Surely he must have made some effort to receive treatment.'

'He prescribed what drugs and potions he felt useful,' said the widow. 'Then Edward here made them up and administered them.'

'They were bland and empirical salves, the accepted treatment for trying to get rid of toxic substances,' said the dispenser. 'Charcoal to absorb noxious material and general supportive treatment. There is little else one can do, especially if the nature of the poison is unknown.'

'Did your master suggest what the poison might be?'

Stogursey nodded. 'We spoke at length about it, sir. But there are scores of plants and fungi in the countryside that can maim and kill. There is not enough difference between their effects to identify them.'

'Though, at the first bout of illness in February, he did wonder if something like ragwort might the cause,' cut in Eleanor Giffard. 'That is well-known to cause disorders of the bile, especially in livestock.'

Edward looked dubious. 'Though I defer to my master's far greater knowledge, it seemed unlikely. Firstly, because ragwort, that yellow weed that abounds in the countryside, flourishes and flowers in high summer, so would not be available in February. Also, how could it be administered? For a horse or donkey to be poisoned by it, they have to eat considerable quantities.'

Eleanor was not going to let her husband's opinion be dismissed so lightly, especially by a servant.

'He said, when faced with these objections, that ragwort was even more poisonous when the plant is dried, making it dangerous for beasts to eat hay that contained the dead weed. So it could be collected in the summer and used in the winter.'

'But if large quantities were needed, how could it be administered?' asked William.

'It could be markedly strengthened by extraction as a tincture,' admitted Stogursey, somewhat grudgingly.

Eleanor became impatient. 'But we waste time and breath, sir. The jaundice passed off and the symptoms of the latest illness was quite different.'

'How so, madam?' asked the officer.

'My poor husband developed palpitations of the heart, sometimes so severe that he fainted. He also had tremors of the limbs and feelings of great coldness.'

'Unfortunately, such symptoms are so common in a whole range of poisonings that they do not help much in identifying the cause,' added Edward Stogursey.

William pondered the answers for a moment. 'You say he refused to be seen by any of the other doctors in Bristol – but did he not seek an opinion from elsewhere? He must have known some eminent physicians who might be able to help.'

The elegant widow nodded at this. 'I sent for one myself, only yesterday. We had good reports of the new infirmarian at Keynsham Abbey, a man well-qualified at one of the finest schools in Europe.'

'And what was the result, madam?'

Eleanor shook her head sadly. 'We had left it too late, I fear. He came and agreed that some form of poisoning was the most likely cause, but said that the effects had gone too far. He held out no hope for my husband's survival – and tragically, his opinion was proved right within a day.'

Hangfield noticed that the widow's iron resolve appeared to be weakening. She became pale and her strong voice faltered.

'I have troubled you too much at this time of melancholy, Mistress Giffard.' He rose from his stool and bowed again to the woman in black. 'I will leave you to your grief and return to make my report to the coroner. It will be necessary for me to speak to all your servants later – and I will have to hear what the physician at Keynsham has to say, but I will not trouble you again, unless some new matter arises.'

Stogursey accompanied him out of the room and down to the front door, where a portly man, whom he presumed was the bottler, opened it for them. William hesitated, wondering whether he should start interrogating the other servants now, but decided he had better report back to the coroner without delay, as this was likely to become a major issue in the city, given the influential people who knew the physician.

When he arrived at the castle, he went straight to Ralph fitz Urse and told him what he had learned at the Giffard house.

'They seem convinced that Robert was poisoned, but with what, and by what means is unknown,' he finished.

The coroner, hunched over his table looking like a bad-tempered bear, scowled at him. 'Are you sure they are not suffering from some delusion, some fantasy about a conspiracy, born of their bereavement?'

Hangfield shook his head. 'It has been going on for some months – and this renowned infirmarian from Keynsham is said to have confirmed it only yesterday.'

Fitz Urse grunted, still doubtful about the story. 'You'd better get up the river and see this monk. When I told the sheriff about this after you left, he was most agitated – Robert Giffard was so well known and well-regarded in the city that everyone who matters will be seeking an explanation.'

'I expected that, sire, but we can only do what is possible in seeking into it,' said William, slightly aggrieved that his efforts went unappreciated.

The coroner ignored his tone. 'And what about this tale that the three physicians in the city may have wanted Giffard dead?'

His officer shrugged his broad shoulders. 'Seems far-fetched to me! The widow said that it was her husband's idea that his competitors were envious of his success and of his monopoly of rich patients.'

The coroner scratched the stubble on his jowls; he shaved only on Fridays and it was already Wednesday. 'So these rich patrons will have to go elsewhere now. At least Giffard was right there.'

'I'm not so sure about that,' said William dubiously. 'This Stogursey fellow has been acting as the physician's right-hand man for years. Perhaps he can keep the practice going until Mistress Giffard arranges for another doctor to take over, if that's what she desires.'

'She's a fine-looking woman, from what I've seen of her at feasts in the Guildhall and elsewhere,' muttered fitz Urse ruminatively. 'Much younger than Giffard himself, though he was comely enough.'

William could not see where this line of thought was going, but in spite of the coroner's appearance and uncouth manners, he was a wily fellow, with much experience of human nature gleaned from years as a soldier and even more as a coroner.

'It occurs to me, William, that since the world began, wives have been getting rid of their husbands when they desire a different man. Who better has the opportunity to poison their spouse than a wife?'

His officer was reluctant to accept that this elegant woman could be a killer, but part of his mind recalled her dry eyes and her lack of obvious grieving, even though he had earlier told himself that such outward sins were not to be trusted.

'But how would she gain anything by that?' he said defensively. 'Robert Giffard was a successful man, looked upon with favour by the aristocracy of this city – and he was undoubtedly rich. His grand house and many servants confirm that.'

Ralph fitz Urse's reply was cut short as the door of his chamber was thrust open to bang against the wall and a corpulent figure strode in.

'The news is all over the town!' howled the new arrival. 'What are you doing about it, fitz Urse?'

This was the Mayor of Bristol, Richard de Tilly, the leader of the civic and merchant community of the city, who vied with the sheriff for pride of place as the most important figure in the county. A fat, self-opinionated man with a face as fleshy as the coroner's, but one that was more podgy and soft. Piggy eyes peered out suspiciously at the world, always looking for slights and offence. He was over-dressed in a red velvet cotta down to his knees, the flowing sleeves and green leggings too hot for the day's weather. On his head was a green brocade creation, which flopped down into a wide curtain on one side, reaching his shoulder. He was always to be seen with his gold chain of office hanging around his neck, and William sometimes wondered if he wore it to bed.

The coroner, who despised the mayor for a self-seeking tyrant, glowered at him. There was little love lost between the King's men and the civic authorities at the Guildhall.

'What are you talking about? Has the river dried up?' he snapped. This was a gibe at the city merchants, whose wealth depended almost totally on the free passage of trading ships down the Avon to the sea.

'You know damned well what I mean!' stormed de Tilly. 'Our physician suddenly dies and you ask what's wrong! How are we all to survive without his expert knowledge?'

'There are three other doctors in the city – use them,' grunted fitz Urse indifferently, seeking to annoy the other man.

'Those incompetents? I wouldn't take my dog near any of them. So what's happened and what's being done about it?' he demanded. 'It's barely an hour since I heard of the death and already half a dozen of the most influential merchants have been invading the Guildhall, demanding to know what happened and asking who are they going to find to treat them and their families!'

As Richard de Tilly continued to berate the coroner, William Hangfield took the opportunity to sidle towards the open door and vanish into the passage outside. He knew from experience that the coroner and mayor would argue until they started to trade insults, fitz Urse pointing out that the administration of justice was the King's business and de Tilly countering with blather about his responsibility to the citizens of Bristol. The sheriff would sometimes be drawn into the altercation, as a royal servant always taking the coroner's side, the whole fracas usually ending in the mayor stalking away, muttering under his breath.

It was still only mid-morning and as Ralph fitz Urse had specifically instructed him to speak to the physician at Keynsham Priory, William decided to go there straight away and leave the Giffard house servants until later. Making his way to the castle stables, he had his horse saddled and thankfully crossed the bridge into the country beyond, to enjoy the green woods and pastures of the Avon valley.

At noon that day, Bristol's three remaining physicians met again at the Anchor alehouse in Corn Street. Erasmus Crote, who had heard the news first from a patient who was one of the city watchmen, had sent a couple of urchins around to Humphrey de Cockville and William Blundus, calling an urgent meeting to discuss the passing of Robert Giffard. They sat in a corner this time, pots of ale before them, but no bread and cheese.

'There are all sort of rumours going around already,' announced Erasmus. 'Whispers that he was poisoned!'

Blundus nodded his agreement. 'I heard the same from a

fellow in the street,' he said anxiously. 'No doubt the town crier will be yelling it abroad in the next couple of hours.'

Fat Humphrey de Cockville slurped his ale, wiped his thick lips and sneered at their concern.

'What of it? It's nothing to do with us, unless one of you two has been lacing his victuals with deadly nightshade!'

Blundus scowled at him. 'Robert Giffard was a good, upright man – and a good physician. We are his only professional colleagues in the county, we cannot just ignore his passing.'

Humphrey leered at the others. 'Then we will all attend his funeral and shed reptile's tears – before rushing off and stealing his rich patients.'

'That's what concerns me,' said Erasmus, in a voice loaded with worry. 'Why should anyone murder a doctor, unless there was something to be gained? Suspicion must fall upon us, sooner or later.'

William Blundus, looking more stooped and emaciated than usual, grunted a disclaimer. 'I know I'm innocent of anything, so what's the problem? If one of you sent Giffard to his death, that's your look-out, but I'm not feared of any probing by the law.'

'Of course none of us did!' snapped Humphrey, impatiently. 'But are you so naïve as to think that the arrogant bastards that run this city care about justice? Giffard was so popular and useful to them and their families, that they need to find a scapegoat and to hell with any firm evidence!'

They pondered this, as they drank some of their ale, Humphrey motioning to the skivvy to bring another jug.

'So what do we need to do?' asked Blundus, looking to Erasmus Crote as the eldest of them and presumably the wisest.

'What can we do, other than sit tight and play the innocents – which is what we are?' grunted Erasmus.

Humphrey had other ideas. 'We need to go down to the Giffard house and pay our condolences to the widow – and discover what's going to be done about his patients,' he said decisively. 'It's an ill wind that blows no good – and I intend to pick up any good that's going!'

The coroner's officer covered the few miles to Keynsham in an hour and a half, having a good horse, a decent road and dry weather. The village was near a double bend in the River Avon and depended for its existence on the large abbey founded a hundred and fifty years earlier by the Earl of Gloucester at the request of his dying son. Hangfield knew this much about the place, but was not prepared for its large size and obvious wealth. A huge church was adjacent to cloisters, courtyards and many subsidiary buildings, one of which must be the infirmary.

He reined in at the main gate and enquired of the porter about seeking Brother Xaxier, the name given to him by Edward Stogursey. His horse was taken to the stables for watering and feeding, whilst the porter called a young novitiate to guide Hangfield to the infirmary. The outer courtyard was thronged with local people, lay brothers and a few Augustinian canons regular in their white habits, but further inside the warren of buildings and cloisters only a few monks were to be seen.

The infirmary was a large building at the back of the complex, and here some villagers and travellers were sitting on benches outside waiting for their ailments to be dealt with.

The young postulant took William to a doorway and into

a passage, where an alcove on one side appeared to be a treatment room, as a lay brother with a linen apron over his cassock was vigorously applying some salve to the legs of an old man lying on a table. Watching the process was a tall man of middle age with a solemn hollow-cheeked face. He wore the same vestments as the other Augustinian monks, but also had a white apron to both denote his status and protect his clothing. The novitiate bobbed his knee to the infirmarian and told him of the visitor from Bristol. With few last words of instruction to his assistant, Xavier came out of the alcove and greeted William, giving him the customary blessing.

The coroner's officer, who was religious from habit rather than conviction, bent his knee briefly, then explained the reason for his visit.

'The poor man died, then, as I expected, God rest his soul,' responded Xavier. He crossed himself, then led William to an adjacent room, little more than cubicle, which from the scrolls, books and pieces of medical equipment on a table, was the infirmarian's office. Seating himself behind his table, he motioned the officer to a stool.

'How can I help you and your coroner?' he asked. 'I saw the deceased only once and that very briefly. By then, he was unable to speak, so I could not discover anything about his symptoms, other than from the household.'

'I realise that, Father, but the widow seems convinced that he has been poisoned and I understand that you did not disagree.'

Xavier nodded. 'I am sure of it, my son. It did not show any of the signs of a disease – and the fact that there was a previous episode that abated as soon as he went away from home is good confirmation.'

'But Mistress Giffard said that you could not tell what noxious substance was involved – nor how it was given to the victim?'

The Augustinian nodded. 'That is true. The symptoms were common to many poisons. The obvious route of administering them is through the mouth, in food or drink, but the lady was adamant that for weeks past, all food had been tasted, much of it by herself.'

William Hangfield could see that he was not going to learn much that he didn't already know. He tried to extract a little more to make his journey from Bristol worthwhile.

'If this does prove to be a deliberate poisoning, we will have to try to find any residue of the evil substance, which may lead us to the person who used it. So can you suggest what we may have to seek?'

The canon considered that for a moment. 'As I have said, a number of poisons can cause the symptoms that the poor man suffered. But we can also eliminate others that would have led to signs he did not have, such as wolfsbane, hemlock, belladonna or foxglove, though there are many others.'

'What about any other means of the poison being given to the victim, Father?' asked William, as he prepared to leave. 'Could there be any way other than by swallowing it?'

The canon pursed his lips in doubt. 'It is hard to think of any that could be practically carried out. Noxious gases, such as from a volcano in Italy or even a lime kiln, could not apply here. I suppose that a pessary or enema could carry a poison into the bowels, but again that is out of the question here.'

Having drawn a blank on this line of questioning, the coroner's officer thanked the learned monk and took his leave, gratefully accepting the suggestion that he called at the abbey guest-house for some food and drink before riding back to Bristol.

He doubted whether he would have the chance to go to his home until later than evening, given the fuss the city leaders were making over the loss of their favourite doctor. However, his wife and son were used to him being away at all hours – or sometimes even days, if a case arose elsewhere in Somerset. Sighing, he clambered on to his horse and set off for Bristol.

That afternoon, the three physicians, having seen the dismal collection of patients at each of their doctor's shops in the middle of the city, met at Blundus's premises, ready to set off together to visit the Giffard household. Humphrey wanted each to go separately, but the others, suspicious of any purloining of patients being made by another, insisted on a communal approach.

'I wonder if Mistress Giffard will even see us?' asked Blundus.

'And if she does, what are we going to ask her?' added Erasmus.

Humphrey de Cockville, who always tried to assume the leadership of any group, was scathing of their doubts. 'We express our sincere sympathy, ask if there anything we can do to help her and then raise the matter of who is going to look after the sick and injured of this city!'

Still muttering doubts, the other two let Humphrey lead the way to High Street. He looked like a fat cockerel, with a red-feathered velvet hat and a bright blue surcoat over his black tunic. His companions were much more soberly dressed in greys and browns – and Erasmus Crote looked definitely shabby. When they reached the house, the front door was answered by the bottler, Hamelin Beauford, who seemed to double as a general factotum in the household, as well as looking after the supply of ale and wine. He was a big man, but was pasty-faced and looked unhealthy to the trio of physicians who now confronted him.

'You will know that we are your late master's medical colleagues in the city,' Humphrey began imperiously. 'We have come to express our condolences to your mistress and to offer any assistance we can.'

Hamelin looked distinctly unimpressed and made no attempt to invite them across the threshold. 'I will fetch Edward Stogursey to see what he has to say about that,' he grunted. He vanished into the house, leaving them on the doorstep, with the door almost closed upon them.

'Insolent fellow, he needs a clip around the ear!' snarled Humphrey. 'We are professional men, not some poxy apothecary,'

'This Stogursey is not even that; he is a servant with ideas above his station,' agreed Erasmus. However, short of barging into the house uninvited, they had little choice but to wait, and in a few moments Edward appeared, the bottler standing behind him as if to repel any invasion.

'We have come to offer our felicitations to Mistress Giffard at this sad time, my man,' said Humphrey in his grand manner. 'Please conduct us to her.'

Stogursey made no reply at first. He stared at the three men, then his eyes returned to Erasmus Crote.

'You were here yesterday,' he stated flatly. 'I conveyed your good wishes to my mistress then.'

This exhausted Humphrey's limited patience.

'Listen, fellow! We are the only other physicians in this city and it is a matter of civic importance that the citizens can all have the benefit of our skills. We need to speak with Mistress Giffard.'

Edward Stogursey regarded them for a long moment, until it was almost insolent. Then he shrugged and raised his hands. 'She is in no mood to receive visitors, but I will enquire.'

He grudgingly allowed them into the hallway and told them to wait, though there were no chairs or benches in evidence.

'That insolent bastard treats us like servants,' growled Blundus. 'It's a wonder he didn't make us go around to the tradesmen's gate at the back!'

They fretted for another ten minutes before Edward returned and grudgingly told them that Mistress Giffard had agreed to see them, but that they must not detain her for longer than a few minutes, as she was sorely distressed over the loss of her husband.

With Hamelin Beauford still lurking behind them, Edward led them to a staircase and then to a solar at the back of the house, which looked over the garden. Eleanor Giffard sat on a chair near the glazed window, gazing through it at the bench upon which Robert had rested during his illness. In a long black gown with widely flared sleeves, she possessed an elegance that the perceptive Erasmus thought was the reason why so many young widows were soon remarried. Seated on a stool in a corner was Evelyn, a stout middle-aged woman who was her personal maid and now apparently acted as her chaperone.

Eleanor stared coldly at the three men, who now stood awkwardly in the centre of the room. She recalled what her husband had said about them, their poor showing as physicians and their envy at his monopoly of the medical trade in Bristol.

'You wished to see me?' she asked stonily.

This time, Erasmus Crote hastened to reply before Humphrey.

'As you probably know, madam, we are the other three physicians in this city – now, alas, the only three since the tragic loss of your husband. We wished, as his colleagues, to offer our most sincere condolences at this unhappy time and to offer you any professional assistance that you might require.'

Mistress Giffard unbent a little and gave a slight nod in acknowledgement.

'That is considerate of you, sirs. My husband was taken from me by foul intent, but the coroner and sheriff will doubtless find the murderer and he will pay the ultimate penalty.'

Humphrey shouldered his way back into the conversation. 'We came not only to offer you sympathy, mistress – but to see how we can best assist you in the continuation of your husband's medical services to the citizens – if indeed, you desire to continue it.'

William Blundus, afraid of being left out of any negotiations, stepped in hastily. 'We are ready to accept any of Robert's patients who are in need of attention – it can be harmful and indeed dangerous for there to be an interruption in treatment.' He saw the lady exchange a look with the Stogursey before she replied.

'That will be no problem, thank you. Tomorrow, I am sending a messenger by the fastest route to the prior of the hospital of St Bartholomew in London. My husband, who trained and worked there for some years, was well known to him and he will undoubtedly find a worthy physician who can take over this practice.'

'But that might take many weeks, madam!' protested Humphrey, aghast at the proposition. 'What is to happen to your patients in the meantime?'

'Edward here knows all of them and is well acquainted with their diagnosis and treatment, as he worked alongside my husband every day. Until permanent arrangements are made, he can tide us over the problem.'

Erasmus made an attempt at protesting: 'But with respect, Mistress Giffard, this man is totally unqualified. He has never attended a medical school nor walked any wards – nor even mastered the art of an apothecary. It is unseemly for such a person to masquerade as a physician, especially to such eminent people who are some of your late husband's patients.'

Edward Stogursey glowered at this naked insult, but Eleanor was dismissive of Erasmus Crote's objections.

'Perhaps he has no formal credentials, but our patients know him and trust him as a faithful assistant to my husband. It is up to them whether they cleave to his ministrations in this urgent situation. I suspect most will, but if not, they are free to seek the aid of common apothecaries in the city or transfer their trust to one of you gentlemen.'

She sat down again and, pulling a kerchief from her sleeve, buried her face in it. Her tire-woman, Evelyn, at once moved to her side and put an arm around her shoulders.

'The lady is overwrought, sirs!' she protested, throwing an urgent glance at Edward, who immediately stepped forward.

'I think you should leave now,' he said harshly. 'My mistress is no state for further conversation.'

He made it an order, not a request and, opening the chamber door, stood by it until they filed out. Hamelin, the bottler, received them outside with a sour face and escorted them down the stairs and out of the front door, which closed firmly behind them.

In the street, Humphrey, unaccustomed to such slights, turned furiously to his companions. 'Getting rid of us was arranged beforehand! That woman is as hard as iron. She put on that weeping fit just to get rid of us.'

They began slouching their way back towards the High Cross, dispirited and annoyed at their lack of success.

'She did say that their patients were free to choose someone else to treat them,' offered William Blundus, to salvage something for their pride.

'Ha! Did you notice that she put apothecaries before us in that choice?' he snarled. 'That was a calculated insult!'

Erasmus raised a placatory hand. 'We've done all we can . . . now we can only hope that common sense will prevail amongst at least some of their customers. When they find that they have a charlatan as their only recourse when they're ill, maybe they'll see that a proper doctor is preferable.'

Though the three discomforted physicians assumed that they would never be allowed to darken the door of the Giffard house again, circumstances dictated otherwise. As soon as William Hangfield had returned from Keynsham, he went straight to the coroner and reported the meagre information that he had gained from Brother Xavier.

'Doesn't take us much further,' grunted Ralph fitz Urse grudgingly. 'I've had the sheriff and that fat bastard of a mayor on my back while you were away. They want this matter settled as quickly as possible, for it seems that some of the high and mighty of the city have taken the loss of their favourite doctor very badly.'

'Why should that be?' asked his officer. 'After all, he was only a physician.'

Fitz Urse shook his grizzled head. 'You did realise that his wife, the fair Eleanor, was a daughter of Maurice, Lord of Berkeley Castle? It seems he's been stirring it up since he heard that his son-in-law has been murdered.'

Hangfield knew only too well how the ruling classes still held sway over the public servants when anything went wrong. The kicking began at the top and ended with the lowest men, of which he was one.

'There's an even further complication,' muttered the coroner, morosely. 'Ranulf fitz Hamon, who as you well know is the commercial king of Bristol, owning almost half the ships that trade out of here, was a close friend of the Giffards. Not only did Giffard look after the health of all his shipmasters, but gossip has it that Ranulf wanted his son Jordan to marry Eleanor, the daughter of an earl, but Robert Giffard got in there first.'

William could hardly see the relevance of this in a murder investigation.

'You're not suggesting that could be a motive for getting rid of Giffard – to make his widow eligible for Jordan, are you?'

The burly coroner shrugged. 'I've learned in this job that nothing's impossible, though I admit it's a bit far-fetched.'

He suddenly stood up and slammed his big fist down on the table, making his ale-cup and inkpot rattle.

'Anyway, these people are nagging at the sheriff and he's nagging at me, so now I'm nagging you to get something done! First of all, as coroner, I'm obliged to view the body – for God's sake, we only have hearsay that Giffard is even dead!'

'I don't think there's much doubt about that, sir,' said William, trying to avoid one of fitz Urse's rages.

'Well, we'll go and make sure! I have to hold an inquest and so far there's damn little evidence to present.'

Hangfield was looking forward to going home to see his wife and son and have a meal and some rest, but it looked increasingly unlikely that this would be for some time. The coroner was already reaching for his surcoat and flat hat.

'We need a doctor to see if there are any signs of any violence on his body – and to suggest what sort of poison was used,' he rasped. 'Who can we call upon?'

'There are three others in the city, sir. Which one would you prefer?'

'I don't give a damn!' snarled fitz Urse. 'Call them all. Three minds may be better than one, especially if they are idiots or charlatans, like most physicians.'

On the way out, William called urgently for one of the castle messengers and gave orders that he find the three doctors and order them, on pain of dire penalties from the sheriff, to come to the Giffard house without delay.

The coroner and his officer stalked across the castle bailey and into the city, fitz Urse shouldering aside any luckless pedestrian who got in his way in the narrow streets. Though most trading had ceased, as it was now early evening, there were still plenty of people about, many going in and out of alehouses and eating shops. They marched down High Street in the direction of Bristol's only bridge across the Avon, until William indicated the large house that was the Giffards'.

'Must be plenty of money in doctoring, by the look of it,' growled the coroner. 'Though if the woman is from the Berkeley dynasty, maybe they bought it for her.'

William banged the front door once again.

'They're not a very welcoming lot in here,' he warned fitz Urse. 'Even the bloody servants think they are royalty.'

The coroner soon saw that for himself, but he was the wrong man to try to obstruct. Hamelin the bottler opened the door and was about to make some obstructive remark when fitz Urse pushed past him and demanded to be taken to Mistress Giffard. Hamelin's attempted protests were met with an offer to take him to the castle dungeons if he didn't comply instantly with the order of a King's officer. Brushing him aside, they went upstairs to the door of Eleanor's solar, but here they met another obstacle, which was harder for the coroner to overcome.

Sitting on a stool outside was Evelyn, the mistress's handmaiden, though it was many years since the elderly woman had been a maiden. She rose as the two large men clumped up the stairs and along the passage, followed by an outraged Hamelin.

'You can't go in!' cried Evelyn in a wavering voice. 'The mistress has a visitor.'

'I tried to tell you, sir,' cried the bottler. 'But you wouldn't listen.'

'This is King's business!' snapped the coroner. 'I'm the only visitor that matters at the moment.'

'Who is it?' asked William Hangfield in a more moderate tone. 'We need to speak with your mistress urgently.'

Another voice came from their rear, that of Edward Stogursey who had followed them up the stairs.

'It is Jordan fitz Hamon, come to convey the condolences of himself and his father, Sir Ranulf!' he said in acidulous tone. 'And the Earl of Berkeley is expected at any time, to comfort his daughter in her hour of bereavement.'

This was name-dropping on a massive scale, designed to

dissuade fitz Urse from intruding on their private affairs, but it had no effect on the pugnacious coroner.

He gave a perfunctory rap on the solar door and without waiting for a reply, pushed it open. William, peering past his master's bulky body, saw Eleanor Giffard in the centre of the room, again dressed in black, but this time in an even more elegant gown of silk, with a filmy black veil covering her hair. But what was more interesting was the back view of a tall man who had been facing her in close proximity, but who had stepped back suddenly when the coroner intruded.

This man now swung round to demand to know who had disturbed them. As soon as he and the coroner saw each other, there was mutual recognition, if not pleasure.

'Do you always blunder into a lady's chamber without her permission, fitz Urse?' he demanded.

A slim, athletic man of about thirty-five, Jordan fitz Hamon had the haughty air of a man whose family could have bought and sold most of the local nobility, if he chose. A long face with a straight nose, which usually seemed to pointing above the heads of lesser mortals, he was dressed in the latest fashion. A scarlet cote-hardie came to his thighs, belted with an elaborate band of embossed leather. His breeches were tight-fitting and ended in soft leather shoes with long toe-points. He wore no hat indoors, but William saw a green velvet creation with a vivid peacock feather, lying on a chair.

The coroner, who knew both Jordan and his father by sight – and had little wish to deepen the acquaintance – ignored him and addressed the new widow.

'I regret the necessity of troubling you on a day like this, mistress, but I have legal duties to perform.'

This was as near an apology as fitz Urse was ever likely to make.

'Damned insensitive and unnecessary, if you ask me!' snapped Jordan, but no one was asking him, as the coroner continued to speak to Eleanor. 'A King's coroner is obliged to view the body and to hold an inquest, madam. I also need to have the corpse examined by a physician, in circumstances such as have been alleged here.'

Mistress Giffard frowned and looked to Jordan fitz Hamon for support. 'But the best doctor in this part of England examined him only yesterday, coroner – Brother Xavier from Keynsham Abbey. Is it necessary to further disturb my poor husband?'

'Intolerable interference, fitz Urse!' brayed Jordan. 'I shall complain to the sheriff about this unwelcome intrusion into a lady's grief.'

Ralph briefly acknowledged Jordan's existence with a curt nod.

'It was the sheriff who insisted that we leave no stone unturned to find the perpetrator who has deprived this good lady of her husband!' he growled. Then he turned back to Eleanor. 'I presume that Robert's body is still in the house, madam?'

She nodded wordlessly, holding a scrap of lace kerchief to her eyes, though William could see no sign of tears. 'Edward will show you, if it is really necessary.'

The coroner nodded and had one last remark. 'I have ordered the other three physicians to contribute their knowledge to the solving of this heinous crime – they will be here directly to assist me.'

Eleanor's doubtful sorrow cleared up instantly. 'What, those awful people from the town? They've already been pestering me today, trying to steal patients from us!'

William noted that she said 'us' rather than 'me', and

wondered again what status Edward Stogursey had in this household.

'Well, they'll be here again shortly, though I'll see that they do not bother you this time. But my officer here will be bothering all your servants to see what they know.'

With a perfunctory bow, the boorish coroner took his leave and as William Hangfield followed him, he saw Edward make a covert sign to Evelyn to enter her mistress's chamber, presumably as a belated chaperone. The presence of Jordan fitz Hamon alone with her in the widow's solar had not been lost on the coroner, for as they clumped along the upper corridor after Stogursey, he muttered to William, 'What's that dandy doing in her boudoir, eh?'

His officer had no answer to that and, in a moment, the sullen servant showed them into a small room that appeared to be a spare bedchamber. On a mattress lying on a low plinth was a sheeted body with two lit candles at the head end.

'Did he die in here?' demanded fitz Urse.

Stogursey shook his head. 'He passed away in the main bedchamber, sir. But in this hot weather, we felt it better to remove him to this cooler room,' he added meaningfully.

'Let's have a look at him, then,' ordered the coroner.

William pulled back the linen sheet to the corpse's waist, revealing the pallid features of Robert Giffard. He was dressed in a thin night shift, with his hands crossed over his breast. The face was peaceful and showed no signs of any obvious disease or injury.

'Do you want to see the rest of him?' asked William.

Fitz Urse shook his head. 'May as well leave that for those medical fellows from town, so you can stay for that. All I needed to know was that he really was dead and to see the corpse, so that I can hold my inquest tomorrow.'

He turned to Stogursey, who had been lurking behind them, disapproval written large on his face.

'I will hold my enquiry at the second hour after noon tomorrow, in the Shire Hall at the castle. See to it that every member of this household, from your mistress to the boot-boy, is present. I will send for the body around noon, as it must be before me during the proceedings.'

The servant-cum-physician looked shocked. 'That is almost impossible, coroner! There are patients to see and a household to run, to say nothing of the strain upon my poor mistress!'

Fitz Urse was unmoved; he had heard it all many times before. 'You will do as I say or you will all be amerced with heavy fines.' As if sweetening his threats, he added, 'You may make arrangements for the disposal of the body after the inquest.'

After the abrasive official had left, William got Edward to round up the servants one by one for him to interrogate them. He did this in the lean-to shelter used as the patients' waiting-room. It was a quick and largely fruitless exercise, so he needed to take no formal statements, as no one knew anything of any value.

Edward had already explained what he knew of the illnesses of his master and neither the cook, housekeeper, lady's maid, kitchen skivvy nor the outside servants had any knowledge that could throw light on the death. Even little Henry, the boot-boy and general dogsbody, who seemed to pick up more gossip than any of the others, had nothing to offer him.

Just as he had finished with the servants, the three physicians arrived, looking anxious and guilty, half-afraid that they were to be accused of something by the officers of the law. William knew them all by sight and had actually consulted Erasmus Crote some months earlier, when his small son had developed a skin rash, which had cleared up after applying some foul-smelling lotion provided by Erasmus.

He quickly set their minds at ease by explaining that the coroner wanted a further medical opinion upon the cause of Robert Giffard's death, even though Xavier, the eminent infirmarian from Keynsham, had admitted being baffled by the death. Relieved, the three men immediately started arguing as to who should go first, but William firmly quashed this by telling them to examine the body together – and that this was a duty demanded by the King's coroner, so there would be no fee.

He marshalled them up to the room where the cadaver lay, with Stogursey hovering in the rear, wearing his usual disapproving scowl. This time, he removed the sheet completely to allow them to view the whole body.

With much muttering and prodding, they examined the entire body surface, the intimate orifices and squinted into the mouth, ears and eyes, before allowing William to cover up the body once more.

'Can you tell us exactly what was the progress of this affliction?' asked the pompous Humphrey de Cockville.

The coroner's officer explained the sequence of events, the attack of biliousness of the skin and eyes some months earlier and how it had cleared up as soon as Giffard went to London, then the recent attacks of malaise, tremors, palpitations and collapse, which ended in his death that very morning.

'And it is said that there was no way in which poisoned food could have been taken in the recent past?' asked de Cockville.

William shook his head. 'Mistress Giffard and all the servants swear that recently, since he was taken ill again, every morsel and every glass has been checked. In the past few weeks, both Edward Stogursey and indeed, the wife herself, have tasted every item of food given to the deceased.'

The only comment was from William Blundus. 'That's all very well, but what if one of those who was responsible for the cooking and tasting, was the murderer?'

'Don't be a fool, Blundus!' snapped Humphrey. 'The lady of the house, his own wife, was one who put herself at risk by sampling everything he ate. And is it likely that she would kill her rich husband, the source of her comfortable life?'

'Her father was far richer, remember,' grumbled Blundus, but he was ignored. William was anxious to complete his tasks, then hurry back to the castle and eventually, to his home. 'You three have now had an opportunity to examine him – and I've told you all we know about the circumstances. So have you any suggestions as to what the poison might be – and how it was administered?'

Again they went into a huddle, muttering amongst themselves, and eventually Humphrey de Cockville appointed himself spokesman, not that he had much to offer.

'There are so many poisons to be extracted from the plants and herbs of the countryside that it's impossible to be sure what it might be. It was certainly not deadly nightshade or any of the potent mushrooms. It could have been wolfsbane or foxglove, or perhaps extract of yew wood, which would fit with the symptoms, but there's no way of knowing.

'Possibly a good apothecary might make a better guess,' suggested Blundus. 'After all, we are physicians, dedicated to curing people, not killing them. Apothecaries spent more time collecting and extracting plants than us, so you could ask one of the better ones in the city.'

Humphrey, determined to keep the lead in any dialogue, nodded at this. 'A reasonable idea, but surely it matters little what it was that killed Giffard – what you need to know is how it was given to him, for that should lead you to his killer. I see no other means other than through his mouth, so maybe those who claim that all his food was tasted are lying?'

'Could it have been in an enema or an ointment?' suggested William Blundus, in a glum voice that indicated he had little hope of this being true.

'How could an ointment kill him?' said the coroner's officer, rather scathingly.

Blundus shrugged. 'Just a suggestion. Many drugs are absorbed through the skin – otherwise it would be pointless in us prescribing salves, lotions and ointments.'

'Well, I'll enquire,' replied Hangfield, in a tone that indicated he would be wasting his time. 'But maybe the coroner will take up your idea that an apothecary might be able to help us.'

Within the hour, William was back in the castle, where he routed out their old clerk, Samuel, to dictate a brief résumé of what he had learned, which was almost nothing.

'The coroner has gone somewhere, he'll not be back here until the morning,' announced Samuel in his quavering voice. 'He said that he was having a meeting with the sheriff and the mayor before chapel to discuss the physician's death.' The old man snorted in disgust. 'Just because the fitz Hamons and other wealthy merchants are upset over losing their doctor, we all have to run round in circles to appease them.'

William sighed, as it meant getting up early in the morning. He lived in a little house at the north side of the city and as it was obligatory for all the castle's officers to attend early Mass in the chapel at the seventh hour in the summer, he would have to leave home before he was properly awake.

He trudged back to his house in the early evening, enjoyed a good meal of pork and beans that his wife prepared for him and told her of the day's events. His six-year-old son, Nicholas, listened open-mouthed at the tale and, though he did not understand much of what his father was saying, he knew the dread implications of the word 'murder', which usually ended with a public ceremony at the gallows just outside the city wall.

It was an ill-tempered group that met in the sheriff's chamber early next morning. Nicholas Cheney and Richard de Tilly had both been at a feast in the Guildhall the previous evening, and the notorious lavishness of the Guild of Vintners, especially when they were celebrating the inauguration of a new Master, had left them with aching heads from the abundance of wine provided. The coroner had been at a different, more private celebration after attending a cock-fight and was also feeling as if the drummer of a war galley was performing inside his skull.

They listened in silence as William Hangfield read out his report of his activities the previous day and elaborated on a few of the points, to make it sound as if there was slightly more substance than it actually possessed. When he had finished, the silence continued for a moment, until it was broken by a rustling sound as the overdressed mayor fished around in his belt-pouch and pulled out a crumpled piece of parchment.

'Before we start discussing this shocking affair once again, what do you make of this?'

He slapped the parchment on to the sheriff's table and smoothed it out with a podgy hand.

'Some urchin slipped it into my under-clerk's hand as he arrived at my chamber this morning. The boy ran off as if the Devil was chasing him, but even if we had caught him, he would only have said that some stranger gave him a penny to deliver it.'

The coroner, who had flashing zigzag lights in his eyes as a harbinger of a migraine, did not attempt to read it. 'What does it say?' was his only question.

Sheriff Cheyney picked it up, being proud of his literacy in a society where that was mostly confined to clerics and merchants. In fact, the mayor could not read or write and the contents of the note had been read to him by his under-clerk.

'A scrawled hand, I suspect to disguise the penmanship,' muttered the sheriff. 'It reads, "Look to the killer in he who woos the lady."'

'And what in Hell's name might that mean?' growled the coroner, as the effort of thinking seemed to make his headache worse.

'It's blatantly obvious,' said the sheriff impatiently. 'Someone is claiming that Eleanor Giffard had a lover who wished to rid her of the encumbrance of a husband.'

The mayor had already worked this out for himself and the dangerous significance of it was not lost upon him. 'We would be entering hazardous waters if we took any notice of this foul accusation. It is obviously nothing but some evil libel made up by some malicious enemy.'

Nicholas Cheyney was inclined to agree. 'Even if only a

breath of such scandal were to become common knowledge, Maurice, Earl of Berkeley, and his powerful retinue would descend upon us like avenging angels, to defend the honour of their kinswoman.'

'To say nothing of the fitz Hamon family, if they became embroiled in this foul defamation,' growled the coroner, the flashing lights in his eye becoming more aggravating.

'Why should they be involved, for God's sake?' demanded the mayor.

Fitz Urse turned to his officer. 'Tell them what we saw at the Giffard house yesterday, William.'

Rather reluctantly, Hangfield related how they had called upon the widow and found her closeted alone in her solar with Jordan fitz Hamon, the lady's chaperone having been banished outside.

The sheriff, to whom this revelation was new, looked thunderous, while the mayor slammed his hand on the table and jumped to his feet.

'I knew this would lead to trouble!' he bellowed. 'This must not be made public knowledge, whatever happens! Imagine the scandal if the son of our most prosperous ship owner – and most generous benefactor to the city – was suspected of murder.'

'And even more if he was tried at the Eyre of Assize and hanged,' added the sheriff, with grim satisfaction.

The coroner overcame his headache to add fuel to the flames of anxiety. 'You are assuming that it is a man who is the culprit . . . but what if the wife wanted to be free to marry a younger man? Would it not be an even greater calamity if the daughter of Maurice of Berkeley was found guilty of poisoning her husband?'

The sheriff held up his hand for quiet. 'Before we begin to

rant and rave about the calamity that might happen, had we not better decide whether this scrap of parchment has any shred of truth in it? And if not, then let us forget it.'

His rational approach calmed the other two men.

'If true, it is a serious allegation,' said the mayor heavily. 'For a man to be alone with a married woman, especially if her handmaiden has been sent out of the room, can only suggest some impropriety.'

'So can we talk about who might have sent it – and why?' agreed the coroner. 'Either he has some knowledge of the poisoning – or is falsely trying to lay the blame for it on to another person.'

'With what object?' blustered the mayor. 'Could it just be spite – or perhaps he is just a deranged madman, out of his wits?'

'You keep saying "man", but it could equally well be a woman,' objected the sheriff. 'They are well known for both their devious cunning and for being fond of poison for their murderous deeds.'

There was a silence as the men digested these alternatives, until William Hangfield ventured to enter the discussion.

'You asked why he sent this missive, sirs,' he said respectfully. 'Surely, another motive might have been to divert suspicion from himself by falsely blaming others?'

His master, Richard fitz Urse, supported his officer's remark. 'It is certainly something to bear in mind. I suppose we have no notion at all who may have sent this?'

The sheriff looked at the creased strip of parchment again.

'It looks as if it was torn from a larger document, but nothing remains of that to assist us. The writing is in ordinary black ink and the penmanship is very irregular, though individual letters seem well-formed.'

'And what does all that tell us?' demanded the mayor aggressively, partly because, being illiterate, he was suspicious of anything to do with pen and ink.

'At least that he was educated enough to be able to write this, and was not some gutter-cleaner or wharf-labourer,' retorted the sheriff, restraining his desire to add 'or a mayor' to his list.

'Most merchants' clerks, clerics and even many choirboys can read and write to some extent,' countered Richard de Tilly irritably.

The others ignored him as the coroner addressed the sheriff.

'And you suggested that he – or she – disguised their handwriting?' Nicholas Cheyney waved the scrap of parchment. 'It seems strange that though the lines of writing are uneven and ill-spaced, most of the individual letters are well-formed.'

'Are you suggesting that we search a city of fifteen thousand people to find someone whose letters match these?' demanded the mayor.

The sheriff shook his head emphatically. 'That would not only be futile, but impossible! I suggest that we lock away this scurrilous note somewhere safe, but bear its allegation in mind in case any other evidence comes to light.'

The coroner looked dubious. 'I feel I must at least make some very discreet enquiries about the relationship between the younger fitz Hamon and Eleanor Giffard,' he said. 'What other motive can we imagine for this death? It is useless us sitting here, pontificating about it like a bunch of priests arguing about how many angels can sit on the point of a needle!'

He turned to his officer, who sat patiently waiting for someone to talk some sense.

'William, we need you to question those damned servants more rigorously. They must know something – possibly about the widow and Jordan fitz Hamon. And get a decent apothecary to look at the contents of the late doctor's pharmacy, to see if anything is there that might have caused the symptoms from which Giffard suffered.'

'And maybe a good look at the kitchen, the larder and the storeroom might reveal something,' added the sheriff.

A bell began tolling to summon the faithful to the castle chapel, and with some relief William rose and waited for the other men to leave, before they could find him even more tasks to perform. As they filed out to attend the early Mass, he wondered if there would ever come a time when murders were investigated by more than one coroner's officer in a city the size of Bristol.

William Hangfield was a devout man and he was bringing up his small son, Nicholas, to be the same, the family attending their local church of St Mary-le-Port every Sunday. However, at the castle chapel that morning, his mind was more on the tasks the coroner had given him, rather than on his devotions. As soon as the Mass was over, he hurried down Corn Street to the shop of Bristol's best-known apothecary, Matthew Herbert.

The coroner's officer entered his shop, which opened directly on to the street, the shutter of the front window hinging down to provide a counter for the public display of pots of salve, bunches of herbs and bottles of lotions. Within the large room behind, several journeymen and apprentices sat at counters, busy grinding powders and mixing ointments.

The walls were lined with shelves and rows of small drawers, each with a Latin name or cabbalistic sign painted on them to mark the contents. Bunches of herbs and even dried reptiles hung from the ceiling, and at the back of the shop, at a high desk set on a raised plinth, was the apothecary himself.

He was a grey-haired man in his mid-fifties, the most respected of his profession in the city. Matthew was the leader of the small apothecary group in the Bristol lodge of the Guild of Pepperers, which, through its monopoly of the spice trade, also embraced the purveyors of drugs and medicines.

William had met him several times, usually when he required some cure for his wife or son. Most of the city's inhabitants went to an apothecary when they were ill, as doctors were too expensive. Probably, yet more people sought the help of 'wise women' than even an apothecary – and in the countryside, this was universal, as there was usually no one else in a village, other than some widow or midwife, who could deal with ill health.

Matthew Herbert recognised the coroner's officer and came down from his high chair to greet him. When he discovered that William was there in his official capacity, rather than as a patient, he took him into a more private back room, which was a store filled with boxes, jars and bales, redolent with the aromatic scents of herbs.

'You have no doubt heard of the sad demise of Robert Giffard?' began William. 'The coroner would be grateful for your professional assistance in the matter.'

Matthew's bushy grey eyebrows rose in surprise. 'I have heard of the untimely loss of our best physician, but how can I be of any help in that?'

The coroner's officer explained the problem, leaving out

any hint as to possible suspects in the case. 'We have no idea what poison was used nor how it was given, but we wish to know if it might have been some substance already within the household, as naturally a physician will hold his own stock of healing drugs and potions.'

The apothecary was an intelligent and perceptive man.

'You wish to know if some evil person within the household might have been responsible – or whether the vile act came from outside?'

William agreed that this was the general idea, but Matthew was not optimistic about a useful result.

'I know that Robert Giffard held a wide variety of medicaments, as I have provided some of his patients with repeat prescriptions. Every physician will have a range of such materials to hand, as they tend to dispense themselves, rather than send their patients to an apothecary.'

He said this without any rancour, though William knew that it meant competition for his own trade.

'If that infirmarian from Keynsham, of whom I have heard glowing reports, did not know what killed Giffard, I doubt that I can do any better,' he continued. 'But I am willing to look through his stock to see if anything fits the symptoms he suffered. Having said that, many substances in a doctor's house can be lethal, just as the contents of this shop could kill half of Bristol if used improperly.'

He swept his hand around the room to make his point, as William wondered if he knew anything about Edward Stogursey.

'The mainstay of that household appears to be a man who acted not only as a servant, but as the physician's dispenser and even medical assistant. Mistress Giffard has indicated that she wishes this man to carry on dealing with their patients until a new physician can be found, which seems very irregular.'

The apothecary shook his head sadly. 'You meant that fellow Stogursey? We in the Guild have been concerned about him, as he is usurping our professional status in the city. And to hear that he has also been "acting the physician" is even more disturbing.'

'Can nothing be done about it?'

'It is difficult since he is not – and could not be – a member of the Guild, as he is unqualified and has served no apprenticeship. Thus there is no way of disciplining him, other than by physical violence and ejection from the city. As far as the physicians are concerned, they have no professional organisation, being so small in numbers outside London. So there is no one to say him nay!'

The coroner's officer arranged with Matthew to go down to the Giffard house in an hour's time, giving William the opportunity to speak further with the servants before he arrived. As he arrived at the physician's home, he saw a fine horse with an expensively decorated harness standing in the yard that led to the stable behind the house. It was being tended by a groom, who had his own pony tethered a few yards away, and William guessed that a man of substance was visiting the house. Was this person going to be the subject of the anonymous note, he wondered. As a lowly public servant, he felt he could hardly tackle Jordan fitz Hamon, the heir to the richest fortune in Somerset, to ask him whether he had been committing adultery with the dead man's widow. He walked over to the groom, who wore a smart uniform, rather than the usual nondescript tunic and breeches.

'That's a fine mare. Does he belong to Jordan fitz Hamon?' he asked bluntly.

The man, seeing the small badge bearing a crown on the jacket of Hangfield's jerkin that denoted a King's servant, touched his forelock.

'No, sir, it's his father's steed. My master is Ranulf fitz Hamon.'

Surprised, William gave a grunt and moved on rapidly. What was the significance of this, he wondered. He must tread carefully, as he had no wish to be caught up in some inter-family intrigue amongst the upper echelons of Bristol society.

Going into the house through the servants' door at the back, he came across Henry, the young boot-boy, who was struggling to drag a large bundle of clothing tied up in twine. As the lad was a thin, weedy weakling, who looked as if a substantial meal would do him good, William picked up the bundle for him, conscious that the lad was only a few years older than his own son, Nicholas.

'And where were you trying to take this, Henry?' he asked amiably.

'Outside the back door, sir. It is to be collected by someone from St James's, as clothing to be given to the poor.'

The coroner's serjeant hefted the bundle back to the entrance and as he dropped it outside, noticed that the clothing appeared to be of the best quality with no signs of wear.

'Good stuff to be given away so readily,' he remarked.

'That is the last bundle, sir. The mistress is getting rid of all my dead master's clothing. No doubt it reminds her too much of the great loss she has suffered.' William felt that it might also be a token of ridding herself of the last vestiges of someone she wished to replace. If so, she had acted quickly, as her husband had only died on the previous day.

Then he chided himself for his cynical thoughts, as Henry might have been correct with his more charitable version of Mistress Giffard's motives.

'Is she ridding the house of all of his belongings?' he asked, knowing that he may well get better information from the more lowly servants than the likes of Stogursey or Hamelin the bottler.

'I don't know about everything, sir, but I have had to tie up three bundles of his garments and several pairs of boots and shoes, which have already gone to the priory.'

The coroner's officer used the opportunity to pursue another matter.

'That's a very fine horse I saw in the yard. The groom told me it belonged to the father of the gentleman I saw here yesterday. Is he a frequent visitor?'

Henry, always ready for a gossip, shook his head. 'I've never seen the older man here before. The cook said he is a rich man who owns many of the ships along the riverside.'

'Did his son, the younger man, come often?' Henry's ingenuous expression did not falter.

'Quite often, sir, John Black said he was especially helpful to the mistress when Master Giffard was away in London after his first illness.'

It sounded as if the cook was the fount of gossip in the household and William marked him down as the next to be interviewed in more depth. Having squeezed all he could from the boot-boy, William went further into the house, looking for Edward Stogursey. He found him in a small chamber next to the room where the physician used to see his patients. The servant-cum-apothecary was sitting at a table cluttered with bottles and boxes of powders, grinding something in a pestle and mortar.

When he saw who his visitor was, his face clouded in annoyance, but no one could risk offending the coroner or one of his serjeants, on penalty of being dragged to the castle and fined, or worse.

'A senior apothecary will be coming very shortly to examine these premises, looking for anything that might have caused the symptoms your late master suffered,' he announced brusquely. He saw no reason to defer to this man, who was only a house servant, however much he thought he was above that station in life.

Stogursey shrugged indifferently. 'Very well, but it's a waste of everyone's time. All doctors' houses have a score of substances that could cause death, given a sufficient quantity.'

'Well, I'll let Matthew Herbert be the judge of that. You will give him your full co-operation – understand?'

From the deepening of the man's scowl, William guessed that the leader of Bristol's apothecaries was not Stogursey's favourite person, but he continued his questioning.

'I see that Ranulph fitz Hamon's horse is outside. I assume that he is visiting your mistress?'

'I would not know that; it's none of my business,' Edward said sullenly.

'Does he visit often, like his son?' demanded William, being deliberately provocative.

'Again, I don't know. My mistress's affairs are of no concern of mine.'

And if you did, you wouldn't tell me, said William to himself, though he admitted that it was the proper attitude for a loyal servant to take.

'Mistress Giffard seems to depend heavily upon you, from what I heard at my last visit.'

'Only in professional matters to do with the medical

practice!' snapped Stogursey. He began pounding the white granules in his pestle with renewed vigour.

'I see that the lady has been generous enough to give away many articles of clothing for distribution to the poor and needy,' persisted Hangfield.

'My mistress performs many charitable acts in the city – and as her departed husband has no further need of them, she felt that the friars could find a better use for them.'

'But your late master has not yet been put into the earth.'

'That is none of my business, Serjeant,' said Edward, in a tone of finality. 'If you wish to know more of my mistress's personal affairs, you will have to ask her yourself.'

'Oh, I will, never fear. But first, I wish to speak to John Black. Where will I find him?'

'In the kitchen, as befits a cook,' muttered Stogursey, bordering on the insolent, but William ignored him and left to seek the nether regions of the house. He found John Black not cooking, but sprawled in a chair in the large kitchen, a quart pot of ale on the table nearby.

A young girl, little more than a child, was chopping onions in a far corner, the tears in her eyes presumably not because of the death of her employer. The cook was a big, fat man who obviously took sampling his dishes seriously. William thought cynically that if the doctor had been poisoned through the food in the household, John Black would have succumbed much earlier than his master. A florid-faced man with thinning fair hair, he was less than forty years of age, but his teeth were already reduced to a couple of blackened stumps.

'Back again, sir? I told you all I knew last time,' he lisped, having some slight impediment in his speech.

'This is different, I want to learn more about who might have wished your master sufficient ill will to want to deprive him of life.'

Black's pale blue eyes widened in surprise. 'How would I know anything about that, sir? I'm only the cook in this place.'

William slid his backside on to the corner of the table. 'But you seem to know a lot about what goes on in this household. What about visitors? Who comes and goes?'

'This is a physician's house, Serjeant. People are in and out every day.'

William became irritated by the man's evasions. 'You know damned well that I don't mean patients! Anyone of note, friends of the late doctor and his wife? There seems to be one such person here at this moment – don't tell me that servants' gossip hasn't reported it to you?'

Cowed by the change in Hangfield's tone, the cook nodded. 'You mean the prince of shipmasters? He's a new one. I've never seen him visit before. No doubt bringing his commiserations to the mistress at her grievous loss.'

'But no doubt you've seen his son here?' snapped William.

John Black smiled, exposing his horrible teeth. 'Oh, certainly. He came often to visit the master and his good wife.'

'But sometimes just his good wife, eh?' demanded the coroner's man.

This time, the cook leered, rather than smiled. 'Well, quite often, the master happened to be away from home, visiting sick patients, if you get my meaning.'

William frowned; he did not trust this man to tell the truth.

'I have to ask you this, did you ever hear of any impropriety between them.' John Black looked over his shoulder and yelled at the kitchen skivvy to leave the onions and go outside to fetch carrots from the garden. As soon as she had scurried away, he looked back at Hangfield.

'Too many ears flapping and tongues wagging in this house, sir. As to your question, it is not my place to tell tales on my employers, but I would guess that the man in question would dearly like to have taken Robert Giffard's place in my mistress's bed.'

'What evidence do you have for that bold statement?' demanded William.

'Oh, none at all other than idle gossip, sir,' said Black hastily. 'But perhaps Evelyn, my lady's maid, might know more – though as she is so devoted to her mistress, I doubt she would tell you, other than under torture.'

Privately, William tended to agree with him, and saw no advantage in pursuing the matter at the moment, as it did not help in determining how and by whom the death of Giffard had been accomplished. Let someone else grasp that particular nettle if it came to making accusations against anyone in the fitz Hamon dynasty.

After John Black had stone-walled a number of other questions with his repeated claims that as a lowly servant he knew nothing of the goings-on in the upper reaches of the Giffard household, William sought out the remaining servants to question and got precisely nothing useful from them. As expected, the lady's maid, now released from her chaperone duties as Ranulf fitz Hamon and his horse had left, maintained total ignorance of any improper liaison between Jordan fitz Hamon and Eleanor Giffard.

'That one occasion when I was sent out of the room was because of her state of desolation because of the death of her husband that day,' she claimed indignantly. William left it at that, knowing that he was wasting his time. Similarly, the stableboy, the groom and the housekeeper had nothing useful to offer – and as for Betsy the kitchen skivvy, she was too frightened of him to answer even a single question, put however gently.

By this time, Matthew Herbert had arrived, and the coroner's officer took him directly to the chamber where Edward Stogursey was still making his preparations. The steward left immediately, not saying a word to the apothecary, his scowl speaking volumes about the professional man's intrusion into what he considered his private domain.

'I assume that this room and the one next door used by the physician would be where all the medicaments were stored,' said William, waving a hand at the rows of shelves and drawers around them.

Matthew nodded. 'I can soon check the names on each jar and drawer, though of course whether that is actually in them may be another matter. I'll do that within the hour and let you know if anything unusual is kept here, though I doubt it will help, as many substances, innocuous in medicinal doses, can be harmful or even fatal in excessive amounts.'

As this was exactly what Stogursey had told him, William had little expectation of anything useful coming from the exercise, but if the coroner wanted it done, so be it. He left Matthew to his task and made his way back to the castle, to get the old clerk to write a short account of his activities to present to Ralph fitz Urse, when he arrived back from the Great Hall where he had gone for his midday dinner.

Then, thankfully, William made his own way back to his house in Vine Street, where he could enjoy an hour's rest and a good meal prepared by his wife Marion. Then, with a mug of ale in one hand, he sat his small son on a stool in front of him and told him of what he had been doing that day.

The funeral of Robert Giffard took place two days later, after the coroner had held a brief inquest over it in a side room of the castle chapel. This merely identified the body and allowed the dozen jurors, dragooned from the Giffard servants and castle retainers, to parade solemnly past the corpse and note that there were no visible injuries. Ralph fitz Urse called a few witnesses, including the widow, Edward Stogursey, the cook, the bottler and, rather surprisingly, Humphrey de Cockville. The latter, having pushed himself forward as the spokesman of the three doctors, merely concurred that the symptoms of the final illness were consistent with poisoning, but that the nature of it could not be determined. After the inevitable verdict of murder by persons unknown, the coroner announced that the record of the inquest would be presented to the King's judges at the next Eyre of Assize and that any further information would be considered if and when it arose.

The funeral cortège set off towards St Augustine's Abbey, across the River Frome, and a considerable number of the city's great and good walked behind the cart pulled by a plumed black horse. The widow, supported by her maid and flanked by several of her female friends, walked immediately behind, with a score of well- dressed citizens following. Chief amongst them were her parents, the Earl of Berkeley and his lady, then the sheriff and the mayor, then Ranulf and Jordan fitz Hamon, with a number of prominent churchmen and a gaggle of the more important ship-owners plodding behind.

Quite a number of Giffard's patients made up the tail of the procession and the three other physicians were spread amongst them, not being averse to canvassing for business as they walked, as there was yet no sign of the new doctor allegedly coming from London.

Once Robert Giffard had been reverently put to rest in the graveyard of the abbey, the investigation seemed to come to an end. There was no new information in the following two weeks and though there were rumbles of discontent from Berkeley Castle and to a lesser extent from the fitz Hamon household, there seemed nothing that the coroner or sheriff could do to move things forward.

Gradually, the public interest in the death waned and was replaced by news of King Edward's increasing problems. The new doctor arrived from St Bartholomew's Hospital and virtually all of Giffard's patients resumed their attedance at his consulting room. Even the few who had drifted to the three lower-level doctors returned to the High Street practice as soon as good reports came of the younger and more energetic physician now installed there.

'What is the town gossip saying about this new fellow?' demanded the coroner of William Hangfield one morning. 'Is he living in Giffard's house now – and possibly in Giffard's bed?'

His officer grinned at his master's salacious mind.

'I doubt that very much, sir! He has taken lodgings in Queen Street and, though he is apparently a good-looking fellow of about Eleanor Giffard's age, the gossips still have their money placed on Jordan fitz Hamon as the next occupant of her bed.'

The routine of coroner's work soon displaced the death of the physician as the centre of discussion between the coroner and his officer. As well as the usual run of fatal stabbings in the wharfside alehouses, deaths under millwheels or the occasional hanging, William's time was occupied by a collision of two vessels in the narrow Avon Gorge during a gale, which led to the drowning of a dozen seamen. Recovering and identifying the bodies from the several miles of tidal mud and turbid water then took him several days. It was at the end of this that the Giffard murder reared its head once again.

When William arrived at the castle one morning, the old clerk said that one of the city watchmen was waiting in the Great Hall to report a death. The Watch was the rudimentary police force of Bristol, a handful of men each armed with a staff and a cudgel, who attempted to keep order in the city streets, especially at night when drunken sailors were brawling outside every alehouse. The coroner's officer knew them all and he soon found Egbert, a tall blond man of Saxon descent, sitting at a bench in the hall, drinking from a pint pot of cider.

'What have you got for us this time?' he asked. 'Not another boatload of drowned shipmen, I hope.'

The watchman shook his head. 'Just a dead beggar, William. As usual, it was a boy with a dog who found him, in a hovel along Welsh Back.'

This was part of the long quayside along the river, between the city walls and the bend in the Avon where it turned down into the gorge.

'He's gone off a bit, but no signs of violence,' he added.

William decided he had better look for himself and the two men set off for the riverside. They crossed the entry of the Frome stream into the Avon, dug out in the last century to divert the smaller river, to act as an additional defence to the city and to give some extra space for the burgeoning number of ships coming up from the sea. This was the maritime heart of the city, the second busiest port in England. An unbroken line of ships lay against the wharfs, riding high on the flood tide.

Labourers ran up and down gangplanks with sacks of merchandise on their shoulders, taking them either in or out of the warehouses set back from the quayside. Wooden derricks craned bales and barrels from the ships' holds, and the scene was one of prosperous activity. For a moment, William was reminded of Jordan fitz Hamon and his wealthy father, who probably owned many of these vessels.

As well as storehouses and barns behind the quay, there was a variety of other buildings, a few alehouses and some private dwellings, mostly small and often semi-derelict, to the point of being little more than heaps of rotting timber. Many of the stevedores working the ships lived there in mean circumstances and it was towards one of these that Egbert made his way.

'He's in that one, probably been dossing down in there for weeks,' he said, leading William to a ramshackle hut, which still had a sagging roof of mouldering thatch on walls of rotting wood. There was a door, but it was half open, tilted back on the one remaining hinge.

'Stinks in there, mainly due to the corpse itself,' warned the watchman.

Once inside, Williams saw that the single room was half-filled with rubbish, but on the beaten-earth floor a figure lay on its side. It was fully clothed but the skin visible on the back of the neck was swollen and greenish in colour. Several dead rats lay on the floor a few feet away.

'He's been dead a couple of days, given this hot weather,' said Egbert. Both men were well used to visiting corpses in all states of decay, and the sight and smell did not cause them any distress, The coroner's officer pulled on the dead man's shoulder to roll him face up, when an elderly man with grey hair was exposed. The features were distorted by pressure against the floor as well as early putrefaction and a number of rat bites, but the watchman immediately said that he knew the man.

'Don't know his name, but I've seen him about the city for years, usually rooting in rubbish middens for something to eat.'

William crouched to make a cursory examination of the neck and head to exclude obvious injuries, but given the state of the flesh, he made no effort to look at the rest of the body under the clothing.

'Best get him taken on a handcart up to the dead-house in the castle, where we can have a better look, before he gets a pauper's burial,' he said, rocking back on his heels. He looked around the derelict room and then frowned. 'It's strange that he has such good clothing upon him. This cote-hardie is of best wool under the dirt. Odd that such a beggar as this would be so well-dressed, unless he stole the clothing.'

Egbert agreed, pointing to the man's footwear. 'Those boots are very fine, if you like toes as pointed as that. They must have cost a few shillings – and they are hardly worn, if you ignore the rat bites.'

William looked more closely at the boots, which were of fine soft leather. In a number of places, this had been nibbled away, the edges being serrated, typical of rat bites, which were also present on the old man's face and hands. The woollen hose underneath was exposed in places, ripped and torn by the rodents' sharp teeth.

Something in William's memory clicked into place as he recalled helping the boot-boy shift some of his master's clothing.

'I wonder if he got these from the monks in St James's?' he said to Egbert. 'The widow of Robert Giffard gave away a lot of clothes for charity.'

The watchman shrugged. 'Maybe, but this poor old soul didn't enjoy them for long.'

He suddenly turned away and stamped hard on the floor with his heavy boot. William saw that he had crushed the head of a rat, which had still been moving slightly.

'May as well put the thing out of its misery,' he said laconically, showing a compassion that was unusual in that day and age.

William looked more closely at the rats on the floor. There were three that were obviously stone-dead, though not decomposed in any way. Then his eye caught a movement under a pile of rubbish and he saw another rodent, twitching and jerking slightly, its back arching spasmodically. Then it sudden went limp and lay still, obviously dead.

'What's killing these vermin?' asked Egbert. 'Is there something poisonous amongst this rubbish?'

The coroner's officer rubbed his stubbly chin thoughtfully. 'You may be nearer the truth than you imagine, Egbert. Let's get this old fellow's cadaver taken back to the castle dead-house as soon as we can, before he goes off any further.'

The watchman went off to the quayside to commandeer a handcart to shift the corpse up to the castle, where a lean-to shed in the outer bailey was provided as a temporary mortuary for bodies awaiting burial. While he was away, William found an old sack amongst the debris in the hut and dropped the four dead rats into it, carefully picking them up by the tails, using a piece of rag to protect his fingers from any noxious substance that might be exuding from them.

An hour later, they had pulled the clothing from the beggar, not without a few choice oaths at the smell both of the putrefaction and of the filthy state of the old man, whose last wash must have been long before the King's coronation. The boots and brown woollen hose were placed in a clean sack, the rest bundled up and put on a shelf in the dead-house.

After thanking Egbert for his help, William went off to report to Ralph fitz Urse about his suspicions that there might be a connection between the beggar's death and the tragedy at the Giffard household. At first, the surly coroner ridiculed even the faint possibility that the two events might be related, but in the absence of any better explanation, fitz Urse grudgingly agreed to his officer following up any leads that might strengthen the suspicion.

The first place that Hangfield went was St James's Priory, to enquire what happened to the clothing that the compassionate Eleanor Giffard had caused to be sent to them. He found a lay brother who worked for the almoner, who dealt with alms and all other charitable activities. This man, himself a Bristolian, knew at once who had been given some of the clothing.

'So old Gilbert is dead, is he?' he exclaimed. 'May God rest his soul; he deserves it after the poor life he had. He was an archer in the King's army years ago, but fell on hard times.'

William, anxious to strengthen his tenuous case, cut short the brother's reminiscences. 'So you say it is certain that the boots and hose, together with a cote-hardie that you gave him, came from Mistress Giffard?'

The other man nodded. 'No doubt at all. It was I who received the bundle from that young lad who brought it from the physician's house – and I handed some of it on to old Gilbert.'

Satisfied that he was at least confirming some of the links in the chain, William's next stop was the apothecary's shop in Corn Street. He carried the sack containing the boots and hose in one hand and, because of the stink, left it outside the door whilst he went in to seek Matthew Herbert.

The apothecary listened patiently while William explained the events of the morning and his idea that there might be some connection between the clothing and the death of both the beggar and the physician.

'It was the dead rats and especially the way one of them died that struck me,' he said earnestly. 'The spasms and the twitching, then suddenly dropping dead, was similar to what happened to Robert Giffard. Surely, the fact that the clothing came from that house and was given to the beggar, who died soon afterwards, could be significant?'

Matthew was too polite a man to have the same scathing reaction that the coroner had shown, but he wondered if Hangfield's devotion to his duties was stronger than the evidence he was proposing. However, he was intrigued enough to humour the officer.

'You say you have brought these boots and the hose with you?'

William nodded. 'I left them outside on the street – I doubt anyone will have stolen them, as they smell quite badly.'

'Bring them through to the back yard, where we can stay in fresh air.'

When William brought the sack through, he found Matthew sitting on a bench in the small cobbled area behind the shop. He had brought a metal tray, which he placed on the ground and asked the coroner's officer to place the boots and hose upon it. The smell was not too bad in the open air and William first lifted out the boots to show Matthew.

'See the way those rats had devoured parts of the softer leather of the uppers?' he said, pointing with a finger. 'They must have found it tasty, as about a quarter of the boot has gone.'

'And you say the hose was poking out of the holes?'

William nodded, pulling out one thigh-length stocking from the sack. 'Those vermin had chewed part of this as well; there's a hole in the toe where it was sticking out of the shredded boot.'

The apothecary studied the items, peering into the boot, apparently oblivious of the slimy state of the inside. He poked around with his finger, then studied its tip short-sightedly.

'I'll have to get one of my apprentices to look at this stuff; he's got far keener sight than me.'

Then, Matthew picked up the stocking, made of fine brown wool, and peered at the ragged edges of the holes made by the rats. He took a small wooden spatula from a pocket and scraped around inside the boot, then turned the hose inside out and scraped some of the slimy mess from the foot. William watched this with interest.

'Is there something there?' he asked.

The apothecary grunted. 'I'm not sure. There is so much slime from the sloughing of the dead man's skin that it's hard to tell. As I said, I'll get my lad, Stephen, to go through it with his sharp eyes. Come back in the morning and I'll tell you if I've found anything significant.' With that, Hangfield had to be content, though he was not sure if the apothecary really was hoping to make some discovery or whether he was just humouring him.

'Do you want to see the dead rats?' he said hopefully. 'In case there is anything you can tell from the way they died?'

Matthew Herbert shook his head. 'I don't need dead rats, but I may have a need for some live ones,' he said enigmatically.

Given the coroner's lack of enthusiasm for William's latest theory, the officer did not report his visit to the apothecary and carried on with his normal work, checking on witnesses for an inquest next day on a boy who had been crushed by a collapsing wall in the city, a not infrequent accident, given the cramped building conditions and often the shoddy workmanship.

That evening, he went home and again regaled his family with the day's events. His small son, Nicholas, was fascinated by his account of the dead rats and chewed boots, asking for more details of each morbid episode from the hovel on Welsh Back. His mother was afraid that this might give him nightmares, but with the resilience of the young, Nicholas slept like a log all night.

Early next day, his father escaped from the castle chapel as soon as possible and made his way down to the apothecary's shop, hoping against hope that Matthew Herbert would have found something to bolster the conviction that the clothing had something to do with Giffard's death. The apothecary left his desk and motioned him into the back room.

'See those? Dead as mutton,' he said, pointing at three dead rats on the floor.

'But I didn't leave them with you,' said William, puzzled at the sight.

Matthew shook his head. 'No, they're not your rats, they are ones my apprentices caught for me yesterday. I needed them for a test.'

He explained that he had locked the three rodents in a large box, giving them some cheese and meat mixed with a substance he had scraped from the inside of the boots and soaked from the lower part of the hose.

'It killed them overnight, with the same symptoms of twitching and fits that you saw in your hovel on the quay-side!'

Hangfield stared at the dead rats with fascination. 'So what was it that killed them?' he asked excitedly.

'That was the hard part,' said Matthew with satisfaction. 'I thought I saw something in the slime in the boot when you were here yesterday, but my apprentice did much better and picked out a few of these.'

He held out a small dish on which was a smear of brownish slime, embedded in which were a number of tiny yellowish spheres, each the size of a pin-head.

'What the devil are they?' demanded William, whose fairly good eyesight could just about see them.

'You may well call upon the Devil, for these little things killed those rats – and maybe killed that poor beggar, as well as your physician,' announced the apothecary firmly. 'They are the seeds of the yew tree, and are extremely poisonous.'

Hangfield felt a wave of exultation that his intuition had proved correct, though he soon tempered this with thought of the difficulties that still lay ahead, such as how was it done and by whom?

'But how could seeds in hose and boots kill a man?' he

pleaded. 'The death of the rats I understand – you gave it to them in food. That could not have happened to either the beggar or to Robert Giffard.'

'The seeds did not kill them,' Matthew replied. 'It was the substance around them that conveyed the poison, though that was originally made from the seeds.' He sat on the edge of a box in the storeroom. 'Look, everyone knows – certainly all country folk – that the yew tree is very dangerous. Branches lopped from yew are never left on the ground, because if livestock eat them, they may well die. All parts of the yew contain this poison, except the pulp of the berries. Yet the tiny seeds in the centre of the berries is very poisonous indeed!'

William still failed to see where this lecture was going. 'So what killed the rats and the others?'

The apothecary patiently continued his explanation. 'I gave the rats some scrapings from inside the boots and on the hose – it was virtually a paste, but that was because the rotten skin of the beggar, together with dirt from his feet and sweat, had probably softened what I suspect was originally a dry powder made from pounding a large number of seeds extracted from yew berries.'

William was still confused. 'But how could that kill a man – in fact, two men, if you count the beggar?'

'In my profession, we very often apply our medicaments through the skin – apart from giving cures by mouth, that is about the only other route available, other than by a clister through the back passage. Rubbed into the skin, especially with some kind of fatty base, some of the drug gets absorbed into the body.'

William Hangfield frowned as he digested this information. 'So someone would have to sprinkle the powdered yew seeds into the boots and hose undetected, if he – or she – wanted to cause harm to the victim?'

Matthew nodded his agreement. 'It would be a brownish colour and as the clothing was the same hue, it might well go unnoticed.'

'Would this be effective in a single dose or would the effect only work over a long period?

'I have seen two cases of yew poisoning in my lifetime, both in children who ate the attractive berries. Thankfully, both survived after forced vomiting and energetic purging, but they became very ill within a few hours, again with twitching and fits and a very irregular pulse. So a single large dose can kill quickly, but I doubt that could be achieved through the skin, so a more long-term application would be needed, which could build up to dangerous or fatal levels.'

William had by now grasped all the essentials of the method of killing, but the vital question now remained – who was responsible? He had one last question for the apothecary.

'The previous illness, which cleared up when he left the house for London – have you any idea what that might have been?'

Matthew considered this for a moment.

'It was certainly not the yew poison. He had an obvious excess of bile in his system and there are a number of poisons obtainable from plants in the hedgerows and woods that would do that. I would suggest it might have been an extract of ragwort, that tall yellow weed that grows everywhere. That sometimes kills horses and asses, even when they merely eat hay that contains the dried plant – but there is no way of being certain.'

William thanked Matthew Herbert sincerely for his help

and asked him to keep the evidence safe until he knew how the coroner wanted to proceed. It was about time he told Ralph fitz Urse that the investigation had been revived, so he trudged back to the castle with the news.

As luck would have it – though possibly bad luck – he found the sheriff in the coroner's chamber, sharing a jug of red Anjou wine as they chewed over the latest news of King Edward's problems. It was not long since the humiliating defeat at the battle at Boroughbridge and though Bristol was a royal stronghold, the tide was turning against him, mainly from the Scots and his own barons, though even his wife was beginning to lose patience with her husband's infatuation with the Despensers, both father and son.

The two men were arguing about the prospects of war when William came in, and he had some difficulty in bringing them back to the problems of the immediate present.

'I know how Robert Giffard was murdered, sirs,' he announced as soon as he had managed to get their attention. 'But I have no idea who did it!'

Nicholas Cheyney stared at him as if he had suddenly lost his wits and the coroner glared at him ferociously.

'What are you talking about?' he barked. 'We'll never know what happened to Giffard. There's nothing left to discover.'

His officer tried to keep a smug expression from his face. 'But I've just discovered it, sir. He had poison put in his boots and hose!'

'In his boots!' yelled the sheriff. 'Are you quite mad, William Hangfield?'

Hurriedly, the serjeant explained, before the others had apoplexy. He told them the whole story of the beggar, the dead rats and his involvement of Matthew the apothecary.

'He says there's no doubt about the yew being the poison, and though he has never heard of it being used through the skin, there is no medical reason why it shouldn't work.'

Eventually, the two senior men grudgingly accepted that the officer was neither mad nor playing some inexplicable practical joke.

'We must hear this from Matthew Herbert's own mouth,' growled the coroner. 'Then discover who the culprit must be.'

'It has to be someone in the Giffard household,' snapped the sheriff. 'No one else would have access to either his boots or, in the previous suspected poisoning, to his food.'

'And it must be someone who knows a great deal about yew poison and how it could be absorbed through the skin,' added William, sagely.

'That servant who acts as an apothecary fits the bill best,' grated the sheriff. 'What was his name, Stogursey or some such?'

'Remember that the lady Eleanor had the same access to his food and his boots,' objected fitz Urse. 'And there is this suspicion that she might be carrying on with Jordan fitz Hamon.'

'But she would not have enough knowledge of poisons to pull off this yew-in-the-boots trick,' scoffed Nicholas Cheyney, always ready to contradict the coroner.

Again, William threw in a reasonable contribution. 'The one who knew about the yew seeds and was able to prepare them need not be one who actually administered them, sirs.'

The other two digested this for a moment. 'If so, then even Jordan fitz Hamon could be behind the murderous plot!' said the coroner.

The sheriff, who was ultimately responsible for law and

order in the county of Somerset, turned to William with new orders.

'We need to shake the tree of the Giffard household and see what falls out. Take a couple of men-at-arms with you and get to the truth of this affair, even if you threaten them with torture.'

Hangfield sincerely hoped it would not come to that, but he touched his forehead respectfully and left to carry out his orders.

At the house in King Street, he sought an audience with Mistress Eleanor, brushing aside any delaying tactics by Edward Stogursey. She was in the doctor's chamber with the new physician, a pleasant-looking man of about thirty, but William, invoking the command of the sheriff, asked her to step into an empty living-room nearby.

'Madam, we have now discovered how your husband died – he was murdered by the poison from yew berries,' he announced bluntly. 'The deadly substance could only have been administered by someone in this household – and his previous illness in February may have been from putting a tincture made from ragwort in his food, again obviously by someone in the house.'

The new widow paled and clutched at her throat in a typically feminine gesture of shock. 'Are you sure of this? Who could have done such a terrible thing?'

'No one is above suspicion, madam,' said the serjeant, drily indicating that even the lady of the house herself was a candidate. 'I need to interrogate every servant immediately, to get at the truth.'

The two soldiers that he had brought with him rounded up all the staff and drove them into the back yard, where they stood in trepidation. William, wearing his most ferocious expression, repeated the news he had given to Eleanor Giffard and then demanded that anyone who had any information must give it that instant or suffer the consequences, which included a hanging for conspiracy to murder.

Edward Stogursey typically protested that he objected to being humiliated like a common criminal, but William pointed out that he was the best candidate, due to his knowledge of herbs, plants and drugs generally – and as the most senior servant, his easy access to every household activity.

'The poison was sprinkled or smeared into the victim's boots and hose!' he thundered. 'I am going to discover who did that, even if it means putting everyone to the Ordeal!'

This was a blatant bluff, as the Ordeal as means of divining guilt had been abolished in the previous century, but his meaning was clear and there were moans from some of the men and muffled shrieks from the two women.

'Who would have dealt with the master's boots, such as cleaning them?' rasped Hangfield, glaring around at the servants huddled in the yard.

A small voice piped up, hesitantly. 'Me, sir, but I didn't do anything bad, honest!' It was Henry, who came forward and dropped to his knees in front of the coroner's officer. 'I loved the master, sir; he was always kind to me.'

Eleanor gave a sob and ran forward to pick up the little lad to comfort him. 'Of course you did nothing wrong, Henry, we all know that!'

There was a sudden commotion at the end of the short line of servants as one man made a sudden dash for the back gate. One of the soldiers ran after him and sent him crashing to the ground before he could escape, dragging him back to throw him in front of William Hangfield.

'So, you do more than cooking here, John Black! Since when do cooks see to their master's boots and hose, eh?'

The fat man crawled to his knees and tried to embrace William's legs in supplication. 'I thought the powder was doing him good, sir, after his illness in the winter,' he blubbered unconvincingly.

The serjeant gave him a kick that sent him sprawling.

'You damned liar! And it must have been you that put the ragwort or whatever it was in his food that caused that disorder of bile!'

'He said it would do him good . . . I did it from the best of intentions,' wailed the cook, with the prospect of the gallows opening before his cycs.

'And who was "he", may I ask?' shoutcd William, relentlessly. 'Where did this evil powder come from, eh? And who paid you to put it in his hose and boots?'

The man grovelling on the ground whispered a name, and the officer gave him another kick.

'Mcn-at-arms, come with me!' he yelled. 'And bring this wretch with you!'

At a shabby house in a side lane off Corn Street, the group that had left the Giffard residence came to a halt outside the door. William Hangfield hammered on it with his fist and when there was no response, repeated the action with the pommel of his dagger.

'Open up in the name of the King's coroner!' he yelled, but again there was no reaction from inside the dwelling.

'There's someone in there, sir,' called one of the soldiers, who had seen a shutter open slightly on a window to their right. 'I saw a face looking out for a second, then it was slammed shut again.'

'Right, give him another minute, then kick this door down!' ordered the serjeant. As no movement was heard inside and the door remained firmly closed, one of the men-at-arms relinquished his hold on John Black and began attacking the stout oak door. He had nothing but his foot to smash against it and it was soon obvious that he was making little impression.

William grabbed the other arm of the cowed cook so that the other soldier could join his companion. Using their shoulders and feet, they thundered against the planks for several minutes until eventually they weakened the fastenings of the bolt inside so that with a splintering noise the door swung open.

'Find him! He's here somewhere!' howled William, still hanging on to the sagging John Black.

The two men rushed into the house and began searching the few sparsely furnished rooms on the ground floor. There was a shout from somewhere in the back and William answered with an urgent cry.

'Hold him, don't let him get away!'

However, when he reached the room, still dragging the cook, he saw his command had been unnecessary, as the fugitive was sitting calmly on a chair, his hands folded on his lap.

'Erasmus Crote, you'll hang for this!' said Hangfield fiercely. The physician shook his head and held up a small empty flask.

'I'll not end on the gallows, unless revenge leads you to string up a corpse,' he said mildly. 'I've just swallowed all that remained of the poison that killed Robert Giffard. There's no antidote. I'll be dead within a couple of hours at most.'

William grabbed the bottle from his hand and stared at the yellowish-brown dregs that lay in the bottom. 'We'll make you vomit, wash your stomach out with water!' he said wildly.

Erasmus shook his head and smiled at the officer. 'It would be useless; I took enough crushed yew seeds to kill a dozen cows. It's far better this way – better for us all.' His eyes moved to the fat cook, cowering in William's grip. 'So you betrayed me, John Black! I suppose it was to be expected.'

The cook shook his head vigorously. 'I had no choice. They were blaming it all on me. I would have hanged!'

'You'll hang anyway,' grated William, 'in place of this evil man, if what he says is correct about the poison.'

Black began blubbering again and Hangfield contemptuously pushed him back into the custody of one of the soldiers.

'You still seem quite healthy, Crote!' he snapped at the physician. 'We'll keep you locked up and, if you don't die, you'll swing from the gallows tree.'

'Give it time, officer,' replied Erasmus calmly. 'Though already I can feel the first twitches and racing of my pulse.'

'Why have you done this evil thing?' demanded Hangfield.

The lean physician, his sallow face resigned to death, sighed. 'Envy, officer! Just envy, pure and simple. You see, I loved my profession, yet have been dogged by ill luck and feelings of inferiority all my life.'

William frowned. 'I don't understand you, man.'

Erasmus gave a slight twitch as one of his shoulders had a spasm. 'I was a good doctor, but never had a fair chance. I never was properly trained, I picked it up from years as an apprentice in Dublin, walking the wards of a poorhouse and following a drunken doctor around a public refuge. I never had the chance to study the theory or read the famous texts, and never had the opportunity to listen to learned teachers.'

He sighed again and in spite of himself, Hangfield began to feel a little sorry for this gaunt man.

'Even those two buffoons who call themselves physicians in this city had the benefit of proper education, one at St Bartholomew's and the other at Montpellier, which he never let us forget.'

'What has this to do with murder?' growled William.

Erasmus Crote suddenly put a hand over his heart, feeling a sudden racing of the beats. 'It's started, there's not much time,' he muttered. 'There must have been more left in that flask than I expected – but all to the good.'

He brought his eyes up to meet Hangfield's again. 'I was better at treating diseases of the skin that all of them put together – including Giffard, though he was a good physician. But where did it get me? Nowhere! I scratched a living amongst the poor, treating sailors with scurvy, stevedores with sores on their jacks and urchins with ringworm, often for no payment at all. Yet in King Street, all the rich and notable citizens, as well as half the nobles of the county, beat a path to Robert Giffard's door.'

His head jerked back as a rictus of pain shot through his neck muscles.

'I was envious of his status, envious of the large fees his rich patients lavished on him! I was even envious of his comely wife, though God knows that, as a widow, she would never have looked twice at me. She was the daughter of a baron and Giffard himself came from a prominent family with high-placed friends in Westminster. What chance did I have of making a name – or even a living – for myself against such competition?'

He jerked again and sweat began glistening on his forehead as he felt a rush of palpitations in his chest. The coroner's officer now knew that Crote was soon going die, but hoped that it would not happen until he had the complete story of this sorry tale of envy and professional jealousy.

'And for that, you committed murder?' he snapped, almost incredulous that a man who spent his life trying to heal the sick could take life so cold-bloodedly.

Erasmus Crote was now flushed and shivering, but quite rational.

'You as a coroner's assistant must have known many murderers who killed for gain, whether it be for money, lust, love or hatred. They were no different from my overweening ambition to be looked up to in my profession, just as Giffard was a friend to all in this county who were its leaders. What difference is there between a thief who robs a merchant for his purse, and a doctor who tries to wrest a good practice from another?'

William Hangfield pointed out the obvious fact to him that he had failed. 'And what good has it done you, even if you had not been caught? Giffard's widow has just imported another good physician from London and with her lofty social connections, all the grand patients will remain there – especially now that it looks as if she will soon be taken into the bosom of the fitz Hamon family.'

Erasmus seemed to droop in his chair, his inflamed complexion suddenly turning into a deathly pallor.

'It is the story of my life, sir. Failure at everything, even the attempt to turn my life around. I wanted what Robert Giffard had and a growing obsession made me strive for it, without regard for the consequences. Envy overrode everything else – I was mad with envious ambition and it has brought me nothing, except death!'

'Was it you who wrote that letter to the mayor, to mislead us by hinting that it was Mistress Giffard's lover who committed this crime?'

Erasmus nodded, then with a groan, his head flopped on to his chest and his arms dropped to his sides.

'Is he dead?' asked one of the soldiers.

Hangfield pulled back Crote's head by the hair and thumbed up his eyelids to look at his pupils, then placed a hand on his chest.

'No, not yet, though his heart beats like a kettle-drum played by a madman. Lay him on the floor. There is nothing we can do for him.'

At the castle later that day, the coroner's officer related the whole sorry episode to Ralph fitz Urse and the sheriff, while Erasmus Crote's corpse lay in the dead-house and John Black was incarcerated in the cells in the castle undercroft to await his fate in front of the King's justices when they next came to Bristol.

'So why did this bloody cook agree to commit murder for the physician?' demanded the sheriff.

'Crote paid him money and the greed of John Black overcame any remorse at harming his own master,' replied William. 'He said he knew Eramus from often meeting him in an alehouse and eventually, for a bribe, he agreed to put a strong extract of ragwort into Robert Giffard's food.'

'Must have been a big bribe to get him to risk his neck for an attempted murder,' said the coroner.

'The excuse that Crote gave him was that he only wanted to make Giffard ill for a time, so that he would be unable to look after all his patients and Crote could gain by offering them his own services. However, Giffard going away for several weeks spoiled the plan, as his recovery, then the regime of the strict tasting of his food, restored him to health.'

The sheriff shook his head sadly, deploring of the evil of some men. 'So then he decided to kill him, I suppose?'

The coroner's officer nodded. 'He devised the idea of placing yew poison in his footwear. Being a skin doctor, he knew it could be absorbed in that way, albeit slowly. Giffard again became ill, but the villains did not reckon on the wife and this Edward Stogursey managing to keep the practice going. He gave Black more money, but also threatened to denounce him as his accomplice if he refused to help.'

'So he was determined to succeed or die, as he would be implicated if the cook was found out,' summarised Ralph fitz Urse.

There was silence for a while as the sheriff and the coroner thought about this tale of jealousy and frustrated ambition that led to murder.

'At least I'll be able to finish the inquest on Giffard that should satisfy all the élite of Somerset,' said the coroner. 'A novel verdict, eh? Murder by envy!'

THE SEVENTH SIN

'Pride, vainglory, that's the worst. It's the father of all the other sins,' the voice from the corner growled. 'Every wicked deed in this world was sired by pride, by man thinking himself more deserving than his fellows and wiser than God.'

His fellow pilgrims at the table craned round in surprised. Up to now on this journey, they'd not heard Randal utter more than a few words, so that some didn't even recognise his voice. And now that they had heard it, his tone only confirmed the opinion they'd already formed of the man, for his voice wasn't a pleasant one, more like shingle being dragged out by the tide.

As usual, Randal had taken his food over to the rickety bench in the far corner and had sat, hunched, eating and drinking alone, as if he was afraid his meats might be snatched from him. Even inside the inn, he kept his hood pulled up over his head, the long points wound round turban-style, seeming ready to leave in an instant should the need arise. And in truth his fellow pilgrims privately wished he would leave. Most of those sitting around the table had hoped he would go on ahead with the other group to Thetford, while those in the group who had braved the rain and travelled on were much relieved he'd elected to stay behind. Randal's presence unnerved everyone.

On the road, he'd always trailed a little way behind the group or kept well to the side of them, as wary as a stray dog. The others had tried to speak to him, but only received the briefest of answers, which had revealed nothing about the man, and even when he did speak he had the disquieting habit of looking over the shoulder of the person he was addressing, as if there was someone standing just behind them. The look was so intense, people would turn to see what he was staring at, but saw nothing.

There was more than enough to make even the boldest man wary on these roads. Any clump of trees or tall rushes might conceal a band of robbers lying in ambush or the next turn might find you stumbling into the deadly embrace of the pestilence, if the chilling rumours were to be believed. Those were fears enough for any man. They didn't need the additional anxiety of travelling in the company of a fellow who gazed at things no one else could see. Only the mad or those who commune with ghosts and demons do that. In the large group they could avoid him, but now that they were fewer in number, their unease returned.

Randal's remark about pride might have been left hanging in the air like a stray wisp of smoke had it not been for Laurence, ever the genial host. He could tell from the moment the group arrived that this man had not struck up any friendship among his fellow pilgrims, and reckoned this to be the perfect chance to draw him into companionship.

'You have a tale for us, sir? Come, we are all eager to hear it, aren't we?' he said, nodding vigorously at the others to lend their encouragement to the man. But the grunts and murmurs he received in return were not quite as enthusiastic as he hoped for.

'Come closer. Join us,' he urged, but Randal did not move.

He clasped his beaker of ale in both hands and stared into it as if he could see shapes forming in it. Katie Valier shuddered and found herself tucking her thumbs beneath her fingers to ward off evil, as Randal began his tale of . . .

Pride

My tale takes place in the wealthy city of Lincoln, Randal began, not more than twenty years ago, though at times to me it seems like two hundred. It should be a holy city for it's a city of many churches, some reckon there to be as many as forty-six within its walls and that's besides the great Cathedral, the Bishop's Palace, the chantry chapels and the religious houses. So there are a great many priests in the city and most have precious little to occupy their time, save for saying Masses for the dead, for which the wool merchants pay handsomely.

But the hours that God does not fill, the Devil will. And there was in that city a group of five young clerics who regularly met in the evening to drink, eat and gamble at dice. Their chief amusement was to set challenges for each other –

dares, if you will – and wager on the outcomes. They frequented a tavern near St Mary Crackpole, which inspired the name for their little circle – the Black Crows. The owner allowed them to use the cellar, trusting that the priests would not steal from the kegs and barrels. It suited both parties: the young men didn't want rumours reaching their superiors that they were spending long hours in the tavern and the innkeeper didn't want the presence of a group of clerics to prick the consciences of his other customers and put them off their drinking and wenching.

Randal paused to take a gulp of his ale and the pilgrims' host, Laurence, chuckled heartily, nodding as if he understood the problem of entertaining clerics only too well, but his laughter died away under the stern glare of Prior John Wynter, who clearly disapproved.

'It seems to me this is a tale of greed or gluttony,' the prior said coldly. 'I hardly think that these young men can have had anything to be proud of. Shame is the only thing they should have been feeling.'

'Ah, but they were proud,' Randal said. 'Listen and you shall see.'

They sought out each other's company because they considered themselves to be far more interesting than the dull-witted clergymen who infested most of the city. There was one of the Black Crows in particular who took great pride in his talents and intellect, a young priest by the name of Father Oswin. He'd come to the attention of Bishop Henry Burghersh as someone who would do well in the Church, destined for great things and high office, many said. Oswin could read and write prodigiously well in several languages in addition to Latin, standing out markedly against his fellow priests, many of whom could barely gabble a Latin prayer by rote and that with little idea of what it meant.

Thus it was that Father Oswin, a man of no more than twenty-five, was selected, as one of the youngest men ever to be trained in the art of necromancy and other spiritual defences in the service of the Church. Subdean William and a few other members of the Cathedral Chapter had counselled strongly against it. It took a wise head and a steady nerve to wield power over spirits and angels, they said. No one under the age of forty was mature enough to handle such a role. But Dean Henry pointed out that wisdom did not necessarily increase with age. Many priests were just as addlepated and vacillating at sixty as they had been at sixteen, probably more so, he added, pointedly staring at several of the members of the Cathedral Chapter. The will of the dean, as head of Chapter, prevailed and Father Oswin entered into training.

Although Oswin was supposed to discuss his training only with his tutors, he could not resist the temptation to impress his fellow members of the Black Crows with little hints about the mysteries he was learning and, out of curiosity and perhaps a little jealousy, they constantly pressed him to tell them more.

One cold December night, the members of the Black Crows began to make their way towards their favourite tavern. There was a bitter wind blowing, carrying with it a fine misty rain, which clung to clothes and quickly soaked them.

First to arrive was Deacon Eustace, a thin-faced man with a long nose, which was always dripping and red, for he seemed perpetually to have a cold. He was dismayed to find himself the first, for he hated being down in the cellar alone. It was a gloomy place. Barrels and kegs of wine, flour and salt were stacked around the mildewed walls, and slabs of salted goat and bacon hung from the great hooks in the arched ceiling. The floor had once been the street on which Roman soldiers had marched and some in the town claimed their ghosts still did. It was only too easy to believe in ghostly soldiers in the flickering candlelight, which sent strange shadows creeping around the barrels and boxes.

Eustace had just made up his mind to wait for the others up in the warmth of the crowded ale-room, when he heard footsteps on the stairs and John ducked his head under the arch. He grinned cheerfully on seeing Eustace and clattered down the remaining steps into the cellar, stripping off his cloak as he came and shaking the rain from it. Eustace was still sitting huddled in his, for even in summer he complained constantly about the cold and damp of the cellar.

'Good,' John said, rubbing his meaty hands and straight away pouring himself a beaker of wine from the flagon on the table, which had been set ready for them. 'Thought I was going to be last, and I'd have to drink fast to catch up.'

John had the build of a blacksmith rather than a cleric, with a strength to match. Indeed, that was the trade of his father and older brothers, but there wasn't enough work in the smithy for all of them, and he, being the youngest, had taken minor orders simply to get an education, but he had no intention of remaining in holy orders. His talent lay in gambling, and he was convinced that if only he could scrape some money together, he could make a comfortable living as the owner of an honest gambling house, which would surely prosper if word spread that his tables had not been rigged, nor the dice weighted.

Footsteps clattered on the stairs again and Giles and Robert descended into the cellar. Giles, like John, was also in minor orders as the parish exorcist, his main duties being to exorcise infants at the church door prior to their baptism and organise the parishioners who were to receive the host at Mass and ensure they didn't smuggle the bread away uneaten to use in spells and charms. Giles bitterly resented this lowly role. Unlike John, he desperately wanted to be a priest, but he could not be ordained into major orders until he could find a living to support him. Without a wealthy patron, that was proving impossible.

He wiped the rain from his freckled face and threw himself down on the bench. It was evident to all that he was in a foul temper. 'I swear one day they're going find that old priest hanging from the rood screen with his tongue cut out. If I could carry him up there I do it myself.'

John leaned across the table and good-naturedly poured a beaker of wine for Giles.

'Get that down you, lad, you'll feel better. Giving you a hard time, is he?'

Giles made a growling sound at the back of his throat. 'I swear that man's mother was frightened by a viper when he was in her belly and he was born spitting venom. That's if he was actually born at all. His parents probably dug him up from under a stone.'

Robert took the beaker that John, in turn, held out for him, and drained it gratefully in one long swallow, shuddering slightly at the sour taste. 'Think yourself lucky you've only one like him to please. I've a hundred of them each worse than the last.'

Like Oswin, Father Robert was already ordained, but had no great liking for his post. His uncle, William, who was subdean of the Cathedral, had secured him a minor position there, but Robert spent as little time working as possible. As he was forever telling his friends, the one and only benefit of being employed in the Cathedral was that it was so large that, with a bit of ducking and weaving, you could always ensure you were somewhere else whenever anyone was looking for you.

'And where is the divine princeling?' Eustace enquired in his nasal tone, dabbing his dripping nose. 'You two normally arrive together.'

Robert grimaced. 'Taking instruction behind locked doors, or so some brat informed me. Probably summoning the Archangel Michael to do his bidding,' he added sourly.

Giles rolled his eyes and John chuckled.

'Anyway, I wasn't going to hang around waiting for him. I've been trying to dodge my uncle all day. Probably noticed I wasn't at Mass this morning and wants to blister my ears.'

Although Robert had no intention of exerting himself in the service of the Church – at least not in the position of dogsbody in which he found himself – all the same, he had been annoyed that his uncle had not suggested him for training in place of Oswin. He was kin, after all, and the post commanded a good stipend, and a great deal of respect. Most importantly of all, everyone knew it was a stepping stone directly into high office, and Robert thought the post of bishop would suit him well. He'd rather fancied living in sumptuous rooms and having a host of minions to wait on him.

'So where were you that you missed Mass?' John asked.

'Still abed,' Robert said.

'And I wager it was not your own,' Eustace muttered darkly.

Eustace took the vows of celibacy extremely seriously, unlike many of the clergy in Lincoln. He wouldn't look at a woman, even turning his face away when one of the older serving women at the tavern approached. Oswin often teased him about it, saying he was scared he'd not be able to resist the temptation to jump on her, but in truth, Eustace gave every impression of loathing all females.

John, grinning broadly, shoved the flagon of wine towards Robert, almost tipping the whole lot over with the strength of the push. Eustace made a grab for it and succeeded in righting it just in time, shaking his head despairingly at John. If there was any object that could be tripped over, broken or crushed, you could always count on John to do it.

'It's as well you've no ambitions to priesthood,' Eustace said. 'You'd drop the infants in the font and knock out half your parishioners every time you tried to put the host in their mouths at Mass.'

As John opened his mouth to retort, the door creaked ajar once more and they glimpsed the hem of Oswin's robes as he sauntered down the stairs. He ducked under the archway and descended the remaining steps. He was closely followed by the serving maid staggering under the weight of a steaming pot, a basket of bread trenchers and another of fresh bread. She lumbered over to the table and heaved the pot of civey of hare onto it, and handed round the bread trenchers. The young men made no attempt to help her, and she expected none. Clergy, she had long ago concluded, would leave you lying in the street in the path of a stampeding bull, sooner than soil their hands to help you up.

She tucked a greasy lock of russet hair back under her voluminous cap and retreated back upstairs with a promise to return with another flagon of wine as soon as she had a moment, which judging by the laughter and shouts above them wasn't likely to be soon. The men ignored her and concentrated on the meal, as if it had arrived on the table by magic.

Oswin stripped off his damp cloak, tossed it onto a barrel and settled himself on the bench. He was a well-favoured young man and a fringe of dark hair curled becomingly round his tonsure, making girls and matrons alike sigh that it was a pity that all the good-looking men ended up in the priesthood. Before anyone else could reach for it, Oswin leaned across and helped himself to the stew, sniffing appreciatively at the rich spicy steam.

'Never realised exorcism could give a man such an appetite.'

Giles snorted. 'It's not that taxing. I do it every week, several times in fact.'

'Saying a few words over a bawling infant or some crazed old woman is hardly the same thing. Even a *boy* in minor orders can do that.' Oswin leaned forward eagerly, waving his knife on which he had speared a large piece of meat. 'I'm talking about wrestling with demons, evil spirits, dark angels.' His eyes glittered with excitement.

A dark flush spread over Giles's face at the barely veiled insult. 'And how many demons have you managed to subdue today? Send them all howling back to Hell in chains, did you? Have you actually read the book of exorcism they gave me when I was made exorcist? Banishing demons is in the book, too, you know.'

'But divining isn't, nor summoning spirits,' Oswin retorted. 'Divining the hidden holy objects. Now that's a rare skill.'

'And I suppose you can do that, too. Go on then, show us!'

Hearing the savagery in Giles's tone, Robert glanced up from his meticulous dissection of the hare's flesh from its bone. He cast about for a subject that would divert them and unfortunately blurted out the first and only thing that crossed his mind.

'They've a new girl at the stew, backside sweet as twin peaches.'

'Which you know, because you've been biting into them!' Eustace snapped. 'I don't know how you can face your confessor.'

'We all have our weaknesses and we all know what yours is, Eustace,' Giles said acidly.

'What's that supposed to mean?'

'Hold your peace, lads,' John said, doling out what remained of the wine into each beaker in equal measure. 'I reckon one of you brought the Devil in here with you tonight. I'm away to fetch some more wine, 'cause I reckon Meggy's forgotten we're down here. So shift your arses and get out the dice. More gaming, less talking is what we need.'

It took John a fair time before he could finally waylay one of the scurrying tavern girls and cajole her into ignoring her other customers and bringing wine from the broached barrel in the yard. Meggy was clearing the gravy-soaked bread trenchers from the table as he lumbered down the steps. John groaned, hearing again the sound of an argument in progress. Mischief rides the east wind, his mother used to say and she wasn't wrong. It was a spiteful wind that always set men in an ill humour. He set the wine on the table, spilling some of it onto the basket of fresh bread. Unwilling to see either wine or bread go to waste, he crammed the soggy bread into his mouth as he poured the contents of the flagon into the Black Crows' beakers.

'So where's the dice, lads?'

'We,' Giles said, with a note of triumph in his voice, 'have found something far more interesting to wager on, something that should be a challenge even for you.'

They all knew that if women were Robert's vice, then John's was definitely gambling, not that he would have considered any pleasure that was so exhilarating to be a vice.

John flopped down on the end of the bench with such a thump that Giles, sitting on the other end, felt it lift beneath him. John leaned forward eagerly.

'So what's to do? What's the wager?' he demanded.

'Our princeling here has been boasting that he can find any holy object that's been hidden,' Eustace said. 'Giles has challenged him to put it to the test. Robert is to take something from the Cathedral and hide it. The wager is that Oswin won't be able to find it, using divination alone.'

'And when I win,' Oswin said, 'Giles will do a penance of my choosing in front of all the Black Crows for accusing me of lying.'

From the malicious expression on Oswin's face, it was plain he'd already decided any penalty was going to be as humiliating an ordeal as was in his power to devise.

'And when you lose,' Giles countered, 'you will confess the sin of pride and vainglory to your confessor and I trust he will impose the full penance that is laid down by the Church.'

A spasm of alarm flashed across Oswin's face. The full penance for the sin of pride was, as they all knew, that for seven long years the sinner must abstain from meat every Wednesday, in addition to the regular fish days, and consume only dry bread and water on Fridays. In practice, it was considered so harsh, it was seldom given any more but, for a man in training to do battle with the forces of darkness on behalf of the Church, there was every likelihood the penance would be imposed exactly as written. For a man with such sin on his soul could certainly not fight demons and hope to survive.

'Never mind that,' John said, ignoring the serious faces of his companions. 'What's the stake to be?' His eyes were ablaze with a fierce excitement that only the cockfights or gaming tables could normally engender.

'One full mark,' Oswin said, staring unblinking at Giles. 'Each.'

Giles swallowed hard and he swayed slightly on the bench, as if he'd been struck.

'Don't be ridiculous. That's far too rich for our stomachs,' Eustace protested. 'It's all very well for you and Robert, but John and Giles are only in minor orders. They're paid a pittance, and a deacon's stipend's not much better,' he added, ruefully patting his own purse.

Oswin raised his eyebrows. 'Well, of course, if Giles can't afford to pay then we'd better call it off.'

'Scared, are you? Trying to find a way of weaselling out?' Giles said. 'Don't worry about me finding the money, Eustace. We won't need to pay, because this braggart isn't going to win.'

'Hold the lantern up higher, the keyhole's not at my feet,' Robert whispered fiercely.

John obligingly tipped the horn lantern, almost smashing it against the door as he did so.

The wind screamed through the bare branches and rattled the shutters of the tiny chapel. On either side of the lonely track, trees and bushes bowed and swayed, and in the darkness it was only too easy to see them as robbers or wolves advancing. The men clustered around the door drew their cloaks tighter about them, shuffling impatiently. There was nothing, save for their tonsures, to mark them as clerics, for like all priests they dressed in the same clothes as those worn by the laity, except when they were on their way to and from church, and when performing, their duties.

Cursing under his breath, Robert finally wrangled the great iron key into the lock and eased the door open. A stench of mice, mildew and rotting wood rolled out to greet them, but the men jostled each other to get inside, anything to be out of that cutting wind. Tiny creatures scurried into the shadows, as the light of the swinging lantern disturbed their nocturnal foraging. Stagnant puddles of water on the floor glistened black under the candlelight. The roof was evidently leaking in several places. The low door opposite the main one still had its key rusting in the lock though it was evident no one had entered that way for years, since it was draped beneath a thick swathe of dirt-encrusted cobwebs.

The dim yellow light from the lantern revealed a stone altar with a cross cut into each corner, and a heap of bird droppings on top. But filthy as it was, all the men turned as one to face it, kneeling and making their obeisance. They gave the gesture no more thought than breathing.

Eustace took the lantern from John, before he could smash it or drop it, and set it down in a deep niche, the length of a man, built into the wall to the left of the altar. It was the Easter Sepulchre in which the statue of Christ was placed on Good Friday and brought forth from on Easter Sunday. A crumbling wreath of yew branches and the ancient stubs of candles lay among the dirt that had accumulated in there.

He hoped that keeping the light low down would prevent it from being seen outside, shining through the broken shutters. He'd no wish to attract the attention of the kind of men who roamed these tracks at night.

He sniffed, wiping his dripping nose with his hand. 'This place is a disgrace. Who says Mass here?'

'No one any more,' Robert said. 'Family that endowed the chantry all died out and eventually so did money they'd left to pay the priests to say the Masses for their souls.'

'Is it still consecrated?' Oswin said. 'This must be done on consecrated ground.'

'Trying to find another reason for backing out?' Giles said, from the shadows.

Robert jumped in quickly, before another argument could break out. 'The relic's still beneath the altar; so long as that remains, it's as holy a place as St Hugh's shrine at the Cathedral. See for yourself.'

He beckoned Oswin to the altar and, taking his hand, pressed it against a small gap beneath the altar slab, which was invisible in the shadow. 'Put your fingers in there if you don't believe me. Can you feel the little wooden box? Earth taken from St Guthlac's grave. Not as valuable as a saint's bone or teeth or cloth from his cloak, I grant you, but it is a relic none the less.'

'Satisfied, are we?' Giles sneered. 'Then let's get on with it.'

'Anxious to part with your money, Giles?' Oswin retorted.

'Like the rest of us, he's anxious to return to a warm bed,' Eustace grumbled.

'Not before I get that cross back where it belongs,' Robert said. 'I came far too close to being caught, taking it from the chest. The Treasurer has the eyes of a falcon. I'm sure he suspects me of stealing something. You'll see – come morning, he'll be making those poor clerks of his check every candle and spoon in the entire Cathedral against the inventory. If he finds the cross missing, not even my uncle will be able to defend me. In fact, knowing Uncle William, he'll be the first to suggest I should be exiled to some barren rock in the middle of the sea to spend the rest of my life as a hermit. He more or less threatened as much when I was caught with that girl in my bed. Probably have me flogged round the Cathedral for good measure, as well,' he added gloomily. 'I don't know why I allowed you to talk me into this.'

'Because,' Oswin said, with a humourless smile, 'you want to see me fail as badly as Giles does. But you are both going to be sadly disappointed.'

Robert bleated that it was a gross slander and he had no such desire, but it was apparent he couldn't think of any other convincing reason for agreeing to do this.

'Describe the cross,' Oswin said, cutting through his protests.

'Silver.' Robert held his hands about a foot apart. 'This tall. With blood garnets marking the places of the five wounds and in the centre, a piece of rock crystal covering three strands of hair from Bishop St Hugh.'

'You addlepated frogwit!' Giles exploded. 'What in the name of Lucifer possessed you to take anything so valuable? If they discover that's missing, they won't just lock you up, they'll wall you up for good and leave you to starve to death.'

Robert raked the stubble of his tonsure distractedly. 'Oswin said he needed something holy, and I thought if I just took a candlestick, he could claim he couldn't find it because it wasn't powerful enough to cry out. Besides, they put the cheap stuff out on display and they'd notice any gaps immediately. They check those night and morning to make sure the pilgrims haven't stolen anything, but the valuables are kept in the chests. They're only brought out for the big festivals, so they won't know the cross is gone.'

Oswin laid his hand on Robert's shoulder. 'And it will be back before anyone discovers it's missing, trust me. But I must prepare. And I need silence, absolute silence.'

The other four backed away from him, retreating as far as the small chapel allowed. Oswin kneeled and then prostrated himself before the altar on the dirty, wet tiles, his chin resting on the floor, his eyes fixed on the dim outline of the altar that covered the reliquary of St Guthlac.

He had been certain that he could do this, but now that the moment had arrived, his confidence leeched out of him like the heat from his body into the cold ground. He'd fasted all day, prayed and bathed. Now he tried to clear his mind, calling on the powers of St Guthlac, St Hugh, the saints and all the Holy Virgins to prove as much to himself as to his brothers that he was worthy, that he had the skills denied to other men, skills that he swore before all the saints he would dedicate to the service of the Holy Mother Church.

'If that which is holy is lost or stolen it will cry out like a child for its mother, calling out to the priest of God and guiding him, until it is found and restored.'

That is what was written. All he had to do was to believe it. He rose to his knees and taking the flask of holy oil from his scrip, anointed his head, hands, feet, ears, eyes, lips and breast, drawing on each the sign of the cross with the chrism. He moved closer to the lantern and, pulling a bottle of water and a tiny bowl from his scrip, he poured the water into the bowl and carefully tipped three drops of the oil into it, watching the pattern of the oil as it swirled in the water.

'Hair of the blessed St Hugh, call out to me, cry to me, that I may find you.' He murmured the words over and over again in a fever of prayer.

Finally, Oswin bowed his head to the altar, then clambered to his feet, turning slowly to face the four men. Even though they couldn't read his expression in the dim light, there was no mistaking the confidence in his stance.

'I know where the cross is hidden,' Oswin announced, triumph ringing in his voice.

Giles exchanged an anxious glance with John, 'Where?'

But already Oswin was making for the door.

The wind, if anything, seemed to have strengthened, hurling them back into the chapel as they tried to force their way out. It seemed to take Robert longer to lock the door than it had to unlock it and Oswin impatiently seized the lantern and strode away into the darkness, with the others scuttling after him. Eustace trailed along behind, sniffing like a bloodhound, as the bitter wind brought tears to eyes and set his nose streaming.

Giles hurried to catch up with Robert.

'Is he heading in the right direction?' he whispered, though he was forced to repeat the question several times, almost shouting into Robert's ear as the wind snatched up the words.

Robert shrugged. 'It's not the route I would have taken,' he said cautiously, 'but it might lead us there.'

Oswin was out ahead, the feeble light of the lantern bobbing up and down at his side, but even he kept turning his head to make sure the others were following. No one wanted to find himself alone in the darkness on a foul night like this. The trees on either side of the path bent and groaned in the wind, creaking like gallows' ropes, and somewhere in the distance a dog was howling. Behind them lay the massive city walls. A flickering red glow was just visible above them, from the torches that burned on the walls of its streets, as if the great gate was the entrance to Hell itself.

Ahead of them, Oswin's tiny lantern light had stopped moving and then it suddenly vanished.

'He might have waited for us to catch up,' Giles said indignantly. 'I can't see the hand in front of my face. Is he deliberately trying to give us the slip? I knew the cheating—'

But his words were cut off abruptly as John slapped a great hand across his mouth, almost suffocating him.

'Get off the track. Horses!'

They didn't hesitate, but scattered and forced their way through the tangle of old undergrowth into the cover of the bushes, smothering curses as hose, cloaks and skin alike tore on brambles. Almost at once they heard the striking of iron on stone and the creak of leather harnesses. Two riders were trotting down the track, heading for the town. Their faces were muffled in hoods and their cloaks billowed behind them.

Each of the clerics crouched lower in his separate hiding place, his ears straining to hear if there were more riders following. Finally, when all seemed quiet, the Black Crows emerged one by one, dragging themselves free of the snagging brambles, and lumbering back onto the road.

'Messengers?' Eustace asked, jerking his head back in the direction the riders had taken.

'Or robbers,' Giles said. 'I wasn't going to stop them and ask. More to the point, where is Oswin?'

'Behind you!' a voice shouted into his ear, and Giles jerked round so violently, his foot slipped and he found himself grovelling on his knees in the dirt.

Oswin stood over him, laughing. 'Why thank you for your obeisance, Giles. I always knew you'd bow to my superior talents one day.'

John hauled the cursing Giles upright, dumping him on his feet as if he was a small child.

'Where to now?' John asked.

'Through here. I've found the place,' Oswin exclaimed.

He plunged back into the grove of trees and they followed, and presently above the wind, they heard the sound of running water. Oswin held up the lantern. They were standing in a small clearing, at the centre of which a spring bubbled up into a pool before trickling away into a stream. They caught a glimpse of something flapping in the wind. As the light fell on it, they saw it was a thorn tree, leafless in winter, but not bare, for it was covered with hundreds of strips of faded rags, teeth strung on cords, locks of hair bound in coloured threads and strands of sheep's wool, all fluttering wildly in the wind.

Next to it stood a small beehive-shaped shrine made of rough stone. The wooden statue that stood on the shelf inside was protected by iron bars, but that hadn't prevented other offerings being stuffed through them, mostly crude little dolls in the form of swaddled babies, like the model of the infant Jesus placed in the crib at Christmas, except these were no more than an inch or two long and fashioned from cloth or wood.

'What is this place?' Eustace said, eyeing the tree with disgust.

'St Margaret of Antioch's well,' Robert replied. 'Folk come here to ask her aid.'

They all nodded. Margaret was a popular saint. It was said that any who lit candles to her would receive anything good they prayed for. She could also shield the dying from the Devil if they called on her name and protect women from the many dangers of childbirth too.

'The cross is here?' Giles demanded, looking from Oswin to Robert.

All eyes turned to Robert. He nodded slowly. 'And you have to admit it's not the most obvious hiding place. I only found it with difficulty and then only because I heard my uncle talking about it a while back.' He gestured towards the thorn tree. 'The locals say the tokens they tie there are to ask the saint to intercede for them, but the priest here in these parts reckons they're offerings to the old goddess, says its pagan. He wanted to chop it down, but his parishioners got wind of it and threatened to chop him down, if he did.'

'All very interesting, I'm sure,' Giles said impatiently. 'But we're here to find the cross, so where is it?'

Oswin pointed to the shrine.

'He's right,' Robert said. 'At the back there's a loose stone. The base of the shrine is hollow.'

All of them crowded round behind the shrine. Oswin placed the lantern close to it, then, pulling the knife from his belt, slid the blade between two of the stones and gently prised the stone forward, first on one side, then the other, until he could get enough of a grip on it to drag it from its resting place. He reached in, a look of undisguised elation on his face, but as the others watched his expression changed to a frown.

'It was a snug fit,' Robert warned. 'You'll have to tilt it backwards to get it out and in the name of the Blessed Virgin whatever you do, don't damage it.'

But when Oswin's hand emerged, it was clutching only a

wad of sheep's wool, tangled in a piece of cord. 'There's nothing there. It's empty!'

'That's impossible,' Robert cried. 'You can't be reaching in far enough. You've pulled the wrappings off, that's what you've done, and left the cross in there. Here, let me.'

He almost flung Oswin aside and kneeled on the wet grass. Pulling up his sleeve, he reached into the shrine, twisting and turning his arm as he groped his way over every inch, his expression becoming ever more frantic.

'It's gone. It's gone,' he shrieked.

John hauled him out of the way and stuck his great fist inside and flailed around, bringing down a shower of dirt and small stones, but he could find nothing. Eustace followed, methodically working over every surface, but in the end he also was forced to withdraw empty-handed.

'It's not there,' he announced, as if there could be any doubt in the matter. 'That space would only just have contained it, as Robert says.'

'Could some stones have fallen down on top and buried it?' Giles asked, the only one not to have tried feeling for it.

'It's just bare earth on the bottom, nothing fallen, as far I could feel,' Eustace said, 'apart from what John brought down, of course. Besides, any fall would have covered the wrappings too. He pointed to the wool and cord still gripped in Oswin's hand. 'That is what you wrapped it in, Robert?'

He didn't answer. He was sitting on the wet ground, his head clutched in his hand, groaning and rocking.

'Someone must have watched you put it there and taken it,' Eustace said.

'But I was so careful,' Robert wailed. 'I waited until it was dark this evening and searched round thoroughly to make sure I was alone. What am I going to do? If it isn't back by morning . . .' He buried his head in his hands again, muttering what might have been either a prayer or a curse.

'You told us this was a pagan place,' Oswin said. 'Witches and sorcerers use familiars in the form of hares, cats or ravens to bring them word. Was there an animal or bird close by?'

'What would a witch want with a cross?' Giles said. 'It'd burn her if she touched it.' His eyes narrowed as he stared at Oswin. 'But you, on the other hand, you knew where the cross was and you disappeared with the lantern while we were hiding from the two riders. When you came back to find us you admitted you'd already been here. You had plenty of time to take it.'

'And why, in heaven's name, would I do that?' Oswin demanded. 'The whole point of the wager was for me to prove to you I could find it.'

Robert's head jerked up. 'Maybe being necromancer isn't enough for you.'

He scrambled to his feet to face Oswin, his face contorted in anger. 'You want to ingratiate yourself still further by discovering a thief. That would certainly get you noticed, wouldn't it? You always said you'd be a bishop before you were thirty. What are you planning to do? Wait until they discover the cross is missing, then produce it before the whole Cathedral Chapter, claiming you'd divined where the thief had hidden it? It's not enough for you to have us humble clerics admire your talents. That won't help you advance. No, you need the bishop and every priest in Lincolnshire to know just how clever you are. Maybe if you're lucky, word might even reach the Archbishop of Canterbury himself.'

Oswin fumbled with the buttons fastening his cloak and

wrenched it from his shoulders, throwing it on the ground between him and Robert. He held his arms out wide.

'Come on then,' he taunted. 'If you really believe I have the cross why don't you search me? Want me to strip naked to make it easier?'

He whipped round to face Giles. 'As for me having time to take it when the riders were passing, that applies to every one of you. Any of you could have slipped to the shrine while the others were hiding and taken it. And unlike me, you all had good reason. You all wanted me to fail to find it, so I'd lose the wager. You most of all, Giles, and you, John, because neither of you could afford to pay. You both admitted as much in the tavern. And with your fondness for gambling, you'd find the money very useful, if I had to pay you, wouldn't you, John? So let's search everyone, shall we?'

John pushed his way in front of Giles, his huge fists clenched. 'Are you calling me a swindler, you steaming pile of pig shit?'

Before Oswin could reply, Eustace had stepped between them. 'You claimed to have found the cross once already tonight, Oswin, so why can't you tell where it's gone now, or was that just a lucky guess? After all, you too dine with the subdean, so you could just as easily have heard about this place as Robert did.'

'I've heard about a hundred places, how would I know which Robert would choose?' Oswin said indignantly.

'Unless you two are in collusion,' Giles said. 'Brothers of the glorious Cathedral are bound to stick together against us mere scullions who labour in the common churches. But Eustace is right. Here's your chance to prove your talents to us once and for all. Go on, find the cross now!'

Oswin was almost white with rage. 'I told you,' he said,

through gritted teeth. 'The rite can only be performed on consecrated ground. Why do you think we went to that pigpen of a chapel? Because, unlike a shrine, it has a relic. I could go back there, but the time that would take would give the thief ample opportunity to whisk the cross far away. Or is that the idea, Giles? Get us out of the way, so you can carry it off?'

Oswin was breathing hard, trying to control his temper. 'Look, if one of us took it, he would have had to conceal it somewhere nearby, under some fallen leaves or in a hollow tree, with the intention of returning for it later,' he added, glaring pointedly at Giles. 'There wouldn't have been time for any of us to carry it far and return to the track again. So I suggest we search for it.'

The Black Crows eyed each other with hostility, but since no one else seemed to have a better solution, they reluctantly agreed to separate and search, drawing lots with dice as to who should go in which direction. After further heated argument as to who should get the lantern, it was decided to leave it in the centre of the clearing where its light could guide them back.

They disappeared into the trees. The whining of the wind in the branches mingled with the sounds of shoes shuffling through fallen leaves, of sticks poking under sodden vegetation, and the occasional cry of hope as they struck against something hard, only to find it was a stone or a rusting horseshoe. In front of them, the wind-whipped bushes and trees loomed out of the darkness as assassins waiting to trip and tear, scratch and strike. Like sailors in a storm, they kept glancing back towards the clearing, fearful of losing sight of the faint yellow glow that appeared and disappeared behind the swaying bushes.

A shriek tore through the darkness, freezing every man in his tracks. They held their breath, listening, frantically trying to decide which direction it had come from, but the cry had been too brief and the wind distorted every sound. So, they turned, stumbling back towards the fragile safety of the clearing, the blood pounding in their ears, as if the Devil's black horse was galloping behind them.

One by one, they burst out of the trees, staring at each other. What was that? Who was that? Where did it come from? Did you hear? It took several minutes before they realised that only four men stood in the clearing. Where is he? Which way did he go? Come on! Hurry!

Huddling together in a little knot, they edged back into the wood, taking the lantern with them, holding it up high, as monstrous shadows ran beside them.

Over there. What's that?

His body was lying curled on its side, his back towards them. They hurried across and crouched down. His eyes were staring sightless out into the darkness beyond. His mouth was wide open, in pain and shock, one hand still lying across his chest as if he'd clutched at the wound, trying to stanch the blood that had gushed out over his fingers. The Black Crows did not have to touch him to know at once that Giles was dead.

They stared at one another in shock and fear. But who? Why? They peered into the darkness, staring wildly about them for any sign of an assailant, but only the trees stirred.

Robert was visibly trembling. 'What are we going to do? If . . . if we take him back to Lincoln, the whole story will come out, and what if they think one of us killed him?'

'What if one of us *did* murder him?' Eustace said, looking from one to the other of his companions. 'I don't see anyone else out here, do you? If Giles stumbled upon the cross before the person who stole it had a chance to recover it . . .'

'God's bones, you surely can't believe that,' John said aghast. 'None of us would kill for that cross.'

'One of us might,' Eustace, said, staring at him pointedly, 'if he was desperately in need of money. People have been known to run up quite a debt at the gaming houses or cock-pits, and they say the men who own them are not known for their patience.'

With a bellow of rage and indignation, John aimed his huge fist at Eustace's jaw. If it had connected, Eustace would probably have lost a few teeth, but he managed to stumble backwards just in time.

'Stop it!' Robert pleaded. 'It's bad enough one murder's been committed without adding a second. No one believes you killed him, John, but the point is they're bound to think one of us did. And how are we to prove otherwise? And once they learn we all took the cross, they might even think we all had a hand in his murder as well.'

'It was you who took it,' Eustace said. 'The rest of us had nothing to do with it.'

'But we all knew he was going to do it,' Oswin said quietly. 'And we told him to do it. That's conspiracy and it carries the same punishment. Robert's right, we can't take Giles back, nor can we let the body be discovered.'

'We could bury him out there among the trees,' Robert said. 'The grave wouldn't be noticed, if we covered it with the fallen leaves and the old bracken.'

'Can't dig with your bare hands,' John said, still glowering at Eustace. 'Need a spade to dig a deep enough hole and you'll be digging through roots. Not an easy job, nor a quick one. Too shallow and he'll be dug up by any passing dog or fox. I can fetch us a couple of spades. I know where our sexton keeps them. But I'll not be able to get back with them till tomorrow night. So what'll we do with the body till then?'

Oswin gnawed at his lip. 'That chapel we met in, you said no one ever uses it, Robert. We could hide him in there until we can dig the grave.'

It took them some time to retrace their steps to the chapel, for even in the dark they dared not risk using the track and had to wind their way through the trees. John carried Giles's corpse all of the way, slung over his shoulder like a sack of wheat. But by the time they got inside and thankfully locked the door behind them, even he was staggering and he dropped the body onto the tiles with such a crash, that if Giles hadn't already been dead, the fall probably would have killed him.

'Where . . . where do we put him?' Robert asked, despondently. 'It doesn't seem right just to leave him on the floor, and the shutters are broken in places. Someone could peer in, when it's light.'

They gazed around. The chapel was so small that there weren't many hiding places.

'Behind the altar?' Eustace suggested.

Oswin shook his head. 'He could be seen by someone looking through that casement above it. There . . . in the Easter Sepulchre. We can use the wooden cover to seal it, as they do on Good Friday.'

With Oswin taking the feet and John the head, they carried the body to the long alcove and with much pushing and shoving managed to ease it inside, crossing the hands over the breast. From his scrip, Oswin removed the flask of chrism for the second time that evening. Eustace grasped his sleeve, shaking his head.

'You cannot. He died unshriven.'

Oswin angrily jerked his arm from Eustace's grip, and dipping his fingers in the holy oil, made the three-times-seven crosses on Giles's body. Eustace turned away, but John and Robert murmured the words with Oswin. 'I anoint thee with holy oil in the name of the Trinity, that thou mayest be saved for ever and ever.'

When all was done, they heaved the dusty wooden cover into place to seal the side of the alcove and, in silence, hastened away out into the bitter night.

A man clad in deacon's robes standing in a Cathedral Close is as near as any person may come to being invisible. Beggars, pilgrims, thieves and clerics alike keep a sharp lookout for those dressed in the robes of high offices, but those wearing the robes of deacons, priests and clerks are as common as dog dung and few men even bother to look at their faces.

The Cathedral Close was crowded. Priests sauntered by in twos and threes, while clerks with arms full of scrolls scurried past them. Pilgrims in little bands jostled to get ahead of their fellows and be first in line for the queues to the shrine of St Hugh. Men hefted bundles of dried fish, whole pigs' heads and planks of timber. Women clustered round the stalls selling boiled sheep's feet, spices or herring. A group of choristers dodged round the legs of horses as they chased a ball, kicking it from one to the other, ignoring the bellows of the woman whose pots it came within a whisker of smashing.

No one took any notice of Eustace as he swiftly mounted the outside stairs to Robert's chamber. Thanks to his uncle's influence, Robert had managed to secure lodgings in one of the many little houses that surrounded the Cathedral, though such chambers were normally assigned to clergy far more senior than he. A wooden shelter protected the top of the stairs and prevented the rain being driven straight in whenever the door was opened. Eustace groped along the top of one of the beams inside the roof of the shelter, until he found the nail on which Robert kept his key. Robert constantly mislaid his key and as Eustace had discovered on a previous occasion when he accompanied Robert home, he had taken to concealing it rather than carrying it around with him. Eustace swiftly turned the key in the lock and slipped through the door, closing it behind him.

The chamber was scarcely more than a loft in the roof space, with only enough room to stand fully upright in the centre, but as Robert had said, at least he was the sole occupant, unlike many of his fellows who were obliged to share the bigger rooms. Eustace scowled. He knew exactly why Robert thought this a virtue, because while he might live alone, he certainly didn't sleep alone.

Eustace gazed round the room. Robert was fastidious about his clothes, if not about his bedfellows, and the room was stuffed with chests holding linens, hose, and tunics, while a line of well-crafted leather boots and shoes stood along one wall, like an army ready to march.

As Robert had feared, the treasurer had called for every artefact in the Cathedral to be checked again the inventories. It was only a matter of time before the cross was reported missing. Eustace had already searched the rooms of Oswin and John, but found nothing. He'd left Robert till last, certain that if he had retrieved the cross, unlike the others, he would have smuggled it back into the Cathedral chest. But supposing he hadn't had a chance to do that, and it was still hidden in his room somewhere?

Eustace worked his way methodically round the chamber

twice, first searching in and behind boxes and the bed, then with the help of a chair, running his hands along the top of the beams, but he found nothing. That, Eustace thought, left only one culprit – Giles. He had not had the cross on him when he . . . when he died. So either he hadn't retrieved it from where he had hidden it, or he had stowed it in another hiding place in the grove. It had to be there somewhere among those trees. There'd been no time to take it anywhere else. Eustace would have to return to the forest and search again, this time alone.

The wind was no less fierce on the following night, but at least it was dry. Oswin was grateful for that much at least as he trudged up the dark track towards the chapel. He had brought his own lantern this time, but kept the light muffled by his cloak, trying to ensure that it illuminated only the foot or so of the ground ahead of him. It was law that any man walking abroad at night should carry a torch or lantern to prove his good intent. Unfortunately, it also proclaimed to all those whose purpose was not lawful just where the honest man was walking. Not that what Oswin was about to do was either honest or lawful.

Every step along the track was a forced one. He had to goad himself forward, for his brain was screaming at him to turn back. Let the others do it. Walk away from this while you can. What could they do about it anyway if you didn't come? And what if they don't turn up and leave you to bury the corpse alone? But he had not managed to sleep during what remained of the night yesterday and he knew he'd never sleep until he'd seen with his own eyes that the corpse was safely buried where no one could find it. Only then could he breathe easily again.

If Robert kept his wits about him, there'd be nothing to link any of them to the missing cross. As to the disappearance of Giles, no one knew of the Black Crows' existence, save for the tavern-keeper, and why should anyone start asking questions at the tavern? There were thousands of men in minor orders who became discontented and left to take a wife or to seek more profitable employment as soon as they got the education they needed. Unlike deacons and priests, those in minor orders did not take lifelong vows. All someone like Giles legally had to do to return to the life of a layman was grow out his tonsure. His parish priest might call him an ingrate, but no laws had been broken if such a man simply wandered off. There was no reason for anyone to start looking for him.

As Oswin approached the chapel, he saw the flicker of a light behind the broken shutters, as someone passed across in front of a lantern. His relief that the other Black Crows had come was mixed with annoyance. Did those fools not realise their light could be seen? Why hadn't they the sense to shield it inside the Easter Sepulchre as before? Then he realised why and shuddered.

Pressing his ear to the wood of the door, he could hear the shuffle of feet inside and the low murmur of voices. He rapped softly. Instantly all was still. He knew those inside were listening, as tense as he was himself.

'It's Oswin,' he called, as loudly as he dared. He heard the footsteps crossing the stone flags and the door was opened a crack, impatiently he pushed it wide enough to get in.

The stench in the chapel was worse than he remembered. Damp, rot and mice as before, but something even more unpleasant. But Oswin only vaguely registered it. He was impatient to get this business safely over as quickly as possible.

'Is Eustace not with you?' Robert asked, the moment Oswin had turned the key in the lock.

'No sign of him on the track,' Oswin said,

'I knew he wouldn't come,' Robert grumbled.

'Typical of him to leave others to clean up the mess while he keeps his hands clean,' Oswin said.

'Happen he's afeared that if he came we'd discover who murdered Giles,' John muttered. 'If a murderer touches his victim's body, the corpse'll bleed afresh.'

'You think it was him, then?' Robert asked. In spite of the cold, damp air, beads of sweat were running down his face.

'He's the only one of us who isn't here,' John said. 'I reckon that proves it.'

Robert unfastened the two buttons that closed his fur-lined cloak and cast about him, trying to find somewhere to drape it, other than on the filthy, wet floor. A small handcart stood ready in front of the altar, with two spades propped up against it. He dropped the cloak into the handcart.

John scowled resentfully. Unlike Robert, who could afford both summer and winter cloaks, John possessed only one of plain homespun, and he'd been forced to discard that in the water-filled ditch on his way home last night, because thanks to the others leaving it to him to carry Giles's body, it was soaked with blood. But he didn't hear any of them offering to share the cost of buying a new one or even bothering to ask if he had another.

The three men approached the wooden board that sealed the Easter Sepulchre. They hesitated, grimacing at each other. Was the same thought going through each man's mind? What if the corpse starts to bleed?

Oswin took a deep breath. 'The sooner we get him in the ground, the safer we'll be. The corpse'll probably still be stiff, so we'll roll the body out onto the board. Did anyone bring anything to cover it?'

By way of an answer, John pulled a folded length of sacking out from the front of his tunic. His jaw was clenched so hard, it seemed impossible for him to speak.

Oswin kneeled down beside the sepulchre. The terrible stench he'd noticed when he first entered the chapel was much stronger here, and indeed seemed to be coming from the sepulchre itself. But surely it couldn't be Giles's corpse. It was the middle of winter and cold enough in the stone chapel to keep ice from melting. His stomach heaved, but he swallowed hard and, trying to ignore the smell, seized the top of the wooden board and pulled it downwards towards him. A stench of rotting flesh billowed out and even John and Robert, standing some way behind him, began to gag, hastily covering their noses and mouths with their sleeves.

The recess was deep and low to the floor and John and Robert were standing between the lantern light and the sepulchre, but even before Oswin's brain had made sense of what his eyes were seeing in the half-light, he knew that something was terribly wrong. He jerked back. The long board clattered to the ground. He scrambled to his feet and, snatching up the lantern, he held it close to the recess. John and Robert gasped, crossing themselves as they rapidly backed away.

Giles's copse was lying in the sepulchre, his hands folded across the blackened bloodstain that covered his chest, just as they had arranged him the night before, but he was no longer lying alone. A second body had been pushed in beside him, a body so rotted and putrid it must have been dead several months. Her gown was the only sign that the corpse had once been a woman. They lay side by side, as if whoever had put her there intended some cruel mockery of the carvings of knights lying beside their wives on the tombs in the great Cathedral itself.

Even as the three men gaped wordlessly at each other, a great hammering sounded on the wooden door of the chapel, as if someone was striking it with a sword hilt.

'Open up, in the name of the King!'

For a moment, they stood frozen, then they sprang into action. John threw the spades into the handcart, covering them with the cloth, while Oswin struggled to try to fit the wooden board back into the side of the sepulchre.

The hammering sounded again. 'Open up, or we'll smash the door down.'

The splintering of the wood of the rotten door suggested they were attempting to do just that.

Robert sprinted the few yards down the small chapel. 'Hold fast, hold fast!' he begged. 'I'm trying to turn the lock, but it's rusty.'

He jiggled the key as if he was struggling to turn it, but the hammering redoubled and he dared stall them no longer.

As he opened the door, he was almost smashed against the wall as three men came charging through, their swords drawn.

The sergeant-at-arms gestured with the point of his sword. 'You three, against that wall where I can see you. Search them,' he commanded the man beside him. 'God's arse, what's that infernal stink?' he added, screwing up his nose. 'Smells as if an animal got itself trapped in here and died.'

The pimpled-faced youth ordered to do the searching carried out his duty with undue diligence, tossing their knives with a clatter onto the floor and running his hands over every inch of their bodies that might be concealing any weapon or stolen item and a few parts of their anatomy that plainly couldn't. The other man-at-arms, an older and considerably stouter man, grinned as he collected the knives from the floor, clearly enjoying watching the prisoners squirm.

'So,' the sergeant said, 'what mischief are you three making? Someone reported seeing a light in here two nights running. They thought the place was haunted the first night, until they saw you lot creeping in tonight.'

'Can't you see we are clergy?' Oswin said sharply. 'And in case you hadn't noticed, this is a chapel.'

'Can see your tonsures, right enough, but that still doesn't explain what you're doing in here behind locked doors in the middle of the night. This chapel's not been used for years.'

'If you ask me, Sergeant,' the older man said, 'I reckon they fancy each other and this is where they come to do it, 'cause they know they'd get their balls sawn off if they was caught at it.'

John gave a roar of outrage and tried to take a swipe at the man. He was only prevented by the prick of the sergeant's sword in his chest, forcing him back against the wall.

'Listen, you imbecile!' Oswin snapped. 'We came to offer prayers for the souls of the family who endowed this chapel. We're in Holy Orders and you have no authority—'

His words were severed by a crash, as the board in front of the sepulchre slipped from the stone and clattered onto the floor. All eyes swivelled towards it.

'What the Devil . . .?' His curiosity evidently aroused, the sergeant took a few tentative paces towards it, his sword held defensively in front of him. Oswin closed his eyes and prayed. But it seemed that not even the most fervent prayers could make one corpse vanish, much less two.

Every prisoner knows there are a few blessed moments that creep between sleeping and waking, nightmares and misery, in which you briefly imagine all is right with the world. You are safely dozing in your own bed, in your own house. You are happy. Then, as you open your eyes, reality douses you with a bucket of filthy, icy water. You realise where you are and what lies in wait for you. So it was for Oswin, as he awoke the next morning to find himself in the bishop's carcer.

Not even Oswin had been able to think of a convincing explanation for the two bodies. But in truth it scarcely mattered, for the sergeant-at-arms, though well used to seeing the worst depravities that a sinful city could conspire to produce, was so shocked by the sight of those two corpses, one fresh, the other rotting, that if St Michael himself had appeared with flaming sword and attempted to defend the three clerics, the sergeant would have arrested him as well.

Before they could even open their mouths to protest, all three Black Crows found their arms bound behind them so tightly they were in danger of losing both limbs, and they were being marched, at sword point, back to the city gate. Once inside the walls, they were taken at once to the Bishop's Palace, opposite the Cathedral, for clergy could neither be detained nor punished by the civil courts. Which, the sergeant muttered beneath his breath, was a gross injustice, for he'd have willingly hanged them from the castle walls himself, for what he had witnessed was surely more foul and depraved than any crime a layman could commit.

There was nothing to be done that night, so all three men were marched to separate cells and ushered, none too gently, inside. Oswin found himself alone in a tiny cell below ground, with nowhere to sleep save in the straw on the floor. There was a single narrow window so high up on the wall, that its only real function was to add to the prisoner's misery by admitting freezing winds, rain and snow, and the occasional piss of passing dogs or choir boys, the latter finding it highly entertaining to compete as to which boy could most accurately drench the incumbent below.

Oswin sat huddled against the wall, his fingers pressed to his forehead, trying to make sense of all that had happened. If only he could work out how or why the second corpse had come to be in the chapel, he might be able to come up with some sort of defence. But he couldn't. Only the fact that he was sitting in the cell convinced him that what he'd seen hadn't been some ghastly nightmare or vision. He was still trying in vain to reason it out when he heard a jangle of keys outside the stout oak door. He clambered stiffly to his feet as the door opened.

The gaoler, a grizzled man with a belly as round as a farrowing sow and tunic that bore testimony to every meal he'd ever eaten, regarded his prisoner in silence for several long minutes, as if Oswin was some unknown creature he'd never before encountered.

Finally, he jerked his head towards the passage. 'Sent for you, so they have.'

Without warning, the gaoler reached in and grabbed Oswin's arm, gripping it so tightly that Oswin was sure he was going to snap the bone.

As he dragged Oswin up the stairs at the end of the passage and out under the grey skies, the gaoler added cheerfully, 'You're the first. Means you can get your story in afore the others. Mind you, that's not always a good thing. If the others gainsay you, you'll look like a liar, so you will. If they think you're lying, they're bound to think you're guilty. So what you been up to, then?'

'Nothing!' Oswin said hotly. 'And there's no need to break my arm. I can't exactly run off, can I?'

The courtyard was closed in on all four sides by high-walled buildings and all the doors were firmly shut.

'If I was you, I'd admit to whatever they say you've done. Throw yourself on their mercy. Swear you repent. Go at lot easier on you, they will, if they think you're contrite. You deny it and they'll come down as hard as an axe on wood, 'cause that's the sin of pride, so it is, refusing to admit you're a miserable worm.'

They'd reached a narrow archway in one wall, which opened onto a spiral staircase. Here, the gaoler was finally forced to let go of Oswin's arm, since they couldn't climb the stairs side by side. He flung Oswin in front of him with such force, he fell onto the steps, banging his knees. The gaoler prodded him to his feet and he limped up the stairs, rubbing his bruised arm, his stomach knotting tighter with each step.

At the top, the gaoler reached around him and rapped on the door at the head of the stairs. The mumble from inside might have been, 'Come in' or 'Go away,' but the gaoler evidently took it for the former. He twisted the iron ring and, once more gripping Oswin's arm as tightly as if it was a live eel, propelled him into the room.

Oswin found himself in a richly decorated chamber. The plaster above the wainscoting was painted with colourful scenes from the life of the blond and bearded Edward the Confessor. Gold leaf glinted on his crown and on the ring he was holding out to a beggar.

Below the painting and behind a long, heavy oak table sat three men, who Oswin recognised as the Subdean William de Rouen, Precentor Paul de Monte Florum and, to his dismay, the Treasurer of the Cathedral, Thomas of Louth. Ranged along the table were platters of mutton olives, roasted quail, and spiced pork meatballs set amid flagons and goblets. At the sight of the meats, Oswin's stomach began to growl. Supper the night before was now but a distant memory.

The only other occupant of the chamber was a pallid man who was hunched over a small table set in front of the casement, angled so that the light from the window might best illuminate a stack of parchments on it. He had the wary look of an ill-used hound.

'Here he is, Fathers,' the gaoler announced cheerfully. 'This 'un's Father Oswin.'

'We know who he is.' The subdean impatiently flapped his hand at the gaoler, his florid jowls wobbling, like the wattle of a chicken. 'You may go. I'll toll the bell when Father Oswin's to be taken back to his cell.'

Oswin had thought his spirits could sink no lower, but they did. It seemed his superiors had already made up their minds, before a single question had even been asked, that he was not simply going to be released.

'That,' Father William continued, indicating the man at the writing table, 'is my clerk. I will conduct this interview in English, but he will take note of your answers and later translate them into good Latin, so that they may be entered into the record books.'

Subdean William had become even more punctilious since the death of the dean, Henry Mansfield, a week earlier. It was widely rumoured that he was expecting to be appointed dean himself now that the post was vacant, and he was determined that nothing should prevent that. Oswin knew he would be far from pleased that his nephew had got entangled with one corpse, never mind two. Even a whiff of scandal would not reflect well on Father William if it was thought he couldn't keep his own family in order.

Father Paul selected a mutton olive from the platter and delicately bit into it. He had one eye that wandered off at a slight angle so that it was hard to tell where he was looking. Strictly speaking, as precentor he was the senior in rank after the dean and should have temporarily assumed the dean's duties following his death, but everyone knew Father Paul had little interest or aptitude for anything other than his music and was quite content to let Father William take over the role until a new man should be appointed.

But it was the treasurer, Thomas of Louth, whose presence most worried Oswin. The disciplining of clerics was not normally something he needed to involve himself in. Was he here because he'd discovered the cross was missing? He was a man who, it was whispered, had never heard of the concept of forgiveness or mercy, and to add to his fearsome reputation he had a puckered white scar that ran from his temple to his chin, twisting his mouth into a perpetual snarl. There were as many stories circulating in Cathedral Close as to how he'd come by that as there were tongues to whisper them, and each of the tales was more chilling than the last.

'So, Father Oswin,' Father William said, 'suppose you begin by explaining to us what the three of you were doing in the disused chapel after the curfew bell.'

Oswin, though he knew the question was coming, still hesitated. No better explanation had come to him than the one he had tried to give the sergeant-at-arms the night before.

'We'd gone there to say Mass as an act of piety to pray for the souls of the dead family. We heard, from your nephew,' he added pointedly, 'that the family who had endowed the chapel had died out and there was no one left to pray for their souls in purgatory.'

'Did someone offer you money for these prayers, a family friend, perhaps?' the precentor enquired.

Oswin shook his head.

'You were giving up a night's sleep and putting yourself to this trouble for no payment?' The precentor's eyebrows shot up so high, they vanished beneath the fringe of hair around his tonsure.

'It was a penance,' Oswin said hastily.

'And which of your confessors imposed such a penance on you?' Father William asked.

'We imposed it on ourselves, as an act of piety. We had feasted and drunk too well a few nights before and wanted to make amends with some act of charity.'

'Thereby committing a greater sin,' William said, 'by thinking yourselves wise enough to act as your own confessors and determine the penance for a sin that you were too proud to confess before others.'

Oswin felt his face grow hot, but he could hardly deny it without refuting his own explanation.

The treasurer impatiently shuffled in his feet. 'Whether or not he should have confessed the sin of gluttony, Subdean, is hardly worthy of discussion, given the far more serious matter of these young men being discovered with two dead bodies. That, surely, is what we should be investigating here.'

Before Father William could answer, he turned to Oswin. 'Do you have an explanation for that, Father Oswin?'

'I . . . was just as shocked as the men-at-arms. I swear we didn't know they were in the Easter Sepulchre until the door fell off. The men-at-arms slammed the chapel door as they came in. It must have shaken the wood loose. We were horrified by what was revealed.'

The precentor made a studied selection of a roasted quail and, ripping one of the legs off, dragged the flesh through his teeth before waving the bone at Oswin. 'Surely, you saw the door was on the sepulchre when you entered. You had, after all, been there two nights running. Didn't you think it strange the Easter Sepulchre should be sealed? From Easter Sunday until Good Friday, it is left open to proclaim the joyful news that Christ has risen. Why didn't you remove it straight away?'

'It was dark in the chapel, Father Precentor. We didn't notice. We came in and immediately kneeled to pray and, naturally, we didn't look around as we prayed.'

'Naturally,' the treasurer repeated with heavy sarcasm. 'And I suppose you were so immersed in prayer you didn't notice the stench either.' He turned to address his colleagues. 'I've inspected the body of the woman personally and I could hardly hold onto my breakfast, the smell was so bad.' He picked up a pomander of spices from the table in front of him and wafted it under his long nose, sniffing hard as if the stench of death still lingered in his nostrils.

'It wasn't nearly as strong when the door was in place, and the smell of damp in the chapel masked . . .' Oswin trailed off. It was plain from his expression, Father Thomas believed not one word of it.

'Did you recognise either of the corpses?'

Oswin had prepared himself for that one. 'As the sergeant-at-arms will tell you, Father Thomas, we never got close enough even to glimpse them. He had his men drag us from the chapel straight away. The sergeant was the only one who actually saw them.'

'I think that explains everything satisfactorily,' Father William announced, ignoring the expressions of incredulity on his brothers' faces. 'There is just one tiny detail that still puzzles me,' he continued blithely. 'Do you normally take spades and a handcart when you go to say Mass for someone's soul? I must confess it is a new refinement to me. But then perhaps the archbishop has issued a decree that you, as an eager young student, have read, but I, as a dullard, have not. Have you been privy to some synod council meeting perhaps, to which us lesser men were not invited?'

Oswin's mind raced. 'They were already in the chapel when we arrived, Father William. Labourers making repairs probably left them there for safekeeping overnight.'

Father William glanced along the table. 'Have you given any workman a key, Father Thomas? Given orders for any repairs?'

'None,' Thomas said. 'As our young brother reminded us himself, the family has died out and the money they left for the maintenance of the chapel has run out.'

The subdean leaned his elbows on the table, his fingers pressed together as he gazed at Oswin. 'You see, that is something else that troubles me, Father Oswin. You say that the cart and spades belonged to some labourers, yet when the chapel was searched, my nephew's cloak was found under the spades in the cart. I can understand that if he found the cart and spades already in the chapel, he might have tossed his cloak on top of them. But why would he go to the trouble of lifting the spades and placing his cloak underneath such dirty tools. Were you perhaps expecting to be translated from the chapel into heaven in a whirlwind for this act of piety of yours, and my nephew, fearful that such a wind would also carry his heavy fur-lined cloak away with it, felt compelled to anchor it down?'

Oswin tried to speak, but Father Thomas interrupted: 'I've no doubt you can invent an explanation for that, too, but let's stop wasting time. Father Robert's cloak was found in the cart covered with short hairs, which at first I thought might belong to the male corpse, but in fact they match the strangely cropped hair on the woman's skull. The cloak was also smeared with . . .' He wrinkled his face as if he was going to vomit. 'Let us just describe it as other of her bodily remains. Not to put to finer point on it, the cloak stank of the woman's corpse. So, the only conclusion we may draw is that you three covered the woman's corpse in the cloak and used the cart to carry it to the chapel, where you concealed it in the sepulchre, for what diabolic purpose I cannot yet tell.'

The treasurer leaned forward and continued. 'As for the dead man, he has been identified as a young cleric in minor orders from the Church of St Rumbold, who has not been seen since vespers two nights ago. I only had to take one look his body to see he'd been stabbed to death. So what exactly were you planning to do with these corpses, Father Oswin? Use them to raise demons or conjure the spirits of the dead? Then what were you going to do? Bury them together in whichever grave you stole the girl's body from, so that the murder of this poor young man should go undetected?'

Subdean William sucked his breath in through his teeth. 'I

warned the dean that allowing a priest as young and arrogant as Father Oswin to study the arts of necromancy and the conjuring of spirits was a mistake. And I regret to say, I've been proved entirely right. The Devil will turn these Holy Mysteries to his own wicked purposes in those who are too inexperienced to handle such dangerous knowledge. And it seems Father Oswin has dragged other innocent young men, including my nephew, into this foul pit with him.'

The gaoler flung Oswin back in the cell and backed out.

'Am I to get any food?' Oswin called out, as the key grated in the lock. But the only answer was the sound of footsteps walking away.

He slid down the wall and onto the straw. At least they hadn't put him in irons, not yet anyway. And none of the three interrogators had mentioned the cross, so that must mean that they hadn't yet discovered it was missing or they hadn't connected its disappearance to Giles's murder, which was at least something. And with luck, they never would. There was no reason for them to suspect a link, unless the treasurer really did believe Robert a thief. Then he'd only too readily believe him a murderer, too, and Oswin and John at the very least his accomplices.

Although Father William and Father Thomas had made a lot of nasty accusations, they'd as good as admitted they didn't actually know what he'd been planning to do with the corpses, nor could they prove he'd killed either one of them. Oswin was trying desperately to convince himself that things weren't really that bad, but he knew they were.

He banged his head against the wall, trying to think. Nothing ... nothing made sense. And the situation could only get worse when Robert and John were questioned.

They'd surely have the wit to go along with the story that the three of them had gone to the chapel to say Mass, since they'd heard him tell the sergeant-at-arms that tale. But what would they say about the handcart? Oswin realised that he'd no idea which of them had had the foresight to bring it to the chapel. John probably; it was the kind of practical thing he'd think of, and he could far more easily lay his hands on a cart than Robert. But would he have the wit to lie about it?

Father Thomas had said Robert's cloak was soiled with the remains of the girl. So had the traces got there because they were in the cart, which John had used to carry her to the chapel, or had they stained the cloak because Robert had been the one who'd dragged her corpse there?

But why would either Robert or John do such a thing? It was in all of their interests to bury Giles's body where no one could find it and quietly return to their duties. Unless ... unless Eustace was the one behind it. Had he been the person who'd reported seeing someone in the chapel to the watchmen? That chapel was so remote from houses or the city walls, who else would have noticed the light? Was that why he hadn't come, because he knew the men-at-arms were on their way? If he'd stolen the cross and murdered Giles, he might well have alerted the authorities, so the three of them were caught red-handed to divert suspicion from himself.

Had Eustace planted the body of the girl, so that it would appear the corpses were being used in the dark arts, knowing that Oswin would be sure to be accused, given his training? Oswin swore violently, thumping his fists against his head. Why hadn't he thought of that before? The vicious little weasel was certainly clever enough to come up with that as a plan, and spiteful enough to carry it out. But how on earth was he going to prove it?

The key grated in the lock once more, and he raised his head as the gaoler waddled in carrying two pails, spilling water from one of them as he walked. The other, judging by the smell, was the piss bucket He set both down next to each other and drew a flattened loaf of bread from under his sweaty armpit, tossing it into Oswin's lap.

'That's your breakfast. It's your dinner and supper, too, so don't gobble it all down at once; but if I was you I wouldn't try to save any of it overnight, otherwise the mice'll have it afore you do.'

'Bread and water,' Oswin said in dismay. 'How long am I to fast on this?'

'Every day for as long as you're in the carcer. That's the rule in here, so it is. So you'd best get praying they get this business over soon, else it's going to be a long, cold and hungry winter for you.'

Eustace stood in the Cathedral Close, trying to make up his mind what to do. He'd watched the arrest of Oswin, Robert and John from the bushes near the chapel, seen them being dragged out and marched down the dark track towards the city behind its great thick walls. A while later, his legs numb and stiff from the cold, he'd seen a troop of the bishop's men-at-arms ride up to the chapel, followed more slowly by a long covered wagon, which was backed up to the door. After what seemed like hours, the riders and wagon set off back to the city gate, leaving one man standing on a miserable and lonely watch at the door, blowing into his hands and stamping his feet to keep warm.

Eustace had cursed under his breath. His plan had been to

search the chapel, just in case one of the Black Crows had managed to hide the cross in there, but he hadn't bargained on them leaving a guard on the door. Still, they wouldn't leave a guard there for ever.

The question now was what would his three brothers say when questioned? Even though they were all in holy orders, there was no doubt in Eustace's mind they would lie. They'd have no qualms of conscience over that. He'd always been aware that he was the only member of the group who took his vows as a priest seriously. But what form would those lies take? Would they name him, try to put all the blame on him? Would they claim he'd murdered Giles and they'd simply stumbled across the body? If he could only find out which of them had the cross and lead the authorities to it, then it would exonerate him and prove their guilt. But where was it?

He glanced up at the casement of Robert's lodgings, and then looked again. He was certain he'd seen the flash of movement, as if someone had crossed in front of the window. He watched intently. There it was again. There was definitely someone up there, moving around. Had Robert been released already? Well, that wouldn't surprise him, given his uncle's influence. Doubtless, Father William intended to spirit his nephew away, send him to a distant town until the scandal blew over, leaving Oswin and John, and Eustace, too, if he wasn't careful, to carry all the blame and punishment. Robert was probably packing for his journey even as Eustace watched.

Rage boiled up in him. He strode round the side of the building and, keeping to the side of the stairs where there was less risk of the wood creaking, he crept up towards the door. He was determined Robert wasn't going anywhere until he'd discovered the story Robert had sold to his uncle and exactly what he'd revealed about the members of the Black Crows, even if he had to beat it out of him.

The door was not quite closed. Through the narrow gap, Eustace glimpsed the lid of a chest being opened, but the person behind it was hidden from view. He pushed the door open and, as he stepped through, caught it and pressed it closed with his back. There was a stifled cry of surprise and someone rose up from behind the open chest, but it was not Robert.

A woman stared back at him, her expression as startled as Eustace knew his own must be. His gaze dropped to her hand. She was holding a cross – *the* cross, he realised, as a surge of shock and excitement flooded through him. It was exactly as Robert had described, silver, decorated with five blood-red garnets and in the centre the little dome of rock crystal, which held the precious hairs.

'Where did you get that?' Eustace demanded.

A look of panic flooded the woman's face. 'I found it here . . . Father.'

'In the chest. You were searching the chest for things to steal?'

'I . . . I wasn't stealing, Father. I swear on the Blessed Virgin, I wasn't. It was on the table. I . . . was putting it away safely for Father Robert. Anyone might have come and took it, seeing as he always leaves the key . . .'

'How do you know where . . .?' Eustace began. 'Ah, of course, he's brought you here before. You're one of his whores, aren't you?'

'I'm no whore!' The woman's jaw clenched and her expression turned in the instant from fear to hard, cold rage. 'I come to clean for him, wash his clothes. That's how I know.'

Eustace took a step towards her. 'But you didn't find that cross in here, I know that much. It was not in this chamber yesterday. And, if Robert had brought it here, he most certainly wouldn't have left it lying around for anyone to find.' He took another step towards her, his voice dropping to a low and menacing whisper. 'So, I'll ask you again, how exactly did you come by it? Answer me, woman, otherwise all I have to do is call out and a dozen of the watch will come running. You are holding all the evidence any justice could need to convict you of theft. They will hang you and then you will find yourself in the eternal darkness of Hell, forever being spun and hurled in a terrible, howling wind, which is the fate of all whores. So, you will tell me truthfully where you got that cross.'

Eustace expected the woman to look terrified, to plead, beg, fall on her knees, but he was not prepared for the fire of pure hatred that flashed in her eyes.

Eustace tried to open his eyes, but his eyelids seemed to have been turned to stone. His head felt as if it was split into two and a wave of nausea engulfed him. He wanted to roll over and vomit, but he couldn't move, he couldn't even heave. He was dimly aware of sounds around him, voices, footsteps, cries and moans, but they seemed to be a long way off, muffled and distorted as if they were drifting towards him through a dense fog.

'. . . it seems he staggered as far as the stairs, then fell from the top.'

'But you said he was already injured before he fell?'

'It appears that way. Some passers-by heard a cry and it made them glance up. They all reported seeing him standing at the top of the stairs holding onto the doorframe, the side of his face all bloodied. A few ran across to try to help, but it was too late. Before they could reach him, he either fainted or lost his balance, and came crashing down onto the stones below. He might have recovered from the head wound, but not the fall . . . He'll not see another dawn in this world, Father William. Mind you, that might be a mercy, for his back's broken. He'd have been a cripple had he lived.'

'Many cripples live worthy lives,' Father William said sharply. 'Confined to their beds they are able to devote their lives to praying for others, and what life could be better spent than that?'

'If you say so, Father.' The other voice sounded less than convinced. 'Of course, the poor ones don't have the luxury of a bed, they spend their time lying on the streets begging for alms. But I dare say you'll tell me that's a blessing too, for if it weren't for them, the rich would have no one to give their charity to. But that aside, we've done all we can for Father Eustace. You'd best shrive him before it's too late.'

Up to that moment, Eustace's brain had been swamped by the pain of his body and by the terrible sensation of not being able to move. He heard that spirits could be trapped inside the trunk of a tree, and he felt as if some witch had banished him to a tree, encased every inch of him in wood. But now another sensation flooded over him: cold, black horror. He was going to die. He was going to enter that purgatory in which souls are burned and tortured until they are cleansed. He knew as a Christian soul he should be glad of it, rejoice that he was one step closer to heaven. But Eustace felt no such joy. He was terrified.

The infirmarer did not need the art of divination to predict when his patients would pass from this life. He had cared for enough men to read the signs in a man's body that warn that death is fast approaching. Besides, he'd learned that a strong draught of poppy juice in spiced wine administered just before the last rites, then jerking the feather pillow out from beneath the patient's head after he'd been shrived, was usually enough to help him pass swiftly and painlessly into the next world, for it is well know that a man cannot die on feathers. The infirmarer was a compassionate soul and he knew how to bring a merciful end to a man's suffering in this life, though sadly not in the next.

Father William had performed the last rites with devotion and diligence, and Father Eustace had seemed sensible of what was happening. Without even waiting for the questions his confessor was obliged to put to him, Eustace had tried desperately to make a full confession, indeed the words had vomited out of him in a torrent. The only trouble was, very few made any sense.

There was no doubt in Father William's mind that Deacon Eustace had wanted to unburden himself of some great matter that clearly weighed heavily upon him. His sincerity was evident in his tone, his urgency, his grip. But though he clearly thought he was making himself understood, he was not. The utterances were a random jumble of words and phrases, in English and Latin, some phrases learned by rote from psalters as a child, others vile and obscene. Nonetheless, Father William had absolved him, trusting that God could judge the sincerity of all of His creatures' thoughts, even if man could not understand their speech. And Eustace had sunk back in the bed, seeming at peace and content. The terror had gone from his eyes.

As soon as he had left Eustace's bedside, Father William had summoned the precentor and the treasurer to the dean's private chamber, which he was now occupying. The three of them sat around the fire, goblets of their favourite spiced wine, hippocras, in their hands, and platters of goat chops, spit-roasted chicken and pears in wine on the small tables between them to aid their deliberations. No man, not even a man in holy orders, can think well on an empty stomach.

But for once, the precentor's gaze did not stray to the food. He was staring intently, with his good eye, at the silver cross that stood before them on the table. The reflections of the flames from the hearth flickered deep inside the hearts of the polished garnets, as if five tiny fires were burning on the cross.

'But did he say if he knew how the cross came to be in Robert's chamber, or even what he was doing in your nephew's room, Father William? The way gossip spreads in Lincoln, the whole city knows that Robert lies in the carcer, so Eustace can hardly have expected to find him at home; quite the opposite in fact.'

'I believe we all know why the cross was in Robert's chamber,' Thomas said. 'He stole it. As I told you, Father William, I caught your nephew hanging around the chests on several occasions the other morning. I suspected he'd taken something or was planning to. Not that I blame you, Father William. It's tainted blood from the mother, that's what always turns a perfectly respectable family line to the bad. But I'm afraid I did warn you, and if you'd listened to me and had his chambers searched there and then, we might have put a stop to it, before this business of the corpses.'

'You think the deaths are linked to the theft of the cross?' Father Paul said, apparently unaware that the subdean had turned as red as the garnets and was spluttering furiously.

'Have to be!' Thomas said airily.

'Then,' Father William said, his voice crackling with ice, 'since you are so confident of the fact, perhaps you might care to enlighten us as to exactly how?'

Thomas coughed. 'I . . . what I meant was, it's surely too much of a coincidence that Robert should be involved in two entirely separate crimes within days of each other. Didn't Eustace shed any light on the matter?'

'We have not established that my nephew was involved in one crime, never mind two!' Father William snapped. 'And as I explained, poor Eustace was making little sense. Several times he said something about a woman. But that could have been as much nonsense as the other things he was muttering.'

'Eustace was the last man in Lincoln to have any dealings with a woman. He despised them all,' Father Paul said, finally giving in to temptation and ripping a leg off the roasted chicken. Its skin glistened red-gold in the firelight from the honey and spices with which it had been basted. 'In fact,' he said, wagging it at them, 'there were rumours his tastes ran to . . . But I suppose one shouldn't speak ill of the newly dead.'

He glanced uneasily into the shadows in the corner of the room, as if Eustace's spirit might be lurking there.

Thomas, frowning, suddenly leaned forward and picked up the cross, holding it close to one of the candles. 'Look at this.' He pointed to one of the arms of the cross. 'See the dark stain in the lines of the engraving? I'd say that was dried blood, wouldn't you? This could well be what made the hole in Eustace's head.'

'You think he fell on it?' Father William asked.

'I don't think that would have been enough to cause the

injury. It wasn't fixed to anything so it would have been knocked over if he fell against it. He might have sustained a bruise or gash, nothing more. The infirmarer is sure he was hit with something and the blow was a hard one. This would make a useful weapon,' hc added, brandishing the cross to demonstrate.

He tipped the cross this way and that, angling different parts towards the candlelight, then his fingers pounced on something else. Carefully, he unwound several strands of long, reddish-brown hair, which had been caught under the setting that held one of the garnets in place.

'A woman's hair. Eustace might have had good reason to despise women if one of them struck him with this. The trouble is, that doesn't help us much. There's no shortage of women in Lincoln with hair of a similar shade. Why, even that corpse had hair this colour—' He broke off, frowning.

'Then it must have come from the corpse,' Father Paul said. 'Didn't you tell us hair from the decayed body was found on Robert's cloak? He doubtless wrapped the cross in his cloak to carry it away and that how it got onto the cross.'

Thomas shook his head. 'If he wrapped the cross in the cloak, it would have been before he used it to cover the corpse, not afterwards. Besides, the noticeable thing about that corpse was that the hair was short; it'd been cropped. This is much longer, and see the way the ends taper? It's never been trimmed. But I'll grant you one thing, it's remarkably similar in colour to that of the corpse. Another coincidence?'

Oswin scraped up the damp straw and heaped it over his legs to try to get warm. But the icy rain was driving in through the grating faster than it could drain away down the shallow gulley and out through the tiny hole in the wall. Puddles were spreading ever wider across the flagstones. Oswin wondered, miserably, if anyone had ever drowned down here. Shivering, he clamped his hands under his armpits in a vain attempt to warm his numb fingers. He rolled on his side, trying to ease the pains in his belly. Drinking water instead of wine or ale had given him such a severe dose of the flux that on some occasions he could barely reach the piss-pail before his bowels exploded.

At least today the rain kept away the jeering boys and curious young clerics who came to peer down at him. Anyone crossing the courtyard hurried as fast as they could to get safely to shelter again. Only the bells in the Cathedral ringing out the hours of the services marked the slow crawl of time.

Oswin heard the door at the end of the passage grate open and he sat up. The gaoler had already been round with the daily ration of bread and water, and it was too much to hope that he might be returning with more. He heard voices. Were they bringing another prisoner in or taking one out? He listened for the sound of a cell door being opened further down the corridor, but the footsteps did not pause in front of any cell. Judging by the clatter of wood on stone, one of the people approaching was wearing wooden pattens tied over their shoes to stop them being spoiled by the mud and puddles. Not the gaoler or a prisoner then.

The footsteps stopped outside his own door. He heard the key grinding in the lock and lumbered to his feet, brushing the straw from his clothes, as the door opened.

'We've been taking good care of him, Treasurer,' the gaoler said.

Oswin's stomach knotted. If the treasurer was here, it could only be about the missing cross.

'Wait for me outside in the courtyard,' Thomas said. 'I'll call you when I want the door unlocked.'

'Outside?' The gaoler didn't sound as if he relished the prospect of standing around in the freezing rain, but he shuffled away, not daring to complain, at least not out loud.

The treasurer ducked his head under the low doorway and tottered into the cell. He loomed over Oswin, for the wooden pattens increased his height by at least four inches. He gazed round the cell with curiosity and then down at Oswin, who was suddenly and painfully aware of how dishevelled he must look, and of the stench emanating from the overflowing piss-pail in the corner.

'I will be asking your two companions the same questions, so I'd strongly advise you, Father Oswin, to speak only the truth this time. Your companions do not seem quite as adept at inventing tales as you appear to be and will undoubtedly give you away.'

He held up a bony hand to silence any protest from Oswin.

'Do you number among your friends Deacon Eustace from the Church of St Lawrence?'

Oswin nodded, feeling that the less he said the better.

'Then I regret that I must convey sad tidings. You doubtless heard the death bell tolling yesterday. That was rung for Father Eustace, who died in the infirmary last evening.'

Oswin swayed, putting out a hand to steady himself against the wall. It was not grief that moved him, but the shock of yet another of their circle dying. They were all young men and, while death could strike at any age, the thought that two out of the five of them had died in a week was chilling.

'H. . . how?' he stammered.

'I believe,' Thomas said, watching Oswin closely, 'that his death will be accounted as murder. All the evidence is that he was struck on the head by a cross, a silver cross that was stolen from the Cathedral.'

Oswin tried hard to look both shocked and guiltless. The first was not difficult, but as Thomas continued to stare hard at him, he felt his face grow hot and prayed that in the half-light in the cell, it would not be noticed.

'I think you have kept up this pretence long enough, Father Oswin. No doubt you think it amusing to try to fool the *majores personae* of the Cathedral, but I can assure you it is a dangerous game. You may think that because you have benefit of clergy, the penalties for theft and murder will not be severe. But it is not without precedent that a priest may be tried in the ecclesiastical courts and unfrocked by them, leaving the way open for him to be tried by the civil justices, in which case, as you know, the penalty would undoubtedly be death. And when a priest has stolen a valuable cross and reliquary, in addition to committing not just one, but two murders, I think it very likely he would find himself eventually standing trial in a civil court.'

Oswin was already feeling shaky from the flux, but now his legs threatened to give way altogether. 'But, Father Thomas, you know I couldn't possibly have murdered Eustace. I've been locked up in here and he was fit and well when last I saw him. You know he was, because he was the man who called the watch to the chapel.'

'Eustace?' Thomas frowned. 'The sergeant-at-arms said it was a woman who raised the alarm.' He frowned, staring down at the rain drops pattering into the puddles. 'I hadn't remembered that before,' he murmured. 'So was this another woman or the same one?' He suddenly seemed to recollect that he was not alone and looked up again.

'No one is suggesting you murdered Eustace. It is known all three of you were locked in here at the time he was attacked, but you seem to be forgetting that you were discovered with two corpses. Either you killed both of them, or you are guilty of grave-robbing, which is just as wicked as murder in the eyes of the Church and the law.'

'But, I swear to you, I didn't kill anyone. I never even laid eyes on that . . . that woman until we found her in the chapel.'

'But you did know the body of Giles was there, didn't you?' Father Thomas said sternly. 'You know because you put it there. If you hope for any mercy from the Church, you would be wise to make a full and honest confession to me now.'

Oswin knew he was beaten. Even if he continued to deny everything, he was certain Robert at any rate would spill all, if he hadn't done so already. He was intimidated by his uncle at the best of times. If he had the treasurer and precentor threatening him as well, he'd be crying like an infant.

Taking a deep breath, he recounted the whole story, from Giles's challenge to the night they were discovered in the chapel. It must be admitted that in the telling rather more of the blame found its way onto the shoulders of Giles and Eustace than was strictly truthful, but that could hardly matter to them now.

Thomas listened in silence, his scowl becoming ever deeper. The bone-white scar seemed to glow with increasing intensity in the gloom of the cell, until Oswin couldn't drag his gaze from it. Oswin couldn't tell if Thomas's mounting anger was because of the theft of the cross or the concealment of the body, or if he thought he was being lied to again.

But whatever the cause, that look of fury on his superior's face did not bode well for Oswin.

A throbbing silence stretched between the two men, in which the beat of the rain drops sounded like the thudding of a giant heart. Without warning, Thomas's hand moved to his belt and, for one wild and terrifying moment, Oswin thought he was reaching for his knife. But instead, Thomas fumbled in his leather scrip and pulled out a small, folded piece of white linen.

He laid it on the flat of his palm and peeled back the folds of cloth with the other hand.

Oswin stared in bewilderment. As far as he could see there was nothing in the linen. Was this some new method of divining the truth or unmasking a killer that he hadn't yet studied?

'Look at these strands of hair,' Thomas said. 'Careful! Don't breathe on them; if they blow into the straw, we'll never find them.'

Oswin leaned forward, as Thomas swung his palm towards the grey light filtering down with the rain through the grating. Against the bright white linen, he could just make out three long hairs.

'Have you taken a good look?'

When Oswin nodded, Thomas carefully wrapped them again and put the little package back into his scrip.

'Think carefully. Do you know any women with hair of that colour?'

Oswin was wary. He could make little senses of the question and immediately thought Thomas was trying to trick him to confessing another sin. 'Lots of women come to services in the Cathedral, but I don't actually know any, if you mean like Rob—'

Oswin checked himself. Robert was, after all, the sub-dean's nephew. In his position, Oswin certainly didn't want word to reach Father William that he had accused his nephew of fornication.

Thomas gave a dry little cough. 'I am well acquainted with Father Robert's proclivities, if that is what is concerning you, Father Oswin. I am not necessarily suggesting that this woman is known to you in the carnal sense, but I wish you to think carefully. Have you ever seen a woman with hair of this colour with Father Eustace? You see, these hairs were taken from the cross used to bludgeon him. They're clearly not his, so there is just a chance they may belong to his assailant. Someone who might have had a grudge against him? Someone he denied alms to?

'I've already made enquiries among his congregation at St Lawrence. But of those women who have similar hair, none quite matches these and all could prove they were somewhere else at the time of his attack. I will question every woman with russet hair in Lincoln, if I have to, but that could take some time. But it occurred to me, she might be someone known to Eustace's friends. Someone he mentioned to you that he'd quarrelled with, perhaps?'

Oswin shook his head. 'Eustace didn't ever mention women, except to grumble about their whole sex in general. Even if a woman did speak to him, he wouldn't have known what colour her hair was, because he never looked at them. Why, even—' He stopped. 'There is one he knew with this colour hair, but why on earth should she . . .?'

Treasurer Thomas sat alone in the crowded ale-room of the tavern, watching the people on the benches around him. In truth, he was enjoying himself. He seldom got the chance to listen to the gossip and banter in such places any more, for, when he was in Lincoln, he dined with his fellow clerics, and even when travelling to make inspections of property he was expected to dine in the religious houses along the route, which was in any case safer for a man in his position, who would be marked at once as carrying gold and silver. Not since he had been employed as a spy for the treacherous Queen Isabella had he had cause to lurk in the corners of inns and taverns.

He'd been watching her all evening, but it wasn't wise to tackle her in front of a room full of people. In his experience, the regulars would rally around one of their own and it was common for them to block the path of men-at-arms or mob them, while the wanted man or woman slipped out the back of the inn and fled into the night. So he bided his time and savoured the plainness of the mutton stew in contrast to the rich and elaborate dishes served in his own chambers.

He beckoned to the serving maid. 'I don't suppose you've any fat bacon. I'd pay well for a couple of slices of that.'

She raised her eyebrows. He had just consumed a generous portion of stew, but if he wanted to part with more money, she certainly wasn't going to turn him away.

'I'll have to fetch it from the cellar, sir.'

He waited until she'd descended the stairs, then he gave a single nod to a man sitting on the opposite side of the ale-room and, unobserved by anyone else in the crowded room, he slipped through the cellar door, closing it behind him.

The woman was slicing bacon from a flitch hanging from a large iron hook on one of the beams. At the creak on the stairs, she turned, wary, then relaxed a little as she saw who it was.

'I'm just coming, sir. You go back up and take a seat. I'll not be long. Customers aren't supposed to come down here.'

'Only clerics, is that right, Meggy?'

She shrugged. 'There's a group of them come to play dice sometimes. We let them use the cellars. Puts the other customers off, see, having them around.'

'But they haven't been here for several days.'

'I dare say they'll be back,' she said. 'Anyway, what's it to you?'

Thomas pulled the brimmed hat from his head, revealing his tonsure. 'I was thinking of joining them.'

'You'll have to ask them. They don't just let anyone into their little group.'

'But now that two of their members won't be coming back, they'll surely need new blood. He died, you know, Father Eustace. You probably heard the bell tolling for him.'

The knife jerked in her hand and she swore as it nicked her finger. She sucked at the wound.

'I'm sorry to bring you such distressing news,' Thomas said.

'Why should I be distressed? Salt from the bacon, is all. Stings like the very devil when it gets into a cut.'

But Thomas saw her hands were trembling. She slid the platter onto the table, without looking at him.

'Here's your meats. Eat them down here or take them back upstairs, as you please, it's all the same to me. I can't waste time talking. I got customers want serving.'

She tried to edge past him, but he stretched out his hand to the table blocking the way.

'You didn't ask how Father Eustace died. He was a young man. Aren't you curious?'

'Was he?' She shrugged. 'I didn't know him. One priest more or less in the world, makes no odds to me. There's plenty more to take his place.'

'You didn't know him and yet you served him, served him and all five of them every time they came down here to play dice.'

'Don't know their names.'

'Maybe not,' he said. 'But you'd recognise them, and Father Eustace recognised you, too, didn't he? In Father Robert's chambers? Was that why you hit him with the cross, the cross you were stealing? You wanted to stop him reporting you as a thief?'

Her head snapped up. 'I wasn't stealing it. It was that priest of yours who took it, but they never get punished whatever crimes they commit, do they? Only us. It's always us.'

'So, if you weren't stealing it, why did you hit Father Eustace with it? And don't try to deny it. You've just admitted you knew about it. No one, save for the five members of the Black Crows, knew the cross was missing.'

She was staring wildly about her, panic rising in her face. He guessed she was going to try to make a run for it, but what he was not prepared for was the mask of savagery that suddenly twisted her face. With a shriek, she lifted her knife and lunged at him.

Had it been Father William or Father Paul in that cellar, there was no question the Cathedral bell would have been tolling out their deaths that evening. But Father Thomas had not acquired his scar at the Cathedral treasure house. He dodged sideways, letting her momentum carry her forward and, grabbing her wrist, he twisted the knife from her grasp.

She fell heavily onto the flagstones, but even that wasn't enough to subdue her. She made a wild grab for his legs, sinking her teeth into his calf. Only by seizing her long hair and wrenching her head back, did Father Thomas manage to prise her loose. He flung her backwards then hauled her to her feet, holding her own knife at her throat.

His leg burned. He could feel the hot blood flowing down from where she'd bitten a chunk from his flesh, but he tried to ignore the pain.

He pulled her over to the bench and pressed her down onto it. 'Don't even think of running or calling out,' he warned. 'I've an armed man stationed outside that door up there, with orders to let no one in or out, and more men posted round the tavern outside.'

He hobbled to the bench opposite and sat down, keeping the knife pointed towards her. Her eyes were burning with hatred and he knew if he gave her half a chance she'd tear his throat out with her teeth. The safest course would be to call the men-at-arms down here to seize and bind her, then hand her over to the Sherriff of Lincoln. She'd hang, there was no question about that, but he didn't want her to go to the gallows without learning why she'd done it. She hadn't stolen the cross from the Cathedral – that much he'd already discovered from Oswin – so why had she killed Eustace?'

'Tell me, tell me everything, Meggy,' he urged.

'What good'll that do? You're not going to save me from the hangman's necklace.'

Thomas knew she'd never believe him even if he swore that he would.

'But I can save your soul. If you die without confessing such crimes as you have committed, you'll burn in hell for all eternity.'

'You'd like that, wouldn't you?' she said, her eyes flashing. 'That's where he sent her. That's where they all sent her – to hell. Gives you a thrill, does it, to think of her writhing and naked in the flames.'

'Who?'

Her expression softened and a distant look came into her eyes. 'My sister. She was a rare beauty. Hair same colour as mine, but twice as thick and long. Spent hours combing it, she did. Everyone noticed it. They cut it all off, right in front of the jeering mob. That's what did for her more than anything. The whipping she could stand. We'd more than enough of those when we were bairns to make us hardened to it, but then they made her stand at the Cathedral door in nowt but her shift, for four Sundays, with her head all shorn and folks mocking and laughing. Come the third Sunday, she couldn't take the shame of it no more. She hanged herself.

''Cause she loved him, you know. To him, she was nowt but a creature to pleasure him, but she really loved him, that's why she went to his bed. Course, they wouldn't let her have a Christian burial. Said she'd committed the worst of sins – pride for she'd set herself above God and taken her own life when it was His alone to take. Can't ever be forgiven, it can't, not self-murder. She'd burn for it in hell, they said. They were going to bury her at the crossroads outside Lincoln, and drive iron nails into her feet so she couldn't walk and torment the living. But they'd done enough to her poor body. I wouldn't let them have her. I took her and I buried her in the woods close to St Margaret's well. I thought the saint might bless her and keep her safe, even if the priests would not.'

Thomas was trying to make sense of all this, to tie the

threads between this rambling tale and the death of Eustace, but he could not make the connection.

'Your sister was punished for being a whore?'

'She wasn't a whore,' Meggy said fiercely. 'She was faithful to him; never slept with no one else. She loved Father Robert. She loved him! But to him, she was only one of dozens of girls.'

Suddenly, Thomas understood. There'd been an incident just over a year before. An accusation that several of the young priests at the Cathedral were entertaining the town whores in their beds overnight. The accusation had been made anonymously but, as was always the way in Lincoln, soon the whole town was gossiping about it and the Cathedral officials had been forced to act. They'd raided several of the chambers of the priests and dragged out the girls they found there.

The girls had all been shorn and whipped and forced to do penance at the Cathedral door. Their duty having been seen to be done, things had then returned to normal, and presumably the whores had gone about their business once more.

As for the priests, a few light penances had been imposed, including, Thomas remembered, on the subdean's nephew, who was one of those found in the arms of a girl, but no one was anxious to make much of the matter as far as the priests were concerned. They were all young men, prey to the temptations of the flesh, and celibacy was hard on the young. Who could really blame naïve boys, unused to women's wiles, for being seduced by artful and professional prostitutes? Besides, there was scarcely a senior clergyman who didn't recall, with a slight twinge of guilt, some similar failing in their own distant past, and for some it wasn't that distant.

'The body in the chapel,' Thomas said softly, 'that was your sister.'

'I dug her up and carried her there in a cart. Thought if they was to find them together and not know who she was, they'd give her a proper burial in a consecrated ground, then the Devil couldn't take her.'

'You knew that Giles's body was already there?'

'Saw them take it there.' Her face became contorted again. 'I didn't mean to kill him. It were an accident. I only meant to get them punished, like my poor sister had been punished. I wasn't going to keep the cross, I swear I wasn't. That's why I was putting it back in Father Robert's chamber. Thought they'd find it there and he'd be shamed in front of the world, like my poor sister was. But he came in, that Eustace. Accused me of being one of Robert's whores. I told him I wasn't. I swore to him she wasn't neither. But he laughed. Said all women were whores and it were him who'd reported Robert and the others for fornicating. It was his fault my sister died. All his fault!'

'So you hit him,' Thomas said.

'I'm not sorry. You'll not make me repentant of that. I'm glad he's dead. Glad I killed him, 'cause now he'll be rotting in the ground like her.'

'And Giles?'

'Told you that were an accident,' she said sullenly. 'I heard them talking about taking summat from the Cathedral and how they were going to hide it. They never take notice of me when I serve them, as if I'm nothing but a dumb hound for them to snap their fingers at when they want something fetching. I saw my chance. I reckoned if I could take it from them afore they had time to return it, then I could put it in Father Robert's house and tell someone it was there, just like they was told about the girls being in the priests' houses. He'd get the blame. They all would. I wanted to see them punished.

'I followed them and soon as I saw where they was headed I guessed where Robert had hidden it. We used that loose stone as a hiding place for our little treasures when we were bairns. I took the cross, afore they could find it, but I lost my way in the dark, ran right into Giles and when he bumped against me, he felt it under my cloak.

'He tried to grab me and make me give it to him. I pulled out my knife. I only meant to drive him off, but he came towards me again. He must have tripped over a root or some such in the dark, 'cause he fell forward onto the knife in my hand and the next thing I knew he was dead. I ran and hid; saw them carrying the body to the chapel and knew they weren't going to report it. They couldn't, not without giving themselves away.'

'How did you get into the chapel? The door was locked.'

Meggy gave Thomas a pitying look. 'Door on the other side, small one. Wood was so rotten it was easy to chip a hole in it and put my hand through. Key was in the lock on the other side. Stuffed up the hole up again with a bit of wood and leaves. Who's to see in the dark?'

She looked up at him from under the mob of russet hair. Her expression was almost calm now.

'They'll not be punished, will they, those priests? None of them. They'll punish me, though. They'll hang me. But not them, never them, though they took my sister's life no different than if they'd strangled her with their own hands.'

'Your sister took her own life,' Thomas said sternly. 'The three men have been on a diet of bread and water and slept on straw these past nights, and there will be other penances imposed on them when all this is reported.'

She gave a mirthless laugh. 'There's many a bairn in England who'd be glad of a bite of bread for their suppers and a heap of straw to sleep on and think it heaven. What are they doing penance for? What's their sin? I'd like to see every last priest in England struck down. That's what God wants to do: strike them down like the angel of death slew all the first born of Egypt.'

Without warning, she lunged for the knife and grabbed it. Thomas threw up his arms to protect his face and chest, thinking she was going to plunge it into him, but instead, he heard a scream of agony. Meggy was sitting on the bench, her eyes wide in pain, her fingers still grasping the hilt of the knife that she had plunged into her own chest. A crimson stain was spreading rapidly out over the front of her gown, like a rosebud opening. Then she crumpled forward, her head thudding on the table, her hair tumbling over her face and covering those dead eyes.

There was a silence in the inn as Randal finished his tale. He was staring at rushes on the floor. 'I think,' he added softly, 'the days are coming when Meggy will get her wish. If the pestilence reaches our shores, priests will be struck down in their thousands, as they have already been beyond these seas. Perhaps God has finally woken from His slumbers at last and the punishment we priests deserve is about to fall upon us all.'

Prior Wynter snorted. 'According to your tale it is the women who deserve punishment – luring a priest from his scared vows, desecrating a sacred and holy object by using it to murder a man of God, not to mention the wickedness of suicide. It seems to me you have shown us that lust was the chief sin in this fable and it was lust that was justly punished with the death and damnation of these two wanton females.'

All the women in the tavern bridled and there was an explosion of protests.

'And I suppose the clerics received no punishment at all, just like poor Meggy predicted,' Katie said indignantly, glowering at Prior Wynter, 'in spite of the fact that they'd stolen and lied.'

'There were penances,' Randal said dully, staring at his hands. 'The subdean decided his nephew was too much of a liability to keep him at the Cathedral. So he found Robert a parish on the edge of the fens far from the inns and stews of Lincoln. And he sent a comely housekeeper to cook and clean for him, knowing that even if the housekeeper found more ways than a heated stone to warm his nephew's bed, at least the rumours would never reach as far as Lincoln.

'But as I told you at the beginning, Prior Wynter, it is pride that is the father of the other six sins. Oswin was proud of his knowledge and talent for summoning spirits and demons. He exalted in the glory of driving out the Devil and wrestling with angels. He could control the ministers and minions of Heaven and Hell. But his pride was to sire its own punishment.'

With shaking hands, Randal unwound the long tails of his hood and pulled it from his head. His tonsure gleamed in the firelight. He lifted his head and for the first time met the gaze of his fellow pilgrims. This time, it was they who turned their faces away as they saw the wild and haunted despair in his eyes.

'You see, I did summon spirits and demons, just as I boasted I could. But now they come whether I call them or not and I cannot stop them. I see them everywhere. Imps with leathery wings and cruel beaks peer down at me from the trees. Monstrous creatures with human eyes slither over the stones of the track towards me. Men, long dead, stretch out their rotting hands, trying to pull me back down into their foul graves. Giles and Eustace sit on each side of me at the table whenever I try to eat, the blood still running from their wounds. I see demons crouching on women's shoulders, mocking me. I watch the birds of death hovering over the babies' cradles. I am afraid even to look at a child, in case my evil eye should curse them. I am terrified to sleep, for

in my dreams there is no escaping the wraiths that bite and tear and suffocate me.

'That night, in the disused chapel outside Lincoln, as I prostrated myself before that altar in front of my friends, I prayed that St Guthlac and St Hugh and all the Saints would give me the power to summon the spirits of the air and earth, of the living and the dead, and they heard me. They granted me what, in my pride, I most desired. And that was my punishment. They are dragging me down into their kingdom, the kingdom of the dead. I am already in purgatory and I do not know if I will ever escape it.'

He gazed around at his fellow pilgrims, his face contorted with despair. 'If I die at the holy shrine of Walsingham, will the spirits leave me then? If the pestilence comes to take me, will I finally be free from my torment? For that is my only prayer now.'

Historical Notes

Dean Henry Mansfield died in post in Lincoln Cathedral on 6 December 1328. The position was finally filled in the February, not by the subdean but by Anthony Bek, who had previously been elected Bishop of Lincoln, though he never served as such because the result of the election was quashed. However, he subsequently became Bishop of Norwich.

Divination was practised by trained priests within the Church for a variety of purposes. The instructions they were to follow were carefully written down. There were many methods, but they basically fell into three types. Summoning – the calling up of spirits, angels or demons, to question them directly about the future. Scrivening – where, after fasting, purification and mediation, a priest would attempt to read patterns in smoke or in blood, oil, wax or other substances dropped in water. Casting lots – after fasting and saying Mass, the priest was instructed to sprinkle himself with holy water and ensure that six poor people were being fed as he cast his lots. He would then ask a series of yes/no questions such as: Will this sick person recover? Should this journey be undertaken? Should the building work be begun on this day?

All divination had to be performed before a consecrated altar. Some churchmen denounced such practises, but many advocated them, seeing no difference between divination and trial by ordeal, which in previous centuries had been the principle form of determining the guilt or innocence of the accused.

Crackpole, or krakepol, which gave the area of Lincoln its name, is thought to come from the Scandinavian *kráka*, meaning crow and pol, which in Old English means a small body of water. Crackpole lies just north of Brayford Pool. Clergy were often disparagingly referred to as crows by the laity because of their black robes and the fact that they made a profit from the dead. A crow feeding in a churchyard or sitting on the roof of a house was an omen of death.

In the Middle Ages, most churches had an Easter Sepulchre built into the wall on the left-hand side of the altar. This was a long low recess between two foot and six foot long. At the end of the Good Friday services, a statue of Christ was placed in the tomb and kept there until Easter Sunday morning, when the sepulchre would be uncovered and the tomb revealed to be empty, showing that Christ had risen. Many churches bricked up their sepulchres during the Reformation and many more were lost due to rebuilding in later centuries, but some still remain, such as at St Mary the Virgin in Ringmer, East Sussex, and All Saints Church, Hawton, Nottinghamshire. In some old churches, if you examine the wall you can still see the outline of where the recess used to be.

Clergy, even those in minor orders who did not take lifelong vows, were granted benefit of clergy, which by this period had been extended to include anyone who could read. This meant that, except for those accused of treason, monks and clergy could only be tried in the far more lenient ecclesiastical courts, which did not impose the death penalty, even for murder. However, there were cases of clergy being defrocked in the ecclesiastical courts and then handed over to be tried again in the civil courts, which could hang them, but this was rare.

Punishment, even for serious crimes, usually took the form of penances, such as fasting, pilgrimages or incarceration in a carcer, an ecclesiastical prison, where monks and priests were imprisoned in solitary confinement for misdeeds ranging from breaches of the religious rule to criminal offences. Often, confinement would be for just a few days, though, for serious offences, such as murdering another cleric or monk, it could be a year or more, and after that the offender might be banished to a parish or monastery considered to be particularly austere or remote.

EPILOGUE

With the tale of pride, the seven deadly sins were finished. Although at the beginning of their stay the landlord of the Angel had suggested that the pilgrims might like to debate which of the sins was the worst, the very worst, there was a general feeling that such a difficult question was beyond the reach of human beings to decide. This was a matter best left to God. Besides, it was late and they were tired. In front of them, the pilgrims had the immediate prospect of a second night in the not uncomfortable beds of the inn and then, on the morrow, a resumption of their journey towards Walsingham.

Yet, tired as they were and even before the start of the next stage of their journey, they had been looking at each other with new eyes, a consequence of the stories that they'd heard. There was respect and pity for Janyn the veteran soldier and his tale of lust, and some amusement at David Falconer's account of the man who'd been tricked into eating himself to death. The prior's condemnation of sloth pricked the consciences of some. The misery and confusion produced by sin had been amply demonstrated by the stories of greed and envy, anger and pride.

The next day dawned bright. The sky had cleared and the rain-soaked ground was already drying out in the midsummer warmth. Rest, refreshment and a sunny morning gave new heart to the travellers, despite the tales of death and suffering that they had been hearing for the last two nights. Even the spirit-haunted Randal looked, for the time being, if not cheerful then at least not so despairing.

Perhaps the pestilence would never reach this corner of England, they dared to hope. Perhaps the intercession of Our Lady of Walsingham would protect them, each and every one, from the wrath of God, whether they counted themselves among the deserving or the . . . less deserving. There was a new vigour and determination in their movements as they prepared to set out once more for the shrine. The exception was Katie Valier who, with her young companion, was not bound for Walsingham at all but going in search of her de Foe ancestors in the area round Bishop's Lynn. Nevertheless, she intended to keep company with the group for a while longer. And Prior John, of course, though travelling to the shrine, was making the journey not to atone for his own sins but to pass judgement on those of others in his order, a prospect that he relished.

The sense of kinship that had grown between the pilgrims at the Angel – or between most of them – during their two days and nights in Mundham was strong enough for the landlord to mention casually to his wife that he had it in mind to accompany the group to the shrine. What did she think? But, as far as Agnes was concerned, Laurence was required to stay at the Angel. She did not say this straight out but instead remarked that business was good. As long as summer lasted, and as long as the pestilence did not draw near, they might expect to host other passing groups of pilgrims. Perhaps Laurence would have the chance to exercise his storytelling skills again? All these things were true, but it could also be that Agnes was worried about what – or who – her husband might be tempted by once he'd escaped the bounds of home. Not all of the Walsingham pilgrims were pious or preoccupied with sin and salvation; some of the women were young, or at any rate not so old.

In compensation, Agnes arranged with Nicholas Hangfield, the shipping clerk, that he would bring them back a souvenir from Walsingham: it might be a wax effigy of the Mother and Child, blessed by the monks, or a flask filled with water from the Holy Well or, best of all, a little leaden pouch in which was sealed the sacred water mingled with a drop of the Virgin's milk. Nicholas, who was a helpful sort of fellow, promised to do this. God willing, he was planning to pass through Mundham on his return to London, once he had paid his respects at the shrine.

So, bidding farewell to Laurence and Agnes Carter as they stood at the arched entrance to the Angel yard, the motley band moved off down the principal road through Mundham. Not for the first time, Laurence observed to his wife how remarkably sure-footed the blind man was. Until you got close to Master Falconer, you'd never have suspected his condition. Meanwhile, some of the inhabitants of Mundham came out of their houses or straightened up from working in their cottage gardens to stare at the passing parade. A few waved and others called out requests to the pilgrims to put in a good word for them at the shrine.

Soon, the road narrowed until it was more of a path, and they entered the woods that lay to the north of the village. Usually, this would have been a rather forbidding place – hadn't there been some mention of outlaws hereabouts? – but this morning, the birds were singing and the sunlight spilled out in bright patches on the forest floor. Maybe some of the men touched the hilts of their knives more frequently than they would have done out in the open, even as the women chatted or laughed more insistently while they paced through the woods. But they all emerged safe and sound on the other side and breathed more easily because they now had a view of the road before them and the country on either side.

By the early afternoon, they reached Thetford. There, they heard that the group that had departed from Mundham almost two days before had not been so fortunate. This first group had been set on by outlaws in the very woods through which the pilgrims had just passed. No deaths resulted, but several of the party had been wounded or badly beaten by thieves taking advantage of the poor weather and fading light. The injured were being cared for in the infirmary at the Cluniac priory in Thetford. For the Mundham pilgrims, this sad story was a reminder of the perils that surrounded them on all sides, as well as of human wickedness, which had been their theme. Some felt sorrow but most experienced at least a moment of relief and thankfulness that they had not been part of that earlier company. They had chosen to stay behind and to talk and listen. Perhaps God was looking on them with favour after all . . .

Thetford was a meeting-point for other pilgrims and, as they all pressed forward towards Walsingham, the number of companies grew, so that if you had been able to fly up into the air and then look down from a sufficient height you would have seen them like a skein of streams and tributaries coming together in a greater river flowing towards the shrine of Our Lady.

Who knows how many will have their prayers answered at Walsingham, prayers for themselves and their families, for their towns and villages. Some will return home to find their kin or neighbours already struck down, as if in mockery of their piety. Others will survive the worst of the pestilence and count themselves lucky, only to fall victim as it seems to be in retreat.

One in three of the population will be dead by the end of 1349.

And what of the Mundham pilgrims, the tale-tellers? What of Janyn and Katie Valier, of blind Falconer and the stern-faced canon? Did Laurence and Agnes Carter continue to trade under the sign of the Angel? And Nicholas Hangfield, did he survive to call on them, as he'd promised, on his return to London? Was Randal, once a novice priest and now a broken man, to find any relief from his torment?

We cannot know. Their history stops here.

We have kept company with them long enough. They are part of that great crowd flowing towards Walsingham now, and not to be distinguished from the thousands of others making the same pilgrimage. All we can do is wish them Godspeed.